What Hurts the Most

AMANDA COURTNEY

Cover Design by Kiwi Designs and The Author Buddy

Editing and Proofreading by CJ Editing

Formatting by Katarina Martinez

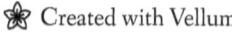 Created with Vellum

Contents

Author's Note

In this novel, you will find journeys of personal growth regarding confidence and self-worth, the importance of surrounding oneself with the right people, and a slow-burn romance. While I tried to keep things lighthearted, the characters in this novel struggle with anxiety, and depression. There is cussing, sexual content, talk of funerals, some dark humor regarding death, an emotional affair, and the main character is cheated on. This is a love triangle, but the right choice is clear.

If you are younger than 18, I'd suggest having a parent approve the content before reading, specifically in chapters 9, 26, 27, 30, and 36. While most of the spice that is written is to compare/contrast relationships and for emotional effect, I'd suggest staying clear if you prefer closed-door/fade-to-black romance.

The following have been created solely for this work of fiction and are not based on any real institution/business:

Lorraine's
North Houston University/Panthers
The Stallions
The Hornets
Francesca's
Houston Roasting Company
Coffee Break

Playlist

Stop and Stare by OneRepublic
Used to Be by Steve Loki & Kiiara (feat. Wiz Khalifa)
Suffering by Melrose Avenue
Perfect by Simple Plan
Heavy by Linkin Park (feat. Kiiara)
Treat You Better by Shawn Mendes
A Symptom of Being Human by Shinedown
Dying For by Rain City Drive
Try by P!nk
Take a Bow by Leona Lewis
Mine by Kelly Clarkson
Somewhere Only We Know by Keane
Leave a Light on by Papa Roach & Carrie Underwood
Fix You by Fearless Soul
Awaken by Breaking Benjamin
Faster by Within Temptation
I Love Me by Demi Lovato
Awake and Alive by Skillet
Here's to Us by Halestorm
My Funeral Song by RØRY & Loveless

Chapter 1
I Don't Want a Funeral

Cori

W hen I die, I don't want a funeral. I don't want a service with less than ten occupied chairs and music no one likes. I don't want a hired preacher reciting the lies from my eulogy that my siblings pulled out of their asses. I don't want anyone standing over my body with dry eyes, struggling to find the words to describe the full life I lived, when all there is to say is, *"She was quiet."*

This epiphany comes to me from the second pew of the funeral home that overflows with people saying goodbye to my grandma while the preacher talks about the amazing woman she was.

The life Grandma lived on the farm with Grandpa was anything but simple. She traveled, taught dance lessons, cussed out people who did her wrong, and gave as much as she could. And when she took over her father's diner, everyone in town came to Lorraine's, looking for more than just food and hot beverages—her infectious smiles and healing hugs could lift the world off your shoulders.

The love she extended to even the strangest of strangers made her everyone's grandma. But she was more than just a

1

grandma, she was my role model and tried so hard to be my anchor in this vortex of a family. Among all the criticisms and comparisons to which I never measured up, she encouraged me never to bow, never to let the words pierce my armor. But I let her down.

What hurts the most about her passing is that her last words to me were, *"I'm so proud of you, Cori."* Because what is there to be proud of?

So, no. I don't think I'd like a funeral.

It's too much to ask of my siblings to waste an hour shedding a few tears summoned forth from obligation. It's too much to ask of them to spend money no one has on a burial site no one will visit. It's too much to ask of a preacher to passionately deliver the eulogy of someone when there's not much to say.

Instead, I want one of my family members, whoever draws the short straw, to take my ashes somewhere, anywhere, and throw me up into the air or dump me off a cliff, allowing the wind to do the rest. Maybe it will scatter each piece of ash somewhere beautiful. Maybe it will rain, dissolving me into nothing. Whatever nature chooses, after it's all over, it will be as if I was never here at all.

I spend most of the funeral praying for the end, but when the end finally arrives, I can't leave. I can't abandon her here, out in the open.

"Cori, let's go. They won't begin until we leave." Mom smiles and waves at the gravediggers standing underneath a tree. But if we don't supervise the burial, how can we be sure she's truly beneath her headstone when we come to visit? How can we be sure they don't take her body back inside, steal her gold wedding band, and sell her body parts?

"Can we at least watch from the car?"

"Fine."

Giving Grandma's dark wood casket one final touch good-bye, we turn toward Mom's SUV. But as my gaze locks with that of two ice-blue eyes, my feet halt in place.

He stands with his hands in his pockets about fifty feet away, leaning against a shiny, black car. Sunlight glints off a silver watch on his wrist.

Somehow oblivious to his demanding presence, Mom sighs when I stop walking. "What now?" But I can't mutter a single word in response because his feet begin moving in our direction.

As he nears, Mom's head snaps to the approaching danger, studying his face until recognition hits. "Samuel!" She embraces him tightly. "Look at you all grown up." Holding him at arm's length, she takes in his broad shoulders, gray suit jacket that strains to hold in his biceps, and the light stubble that grows along his jaw.

"I'm sorry about your mother-in-law, Mrs. Anderson," he says, sympathy painting his face.

"Oh, call me Sarah, like you used to, please. I'm so glad you came." She rubs his arms up and down. "It's so good to see you after all these years. How are you?"

Sam was my best friend growing up. We were attached at the hip from first through eighth grade, only ever at our own homes when the other was right beside us. He was also my first crush, the boy who ruined all other boys that came after.

And the only person in the world Grandma didn't like.

"That boy is too big for his britches," she said. *"Nothing ever satisfies him."* I never knew what she meant by that.

I'm brought back to myself when Sam opens his arms to me for an awkward, stiff hug, probably my millionth of the day.

"I'm sorry about your grandma. I know how close you were."

"Thanks." Words are hard for me, especially during conversations with strangers. Or people who have become strangers. I could make mindless chatter and repeat all the questions that Mom had probably just asked him, like how he's doing, or what he's been up to. Instead, I stand there, my gaze bouncing from the funeral home to the two cars still in the parking lot, to the gravediggers still waiting for us to leave so they can bring the dirt around from wherever they keep it. Anywhere except the eyes that watch me with pity.

I'd love more than anything to fall back into our easy camaraderie, the way we could make each other laugh in any situation, the way the air seemed lighter whenever he was near. But I doubt I'll ever see him again after today, and I'd prefer not to waste my time.

I'd prefer not to kick at the pile where my feelings are neatly collected, sending them flying all over the place.

"Um- would it be okay if I stopped by the house? My mother gave me some food to bring over."

"That was thoughtful. And you're always welcome. You can eat with us and we'll catch up," Mom answers. Mom's car is already loaded down with food from friends and neighbors, and even more waits at Mom and Dad's house to be eaten by my family of eight. And Sam, I guess.

After giving me one more tight-lipped glance, he thanks her and turns for his car, while Mom pulls me toward hers. Despite her promises of watching over Grandma, she tells Dad to drive and we head towards my childhood home.

"That was a great turnout. The service was beautiful," Mom says. She wipes her nose with the thin shreds of a tissue.

"It really was." My fraternal twin, Sage, lays a comforting hand on Mom's shoulder from where she sits beside me in the middle row. In the third row are my two younger brothers, Spencer and Solomon, each lost either to a phone or game device, and my older sister rides behind us with her husband.

"So, did Grandma have money?"

"Sage!" Dad warns.

"What? I'm just asking, jeez." Crossing her arms, she turns to look out the window.

"She and your grandfather were farmers and didn't make much," Mom starts. "They invested most of their life savings into the diner to update things when it was passed down, and whatever they did leave behind is not going to *you*."

"Fine. I'll just get it when *you* die."

In answer, Mom rolls her eyes. Exasperation is a feeling we've all grown accustomed to, thanks to Sage.

Mom turns to me, changing the subject. "That was a nice surprise, wasn't it, Cori? To see Sam."

"Sam Bennett? Is that who that was? Damn. He grew up." Sage bounces her eyebrows.

"It was definitely a surprise," I answer. "How did he even know about the funeral?"

"Well, I posted the details on social media, his mother probably saw it and relayed the news," Mom says.

"I wish he would have come to say hello before I got in the car," Dad says, and Mom pats his arm.

"He's coming to the house, don't worry."

Except I would argue Sam coming over is definitely worth worrying about. Worrying is the only thing I've ever been good at.

My older sister, Stephanie, has Grandma's homemaking abilities and can make a delicious meal out of the barest of ingredients. Sage and Spencer both inherited her athleticism, and her confident and carefree personality; the ability to not let anything crack her nonchalance. And Solomon was blessed with her brains.

I got her love of coffee and reading.

Not bad things to have shared with Grandma. My favorite memories include book sharing and buddy reading with her, and sending her letters with summaries of my latest reads. The only time book reports were fun. But she had so many good qualities, it'd be nice to have gotten something I could use to help make up for my overthinking and sensitive nature.

"Hey, can I have one of these cookies?" Spencer asks from the backseat, holding a plastic bag stuffed full of what appears to be oatmeal chocolate chip cookies. As a junior in high school and outfielder for the baseball team, food isn't safe around him.

Mom turns around in her seat to ensure he captures the seriousness in her eyes. "You can have one." Holding up her finger, she repeats, "One."

I reach my hand back for a cookie but receive a high five instead. Sage turns around in her seat to threaten Spencer, and because her threats are never empty, he throws the bag at her in surrender.

"Oh my God." She holds the bag out for me after taking a bite. "These are fucking heaven."

"Language," Dad warns again.

"She's right," I agree as Sage takes the bag back for another. "Guard those from Spencer with your life."

"If they get seconds, I get seconds," Spencer calls from the back.

"Cori, I thought you were watching your weight?" Mom asks.

"No, Mom. You're watching my weight. I don't care about my weight. Besides," I take a bite and reply, "I'm grieving."

"Well, your bereavement leave ends today, you're both

back to work tomorrow," Dad says to Sage and me. We're servers at Grandma's diner. It's the only restaurant for miles besides a rundown fast-food chain, and it serves everything from eggs to burgers to lasagna. The diner now is rundown as well because, instead of taking over when he should have, Dad hired a manager, Mike, to do it instead. When Grandma ran it, the food was delicious. However, in trying to keep costs low, Mike changed suppliers and hired cooks with no experience.

I graduated with my associate's degree in business last semester, a two-year degree that took me four years to complete because of a lack of funds, but I've had no luck finding a different job. No one wants an associate's degree, they want a bachelor's. And they want experience to go along with that bachelor's degree, but they want to pay as little as possible. So, for the time being, I'm stuck working as a server—an introvert's personal hell. At least it's Grandma's diner, though. Or, used to be.

Admittedly, if Dad allowed me a little more control, I'd love it. Grandma used to tell me it would be mine one day because I was the only child out of my siblings who had any interest in brainstorming ideas for improvement with her: new dishes to try, seasonal items, possible promotions. But I don't see Dad allowing that to happen—he's never been thrilled with the idea of me working at the diner.

"Have you had any more interviews, Cori?" Dad asks. Case in point.

"No, I haven't. I was thinking though..." I summon the courage from deep down inside of me to say what I want to say. Every other time I've stepped up to the door of the plane, I sat back down. But the time to jump has come.

"Now that the diner will officially be yours... What if I took a more active role? Like, an assistant manager? I could be there when Mike can't be, and I can start learning from him. And I have tons of ideas-"

"Cori, you know nothing about running a restaurant."

"Yeah... that's why I said I could *learn*."

Dad actually laughs. "There's a lot more to it than you think. Just focus on finding a big girl job for now. You know I waited tables at that diner when I was in high school, but the minute I turned eighteen I found a job actually worth my time. If you just try harder, I know you can too."

"You just need to have more confidence in yourself, honey," Mom states.

Oh, *confidence!* Why didn't I think of that?

"And ambition."

"Thanks, Dad," I answer dryly, yanking the bag of cookies from Sage and wondering why she never receives this lecture.

"I'm just saying. You need to have more drive and pride in yourself. You're twenty-two and not getting any younger. It's time you move up in the world. Time to..." Dad drones on and on, but I stop listening because it's nothing I haven't heard before. This is the kind of stuff Grandma used to tell me to ignore: Mom's comments about my looks and my Dad's disappointment in my lack of accomplishments.

The only problem is, I agree with them.

Chapter 2
Not a Big Deal

Cori

Wen we arrive at Mom's house, I stay downstairs just long enough to be polite, then make a run for it to my old bedroom. It's not that I don't want to be around Sam, necessarily. But for the sake of my sanity, I shouldn't be within eyesight of his large hands and his cocky smirk that smooths out into a comforting grin whenever his eyes meet mine. And I don't want to be within earshot while my family drills him about his life and what he's been up to since we last saw him eight years ago.

After his dad moved their family of three to Houston for his company, Sam and I promised we'd stay in touch, but we were both kept busy with our new, separate lives. Rather, *he* was kept busy while I wandered around feeling hollow.

Then, he went to college on a full scholarship to play football, and I had a hard time escaping him. When he became the starting quarterback, he rose to fame as a local celebrity, always making the headlines of small-town papers, and even talked about on major sports talk shows. Despite his graduation the previous semester, his name is still mentioned often, only now they wonder why he threw away what could have been a successful career in the NFL to work in real estate development.

I quietly shut the door behind me and take a look around my old bedroom. Mom had it converted into her *crafting* room, although it's really just filled with junk she doesn't want to deal with. There's a box labeled 'Donation' right inside the door, probably shoved in here last minute while she cleaned up. I sit on the floor beside it and pick up the familiar book that sits on top of the pile titled, *Best Poems of Texas,* and turn it over in my hands. But when the door opens, I quickly toss it back.

Sam closes the door before setting down a backpack and sits beside me. I scoot over to make room for him, but we're still too close. My body comes to life with goosebumps at his thigh and shoulder pressed against mine.

"How are you?" he asks, leaning his head back against the dresser we sit in front of.

"Fine." And it's the truth, not just the general answer you give to anyone who asks. I'm sad of course, but Grandma was in her eighties and she lived a full, happy life. I guess there's not much more you can ask for.

He lifts his arm, summoning me to lean into him as if no time has passed and no awkwardness lingers between us. And because I'm not great with rejection—taking it or giving it—I comply. I lay my head on his shoulder, stiff and unsure, but soften at the familiarity of his comforting embrace. Without my permission, my eyes close and my lungs take in a deep breath. His scent, a sweet cedarwood, is very welcome compared to the sharp body spray he used to douse himself in.

"So," he begins, "how's life?"

"Pretty much exactly the same."

"Surely something is different. I see you've gone up a cup size or two."

My head snaps up.

"Sorry. That was inappropriate. But it's hard not to notice. You've grown into a beautiful woman." Either at the shamelessness of his statement or from feeling awkward and unsure of what else to do, I laugh at the unabashed smile that spreads over his face. He wraps his arm around me once more, and we fall into a comfortable silence.

"Seriously though. Did you go to school? Do you have a job? Did you ever write that novel you wanted to write? Do you still live with your nose inside a book?" My thoughts linger on the fact that I already knew all of his answers to those same questions, but he has no idea about mine.

"I only went to school for an associate's degree. I work at Grandma's diner. I didn't write a novel, and I don't really write poetry anymore. And yes, I still live and breathe books."

"Why did you stop writing?"

I reach over and grab the poetry book from the donation box. I hand it over, telling him to flip to page eleven.

"This is yours?" he asks, noticing my name below the poem.

My eyes remain on the door as I explain in a dry tone, "Yep. I won third in a poetry competition. They published the first one hundred in a book."

"That's amazing, Cor."

He reads out loud but stops when I plug my ears. I don't want to hear it.

"Wow. I'm impressed."

Except it's not impressive. If they published *my* poem, it must not be difficult to win a poetry contest after all. The art of poetry is so subjective that anyone could write it; no real talent is required, only feelings. And I have an abundance of those.

"Wait, why did you pull it out of a donation box?" he asks.

"That's where I found it earlier. That's Mom and Dad's copy, I guess they don't want it anymore."

He studies me for a minute trying to understand, but I

11

don't think the situation is understandable. I gave it to my parents as a Christmas present. I had the page of my poem bookmarked and when they unwrapped it, Mom turned to the page, skimmed it, then said, *'That's great, sweetie. But you know, we don't really read.'*

Just then, Mom opens the door and asks if we want more to eat, or if they're good to put it all away. Sam and I both decline before he holds up the book. "This was in the donation box-"

"Oh yes, take it if you want it. I can't for the life of me remember where it came from," Mom says.

Sam looks at me, probably expecting me to say something, but I shake my head. "Thanks, Mrs. Anderson."

"Of course, sweetheart, but call me Sarah, remember?" Once the door is closed, he meets my gaze.

I shrug. "It's not a big deal."

"Well, I'll put this on my bookshelf and cherish it forever."

This is exactly what I tried to avoid: the butterflies in my stomach, the desire pulsating throughout my body at his sweet words, and the flame of hope igniting in my cold heart that maybe our time has finally come.

Sam nudges my shoulder with his. "Hey, I have a surprise for you." He reaches over to grab his backpack and unzips the compartment. "I hid that bag of cookies you and Sage were raving about."

He pulls out the plastic bag and I reach for it, but he yanks his hand behind him.

"I will deck you, Samuel. I'm not in the mood for games." I meant it when I told Mom I didn't have any room for more food, but I'll make some for these cookies.

He laughs. "Then, say yes to the question I'm about to ask you." Our eyes remain locked while my mind spirals with the possible questions he'd want to ask. "Go out with me."

I blink at him.

Of course, I want to scream my acceptance, but I don't fit in his life anymore. I'm a waitress, while he probably makes more money per month than I make in a year, based on the fancy car he drives. How would this work exactly? Even now, he wears an expensive-looking, most likely, custom-tailored suit, while I wear pants I found at Ross for six dollars five years ago. We don't match. No longer are we the snotty-nosed kids that played hard and dreamed big. Gone are the days of blissful ignorance of the realities of adulthood.

"Cori," he says after I stare at him in shock for two whole minutes.

"You heard me when I said I was a server, right?"

His eyebrows furrow in confusion. "Yes?"

"So you know we're in completely different social classes?"

He blows air through his nose. "Cori, I don't give a shit about any of that." He tilts his head. "Do you?"

"No." But it comes out more like a question.

He lifts a shoulder. "Then that's all that matters."

I consider his words. In the grand scheme of things, no, our pay differences don't matter. But pay differences barely skim the surface of my insecurities.

I'd seen the photographs of the beautiful, thin women with smooth, shiny hair that he dated in college all over social media. Women I can't begin to compare to.

"Come on, we'll take it slow, get to know each other again."

"But... why now? Why all of a sudden? I'm just now seeing you for the first time in eight years. I didn't think I'd ever see you again."

"I don't know. When I heard that your grandma had passed, it just got me thinking of all the fun times we had when we were kids. Things have settled down now for me since I graduated and started working for Dad. It just feels right." He takes my hand in his, rubbing his thumb along the back of my fingers. "You know we were headed in this direction right before I moved, anyway. Let's just think of our time apart as a pause. It's better that we waited, though, because now we're adults instead of barely teenagers."

I'm having difficulty breathing. Either I tripped on this junk and hit my head, or I'm grieving harder than I realized and entered a state of psychosis.

"Well, think about it and let me know." He kisses me on the forehead and stands. "I should get going, but let me see your phone, so I can put my number in it." I hand it over, and once he's done, he wraps me in a hug that lasts too long to be considered friendly.

I follow him downstairs and watch as he hugs my mom and shakes my dad's hand, then he leaves with the parting words, "Please, say yes."

My mom, Sage, and my older sister, Stephanie, watch me with hungry expressions.

"What?" I ask.

"Well? What happened up there?" Mom asks impatiently.

"Nothing. We just talked."

"About?" Stephanie urges, moving her hand in a circle for me to go on.

"What I've been up to since we last saw each other."

Sage shakes her head. "Nuh uh, there was more than that, I know it."

"Okay, fine." I take a breath to prepare myself. "He asked me out." I jump at their deafening squeals, but after a moment, Mom's face sobers.

"You said yes, right?"

"I told him I'd think about it."

Too many protests and groans at once, I can't follow who shouts what. Someone calls me "Crazy." Someone else draws out the word, "Why?" There's even a "Cori, you make the worst decisions," in there, and all three of them roll their eyes.

They're right. All the decisions I've made up to this point have been crap. And I know that because people my age are graduating with bachelor's degrees, traveling, and changing the world, while I stand still. When I was a kid, I had big dreams of success and being someone who mattered. But they were childish fantasies that shattered into dust when I smacked into the wall of reality.

"I'm scared he won't like me, okay? Dad's right, I work at a diner. Sage, you're always telling me to stop being so quiet and boring. Mom, you criticize me for being shy and make comments about my weight. And Stephanie, you say I'm going to be the spinster of the family because I'm not flirtatious or cheerful or funny, and I can't cook to save my life. What the hell am I supposed to think?"

"You're supposed to ignore us and have some self-esteem," Sage says.

Stephanie puts her hands on my shoulders and lowers a couple of inches so that her face is level with mine. "You're being ridiculous. Are you really going to let insecurities keep you from happiness? Your confidence is your responsibility. Know your worth, girl." She pushes me playfully, but how does one just *know* their worth? When you're constantly told you're not good enough, when you're constantly compared to other people, eventually it's going to affect me. After all, if everyone has the same opinion, clearly they see something I'm blind to.

For me, confidence feels like arrogance. When the whole concept of *outgoing* is foreign, how does one say what's on their mind without overthinking, or be loud and expressive without annoying people? How do you learn not to care?

"Honey, you've been depressed for a long time. Probably

since Sam left eight years ago. Don't you see how his presence could be a good thing in your life?"

Have I been depressed? I wouldn't say I have, but what do I know?

Sure, when he left, I got more attention from bullies at school, I was lonely at home, and I was jealous of the happiness he easily found without me. And since I've grown up, I've been a little moody with how hard adulthood turned out to be. But I wouldn't say his presence now would fix all that.

Mom continues, "Maybe he'll help you come out of your shell. You could meet new friends and maybe find some job connections." I resist the urge to roll my eyes.

Sage adds, "Look, it's just one date. You're not planning a wedding. Take it from there. You don't turn down someone just because they *might* not like you, or it *might* not work out."

And suddenly, with it broken down into one small step, it doesn't seem like the big deal I've made it out to be. I feel like an idiot. But that's what I do—blow things out of proportion and overthink things until they don't make sense anymore.

If he doesn't think I'm right for him, we'll stay friends or go back to being strangers. Simple. I'll do my best not to dwell on the possibility of that happening, but no promises.

So I ignore all the voices in my head that have claimed dominance over my own over the years. The voices that tell me that I'm too weird and awkward for a guy like Sam, that I'm not pretty enough for him, that I'm not smart or successful enough.

That I'll never be enough.

Then, I wait two days to avoid looking desperate, and send him a one-word text: "Yes."

Chapter 3
Happy for Them

Nick

Eight Months Later

Before I have the chance to knock, the door swings open and a 250-pound ex-lineman slams me to the marbled tile. Tyler stands up, huffing like he's out of shape.

"Pu-" I start, about to call him a vulgar word.

"You shut your mouth!" He points his finger at me. "You don't get to talk. Two years. Two whole years passed without a word from you, and you suddenly reappear back in our lives." My eyes fall to the ground in shame. When I texted Callum and Tyler out of the blue asking if we could have dinner, a hopeful part of me wished everything could be normal between us. That maybe during those two years, the hurt I'd caused would have dissipated.

Sam pokes his head out and points to the only other door on his floor. "Can y'all do this inside? You're going to piss off the neighbor."

Tyler shoots a glare at me, signifying that the conversation isn't over, and gestures for me to go inside first. When the door slams behind us, I turn to see Callum, who is supposed to be the reasonable one, in the corner with his arms crossed.

"You're pissed at me too?"

"You ghosted us. How many of our texts and calls did you ignore? Of course, I'm pissed." He steps forward to stand beside Tyler, both of them looking down their noses at me despite the inch I have on them both. I stare back, taking in Callum's brown beard and Tyler's face thinned from that last little bit of roundness. They're no longer the college kids I once knew. I wonder how different I look to them.

Smiles slowly creep over their faces, dissipating the gloom in the room, and my shoulders relax. "But we missed you too, so we can't stay mad for long." Callum shakes my hand and Tyler tries to tackle me again, but I anticipate the hit.

"Come sit and explain yourself. We have time before the game starts. And the pizza is already on the way," Callum instructs me as he leads us all to the living room with a massive TV on which the NBA pregame plays. He gestures to a black leather armchair for me to sit in while he takes the other, and Tyler joins Sam who's leaned back against the couch scrolling through his phone. A black and white photograph of the Houston skyline adorns the black accent wall behind them.

"So? What the hell have you been up to since you disappeared?" Tyler asks.

"Most recently, working in construction." I rub my hands along my jeans, nervous to admit to them my job. There's nothing wrong with working in construction. But, I promised myself long ago that I wouldn't end up like my father—pissed off at the world because life didn't go the way he planned, wasting away instead of working toward his dreams, and taking out all of that anger on his wife. His loyal wife, whose dreams were also forgotten so that she could fully devote herself to keeping our bills paid.

"Construction, huh? Highways, houses, what?"

"Remodeling houses, building fences, painting, pretty much whatever work is available. The owner takes whatever work comes his way." I'm from a small town where the gas station is also the only restaurant, the plumber also works on air conditioners and does pest control, and the grocery store is combined with the post office. At some point in the past two years, I've worked at all of those places, including the auto shop doing oil changes.

"So why the sudden appearance back in our lives?" Sam asks, eyes narrowed in my direction.

"It's just time for a change. I took a job at a machine shop close to Houston." I pause, wondering if I should wait a little longer before asking what I came to ask. But getting it out of the way would allow for a stress-free evening without the question hanging over my head. "I need a place to stay."

"So, you're moving back?" Sam clarifies.

"Yep."

Tyler excitedly pumps his fist in the air while Callum says, "I've just got a one-bedroom, but you could take the couch if you need to. Or, Sam has an extra room."

"Well, you'd have to pay rent," Sam says. I almost laugh, assuming it's a joke. Obviously, I'll pay rent, but his expression remains stoic, never breaking into a grin like I expect.

"Yeah, I planned on it. I could get my own place too, I just figured I'd ask if any of you needed a roommate first."

"Am I going to wake up one morning to find you gone again?" he asks.

Out of the three of them, I was always closest with Tyler and Callum. Tyler was the friend you asked to go out with when you needed to let loose and forget about the test you bombed, or about the girl that broke your heart. He's not one to turn down a shot, and he'll dance with anyone to anything. I used to be just like that, always up for adventure, never said no to anything. However, quiet evenings at home have become more appealing.

Callum is a much calmer presence, the one back at the table watching over everyone's drinks. The one you go to for advice or the answers to philosophical life questions. He's a closed book himself, but easy to open up to. I had to ignore his calls the most while I was gone because he constantly wanted to check up on me, to make sure I was eating and showering. I don't deserve his friendship.

Then there's Sam. He's an arrogant bastard who thinks he's the main character in everyone's story. Not that I deserved it, but I haven't heard a word from him since I left town. He never came to the hospital, he was never home when I was released, and I never received any worried texts or voicemails from him after I left. Out of all of us guys, he was the one that had changed the least and, simultaneously, the most. His arrogance appears exactly the same, but it's lost its charm. He acts smug. Like he's disappointed in the way I acted after my accident two years ago because he would never have been so childish and run home to his mommy. He never would have allowed the anger to consume him the way I did, and for that, like so many other reasons, he's better than me.

Then again, maybe I'm reading into things that aren't there.

"Not without a heads-up this time. I promise."

Sam strokes his chin, thinking. "Alright. Move in here."

I let out the breath I'd been holding, waiting for his rejection. "Thanks, man. I appreciate it." It's a weight off my shoulders. Although, living with Sam might turn out to be a different weight on my shoulders.

"You want to ask Cori first?" Callum asks, eyebrows raised at Sam.

"Who's Cori?"

"Sam's girlfriend," Tyler sings, mockingly.

Sam rolls his eyes and leans back, crossing his leg over his knee.

"Really? How long have you been together?"

"Only eight months. But we've known each other since we were kids. We reconnected last summer." Eight months is a long time for someone like him. In the three years I knew Sam in college, he never dated seriously. It was always casual hookups with attractive women who deserved much more than Sam was offering.

"It'll be a good story if y'all ever have kids," I say. Sam shifts uncomfortably but nods his agreement.

"Except that's not how their story ends. She'll leave Sam for me one of these days." Tyler smirks until Sam kicks his leg.

"So, will she be okay with me moving in?" I ask Sam.

He brushes off the question. "She doesn't live here."

"Cori's cool," Tyler explains. "A little shy and awkward, but nice."

Shy and awkward is not Sam's type at all, at least it didn't used to be. But it was only a matter of time before his tastes changed—two years have passed and we aren't in college anymore.

"So, give us the rest of the story. You've been doing more than just wielding a nail gun and a paintbrush. I see you have a sleeve." Sam points to my left arm, covered in tattoos of trees and a river. "I see you're still in shape." He points to my other arm, the muscle still toned from manual labor and lifting weights to relieve stress. Then he points to my face. "I see you're still very much alive and didn't fall off the face of the Earth like we thought."

I run a hand through my hair. "Look, I'm sorry. I was in a dark place. I just needed to get away from it all to heal, clear my head, figure out a new plan."

Callum nods. "I get it, man."

I know he means it. Tyler too. Sam is the one who could never understand what it was like for me. How bad it hurt.

Football was his kingdom. He ruled the field and everyone on it. But for me, it was my ticket to freedom. It was money, it was my career, it was life.

"And then Kenna and I broke up." I don't miss the guys shifting uncomfortably. While football was my ticket to the life I wanted, I was hers. And when I couldn't play anymore, she found someone else to give her what she was looking for.

"So, why trees, exactly?" Callum asks, pointing to my arm.

I pull up the sleeve of my shirt to show off the whole tattoo. The mountains start at my shoulder with an airplane flying above them, the tops of the pines at the middle of my bicep, and the trunks end halfway down my forearm. "It's really not that significant. A friend of mine from high school does tattoos now and I was looking at some of his drawings. I just thought this one looked cool. Although, I asked if he'd add the airplane."

I'm grateful that no one mentions the tattoo of my football number that used to be on this arm. The number that was supposed to take me pro. I needed it gone and was lucky that my friend was able to work it into the design of the new one so that you can't tell it had ever been there.

Sam takes me on a quick tour of the apartment and shows me the room that will become mine once I move in. It's a big place with laundry, a full dining room, and three bedrooms, one of which is Sam's office. There are light wood floors throughout, covered in some places by blue rugs, and black metal light fixtures hang low from the high ceiling. It's masculine and a much nicer apartment than I ever imagined living in.

I'm moving from the double-wide I grew up in with outdated, mismatched furniture and wallpaper from the nineties. Although, I'd prefer the double-wide to the cold, staged vibe of Sam's place if the walls back home weren't stained with all the years of struggling Mom and I went through. I almost moved to my own place, a tiny house rental just down the street from Mom's, but I figured there was no sense in being lonely or spending more money on rent and bills for a separate house when I could help Mom pay hers. Give her a bit of reprieve after letting her down with football.

"So what is the new plan?" Sam asks when we're back in the living room. "You said you needed some time to clear your head and figure out a new plan. That's why you ran away. So? Are you going to finish school? Are you going to work at a machine shop for the rest of your life? Or are you going to continue to bounce around from job to job like you've done for the past two years?" There's judgment in his tone.

I shrug. "I don't know. A machinist is a good job. I probably won't ever love it, but does anyone actually love their job?"

"I do," Callum states.

"Me too," says Tyler.

They add context, filling me in on their careers. Callum is a case manager for a charity that helps children from low-income families join sports programs, or take music lessons, pretty much any extracurricular activity. It's a charity Mom and I could have used when I was a kid. Tyler is a PE coach at a junior high, working his way up to high school. And Sam works for his dad in developmental real estate, like he always planned to do.

I'm happy for them, but it's hard not to be jealous. Growing up, I dreamt of being one of those people who loved what they did. Who looked forward to going to work every day instead of coming home on Friday needing to get drunk to forget the week. Who lived to work instead of working to survive. I was supposed to be happy to be like these guys.

But life had other plans.

Two Years Ago

This is what I live for.

The roar of the crowd, each cadence of the drum line, the energy pulsating through the stadium, the adrenaline rush from being part of the team as we burst forth from the tunnel. It's the height of an orgasm, it's riding the Texas Freefall at Splashtown, it's water-sledding through a flood in the street on a trash can lid tied to a bumper. It is unlike any other high I've ever felt.

And it's everything I've worked toward since I was a kid.

When I was five years old, I sat on my Uncle Jonah's lap and pointed to the football players on TV. "I want to be one of them when I'm old."

He tickled me until I almost pissed myself. "Those guys are my age, you knucklehead. And we ain't old yet."

"You are to me." That earned me a noogie.

"You sure you don't want to be an oil man like me?"

"No," I said, unapologetically.

"Yeah, it's not as fun as playing football." Uncle Jonah always came over for lunch after Church and would stay to build blanket forts or have Nerf gun wars, as long as I let him watch the game when it came on.

"You know, I think you could make it, kid." At that point, I hadn't done anything football-related except throw one in the yard, but he still believed in me. I probably could have said I wanted to be an Underwater Flamethrower and he would have supported me one hundred percent.

Now, only a couple more games and one more season stand between me and the NFL, happiness, and enough money to pay back Mom for all the extra shifts she picked up when I was a kid.

Enough money to move her out of the double-wide where my Dad abandoned us.

Mom and Uncle Jonah don't get to come to every game, but they're in the stands today to watch us take down the Spartans in our biggest game of the season. After kickoff, we had possession of the ball. We do okay during the first quarter, but it's the second quarter that things pick up. They've kept us at bay enough to prevent us from scoring, until Sam makes a smooth pass right into the hands of our wide receiver, just a few yards from the end zone.

After he makes the touchdown, the crowd. Goes. Nuts.

Callum stands just feet away, shouting his excitement to me, but I can't hear a word he says from all the cheers, screams, whistling, and chanting. The score now stands 7 to 3 after a field goal. We wait on the sidelines while the defensive line does its job, and when they succeed, we go back out. Another touchdown, this one earned after three first downs. Then it's halftime.

"We could be up by more if Bennett was given more protection." We hear from the offensive coach. "But keep doing what you're doing, keep your eyes open, and finish the fight!"

After the band has their time on the field, something I always hated missing, we run back out of the tunnel. Kickoff has the ball flying past the goalpost, so the play starts at the twenty-yard line. The defensive line isn't able to hold them back this time, and the score is 14 to 9.

But no worries, because we've got this.

"I don't care what the hell y'all have to do, do not let me get hit," Sam calls to us after he tells us the play in the huddle. He's running the ball this time. We line up, and the world falls away around me, my eyes, my ears, my soul, only for the game and the play we're about to run. The ball is snapped, Sam fake passes it to Giles, and we take off ready to block for our quarterback. We make it eleven yards before we lose our hold on their defense. Callum goes down, I go down, Sam goes down. Except our goal was to get the yards to advance, and we did that.

But as I move my arms to push myself from the ground, smile on my lips, pumped for the next round in the ring, the defensive lineman I blocked stands up and takes a step backward.

I've been stepped on a million times throughout my football career. My body's been slammed into the turf, I've torn my ACL, pulled my hamstring, and had a few concussions. This time is different.

This time, when he steps back onto my leg, he loses his balance and falls on my other leg.

And because I was already in a strange position, bone snaps, breaking my heart in ways it'll never mend from.

Chapter 4
The Roommate

Cori

I lie that it's the rain keeping me awake, but I've told myself that too often in the past to believe it now. Some people might drink warm milk, rub some lavender-scented lotion on their skin, or pop a melatonin gummy on nights when insomnia won't allow for sleep. But Grandma always suggested a steaming mug of decaf and a brownie.

"Your belly is just cold and empty," she'd say.

Luckily, I have a meticulously crafted, fail-proof plan for the nights when the critical voice, that sounds suspiciously like my mother's, won't shut up. The nights when I can't figure out what exactly it is that Sam sees in me. The nights when the threat of failure hovers like a dark cloud, ticking faster and faster until I finally give up my act of self-restraint and rise from Sam's bed in search of the closest thing I can find to Grandma's hugs.

I wait for Sam's third deep breath, slowly tiptoe around the bed, avoiding the spot by the bedpost because it creaks, and slip out the door.

If Sam catches me, it's no big deal, but I prefer to avoid the lecture about sugar and eating late at night. And when someone tells me I shouldn't eat something, it only makes me want it more. Sure, I could put on my big girl pants, put my foot down, and tell him to shut it. One day, I'll do that. Until then, it's hard to argue with, *"You shouldn't eat your feelings,"* and *"I'm just trying to look out for your health, I love you."* Unfortunately, the closest thing Sam has in his apartment to a brownie is a brownie-flavored protein bar, which is absolutely not the same. But it'll have to do.

I brew a cup of decaf and listen to the rain pelt the windows until my 'fail-proof plan' fails.

At the jangling of keys unlocking the doorknob, I realize I forgot to adjust the plan to accommodate Sam's new roommate. He moved in two weeks ago and we have yet to meet. For that, I'm grateful because I dread meeting new people. I dread people in general because I don't know how to be warm, welcoming, or likable, and I exhaust myself trying to be so.

I know nothing about this mysterious man except that he used to be Sam's teammate in college, and that he moved back to town because of a job. But I don't know his name, what he looks like, or what kind of job he moved back for.

When he walks in the front door, he drops his keys on the side table. Then, he turns into the kitchen, stopping dead when he sees my shape standing alone in the dark wielding a protein bar and coffee cup as if they're a weapon and shield. Wearing nothing but a short, tight, cotton chemise nightgown that I wouldn't even own if Sam didn't scoff anytime I wore my usual sweatpants.

I can't see him well with only the clouded moonlight streaming through the windows, but I can tell his hair is dark, possibly black. His broad shoulders and build tell me he was probably one of those guys who blocked or something when he played football with Sam.

I want to throw away the rest of my midnight snack and run back to the safety of Sam's room, but his towering frame blocks my exit as we both size each other up. I feel the touch of his gaze skimming down my body, not intimately, but curiously.

"You the girlfriend?" he finally asks, his deep voice smooth as satin.

"Yes. You the roommate?" I cringe. Obviously, he's the roommate, but it's too late with the question already hanging awkwardly between us.

He nods and the AC kicks on, the breeze against my skin alerting me, once again, to how exceedingly little I'm wearing. I hunch my shoulders and bend my knees, trying, unsuccessfully, to urge the white lace trim to fall lower on my thighs. He tilts his head in question at my position before suddenly averting his gaze, then holds out the jacket he had draped over his arm.

"You're cold." It's a statement to be taken as fact, but he misunderstands my reasoning for trying to cover myself.

Confused, I say, "No, I'm good."

"No, you're cold," he insists.

I notice his eyes bounce off my chest before darting away. I glance down to see what he was trying to avoid and notice my hard nipples poking through the thin fabric. My whole face heats with embarrassment. I take the jacket, slightly damp in places from the rain, and slide my arms through, making sure to zip it up all the way. A smooth woodsy scent drifts up from the fabric, subtle and pleasant.

Sliding his hands in his pockets, he rocks back on his heels. "Can't sleep?"

"No," I answer simply.

He jerks his chin toward the food in my hands. "Having dessert?" I search his question for any judgment, but it sounds genuine.

"Yes," I state plainly, daring him to make a comment about eating in the middle of the night.

"Why are you eating it alone in the dark?"

I decide honesty is the best route to take. "I was hungry and Sam was asleep. Plus, I didn't want to hear a lecture about eating sugar or eating too late." He considers my answer for a moment before nodding, and heads to the freezer. He pulls out a pint-sized ice cream container, grabs a spoon, and comes to stand next to me against the counter.

I find myself paralyzed by my uncertainty of whether I should leave or stay, so I nibble on the protein bar, too concerned with the presence next to me to really taste it. If I weren't so shy, I'd ask him his name, what he does for work, the usual small talk. But I'm me, and maybe he doesn't want to talk anyway. The rain outside has softened, allowing the awkward silence to pulse in my ears, magnifying every crinkle of the wrapper, every crunch of the walnuts, and every sound of my swallowing.

He manages to put away the entire pint in a few minutes before pushing off the counter and saying, "Night."

"Goodnight." As soon as he's out of sight, my hands fly up to cover my face. Talk about first impressions.

Once I finish the coffee and snack, I lay the jacket over the arm of the couch and sneak back to Sam's room. I still can't sleep, though now I lay awake mortified over my nipples.

I leave the car running after I park, hoping the AC will help to cool my skin. My mind goes a thousand miles a minute and I struggle to get a full breath, like an over-worked computer whose fans are blocked. But my car blows whatever temperature it is outside and does nothing to bring relief to the sweltering heat.

Going over my answers in my head one last time, I can't be more prepared than I am now, and if I happen to get the job, I promise myself never to leave, so I'll never have to go through this stress again.

I know everything there is to know about the job I'm interviewing for. I looked up the company online and researched the different types of businesses they work with. For example, I know they roast coffee beans and sell them to privately labeled businesses, hotels, and a few smaller restaurants. I know their most popular flavors are their breakfast blends and dark roasts, and their single origin, organic, and unique blends. I know that they have a team of experts who can create pretty much any flavor their customers dream of. I even know that they source their coffee beans from Colombia, Ethiopia, Guatemala, and Papua New Guinea.

I arrived too early to go inside because I wanted to allow for traffic, to prove my punctuality and preparedness. I wish I could tell them about my emergency bag that sat in the passenger seat beside me, but being too prepared is just as unappealing as being unprepared. Inside the bag is my make-up ready to be applied at the last minute so that it doesn't melt off my face, baby wipes, extra deodorant, a lint roller, two extra outfits in case of sweat, and stain remover. I also had an extra copy of my application that I submitted online, my lacking resume, and my references in a black folder that I will take inside with me. The only thing left to stress over is my stuttering and my tendency to forget how to form complete sentences when under pressure.

When it's almost time for my interview, I wipe my face down, reapply my deodorant, run the lint roller over my clothes, and apply my make-up. Then I step out of the car.

Once inside, I approach the lady at the reception desk with a smile that I hope isn't creepy, and let her know my name and why I am here. She asks me to take a seat on one of the gray chairs off to the side, and I act as if the interview has already started. I'm polite as I thank her, and patient as I wait an entire hour for them to call me back. An *hour*. Whereas, if I arrived even five minutes late, they probably wouldn't let me interview at all. I spend that entire hour in physical pain as my heart pounds and my body screams for breath that I can't help but hold. I just want to get this over with so that I can go home and escape underneath my covers.

I am more nervous than normal because a job working for a coffee roasting company is perfect for me. The only business that could top it is something book-related, like a printer or publisher.

When the receptionist finally calls my name, I follow her back to an office where a lady with dark hair and bright pink lipstick sits behind a desk, appearing bored as she looks at her computer. She doesn't say anything when the door shuts behind me, and I stand at a fork in the road—should I introduce myself and take a seat, therefore interrupting whatever she's doing? Or should I wait quietly until she's finished and asks me to take a seat? What is the polite thing to do? The normal thing? The option that won't cause her to dismiss me so quickly?

And why do simple decisions like this one feel like life or death?

She finally spares me a glance over the top of her glasses, and I smile and introduce myself as boldly as I can. If you don't have confidence, you should fake it, Dad always tells me. Because that's *easy* to do.

"Hi, I'm Cori Anderson." I extend a hand over her desk and she takes it, although I almost jerk her arm out of its socket with the strength of my handshake. Dad also tells me that no one wants to shake hands with spaghetti and that a firm handshake shows you're serious and assured. But, as usual, I do the right thing only for it to be the wrong thing.

I mutter a small apology as she rubs her arm.

"Catherine," she states. "Have a seat."

She picks up a sheet of paper from her desk and looks it over. I assume it is my resume and I feel myself start scratching at my wrist, my nerves taking control over my body.

"The position we have available is for an administrative assistant. You'd be filing paperwork, writing emails, taking meeting notes, things like that. I don't see any work history with those duties, do you think you'd be able to handle those responsibilities?"

"Yes, I do. We help out the manager every once in a while at the diner, where I currently work, with paperwork and emails. I'm a quick learner as well, so if there's something I don't know how to do now, I'll pick it up in no time." My words come out too fast and my breathing is ragged.

She stares at me for a second too long, either because she doesn't believe me, she hears that declaration too often from applicants, or maybe she is checking for signs of a heart attack. I adjust the gray blazer I wear over a plum-colored, buttoned shirt and clear my throat. She looks at my resume and asks, "I see you have an associate's in business. Do you have any plans to continue your education?"

"Possibly in the future. Currently, I'm eager to put into practice everything I've learned so far. And to find roots." I'm not quite satisfied with that answer, though, so I continue. "I've also taken some extra courses online, although they weren't accredited courses. Communication and Planning, Fundamentals of-"

She cuts me off. "Yes, I see those listed. What would you say are your strengths?"

I hate the strengths and weaknesses questions. They're hard to get right and difficult not to make yourself look pompous or inadequate simultaneously. But I soldier on because I don't have a choice. "I consider myself to have a lot of strengths such as multitasking, the ability to stay focused and get work done promptly, I'm a quick learner as I said earlier. I'm also reliable and trustworthy." I swallow hard, knowing what her next question will be.

"And your weaknesses?"

"Well, to be honest, I'm... reserved. But- but really that's a good thing." I let out a shaky laugh. "You won't catch me wasting time by the water cooler or getting sidetracked. You know, with coworkers. Chatting." I cringe. I've practiced that exact sentence a thousand times. To sell something, you have to be confident about it, whether or not it's right. But no matter how many times I delivered it to myself perfectly in the bathroom mirror, the judging eyes of each interviewer that I encounter trip me every time.

My wrist is raw; one more scratch and I'll draw blood.

"Do you have any questions for me?" she asks. We've concluded the interview too quickly, a horrible sign.

I know that it's usually good to ask questions whether you care about the answers or not, so I say, "I've done a bit of research on the company, and am passionate about coffee myself, and I think it will be an amazing opportunity to work here. I was wondering what the advancement opportunities will look like for this position. For someone with my background."

She sits up in her chair, her features softening. "Well, you could enter sales and work directly with our clients. You said you've researched us?"

I tell her what I've learned, hoping I'm showing my interest and seriousness without coming off too eager.

"Most applicants come in here not having a clue about us. And a lot of them don't even drink coffee. Not that it's a requirement, but having some knowledge about the taste, and a willingness to try the flavors helps," she states, a small smile toying with her lips.

We end up spending about fifteen minutes talking about the company, then more about coffee, and by the time we shake hands goodbye, Catherine has given me a reassuring smile with the promise to get back to me as soon as possible.

On my way out of the building, I thank the receptionist and walk to my car with footsteps lighter and bouncier than they have been in a long time. I may actually have a shot this time. I want to call Dad and Sam and tell them how surprisingly great the interview went, but I decide not to jinx myself.

Grandma always told me, *"The right thing will come along at the right time. You just have to be patient."* Maybe it's finally the right time.

I t isn't. I realize that shortly after I pull over to the shoulder on my route home.

I was driving down the highway, singing at the top of my lungs, proud of myself for once at how well the interview went when my tire blew.

I just replaced a flat a month prior, after buying a whole new set of tires the previous year, but I wasn't about to let a blown tire take out my mental sanity, so I looked on the bright side of things before I got out of the car. At least it happened on my way from the interview rather than making me late. And at least it's on the right side of my car, rather than the left, which is just feet from traffic speeding by on the freeway. And if a vehicle comes slamming into mine, crushing me against the concrete wall and ending my life, well... then I won't have to stress about finding money for a new tire.

Just as I was pulling the door handle, my phone dinged with a new email.

Ms. Anderson,
I appreciate you taking the time to interview with us today. However, we've decided to go in a different direction.

Catherine Ramos
Houston Roasting Company

Quick and painful.

Now, I stand beside the tire in question, watching a black truck pull over ahead of my car. I hope they're having their own issues and their pulling over has nothing to do with me, but my heartbeat picks up when they start driving in reverse to be closer to my car.

I mentally prepare myself for whatever danger may step out of the truck. It might be an innocent citizen who sees a woman with a shredded tire and assumes she doesn't know what she is doing.

Or it could be a sex trafficker. Or a sicko who likes to make suits out of thicker women's bodies like the villain in a movie Sage forced me to watch once.

I'm armed with a jack, the heaviest thing I have with me, so unless the person has a gun, I have a good shot at survival. If I put all of my hurt from not getting the job and anger at the vindictive tire into my swing, I am pretty much guaranteed to win a fight with just about anyone right now.

A tall, muscular man with dark hair steps out of the truck, wearing a long-sleeved shirt and khakis and carrying a lug wrench. Reason tells me it is most likely for the lug nuts on my tire, but fear tells me it is to knock me unconscious, making me easier to transport.

"You know it's dangerous to be on the side of the freeway?" he calls out. As he approaches, I recognize his features.

"Sam's roommate?" I ask. I still don't know his name.

"Yeah, it's Nick. I thought it looked like you, but I couldn't tell completely."

"Umm... so, where else am I supposed to change this?" I gesture to the tire in response to his question.

"You're supposed to call roadside service, a friend, a tow truck." He waves his hand in a circle indicating the multiplicity of options.

"I can't afford roadside service or a tow truck, and there's no one to call." Sage is never available *if* she even hears the phone ring. I can't call my best friend, Hailey, because she's at work.

"Sam?" His question is sarcastic, but he doesn't seem to understand how unappealing that option is. If I call him, Sam will pay for a tow truck *and* my new tire, then use it against me later. "Or even Tyler or Callum? I'm sure they'd come in a heartbeat."

I lift a shoulder. "I know how to change it myself. There's no point in bothering someone else."

He seems to accept that answer. "You have a spare in the trunk?"

"Yes, but, as I said, I know how to change it so you're free to leave." I wince. I don't mean it to sound rude. My intention is to let him know he doesn't need to burden himself with my problem. Plus, I'd rather avoid the small talk he probably expects.

He takes the jack out of my hand. "If I help, you'll get back in your car, therefore to safety, faster." He jacks up the car before looking over his shoulder at me with his dark brown eyes.

Feeling awkward under his gaze, I quickly move to the trunk and grab the spare tire.

"So, your dad taught you how to change tires?" he asks, as if a woman could only learn such a thing from a man. I leave out the fact that it was a man demonstrating in the video that I watched.

"No. Online videos taught me." I also know how to change my own oil and air filter, change and charge my battery, and check fluids. But the rest of the car is foreign to me. I could learn how to fix other things if I watched enough videos, but car maintenance isn't my idea of fun, only a necessary inconvenience.

As we're putting the jack and wrench back in the trunk, I thank him as sincerely as I can, but it comes out fake and unnatural, almost sounding as if I don't mean it. I add a smile, but that too feels foreign and awkward.

He stares at my face a moment too long, probably weirded out, before saying, "It's no problem. I'm sure I don't have to tell you to replace the tire as soon as possible?"

"I've been through this a few times."

He nods and takes off for his truck. Leaving me alone to wonder what went wrong at the interview.

I walk out of most of them knowing for a fact that I won't be called back and offered a job. But I felt good today. Most of my answers came out clearly; exactly as I had rehearsed them, but without sounding practiced. My tone was friendly, I smiled instead of my usual accidental scowl, and I thought my responses, while not perfect, were acceptable. I arrived a few minutes early, I waited patiently, and my outfit was modest and professional. And the job listing claimed an entry-level, no-experience-required position.

I go home for the thirty minutes before I need to leave for work, wishing I had royally screwed up. Then I'd know what is so unappealing about myself as a potential employee. If I was just given a chance, I could be a valuable asset. Unless I truly am blind to how worthless I am.

Chapter 5
Fine

Nick

Two Years Ago

T he season ended, but my hope of bouncing back persisted. The semester following my accident was filled with physical therapy and sympathy, encouraging words and jokes to mask the pain.

Then summer came. The last summer before senior year. The season that counted because, hopefully, I'd be entering the draft with a degree in sports science I'd never use.

But my coach had called. He needed to see what I could do after months of recovery. Now that I was fully healed, he needed to ensure I could still perform at the level that I was before the injury.

Apparently, he didn't like what he saw.

My leg was different. It had healed slightly shorter than it was before, limiting my speed and agility. Expected after a continuum compound fracture, but still a shock because of my determination to play again.

The coaching staff decided I wasn't what they wanted for the team.

Then, as if that wasn't heartbreaking enough, the admissions office called.

"Unfortunately, Mr. Porter, because you're unable to play, we have to revoke your scholarship. So, unless you're able to come up with the tuition yourself..." the lady trailed off because there was only one way she could have ended that sentence. I worked all of my life to get that scholarship. But that scholarship was to play football. Which I could no longer do. And of course, I was enrolled at one of the schools that doesn't have any heart or understanding.

That happened last week, but I haven't told the guys yet. They've asked me what's wrong several times, to which I respond with, "My leg is bothering me, that's all." They're in their rooms getting ready to go to practice, I'm laying in my bed that I can't seem to get out of.

Callum knocks on the door before poking his head in. "We're about to leave, you need anything?"

I shake my head.

"Alright. Don't make plans for tonight. We're going out or something, to get your mind off that leg." With that, he leaves, Tyler leaves, Sam is already gone, probably with a girl, and I'm left here all alone.

The house falls to a deafening quiet that will drive me mad if I don't get out of here, so I finally roll out of bed. I shower, but don't bother with jeans, sticking to the sweatpants that have become my usual attire, then head to Kenna's. The only good thing I have left in my life.

She opens the door in a towel, her red hair wet from her own shower. "Hey, I didn't know you were coming. Did you text me?"

"Do I have to?"

"No, of course not." But her voice is high and squeaky. She steps away from the door to allow me room to enter and I shut *the door behind me. She points to the couch. "Do you want to sit down? I'll go change and we can go get breakfast or something."*

"Why can't I just come in the room with you?"

"You can. I just thought you could watch TV or something."
She's being weird. I follow to her room, as she walks slowly, periodically looking back at me and smiling.

When she opens the door, she rushes around cleaning up clothes. I tell her that she doesn't have to clean up for me. Her room looks like this every time I come over, why would she suddenly be ashamed of it?

The answer comes in the form of boxers she tries to cover up with her own clothing. Boxers that aren't mine.

As if slapped with an open palm, my face reddens, and my gaze bounces around the room, looking for what I'm supposed to do now.

She's all I have left after losing football and school. I don't know if I have the strength to risk a confrontation or to hear her explanations. Maybe I'm jumping to conclusions—they might not even belong to a guy, they could be hers. Or, maybe they belong to the boyfriend of one of her roommates and they just accidentally ended up in here.

Then, I see a used condom in the trash can underneath her bedside table and I'm no longer able to pretend I didn't notice. I can't pull my eyes away from it as the lump in my throat threatens to choke what little life is left in me.

After Kenna places the clothes in the hamper, she turns to me, then follows my gaze.

"Nick," she says, gently.

"I see why I haven't seen much of you lately," is all I can think of to say.

"Nick." She approaches me, but I back out of her reach.

"I've lost everything, Kenna. How could you?"

She considers her answer for a long while, and when she

finally speaks, I wish she hadn't said anything at all. "Was I supposed to just sit around and wait for you to wake up and remember that I existed? The only thing that has had your attention lately is training." That's not even remotely true, she's the one who's been distant. Always busy when I ask her to dinner, or to just be in the same room at the same time. If it makes her feel less guilty, then I won't say anything to refute it. But I won't sit here and take it, either.

"Whatever, Kenna." I move about the room collecting things I've left here, a couple of t-shirts, a toothbrush and other bathroom items, an extra phone charger, etc. "Have a nice life." Then I leave.

When I get back to that empty house, I can't stand being there either. We'd all been living under the same roof, yet in vastly different houses, pretending everything was still the same. But nothing would be the same again. So I spend the next couple of hours packing all of my stuff into my truck and I run back to Mom's before the guys make it back from practice.

Present Day

S omething went wrong with the play and somehow the ball ended up in my hands. An offensive tackle with the body of a bear and the head of a chicken starts clucking while he pushes off the ground with his huge paws, and I start running as fast as I can for the end zone. Blinding pain starts shooting through my leg anytime I put weight on it, and when I look down, there's a bone sticking out of my shin just beneath my knee. Somehow, I make it to the end zone, but when I collapse on the ground, blood pouring from my leg, I realize I never had the ball after all. What I carried was a clock.

I wake covered in sweat and gripping my leg at the imaginary pain. It's not uncommon for these types of nightmares to occur. They used to happen a few times a week after the injury but had become less frequent.

The clock shows it's just after midnight. I take my shirt off but remember my clean clothes are still in the dryer and I'm dying of thirst anyway. I step out of my room and pass by Sam's door when it opens, revealing a wide-eyed Cori. She stops and averts her eyes at the sight of my bare chest.

She crosses her arms, covered this time by... my sweatshirt? It's a North Houston University football sweatshirt, cyan blue to match the school colors. She probably thinks it's Sam's; most guys on the team had one. But I know this one is mine because of the bleach stain on the sleeve and the image of the Panther— Sam's only had the school name.

I motion for her to go first and she quietly shuts the door before tiptoeing down the hall. When she gets to the end, she turns. "Umm, were you coming to sit out here or something?"

Weird question, but okay. "I just came to get a drink. And a shirt."

She nods and chews on her lip looking conflicted before deciding to continue into the kitchen. I watch after her for a second, curious, as she starts messing with the coffee machine, then head for the laundry room.

After I'm dressed again in a dry white shirt, I fill a glass with water and stand at the counter gulping the whole thing. I refill the glass, then rummage through the pantry for my secret stash of chocolate chip cookies. Cori is already seated on the couch covered with a blanket and coffee cup in hand, no snack this time. I hold a cookie out to her, but she shakes her head.

"It's okay, thank you, though." She had said the other night,

"I didn't want to hear a lecture about eating sugar or eating too late." I assume she's declining now for that same reason, but my mom struggled with her body image and eating habits for years after my dad left. I don't want anyone feeling that way around me.

"There's nothing wrong with sugar every once in a while." I lay a cookie over the rim of her mug anyway and she watches with a blank expression as I sit in an armchair by the window.

"Can't sleep again?" I ask.

"No." Slowly, as if unsure whether it's okay to eat it, she brings the cookie to her lips and takes the smallest bite I've ever seen. Meanwhile, I've consumed two whole cookies.

"Well, I've heard caffeine is good for insomnia."

"It's decaf," she says dryly.

"Then, what's the point?" Coffee is necessary when I have to wake up at five a.m. but the taste is awful and not worth it without the caffeine.

She bites her cheek, watching the steam curl out of the top of her cup, then lifts a shoulder. "I don't know, it's comforting. The heat, the taste. Reminds me of my Grandma."

"Your Grandma tastes like coffee?"

She rolls her eyes, but I get a smirk out of her. "She drank a lot of it, so probably. I just mean, her house always smelled like a freshly brewed pot and she recommended coffee for any ailment."

"And what's ailing you?"

Her eyes meet mine. They're a soft blue, almost gray, like faded denim or a stormy ocean. "Nothing really. Just can't sleep."

I'm curious about this woman, not just because she's one of my friend's girlfriends, but because... well, she's strange. She's guarded and hesitant, but what is there to be wary of? Is she this way with Sam? Or is she unapologetically herself, whoever she is, when you knock those fences down?

"So, you and Sam knew each other when you were kids? Was he just as ugly then as he is now?" I ask, hoping to break the tension a little more.

It almost works. The corners of her lips twitch, but if I weren't watching so intently, I would have missed it. "No, he's always been attractive. It's annoying."

I grin and she takes another sip of coffee. "Where were you coming back from earlier? Or headed to?"

Her eyes remain on her cup as she runs her thumb along the rim. "An interview."

"Oh, did it go well?"

"No."

"Ouch. Well, the right job will come along at the right time." I thought it was a comforting thing to say, but her eyes snap to mine, her brows furrowing as if I offended her. Or maybe she's trying to figure something out. She averts her gaze, but the pinch of her forehead doesn't ease as she stares off into the distance and I'm at a loss of what to do or say next. I consider myself to be a confident person, pretty sure of myself and comfortable in my skin, but here with this woman, I've never felt more out of my element.

I notice a book next to her on the arm of the couch and I jerk my chin to it. "What are you reading?"

"Nothing, you won't stop talking to me." Her words are slow and soft like she's unsure she wants to say them, and I hope she's joking because the air is already suffocating enough. Her features soften into the barest of grins, but it's still just a whisper across her lips as she turns the book around. I assume it's fantasy, based on the crown and dagger on the cover.

"What's it about?"

"A king kidnaps a queen from another land and they fall in love."

I raise a single brow. "Sounds... *romantic.*"

She doesn't respond.

"Do you read a lot?" I realize I've done nothing except ask her questions tonight, but she kills every conversation by not reciprocating. If she gives an answer at all, it's a simple one. I don't know how else to keep the conversation going if I don't continue the interrogation.

"Yeah."

"Why?" An idiot would know it's because she enjoys it. But I've never understood how reading is more enjoyable than watching TV. Your brain doesn't have to work as hard when the visual is already done for you.

"It's a good escape." She chews on her lip, and I fight the urge to ask what she needs to escape from. I can't imagine she'd like that question.

Instead, I choose to state an observation, "You don't talk much." But it becomes apparent I chose wrong.

She rolls her eyes. "Okay."

It's not remotely the response I was expecting. "What? It's just an observation I've made." But I guess it's an obvious one, one she's likely made herself. By bringing awareness to it, I've only heightened the awkward tension between us.

She narrows her eyes again and cocks her head to the side. "I've answered every one of your questions."

"Sure, but I feel like I have to pull words out of you."

"I barely know you."

Don't people have conversations with strangers all the time? "You get to know people by talking to them."

"I don't like talking," she shoots back. At least she's honest.

"Then, I guess we don't have to talk."

"Fine."

"Fine."

She holds my gaze instead of looking away this time, daring me to open my mouth. We sit there, awkwardly studying each other for a few minutes until, slowly, she reaches her hand over for her book, picking it up, and bringing it to her lap. Only after she turns the page to where her bookmark lies does she finally break our eye contact and look down.

For the next twenty or so minutes, she reads and I watch her. I don't know why, but I can't seem to look away. I have an overwhelming urge to understand what's going through her mind, to know why she can't sleep, to know why she doesn't like talking. If for no other reason than she's the exact opposite of any woman Sam's dated before. She knows I watch her because she pins me with her gaze for a few seconds anytime she turns the page, her expression unreadable.

"What the hell are y'all doing? It's after midnight." Sam's voice penetrates the tension as he appears in the walkway between the living room and the hall, rubbing his eyes.

"Sorry, I couldn't sleep." Why is she *apologizing?* Cori rises from the chair, taking her coffee cup to the sink to rinse it out.

"Well, how am I supposed to sleep without someone to cuddle with?"

She dries her hand on the towel and walks toward him. "The same way you sleep whenever I'm at my own apartment." It's a statement, but her tone is lifted at the end.

"It's too late for your sarcasm." As she walks past him, he playfully pinches her butt. "Night, Nick," he says, following her.

I'm left wondering if I'm still asleep and if that encounter with Cori was nothing more than a weird dream.

Chapter 6
Shy or Something

Cori

With ten minutes left in my shift, my best friend, Hailey, walks inside and sits in a booth to wait. After I clock out, we'll eat Mexican food and host our book club meeting, just the two of us—we're too antisocial to ask anyone else to join. We started this book club after high school, and we actually talk about the books we read instead of calling it "book club" as an excuse to drink wine and gossip. Don't get me wrong, there's still plenty of that happening, but we have monthly picks and discussions about the books we read beforehand. The majority of the books we choose may be smut, but I think we've earned the right to read what we want after years of reading classics in school.

Sure, themes of poverty or power are important, but they aren't what I want to escape into after being yelled at by hungry customers all day. Poverty is my reality, I don't need it in my entertainment too. Besides, books provide more than just life lessons and escapism; they are experiences we'd otherwise miss out on. Besides Sam, I've had one other serious boyfriend, and have never experienced the passion and intensity described in these books. When your brain won't shut up and lives in a

49

constant state of anxiety, orgasms are more work than they're worth anyway.

When I'm reading, I'm not worried about the lighting or if I'm hurting Sam with my weight. I'm not worried about the pain from lack of proper lubrication. I'm not thinking back over my day and wishing I could take back every cringy thing I said. So, instead of having great sex, I just read about it, and I'm fine with this arrangement.

Hailey and I try to meet up at least once a month but, too often, life gets in the way. She graduated last semester and now teaches English at a junior high. Her work day doesn't technically end until 5, but she's usually working much later than that, planning lessons, grading, and preparing for the next day.

While Sam was my best friend growing up, he was also friends with the "cool" kids and, before he moved away, those friends of his didn't bother me. But once he left, I lost my protector—the wolf that kept all the other wolves away. I became fair game to cruel jokes and hurtful remarks. The thing is, I didn't sit down and take it back then. I gave as well as they did, but that only made me more fun to play with. And I lost every time because I was always outnumbered.

Hailey had just moved to the district when she and I met freshman year of high school. One lunch period during which she was seen eating with me was all it took for her to become another target.

If you stripped away all those years of bullying that we both endured, you'd find hopeful green eyes that look for the positive in any situation. There'd be welcoming arms ready to provide a comforting embrace to anyone in need of a safe space. There'd be a loving, caring person willing to give the shirt off her back to anyone who needed it. Instead, both of us approach everything with caution and the assumption we'll be bitten with sharp fangs, allowing venom to fill our veins and leave us writhing on the ground in agony.

In the years since we met, her teeth have been straightened by braces and her face has shed the last little bit of baby fat. Otherwise, she still has the same long, perfectly straight black hair and the same freckles dotting her nose.

"Hey, I'm almost off. I just have one more thing to do in the back, then I'll be ready to go," I say.

"Good. It's been a hell of a week. I need a margarita more than I need oxygen right now." She exhales a heavy breath and I wish I could hug her, but it will have to wait.

"Did I hear margaritas?" Sage asks, coming up behind me. "I figured when you told me that y'all were hanging out, that meant the bookstore and coffee."

"We'll probably do that too," Hailey says.

"Well, can I come for the margarita part? Brian is at a Bachelor party tonight. And Cori will need alcohol within reach when I discuss something with her."

"Who's Brian?" Hailey asks, waggling her eyebrows at her.

"He's my boyfriend. He's dreamy and has dimples and plays the drums."

"Discuss what?" I ask, on high alert. Is it about Mom and Dad? One of our siblings? Is there an issue with the apartment? Did she accidentally destroy one of my favorite books?

"We'll talk about it when you have a margarita and queso in front of you." She pats my cheek and walks away. Except alcohol doesn't help me like it does some people. Liquid courage or calming for some, anxiety-boosting for me, heightening every negative thought or feeling, but taking away my ability to control myself. I only drink it for the taste, as long as it's fruity.

My heart beats its way through the last of my side work, then I grab my bag and change in the bathroom into a tank top with a cardigan. I head for the door, digging in my purse to turn the sound back up on my phone in case any important calls come through, like, "Your apartment flooded," or "Mom and Dad's house is on fire." Then, I see six missed calls from Sam, and I stop breathing. Six missed calls mean something bad happened. Six missed calls means my life will never be the same.

"Are you okay?" Hailey asks as I approach them, frantically pressing buttons on my phone.

I don't answer her while I wait for the phone to ring, silently praying everything is okay.

"Cori, I've called you a million times," Sam says upon answering.

My voice shakes. "I was at work, is everything okay?"

But when he responds with his reason for so many calls, I could just kill him for almost giving me a heart attack. "Yeah, everything is fine. I was just wondering when you were going to get here. Nick will probably be here soon and there's a lot of people I want to introduce you to."

"What are you talking about?"

"Nick's surprise party." Only, he says it in the form of a question. "I told you about it a week ago. You're coming, right? I've already told everyone you're coming."

"You never told me about a party." I know he didn't because the word *party* has the same effect on my heart as six missed calls.

"Party? I could go for a party right now," Sage says because she doesn't need days of mentally preparing for social situations. She's spontaneous and there isn't much she'll say no to.

"Yes, Cori, I did," he says, slowly, as if I'm a child and his word is to be taken as fact with no evidence to back it up. "A bunch of my old friends from college are going to be here, everyone is excited to meet you."

I pull the phone away from my ear and fill them in. "Let's do it." Sage steals the phone to tell Sam we're leaving now, and Hailey shoots an expression of disbelief my way.

Hailey and Sam have resisted my every attempt at making them like each other and insist on retaining their disdain for one another. Hailey finds Sam to be arrogant and selfish, while Sam finds her to be rude and judgmental. They refuse to believe that they're simply misunderstanding the other, so in the middle I remain.

I take her hands in mine. "I'm sorry. We don't have to stay long, I'll just meet whoever it is he wants me to meet and then we'll leave and get those margaritas, okay?"

She sighs. "It's fine. There should be alcohol there, right?"

Sage has enough clothes in her car to fill a closet. She grabs a hot pink dress and black heels from her trunk and changes in the backseat while Hailey drives.

"Since we have a moment now, I guess I'll give you the news," Sage says once she's dressed. "But you can't freak out, okay? It's a good thing." When I turn around in the passenger seat to see her better, her finger is pointed at me, as if she knows me and my tendency to panic.

"No promises."

She rolls her eyes before meeting my gaze once again. "I'm moving out."

My eyebrows shoot upwards, and my shoulders jolt as if the words have physically pushed me. "Moving out? Where are you going to live?"

"With Brian, duh. You know our lease is up next month, so I thought now would be the perfect time."

"You just started dating him a few weeks ago. You're moving in with him already?"

"Dimples, Cori." She shrugs. "I know what I want."

Okay. Just breathe. In and out.

My mind spins a mile a minute, thinking of potential room-mates. Taking over her half of rent might be feasible if I eat scraps at the diner, and don't turn the heater on. Or the AC when summer fully arrives. Except this is Texas and I'll die without the AC. Maybe if I-

"Quit spiraling," Sage says with another eye roll.

"I'm not spiraling."

"Yes, you are, I can see it on your face. Your eyes are darting around the car but not seeing anything. You're freaking out in that freaky head of yours."

"I'm just working out how I might be able to afford rent without asking some random stranger to move in with me."

"Ask your best friend," Sage says.

"I just signed another year's lease on mine in January. I'm sorry, Cori," Hailey says from the driver's seat, bringing us back to the issue at hand.

"I already knew that, don't be sorry."

"But, you could sleep on the couch? Or we could get bunk beds? We could share a bed. I'm a cold sleeper anyway, we could cuddle!!" Hailey adds, desperate to present any idea that doesn't involve me moving in with the man she hates.

"Or, I don't know, maybe you could... let's see... *move in with your boyfriend?*" Sage's eyebrows rise.

We've only been dating for nine months. Is that long enough to move in with someone? It's out of the question anyway. I can't just ask him if I can move in and invade his space—he has to be the one to offer it. And if he does, would Nick be okay with me moving in?

Hailey reaches over the center console and grabs my hand.

"I may know someone who could move in, someone I know from college. She's really nice."

Sage throws her hands up. "What's wrong with moving in with Sam? You spend half your time over there anyway."

I repeat my concerns out loud, which causes her to stick her fingers in her eyes. I add, "What if I give up our apartment and it doesn't work out with you and Brian?"

"Thanks for your doubt, Cor. I'm so glad I have your support." She turns to look out the window. "I'll pay rent until the lease is up and then you can either renew it with someone else's name on the paperwork, or you can grow up and communicate with your boyfriend."

On the bright side, the unfortunate news of Sage moving out distracts me from my typical pre-party routine where my insides twist themselves until bile floods my throat. There's sour candy and salt packets in my pocket to ground my senses, just in case I can't ward off a panic attack through breathing, but it also helps that Hailey is here with me. Like a support blanket.

Before we're inside the door, Sam's hand is wrapped around my wrist, pulling me into the hallway towards his bedroom. Once we're inside, he hands me a shopping bag.

"Here, I got this for you."

I peek inside and see red fabric. "What is it?"

"It's a dress. And there are shoes underneath. I thought you could wear it tonight."

I pull it out and find a necklace and lacy underwear as well. "Why? I already changed." The dress is modest but still shorter than I'd like and I'm not sure that I'll be able to walk in the heels.

"It's been a while since I bought you anything nice. And, I'll admit, I was a little afraid you'd show up wearing a t-shirt or something." He smiles, his eyes light.

"Well? Are you going to put it on? The dress is supposed to have shapewear sewn in," he says. I pull my blazer closed and cross my arms over my chest.

"Do I have to?"

"I mean, it'd be kind of rude not to, don't you think? I bought it for you. His eyes narrow. "What? You don't like it?"

"No, it's pretty, it's just... I'm already dressed. And it's so short and probably tight."

"Come on, I went to a lot of trouble picking it out for you, I thought it'd make you happy." More like, his *assistant* picked it out. "It'll look a lot sexier than what you have on. Don't you want to make a good impression? This is a party, Cori. No one else is wearing jeans. No one that matters, anyway." I know he's referring to the dark jeans Hailey wears.

Reluctantly, I start to take off my clothes.

After I'm done, I look in the mirror. As expected, it's too short, too tight, and not me at all. Sam clasps the necklace around my neck, a single, simple diamond embedded in the center.

"And take your hair down. Your hair looks so much nicer down." He unclasps the hair clip and fluffs the waves out over my shoulder.

I swallow hard and attempt to pull the dress down, but it's no use. The cool air against my legs demands my focus as he pulls me back out of his room and toward a group of strangers. It's a good sign that he's so eager for me to meet people, right? Taking a few deep breaths, I mentally prepare myself for the assessment I'm about to undergo from these curious eyes.

Don't panic.

"Guys, this is Cori. Cori, this is-"

I shake hands with each person, but my brain doesn't absorb a single name that Sam says during each introduction. I'm too busy wondering why Sam insisted on showing me off to these people. I'm inferior in every way, a platypus among swans. There are two women and three men within this circle, all shiny and polished in ways I'll never be, but I find myself thankful for the outfit after all. I would have looked ridiculous in my blazer and jeans next to these people.

"It's, uhh, nice... nice to meet you all. You're all friends from Sam's- I mean, *of* Sam's from college?" It doesn't matter if you're an expert at something; watchful eyes apply pressure that could cause anyone to fumble. Sam, noticing my heaving breath, furrows his brows while I feel like I'm running a marathon through mud.

They all nod, and one of the women asks, "When did you two start dating?"

I look at Sam, but he's waiting for me to answer. "About nine months ago." But I guess that wasn't enough of an answer because they continue to stare at me.

Thankfully, Sam chuckles and continues the story of how we started dating, and I use the time to look over my shoulder for Hailey. She stands against the kitchen counter alone sipping her drink. Reading the plea on my face, she comes to stand beside me. Sam tenses when he notices her approach but introduces her despite his disdain, and she presses her lips into a thin line.

After a while, Sam ushers us off to another group of people.

One of the women in this new group, who Sam introduces as Erin, smiles widely, her white teeth almost blinding. Holding out her hand to me, she says, "We're so excited to finally meet the woman who's been putting up with this guy. Sam and I dated a bit in college, but it wasn't really serious. I love your dress! So tell me about yourself. What do you do for work? How did you and Sam meet?"

The introvert in me is shell-shocked by the energy bursting from her tiny frame, but I manage to recover and take her dainty little hand in mine, hoping she doesn't recoil from my sweaty palms. Then I recount the story of how Sam and I met, keeping it short and sweet.

She narrows her eyes at Hailey before I can answer any of her other questions. "You look really familiar, did you go to NHU too? What's your name? I love your hairstyle!" The red-haired woman that stands beside her, who Sam introduced as Kenna, rolls her eyes just enough for me to catch it, but I'm not sure if it's toward Erin or Hailey.

Before Hailey has a chance to answer, Erin snaps her fingers. "We work together! You teach English, right? Wait, do you have A or B lunch?"

"B," Hailey answers, unsure.

"We're so having lunch on Monday. I have a free period before. I'm the cheer coach, but I also teach math. I'll pick up some salads and meet you in the teachers' lounge in the west hall. Oh, I'm so excited to have a new work friend!"

While they talk, I feel like prey beneath Kenna's unimpressed gaze as she studies me, my clothes, my shoes, my hair. I avoid looking back at her, but my peripheral vision is excellent, a skill you pick up on when you're an observant wallflower afraid of accidentally making eye contact. She takes a sip of her drink and talks over Hailey to ask me, "You don't talk much, do you?"

I finally meet her unfriendly stare, unsure of how to answer that dreaded question. Or *observation*, as Nick called it the other night. On one hand, no, I don't talk much. On the other hand, the opportunity for me to talk much hasn't exactly presented itself. I've answered every question I've been asked, but the focus of this conversation has been on other people besides me. Was I supposed to insert myself into the conversation despite my having nothing of value to contribute?

I decide to give her what she wants but without further explanation. "Nope."

"Are you shy, or something?"

It's hard to admit, especially with the negative connotation usually accompanying the label, but there's no point in pretending otherwise. "Yes."

She smiles, feigning innocence, and I brace myself. "Well, don't worry. *I'll* get you out of your shell eventually." As if all I needed to stop being shy was a determined person who wouldn't take no for an answer.

She cocks her head. "What did you say you do for work?"

"I'm just a server for now."

Sam is quick to jump in and add, "Yeah, while she's still in school finishing up her bachelor's degree."

"Oh? What's your degree in?" It's a perfectly reasonable question, but I can't help the feeling that Kenna senses the lie. Because it is.

I look up at Sam. I'm not *still in school*, I'm not *finishing my bachelor's*, I'm *just* a server. That's it.

I thank God when Sam gets a text and calls out, "Okay, quiet down everyone, they're downstairs." He moves around the room, turning off lights and ushering guests to duck down.

Hailey takes this opportunity to pull me off to the side.

"Are you kidding me?" she whispers. "You can't move in with that asshole."

I don't respond. Too much has happened tonight. Our plans were rerouted to a party, of all things, Sage dropped a bomb on me, then I was thrown into a den of hyenas where I discovered that my boyfriend is ashamed of me. After I was made to feel ridiculous for being insecure about our differences in social class and attraction ratings.

I try to stay focused on the task at hand: surprising Nick. Mainly to keep my body from shaking and my insides twisting. Then, I realize I don't even know what this surprise is for. Is it his birthday? Is it a "Welcome back," situation?

Whatever it's for, Nick walks in trailed by Tyler and Callum, the lights flick on, everyone shouts, "Surprise!" and the buzz of chatter resumes.

Chapter 7
Chokehold

Nick

N o one needs to know, but today is my birthday. And the only thing I want for my birthday is to pick up some nachos on the way home, watch the Stallions play baseball with a beer in my hand, and pass out during the post-game show. After work, I head to my truck to do just that, but Tyler calls.

"Nick. Callum and I request your presence for dinner. Tonight at seven. We'll pick you up from your apartment at six forty-five." He hangs up before I can ask any questions.

If Tyler is saying as little as possible, it's because he's trying to keep from spilling whatever secret he's keeping. I guess my plans for the night are canceled; although spending my birthday with these guys will be an improvement.

I head home, shower, and wait for them in front of Sam's—I mean, *my* apartment. For now, anyway. Because my share of rent equals what I'd pay if I had my own place, I probably won't stay here long.

When Callum's truck pulls up, the back window rolls down and Tyler tells me to get in the front. He shakes my shoulders from behind me after I climb in, wishing me a Happy Birthday.

"Thanks. I'll be honest, I was hoping none of you remembered."

"We spent three years with you in college. Of course, we remember. Time has passed, but it hasn't erased our memory," Callum answers, always the wise one.

"So, where are you taking me?" I ask.

"Guess," Tyler instructs, but I don't have time to guess before he blurts out the answer. "That Mexican food place we always go to on our birthdays. It's tradition."

A grin spreads over my face, then my phone rings.

"Hi, Mom," I say, holding the phone up to my ear.

"Happy Birthday to you," she sings. It's the third time I've heard the song from her today, but I don't mind, although her voice carries to the guys. I sit awkwardly listening until she's finished while Callum and Tyler snicker.

"Thanks, Mom."

"Are you still coming this weekend so I can make your birthday dinner for you?"

"Yes, for the thousandth time," I answer, teasingly.

"I'm sorry, I just miss you. This is the first time in two years that I haven't had you home for your birthday."

"I know, Mom. I miss you too." And this is why I worry about her being alone. Why I want her to find someone. Even if it's just a friend.

Then I hear a male voice in the background. "Elaine," it said—Mom's name.

"Who is that?"

"Oh, no one. It was just the TV." My eyes narrow. I figured it was Uncle Jonah, who does maintenance around the house for Mom sometimes. But she wouldn't lie if it were him.

"You know I wouldn't care if you were seeing anyone," I say gently. It's a topic we've discussed so many times it's reached pestering status. I don't want Mom to be lonely, especially since I moved away again, and I wouldn't worry so much if I knew she'd finally lowered her guard and let someone in. Dad really did a number on her.

"I know but I promise it was just the TV."

"Okay, I believe you." Except I don't.

"Hi, Mom!" Tyler calls from the back seat. I put her on speaker and she asks Callum how he's doing, and Tyler if he's behaving.

"Well, I won't keep you, I just wanted to wish you a happy birthday. Again." She laughs.

I say goodbye and hang up just as we arrive at the restaurant. We eat, then a sombrero gets placed on my head and my nose is covered with whipped cream while they sing to me. When we get back to the apartment, I expect them to drop me off at the sidewalk, but Callum parks in a Visitor's spot and turns his truck off.

"Are you coming up?" I love these guys, but I was kind of looking forward to turning my TV on and falling asleep.

"Yeah, we'll come up, maybe watch a movie or something," Tyler says.

He and Callum have been acting weird all night. First, the weird phone call, the impromptu dinner, and insisting on driving me. Then, they didn't stay off their phones for the entire meal, which isn't exactly unusual, but they kept stealing glances, like maybe they were texting each other about me. And now they've invited themselves up to the apartment for a movie?

"Okay, what's going on?" I ask.

"Nothing. We just missed you, man," Callum answers.

"Yeah, we've got some separation issues," Tyler adds. And I might have believed that explanation, except I've been back in town for two weeks and this is only the second time I've seen them.

I narrow my eyes before deciding to let it go and continue waiting for the shoe to drop. It does as soon as we open the door to the apartment and a cacophony rings out, "Surprise!"

"Nick. Happy Birthday, man." Sam walks up, arm wrapped around a miserable-looking Cori. "Were you surprised?"

"Yep. You got me."

"Good. Not that you deserve it, but I figured a birthday party would be the best way to ring in your big return." His glare is piercing, leaving me confused if he's mad I left in the first place or that I returned at all. "You've met Cori, but this is her friend Hailey. I know she looks like a bitch, but she's- no, actually she's just a bitch." He gestures to a dark-haired woman, a scowl on her face.

Cori whips her head towards his and pulls away from his embrace. "What is wrong with you tonight?"

"What? No one can take a joke? I thought that's what we did, Hailey. We poke fun at each other."

Hailey crosses her arms and pokes her hip out. "It's fine, Cori, he's right, that's just the dynamics of our relationship. He doesn't pretend to like me, and I don't pretend to like him."

I reach out my hand to her. "I'm Nick, it's nice to meet you. I'm sorry for this dick," I say, jerking my head towards Sam.

She shakes my hand but doesn't smile or respond.

"Oh, sure. Everyone team up against the guy who threw this party for everyone. And let you come, I might add," he says, widening his eyes at Hailey. Someone from the kitchen calls out Sam's name and he goes to see what they need, leaving me alone with the two most guarded women in this apartment. Possibly this town. They both glance around the room, probably looking for a reason to walk away.

"So, how long do you think I'll have to stay out here and socialize?" I ask, my attempt to break the freezing ice.

"It's your party, these are your friends. If we have to be here, so do you," Cori deadpans.

I smirk. "Are you going to guard the door or something?"

"If I have to." She pins me with that same unreadable expression from the other night. If I'm not mistaken, her tight lips hold back a smile as if I'm not worthy of one just yet.

I meet Hailey's gaze when I feel her studying my face. She returns my grin but an old teammate approaches, pulling me into conversation before I can make one with her. As the two women fade into the crowd, I hear a muffled voice say, "He's cute. Why can't you date him instead of Sam?"

Cori

Hailey and I take a few steps away when Nick gets distracted. "He's cute. Why can't you date him instead of Sam?" she asks.

"Can we not do this? Can you just get my mind off of it all, please? There's too much going on tonight-" I'm interrupted by Tyler and Callum approaching, and Callum asks if Hailey is doing well.

Tyler, on the other hand, looks her up and down and says, "Fine as always, Ms. Weldon." Hailey's glare of steel doesn't crack so he turns to me. "I saw Sage walking around. I keep meaning to ask, is she seeing anyone?"

"Yeah, she just started dating some guy and is apparently moving in with him."

"Damn, too late again." He looks at Hailey, seemingly

considering something. "What about you, H? You seeing anyone?" He flashes a comical smolder her way.

Hailey's arms are crossed and her expression is deadly. Callum grabs Tyler's arm, dragging him off before she pounces. Callum and Hailey have hit it off. Not romantically, but they have a lot of interests in common and always find something to talk about. It doesn't hurt that Callum is a sweetheart. Tyler on the other hand, according to Hailey, is abrasive and thinks too highly of himself. *"Just like Sam, only less stuck-up,"* she told me once.

I thought the same thing at first, only I've come to learn that Tyler had a rough childhood and used humor to distract himself and his siblings from the world crumbling around them. He's a clown, but his compliments are genuine, even if his delivery could use some improvement.

"So, why was this week so stressful? Did something happen?" I ask, now that we finally have a moment.

She gently shakes her head. "It's been a rough *month*."

I turn so that she has my full attention. "Why? What's going on?"

"It's not the time. We can talk later."

I glance around for Sage to suggest we leave, but hear gasps from the kitchen. Sam appears in the walkway between the kitchen and living room, his hand wrapped in a dish towel. Blood quickly spreads over the white cotton.

I shoot an apologetic look at Hailey.

She rolls her eyes, but says, "It's fine. Go take care of your dumbass."

"I promise I'll be right back."

It turns out my dumbass squeezed his glass a little too tight, causing it to shatter in his hand. Once we get to his bathroom, I examine the cuts quietly. Despite the amount of blood on the towel, I don't think any of them are deep enough to require stitches, and Sam rejects any idea of going to the ER anyway.

I get to work cleaning his hand and checking for stray glass, but I'm not entirely confident in my healer abilities.

"Are you okay? You seem off tonight?"

My head snaps up. "Off?" I ask, sharply. "I don't like crowds or strangers or small talk. How do you not know that by now? And, you know," I look back down and flip his hand over, preparing for the bandage, "I found out tonight that you're ashamed of me."

"What? How could you think that?"

"You told that lie about me only working as a server while I finish my bachelor's degree." I wrap the bandage around his hand, a little too tightly, based on his wince.

"Well, aren't you?" Another wince.

"No, and you know this."

"You are trying to find another job, aren't you? I just assumed at some point you'd go back to school since you can't find anyone to hire you as is. Besides, you can't be a server forever," he states, sounding identical to my father.

"Why not?" I have my reasons for wanting out of serving, but I'm tired of everyone looking down on the position. "You know, the job is important. I handle the food people consume. There's a lot of responsibility and stress that comes with that."

He snorts. "Sure. Anyway, you hate it."

I struggle to find the words to refute his point because... well, I do hate it. So I say, "Okay," because I'm eager to end this nonsense, find Sage, and leave. Maybe Hailey was right—I need to reevaluate this relationship.

Except, Sam is the only thing I've done right according to my parents. Would I really let him go because he wants better for me than a job that I already hate?

Without another word, I leave him sitting on the counter of

his bathroom and go back out to the living room. I finally find Sage, but she informs me that Hailey wasn't feeling up to a night out after all and left.

"We'll just order a ride home. Unless you want to stay and start getting used to living with a boy?" She doesn't wait for my response before bouncing off to go make friends with anyone and everyone. It's so easy for her. She doesn't overthink or stress or care about what others think of her. She just says and does what she wants, simply shrugging off the consequences.

There's no answer when I call Hailey, so I send a text message instead. *I'm sorry. We'll talk tomorrow, just you and me. No interruptions.*

I'm left standing there against the wall, my eyes flitting across the room looking for Sam or Tyler or Callum, anyone I can go stand beside just for comfort. I see a familiar woman who Tyler had a casual relationship with a few months ago. I've only met her once, so I don't know her very well. I want to go up to her—scratch that, because *want* is a strong word. What I *want* to do is run away and never have to meet or make small talk with another person ever again. But I *wish* I was the sort of person who could go to her and say hi, tell her I like her blush-colored, a-line dress with the lace neckline. Maybe ask her how her dog is, the pinscher she said had a thyroid issue.

But a million ridiculous what-ifs siege control over my body, trapping me in place. Like, what if I accidentally make her uncomfortable by commenting on her dress? Or what if something has happened to her dog since the last time we spoke and I make her cry by bringing it up? Or what if she doesn't remember me? Or thinks it's creepy that I remember one small part of a conversation we had a couple of months ago?

So I stay put, appearing standoffish and rude when really, anxiety has me in a chokehold.

Chapter 8
Just Don't Be Shy

Nick

I spend the next couple of hours repeatedly answering the same questions.

"What have you been up to?" *Working.*

"Are you going to go back to school?" *Haven't thought about it.*

"How's the leg?" *Fine.*

"If you're not going back to school, what are you going to do?" *I... I...*

I seem to be the only person in the room who didn't finish college. The only person who didn't end up in the field they'd planned to. The only person who hasn't achieved, or isn't actively working towards, their dream. Maybe coming back was a mistake.

I take advantage of the turned heads when Sam cuts his hand, and escape the interrogation. As I'm pouring whiskey into a clear plastic cup, I hear a familiar, dangerous voice behind me.

"Nick." I turn to see my ex-girlfriend, Kenna, her lips as red as her dyed hair. She stands close enough that I see right down her dress, and her sweet perfume takes me back to all the nights we spent entwined.

"Kenna."

"How are you doing?" She puts her hand on my forearm and rubs circles on my skin with her thumb.

I bite the inside of my cheek. "I'm doing good. You?"

"I've been better. I got laid off from the job I started just a few months ago."

"Sorry to hear that." I take a long drink and savor the burn.

She cocks her head to the side. "Are you?"

"Of course I am. Why wouldn't I be?" I need to get away before she sinks her teeth into me.

"We didn't exactly end things on good terms."

"Well, you cheated on me," I state, matter of factly.

"Look, neither of us was in a good place then. Now we are." She bats her eyelashes at me, a flirty gleam sparkling in her brown eyes.

"Okay..." I draw the word out, unsure of where she's going with this.

She runs her long, black fingernails down my arm before wrapping her hand around my wrist. "So... let's talk."

"I don't think that's a good idea."

Her tongue drips with venom as she asks, "Why not?"

I want to say, '*Because I'll always feel as if I'm holding you back. Because I'm still not in a good place. Because I still don't know what I'm doing with my life after two years. Because I doubt I'll ever trust you again.*' But I don't.

Instead, I say, "I don't know. Maybe. I gotta go." I pull my arm out of her grasp once again, my heart threatening to beat itself to death.

I need some fresh air, but we're too close to Houston and the closest thing I'll get is thick and murky. Stepping around her, I escape to the balcony, and stand off to the side where the stone wall hides me from view of the windows. I hold a deep breath of the cool night air in my lungs until it burns, then exhale my frustrations.

I need to learn how to be around them all. How to keep myself in check and not let my jealousy of people like Sam consume me. How to be around people who got to keep their scholarships even though they had money to pay for tuition. People who could have made it to the NFL, but threw it away for a job with *daddy*. People who continued their lives at school and went on to graduate after my world was flipped upside down. People who have a plan for their life.

I need to learn how to deal with hearing news like, *"Coach Resinski signed with the Dolphins."* The coach who kicked me off the ladder before setting the ladder on fire. I know he was simply doing his job. But doing his job is how he rose to the top while I lay writhing at the bottom.

I haven't thought about my future since my injury, and even then, I couldn't consider a future without football. I was going to heal and train, get myself back in shape and back on the field before the next football season. When that didn't happen, I succumbed to my heartbreak, and like someone who writes off relationships to protect his heart, forced myself to work jobs I couldn't care less about. Before life could throw me around again, I'd leave and work somewhere else for a while. Get a change of scenery before the fear of commitment set in.

Now that I'm back here among all these teachers, accountants, and engineers, I want that. I want to *be* someone. I want to be excited about something again. I want to care again. Have a goal and accomplish milestones towards that goal.

But I don't know how to make that happen.

When the door opens, I expect it's Kenna, having followed

me out here to invade my solitude. Instead, it's Cori. I watch inquisitively as she steps up to the railing and closes her eyes, allowing the chill to soothe her red cheeks.

"So, who are you hiding from?"

Her head whips toward me and her hand goes to her heart. "Sorry, I didn't know anyone was out here." She talks around something in her mouth, a cough drop maybe, or piece of candy. "I'm not really hiding from anyone. Or, maybe I'm hiding from everyone." She shakes her head and carefully rubs one of her eyes. "I just needed a moment."

I nod in understanding, and we both turn our heads to the courtyard beyond the rail. The smell of rain from a drizzle lingers in the air, along with something floral that I think might be Cori. I take another deep, healing breath.

The rumble of thunder has us both looking at the sky, hoping the rain holds off until we're ready to face the crowd inside on our own terms.

"Wait. Are *you* hiding from someone?" she asks, turning to face me.

"Originally, from my ex. But I guess my answer is kind of the same as yours."

"Who is your ex?"

"Kenna Armstrong. She has red hair and a black dress on."

Something flashes in her eyes. Disappointment maybe. "Oh. Yeah, I met her."

My body tenses out of defensiveness, but not for Kenna. "What did she say to you?"

She crosses her arms and shoots an irritated look my way. "Nothing much different than what you said the other night. About me not talking much."

"Why does that bother you? Like I said, it was just an observation."

"I know." Another simple answer, a dead end to the conversation. Until she closes her eyes again and breathes before adding, "It's just that I hear it so often. *'You're so shy, why are you so shy? You don't talk, why don't you talk?'*" she says, tone lifted mockingly. "I have many insecurities. Being shy is my greatest one."

"So, just don't be shy. Fake it 'til you make it, or whatever. Do something crazy to get over the fear."

She turns on me so fast I jolt backward, but the fury in her eyes vanishes as she meets my gaze, and whatever words she wishes to hurl at me die on her tongue. She looks away.

"Say it. Whatever it was you wanted to say to me just now, say it." I get the feeling I'm not the first person she's wanted to hurl that anger at.

But she doesn't. She stares off into the distance, guards up and defenses ready, quiet as the night around us.

The door opens then. Sam steps out, shaking his head at us both and crossing his arms.

"Are you hiding?" he asks Cori.

"Maybe." She turns her back to him and he sighs before looking at me.

"And what are you doing?"

I decide to follow Cori's example and give him partial honesty. "Maybe hiding too."

"Why? It's your birthday." He points inside. "These are your friends."

"At one point, yeah. I haven't seen or talked to most of these people in two years. And why the hell would you invite Kenna?" But I forgot. He wouldn't have known what happened between Kenna and me because I left town and moved my stuff out before I had a chance to explain anything.

"Why wouldn't I? She was friends with all of us in college. And, I don't know, I kind of figured you two could reconnect and get back together. You should be thanking me and begging her for her forgiveness."

"She cheated on me," I say quickly, not wanting the words to linger on my tongue. I want them out in the open as fast as possible so we can move on from this conversation.

His expression softens, his mouth opening and shutting a few times before a response comes to him. "Oh, shit. I thought you broke up because you left town without telling anyone."

"I left town without telling anyone after I found out she had slept with someone else." And I left for many reasons, the main one being that I needed space from everyone, like I did when I came out onto this patio. Space to breathe and get my mind off of what I'd lost.

Sam steps closer to me and places a comforting hand on my shoulder. "I'm sorry, man. I didn't know."

I run my hands down my face. "It's not just her, though. Everyone treated me differently after Coach kicked me off the team. You included. Callum wouldn't stop asking if I'd eaten or slept, Tyler could only give me advice about not letting it get me down. And you avoided me."

When guilt and shame should soften his features, he turns it all back on me. "What the hell was I supposed to say to you? I didn't know how to be around you without accidentally rubbing it in your face that I could still play."

I turn towards the rail, bracing my hands on the black wood.

"What is this, I thought you were in a better place?"

I thought so, too. It's easy to stand strong when the winds aren't blowing. I guess, over the last two years, I forgot what the winds felt like.

I face him once again and dismissively shake my head. "I'm just tired. I let my emotions get to me."

"Well, get some coffee. The night is still young." He turns to Cori. "As for you, are you done overreacting?"

She remains with her back to us for so long, that I begin to wonder if she heard him. Finally, she looks over her shoulder and nods, and we all go back inside.

I t's better the second time I make a round through the room. Tyler pulls me into a group with some old friends of ours and informs me that Kenna left. With her absence and the freedom to catch up without having to watch my back, I start to enjoy myself. The *What are you doing with your life* type questions transform into *Remember when* stories, and it's as if the balcony never happened.

Cori still looks miserable being dragged around by Sam, but perks up when Tyler makes me recount the story of the hurricane that flooded the city our sophomore year. Everything was shut down because no one could get anywhere. Even our street had about three feet or so of water. So we got a trash can lid, tied it to the back of Sam's truck, and water sled down the street. And we had a blast doing it until someone called the cops on us.

"Were you all drunk?" Cori asks.

All four of us, Tyler, Callum, Sam, and me, answer simultaneously, "No, why?"

"So, just stupid, then."

Too soon, the party starts to thin and a woman with lavender hair walks up to Cori to ask if she's staying or ready to order a ride.

"Are you Cori's roommate?" I ask her.

"Yep. Her roommate, her twin, her coworker." *Twin?* I look

at Cori's face, then back at her *twin*, apparently. I don't see an ounce of resemblance among Cori's round face and hooded eyes, and her sister's pointy chin and cheerful demeanor.

"My name's Sage. And we're fraternal twins, no different from siblings other than we shared the womb at the same time," she explains, noting the confusion on my face.

"I can drive you guys home if you want, so you don't have to pay someone," Callum offers.

Sam wraps his arms around Cori, practically begging her to stay the night and she relents, though she doesn't look too happy at the idea.

Callum, appearing hesitant to be alone with Sage, bravely takes her home, and Sam goes to bed. Despite her protests, Tyler and I help Cori clean up.

"It's your birthday, you shouldn't be cleaning up after your own party," she says.

"If I help, we'll get it done faster," I respond. Same thing I said about her tire.

After an hour of combined effort, the apartment is mostly back to normal and we all collapse on the couch.

Tyler puts his foot in Cori's lap and says, "Foot massage, please."

"Ew." Her face scrunches in disgust as she pushes on his leg.

"Do y'all mind if I just crash here on the couch?" Tyler's gaze flicks between me and her.

"No, but you're using sheets this time. And a blanket," Cori answers, sternly pointing her finger at him.

He sighs. "If I must."

"Okay, I have to know, what's the story with the sheets?" I ask.

"He takes his clothes off in his sleep. All of them. And I'd prefer if his bare ass didn't touch the very couch I sit on. Or, *other* body parts."

I look over at the shameless, almost proud, grin on his face. "How have I known you for as long as I have and didn't know that about you? How did I *live* with you and not know this?"

"I always had my own room. Plus, I usually go to bed naked, since I wake up that way anyway." He shrugs. "I'm a hot sleeper. The blanket probably won't do any good."

Cori groans.

Chapter 9
Don't Sign a Prenup

Cori

T he realization dawns that I'm being undressed by a blond man, wrenching my mind from what little sleep I had finally found. His hands roam over my breasts and I groan out loud, but not from pleasure. I squint at the alarm clock to find it's only seven a.m. On a Saturday.

I will never understand people who wake up before it's absolutely necessary to force themselves back into reality. And Sam knows this, so what the fuck is he doing?

Maybe I would be more accepting of mornings if I could fall asleep at an appropriate time. But the voices in my head are wired at night and exhausted in the morning, therefore so am I. Maybe it's the threatening darkness at night, the unknown that fuels the anxiety, and the peaceful, bright mornings that calm it; I don't know. Regardless, it's too early for this shit.

Usually, after the deed is done, he leaves to shower or rolls over to his side of the bed, depending on the time of day. So I figure I can get this over with pretty quickly and be dozing off again in a matter of minutes.

Running my hands through his hair, I tug lightly on the golden strands. His darkened eyes meet mine right before he flips over onto his back and pulls me toward him, guiding my head between his legs.

His heavy breath increasing as I move my mouth and hand in tandem is when I feel most intimate with Sam. For obvious reasons, of course, but sometimes I wonder if he even finds me attractive anymore. If he *ever* liked my looks. Even if he doesn't, at least I can still make his eyes roll back in his head and his body tense as he shoots a small boost of confidence into my mouth.

I swallow, expecting him to leave like usual. Instead, he pushes me backward until I'm lying against the pillows once again, and he makes his way back down my body. Each kiss is planted slowly, his tongue slipping out to stroke my skin before he moves lower. And the further south he gets, the more shivers course through me, sending hot waves of pleasure right to my center. Bumps erupt over every inch of my body as a moan escapes my throat.

Putting pressure on my knees until they fall open, he keeps his eyes on mine as he lowers his head and bites his way up my inner thigh. My breath comes out fast with anticipation. His lips land right where I want them, and he sucks until my back arches. My head falls back, my hand finding his hair again. Then his phone rings.

A blast of cold air hits me where his mouth was just a second ago.

"Seriously?" I ask, breathlessly.

"It could be for work."

He answers the call while he slips on his underwear and pants, and disappears to his office. With my heart beating quickly from the cold water thrown on me, there's little chance I'll be able to go back to sleep, so I shower and get ready for the day. Once I'm dressed in fleece leggings and one of Sam's t-shirts, I send Hailey another text to call me when she's awake and we'll make a plan to talk today.

I reach for the doorknob, but Sam steps inside and looks down my body. "You're already dressed? I figured we could finish what we started." He runs his hand down my back to cup my rear as he presses the front of his body into mine.

"The mood has sort of fizzled and I'm showered already."

"Alright, suit yourself." He goes to his closet and comes back out with a shirt. "Come on, I smell bacon. I think Nick is cooking breakfast."

Sure enough, we find Nick laying platters of eggs, bacon, and pancakes, and a bowl of mixed fruit on the table, where Tyler's already seated wrapped in a blanket.

Sam slaps Nick on the shoulder and says, "Good thing we're going to the gym later to work all of this off. Wanna come with us, Cori? I'm going to train Nick, get him back into shape."

Nick gives me a look that suggests he isn't thrilled about this plan. I don't blame him.

From what I see, Nick is still very much in shape. Broad shoulders that barely fit in his gray t-shirt, thick, defined arms that extend from the short sleeves, and thighs that could burst a watermelon. But if Sam's focus is on Nick's body weight, it isn't on mine. He's tried several different tactics to convince me to go work out with him, but I'd rather eat lettuce for a month than work out with Sam again. The one time I did, I found I hated his methods of screaming "One more!" on repeat until I threw up. I also found that the more he yelled, the more I wanted to sit down in defiance and eat a loaf of bread.

"No thanks." I'm reaching up into the cabinet when Nick's towering frame appears beside me, taking the handle of the cup out of my hand.

"I'll get it, you sit and eat."

"Oh, it's okay, I can get it."

"No, let me," Nick insists. A peace offering to make up for the weirdness last night on the patio, maybe? Or, from the other night?

"Just let him get it, he needs to earn his keep," Sam jokes from the table with a smirk aimed at his phone.

I cave and take my seat, giving Nick a thankful smile, but he's glaring at Sam. "I pay rent, asshole."

I spoon a small amount of eggs and some fruit onto my plate, but as I lift my fork to stab a strawberry, my plate disappears. I look up to see Nick loading it down with more eggs, a pancake, and three strips of bacon.

"Syrup?" he asks, lifting the bottle.

"Uhh," I look over at Sam, but he's not paying attention. "No. Thanks though."

Nick considers my answer, probably wondering if I'm declining because Sam is there, but finally sets my plate down in front of me.

I turn to Tyler after biting into the strawberry. "Please tell me you at least have underwear on under that blanket."

He grins. "Nope."

"At the *breakfast* table? Do you have no shame?"

His eyebrows fall. "Did you not know that already?"

I shake my head and Sam chooses that moment to look up and glance at my plate. "Damn, Cori, don't you think that's a little much?"

"No," I challenge, but I'll probably leave the pancake uneaten.

The silence is thick until Sam starts talking about some client from work. I'm not listening, though, because, for every second until my plate is clean, I feel the burn from Nick's watchful stare.

I'm often confused around people in general, but this is one of Sam's best friends. Or, he used to be before he left college.

Nick has seen women much more beautiful than I on Sam's arm. Women who don't struggle with socializing, who don't have to practice a remark in their head ten times before saying it. Women who are much better suited for a witty, poised, elegant man.

But his gaze doesn't feel the same as Kenna's menacing leer did last night. It feels knowing. Intimidating. Intrigued. It feels... risky.

Tyler offers to drop me off on his way home after breakfast, and when I walk into my apartment, I find my parents sitting on the couch. Unfortunately, they see me and it's too late to back out of the door and run for the hills.

"Well, look who finally decided to come home," Mom says as I lean down to hug her and Dad.

"I didn't know you were coming today."

"I texted you," she says, with a lift of her shoulder.

I take my phone out, but there's nothing there. "I didn't get anything, but I'm here now. Sorry."

"We just figured we'd take you both to lunch. Since you never call or visit, we have to make the drive to make sure you're both still alive." I know there's a hint of truth behind her playful tone. Mom has to guilt-trip me for something at least a few times a week. "It's a shame you didn't bring Sam with you."

"Again, I didn't know you were here."

Sage points to a couple of boxes stacked by the front door. "Now that she's here, can I finally know what's in those?"

Mom answers, "Now that I'm finally making progress going

through your Grandmother's things, we brought some stuff we thought you'd want."

"Why don't you let us help go through her things?" I ask.

"I wouldn't want to burden you with helping us."

"Mom, you know it wouldn't burden us. We'd love to help you." Mom doesn't respond, and I know it's because she'd rather do it herself. She likes to be in control and, of course, wants first dibs. But again, guilt-tripping is her favorite thing to do.

Sage opens the box with her name scribbled on the side in black marker and scrunches her nose up in disgust. "Yeah, and if you let us help, we could pick out things we'd actually want."

I peek in her box and my heartbeat picks up at the sight of Grandma's books. "Mom probably got the names mixed up."

"Well, excuse me, it's a lot of work to do by myself. Plus, I've got several boxes to keep track of, one for each kid and your father, a trash box, and a giveaway box, then I have my own boxes."

"I know, I wasn't criticizing you," I reassure her.

I've admired Grandma's books ever since I was a kid. There are so many classics, so many old editions passed down to her from her parents and grandparents. And there are always treasures to be found within the pages—other than the story, I mean. Grandma was a stasher. If she came across a magazine or newspaper article or picture that made her think of the story, she'd fold it up and stash it in the book. She used the most random things for bookmarks, like receipts, photographs, even strips of fabric from her sewing projects, and most of them lie forgotten between the pages.

"Well, are you going to change, Cori, so we can leave?"

My attention is snapped back to Mom and I look down at the leggings and t-shirt I'm wearing. "Right. I'll be back."

Sage is wearing a long, white dress with pink flowers, and

Mom is wearing light gray pants paired with a coral blouse. Even Dad is wearing khakis. So I choose a gray t-shirt dress that hits just below my knees and my off-brand leather sandals instead of my typical jeans and canvas shoes.

Mom has always been critical of my looks and my clothing. I was never much of a girly girl; I tend to gravitate toward comfort more so than looks, and Mom has always wished I was more like Sage in that way.

However, when I walk out to the living room, Mom looks me up and down. "You look cute. I never see you wear dresses anymore."

I blush and look at the ground, suddenly embarrassed by the compliment. "Thanks, Mom."

I follow Dad out to the car, with Mom and Sage behind me.

"Cori, you have stretch marks on your legs." I stop and sigh at the sky. That's why I never wear dresses. "You know what that's from, right?"

I yank open the back door to their SUV. "Yes, I do, I don't need the lecture."

"I'm just saying, it's from gaining weight. I keep telling you to watch what you're eating."

Tune out. Disassociate. Breathe.

We get situated in our seats and Dad pulls out of the parking lot.

"Ugh, Cori," Sage complains, pulling a loose hair off her dress. She rolls the window down, letting it fly off with the wind.

"How do you know that's mine?"

"Because it's brown?" she states sarcastically. "And your hair is all over the apartment." I'm the only one in the family who inherited Mom's brown hair, except she dyes it blonde now to cover the gray, and Sage dyes her blonde locks a different color every few months—it's currently lavender.

"Hopefully, it doesn't find its way to a crime scene. If I'm brought in for questioning for a murder I know nothing about because my hair was found around the body, I'm telling them you framed me."

She and Mom shoot confounded looks at me, identical in almost every way, except for the light lines around Mom's eyes.

"What is wrong with you?" Mom asks.

"Anxiety," I state, plainly. "I thought we all knew that already."

"No, it's all those books you read. Your imagination is too active."

"So, Mom, Dad," Sage starts, looking nervous for probably the first time in her life. She repeatedly smooths the nonexistent wrinkles in her dress. "The lease on our apartment is up next month, and I've been thinking that it's time for Cori and I to go our separate ways. It's probably time for her to move in with Sam, anyway. Don't you agree?"

Mom turns around in her seat, brows furrowed, as Dad looks at her in the rearview mirror. "And where will *you* be moving?"

She hesitates. "With Brian."

"*Brian?* You just started dating him, what? Two months ago?" Mom asks.

"Yeah, so? I practically live there already." Her head whips to Mom's face; I don't think she meant to say that last part out loud.

Mom rolls her eyes and flips back around in her seat.

"You always jump into things, Sage, without thinking it through. Look what happened with college." Sage had a full scholarship to play volleyball at Sam Houston, but left after one year because she was *"sick of school."*

"Yeah, well, life is too short to keep doing what makes you miserable. Or to not do something just because it may not work out. Like it or not, I'm an adult now and can make my own decisions, so I'm not asking for permission." The tension has a strong hand around each of our throats. While I'm proud of Sage for sticking up for herself, I'm also glad the attention isn't on me and *my* horrible life choices for once.

I reach a hand over to hers to show my support, but I can't help but wonder how we have such different personalities after having been raised in the same household. It's as if God got us mixed up and sprinkled confidence into her ingredients twice, leaving me too scared to even tell the barista she got my coffee order wrong.

"Well, I guess there's one thing we can celebrate about all of this," Mom starts. "You moving in with Sam." She turns in her seat again, her smile emanating warmth and pride.

I'm not sure that I am moving in with Sam, but I don't have the strength to let her down just yet. I smile back instead of answering and enjoy the sweet moment with Mom.

But Sage ruins it.

"Except she doesn't want to ask him. She's been thinking of ways to make it work, either by herself or with a new roommate."

"Why don't you want to ask Sam?" Dad asks.

I wonder if I'll traumatize my family too much by jumping out of this car simply to avoid answering. "Because, while Sage doesn't give much thought to her actions, I give too much thought." I relay my list of concerns: I'm not in the same league as him, I'm not sure he'd want me to be there all the time, Nick just moved in, then I admit to them what Sam did last night.

In line with the usual dismissing of my concerns I've come to expect, Dad scoffs. "Sam is the only thing you've done right in your life. Don't throw him away because you're insecure about your job, especially when you have that job because you gave up trying to find anything else. A man like Sam isn't going to wait for you forever, and if you lose him I doubt very much you'd find someone else as good."

My cheeks blaze with embarrassment as Dad's verbal slap rings through the air. I stare out the window, head throbbing from every word I want to say but keep locked inside out of fear of being disrespectful. Besides, I know he's right. He's only repeating the very song I sing myself to sleep every night.

"Is Sam cruel to you?" Mom asks.

"No, why?"

"Does he brush his teeth?"

I draw out my answer, unsure where she's going with this. "Yeah?"

"Is he lazy? Does he cut his toenails? Is he racist, sexist, unkind to people different from himself?"

"No, yes, and no."

"Then, what's the problem?"

I refrain from mentioning how basic those qualities are. Shouldn't a person I might live with require a little extra?

After a painful lunch, during which I was praised for hardly eating and scolded for being closed off and unsociable, we're waiting for the server to bring the check when Dad brings up the diner.

"I've debated selling it. Just get it off my hands, so I don't have to worry about it. But if Mike can get sales up, I might consider putting some more money into it. I need to see that it's worth the investment first."

I look around the table at Mom and Sage, their eyes glossed over as they daydream about literally anything besides the diner, and clear my throat. "You know, Dad, I have tons of ideas for the place. Grandma did great running the diner, but obviously, times are changing and the town is growing-"

Dad holds up a hand. "Cori, we've talked about this."

"I know, but you haven't even heard my ideas. We need fresh ingredients. Whatever food you want on the menu, fine. Just use fresh ingredients wherever possible. And I think we could really do well with an expanded coffee menu. There's no coffee place in town-"

"Costs. It's all about costs. And unless I see how your *ideas* won't break the finances, I won't consider them."

"I can get that information for you. And we can add to the menu with ingredients we already have. I make flavored drinks for customers all the time that aren't officially on the menu."

His eyes widen. "You charge them, right? A cup of coffee is $1.49. If you're using extra ingredients-"

"Yes, I add a charge for everything I use. But it'd be a lot easier if we already had a button for those drinks and a set price..." I smile, hoping to sell the idea, but Dad scowls.

The server drops off the check and Dad slides his glasses on. "It's not a coffee shop. Just leave the brainstorming to the professionals." He looks at the check and gets his wallet out, signaling the end of the conversation. But I'm not done.

"You work for an auto parts factory. What would you know about running a restaurant?"

His head snaps up to mine. "I grew up in that diner, young lady. I grew up in that town. I know much more than you think."

"You tell me all the time that I don't have ambition or drive. I do. But I don't have anywhere to put it."

"Use it to finish your bachelor's and get a real job." Like a judge's gavel, his words slam down silencing my defiance. "And move in with Sam. Before he moves on to someone else."

I escape to the bathroom to wash my hands. I'm scrubbing my hands for the third time, only to stall leaving the peace, when Mom walks in.

She waits for me to shut the water off, then turns me around by my shoulders and dries my hands with a paper towel as if I'm a child.

Pulling me in for one of her bear hugs, she says, "I'm sorry, honey. Sometimes we forget how sensitive you can be." I almost pull back, but I don't have the energy. "We just worry about you. Stephanie is married now with a doctorate to fall back on if anything happens to Adam's job, and Sage is confident and scrappy and can figure out her own problems. But we know how difficult it is for you to talk or make friends. It would be a relief to know that you were secure in your relationship with Sam."

There's too much to unpack in that statement, but I start with, "Why do you worry about me? I'm doing fine."

"Are you? The only reason you have an apartment is because Sage dropped out of college and needed a roommate. The only reason you have a job is because your Grandmother took pity on you and hired you."

Okay, that fucking hurt.

"Even if I moved in with Sam, that's no guarantee that it will last. *Marriage* isn't even a guarantee."

"Maybe not, but moving in with him is the next step towards marriage, and if the marriage doesn't work out, then you leave with loads of money." She raises her eyebrows and points her finger at me. "So don't sign a prenup."

Rolling my eyes, I turn towards the mirror, taking in my dull brown hair, thrown lazily into a ponytail, and my full round face. Honestly, I don't hate what I see in the mirror. My hooded eyes and my lips thinner than the standards of beauty are beautiful to me. But I know that most people don't agree.

"I want to ask him. I'm just scared he's going to say no."

"Well, maybe we'll go shopping soon and give you a makeover. Some new clothes and a new hairstyle?" She tilts my chin up, looking at my skin. "Maybe a facial?"

I yank my chin out of her grip. "Ugh, Mom."

Chapter 10
A Packaged Deal

Cori

After a sleepless night making lists and considering every possible angle until I reach the point where nothing makes sense, I decide to try meditation. It can't hurt, right? So, after work, I sit on the floor of my bedroom, cross my legs, close my eyes, and empty my mind as best as I can. I don't force any thoughts, instead letting them come naturally. But the only thought that pops up is a sudden craving for raspberry scones and how good they taste dipped in coffee.

Next, I try flipping a coin. Heads, I'll ask Sam to move in with him. Tails, I won't ask and I'll look for a cheaper apartment. But the coin lands on tails, and I'm both relieved and disappointed, and just what the hell am I supposed to do with that?

So I make a pros and cons list. Under pros, I write: *it's time, I can't afford rent on my own, Sage wants me to, Sam wants me to, my parents want me to.*

Under Cons, I write: *don't know if it would work out, don't know if I want to, don't know, don't know, don't freaking know!*

So I go buy a raspberry scone from the coffee shop down the street and try meditation again. With the lights turned off

91

and a toasted pecan latte-scented candle burning in the corner, I sit on the floor of my room, empty my mind again, and let my brain do its thing.

How does Sage get her hair so shiny when she uses the same hair products as me?

Why, out of everyone in my family, is mine the only name that doesn't start with S?

Why did God make me so weird and socially anxious?

What the hell does Sam see in me?

If a raspberry scone tastes so good dipped in coffee, would raspberry-flavored coffee taste just as good?

"What are you doing?" Sage's voice interrupts my thoughts, not that I was making any progress.

"I'm meditating."

"Why?" I open my eyes to find her head poking through my doorway and her eyebrows pulled down.

"Because I don't know if I should ask Sam if I can move in."

"So, you're overthinking it as usual?"

"Probably. But it feels like I'm underthinking it."

She sighs impatiently. "It's not an all-or-nothing decision, Cori. If you move in with him and it doesn't work, just move out." As if it were that easy. "Stop trying to have every step planned before you make a decision. You don't need to have every answer to every question."

I've always known I needed a life coach, someone to follow me around with a clipboard and whack me with it when I'm making the wrong choice or overthinking things. Never once have I considered the possibility of Sage being that coach, but I may have found her calling.

She leaves, but yells out from down the hall, "And quit being so insecure. It makes you seem pathetic."

I'm about as insecure as a person can get. But if I'm truly honest with myself, which I'm usually not, the issue isn't that

I'm scared Sam will say no. It's that I'm not sure I want him to say yes.

I still haven't heard from Hailey since she left the party. Because she's ignored my phone calls and responded to each of my texts with vague excuses that she's busy, I try a different approach than the usual, '*Are you okay?*'

> Me: What is going on with you? Are you mad at me or something? And don't just say you've been busy. Tell me the truth.

Hailey: I'm sorry, I've just been busy. There's a lot going on.

> Me: Then let's hang out tonight and you can vent to me about it.

Hailey: Okay. I can come over around 5 ??

> Me: I'll be here.

While waiting for her, I work on my secret blog. I don't want the scrunched-up expressions at the 'shy one' having a blog and social media pages when I hate socializing. It's not like I make dancing videos or anything, just coffee recipes. As someone who can't afford to visit a coffee shop as often as I'd like, I had to get creative with coffee at home, and it's fun to share the recipes I've come up with.

So I don't tell anyone about it, except for Hailey and whoever reads my resume. Not that it makes me more appealing to potential employers. Not even a coffee roasting company.

There are comments to respond to, social media content to create for the new recipes, and some site plugins to update. I make some money off of it, but not much. And most of the money goes back into it, paying for the website, the hosting, the plugins that make it work, and even the ingredients needed to experiment to create new recipes. I could tell Dad about how it brings me joy and could possibly lead to something bigger in the future, like privately labeled coffee once I have enough money saved up. Or, affiliate sales once I get enough email subscribers. But I know what he'll say- *'You still need a real job.'*

When Hailey arrives, we plop down on the pink and green couch that Sage and I found at a thrift shop for twenty dollars. It's hideously ugly and was probably covered in ten different kinds of bodily fluid when we bought it, but after a good cleaning, the wide cushions make for the perfect napping spot. We turn on reruns of The Office, and pick at the plate of random crap I set out: grapes, cucumbers, nuts, cheese, and cookies because balance is important.

After the fourth episode, the food is gone and the looming confrontation eats away at me.

"So, what happened Friday?" I ask, keeping my eyes on the TV.

She sighs, grabbing the remote to pause the show, and we position our bodies to face each other. Dark circles lurk under her haunted eyes as if life isn't letting her come up for air— neither of us should know what that feels like at twenty-three.

My phone dings from where it sits on the table, my text notification tone, but I ignore it. This is Hailey time. She looks at the screen, then raises her brows at me.

"Are you going to check that?"

I shake my head.

"Just check it really quick. You know if you don't, he's going to call." I assume it's Sam's name she saw on the screen.

Sure enough, my phone starts ringing. Rolling my eyes, I tap the answer button.

"Hello?"

"Hey, can I come over?" I pull the phone back to verify the name on the caller ID. Sam hates coming over here and insists on me going to his place every time. I almost feel bad declining the offer.

"Hailey is here. We're talking since we didn't get to at the party."

"Oh. Okay, then." We say our goodbyes and I turn back to Hailey. But the damn phone dings again.

> Sam: Can I come and have girl's night with you?

What is his deal? Any other day and I'm practically begging for his attention, but the nights that I try to hang out with someone other than him, he begs to come over?

> Me: No, Hailey is having a rough time. She needs this. I'm turning my phone off now.

I lay it on the table and turn towards her, taking her hands in mine and giving her my full attention.

"Okay, I'm all yours. What's going on?"

"Nothing, really. I'm just in one of those funks where I can't see the point of anything. Like, we go to work at jobs we hate to pay for food and shelter that only keep us fed and rested so that we can go to work. Or, we do maintenance on our cars only so we can go to work to pay for the maintenance on our cars. And for what? So we can keep going to work at jobs that we hate."

I understand what she means. But this sounds more like a rant that *I* would have, not Hailey. "I thought you loved your job?"

"I do, it's not really about my job. It's just about life sucking right now." I get the feeling that she's withholding something, the real reason for her sadness, but I don't want to push her.

"Why don't we have weekly book clubs instead of monthly? I know it's hard to find a night where we're both free, but I'll move my schedule around." Whatever I have to do, I'll make time for her.

She smiles and squeezes my hand. "That would be great. But it will probably be difficult if you move in with Sam."

My shoulders fall. "Why?"

"Because he won't want me around," she says, impatiently, like I should already know this. And I do, but my coping methods involve sticking my head in the sand and pretending like nothing is wrong. "Are you really considering moving in with him?"

"Ugh." My head falls back on the couch in frustration. "I don't know. My parents and Sage think I'm ridiculous for being scared to ask him, you think I'm ridiculous for even considering it. I don't know what to do."

"Well, what do *you* want to do?"

"It's not that easy." I pull the blanket off the back of the couch and cover my head with it, trying to escape from the issue at hand.

"Isn't it, though? It's not up to me, and it's not up to anyone in your family. It's up to you."

"What if I do want to, but he says no?" I ask, for what feels like the thousandth time.

"Then good riddance. And move on to the roommate."

Poking my head out, I glare at her. "That isn't helpful. Do I need to keep a jar that you have to put money into every time you insult my boyfriend?" I think about that idea for a moment. "Actually, that's not a bad idea. I may do that anyway and fund my book addiction."

"Okay, and then I can borrow the books you buy with it." There's an excited gleam in her eyes that causes me to rethink.

"Never mind. It would only encourage your insults."

"Why would he say no to you?" she asks. "You're beautiful and smart, and he's lucky to have you. I'm not sure what you see in him, but he'd be a moron to let you go."

I study her face for the lie because I don't see what she sees. The irony isn't lost on me that the very things she says about him are what I say about myself, and vice versa- in my eyes, he holds all the beauty and brains and I hold all the luck.

"But don't you think you were happier before him? More confident in yourself?"

"Uhh, no." In fact, moments before Sam and I reconnected, I was picturing how empty and pointless my funeral would be.

"You used to write poetry, you didn't always hide things, like your blog, from everyone. You used to smile."

"I sucked at poetry anyway. I would still be hiding my blog from my parents, and I do smile." I show her my teeth. "See? I'm smiling right now."

Rolling her eyes, she crosses her arms. "Just make sure that if you decide to move in with him, you make the decision based on what *you* want. Deep down in your gut. Not what your family wants, not what I want, not what Sam cons you into." Like the teacher she is, she points her finger at me. "And don't overthink it. Who cares if it's reasonable or what you think is the right thing to do? It needs to be what you want and nothing else." It's almost like she knows me and my tendency to over-think. "I will support you no matter what."

Her face softens and I know what she's thinking before she says it. "You know, I've been thinking." Anytime life gets heavy or complicated, we escape into a dream—a coffee shop that we'll never open, but we plan every detail anyway. "Every coffee shop I know is industrial-themed with exposed brick, black pipes, and metal. I'm thinking we should go Victorian with bold wallpaper and gold and antiques. It's not too different, but it's memorable. More tea-house, but no pastels."

I smile in gratitude and play along. "And we can have a poetry night. And book club night. Maybe a jar on the counter for people to put money into to buy someone else a cup of coffee or snack if they can't afford it."

"Yes! And a 'choose your own mug/glass shelf,'" she squeals.

"And a little free library in the corner where people can leave and take a book. And I want unique blends of coffee, not just flavored syrup."

Her grin fades as she grasps my hand. "You should actually do it. Save up and open a coffee shop. Or find some sort of job in coffee somewhere. Live the dream instead of just talking about it."

Twirling a loose thread from my pants around my finger, I admit the disaster of an interview I had. And her reaction of matched bafflement and outage is why she's my best friend. She suggests emailing them back, asking some follow-up questions to get feedback on what exactly went wrong, and while I'd rather eat my own shirt, it might prove helpful. I pull my phone out to start a draft with her help when a knock sounds at the door.

"I swear to God, that better not be Sam," she says with a groan. I reassure her that it won't be, although I'm not confident in that statement.

I go to the door and open it. It's Sam.

"What are you doing here? I told you not to come," I whisper.

"I'm just a delivery boy right now." He hands me a drink carrier with four iced coffees and two bouquets of flowers. "I wanted to cheer up Hailey since you said she's having a hard time. I didn't know what she drank though, so I got options, and then I got your favorite, an iced caramel latte. Also, there's a bouquet for each of you. Yours is the one with the key tied to it."

I look down and see a small gold key tied to a ribbon around the stems of red roses. "A key for what?" I'm too stunned to say anything else. He's never bought flowers for me before. I'm looking for the prank, waiting for the punchline, but my heart warms at the same time.

"Move in with me."

I gape at him until he explains.

"Tyler let it slip that Sage was moving out. And it's time anyway, don't you think? That we move in together?"

Someone walks up behind me, Hailey, I assume, although I can't be sure. The drinks and flowers are taken out of my hands as I stand there blinking at the hopeful grin on Sam's face.

"Are you sure?" I finally ask. "I'll be there all the time, we won't have our personal space, my stuff will be everywhere. And you know how badly I shed. And how often I lose hair ties." I can't stop rambling. "And my books. Have you seen how many books I have? We'll have to share a bathroom, we'll have to-" I was about to say 'poop in front of each other,' but he cuts me off, thank God.

"Cori, move in with me. Bring your books. Bring your loose hair. Bring your hair ties and scatter them all around the apartment." He stops and narrows his eyes. "Do you have to bring all of your books though?"

I nod. "We're a packaged deal."

"What about your shelves?"

"Well, where would I put the books?"

He shrugs. "The shelf by the TV?"

"I have way too many books for them all to fit on one shelf." Our back and forth is quick, like we're bartering on the price of fish at a roadside market.

"Fine. You can move your ugly bookshelves into the bedroom." I can't fault him for calling them ugly because I found the puke-yellow one at a thrift store for ten dollars, and the hot pink one covered in Barbie stickers on the side of the road.

"What about rent? How much will I pay?"

"Uhh, nothing?" He looks at me like I'm crazy for asking.

"I can't just not pay anything." In other words, *I don't want you to own me.*

"Okay, what if you don't pay rent, but you do the housework?"

I'd rather be eaten alive by a dragon and live inside his belly forever. "Can I just pay rent and we split housework?"

"Or, you could save your money and go back to school?"

And we're back to square one. He sees my expression fall and he grabs my waist, pulling me into him.

"Fine. You can just live with me rent-free, we'll split the housework, and you can save your money for whatever you want- school, books, a whole separate apartment just to house your books, I don't care." He nuzzles his face into my hair and inhales deeply and, somewhat, creepily.

"So?" he asks, urging me to answer.

"What about Nick?"

"It's not his apartment. He doesn't get a say."

I don't agree with that, so I make a plan to ask him when I see him next. And hopefully, that's soon so that I can start forming a different plan if he's not comfortable with it.

For now, I tell Sam, "Then, yes. I'll move in with you."

A fter Sam leaves, I return to Hailey sipping one of the drinks and watching TV again.

"I'll admit, that was nice of him," she says as I sit down next to her.

"Did you overhear me tell him that I'll move in?" I ask, timidly.

She sighs. "No, but I figured you would." Turning to face me, she studies my face. "It's because you want to, though. Right? Not because he just bought you flowers and coffee? If so, you and Sage may have more in common than you think."

"And what is that supposed to mean?" Sage asks as she walks into the living room.

"That you're easy."

"It's called knowing what I want. Both of you should try it." Sage takes one of the coffees from the drink carrier.

"Yeah, I guess you're right." Hailey picks up her phone. "But I do know what I want. And it's pizza."

Chapter 11
Whatever You Want

Nick

The night after the party, I went home to have dinner with Mom and Uncle Jonah. We clogged our arteries with fried chicken and mashed potatoes; my favorite meal. Then, they made me pose in front of a homemade chocolate cake while Mom took pictures and they sang to me like I was five years old again. Overall, it turned out to be a pretty great birthday.

The next day, I hang out with the guys again before running some errands, and when I get home, Sam's kicked back on the couch watching TV.

"Hey, man," he says, as he starts to sit up. "Guess what."

"What?"

"I asked Cori to move in here with me."

I stop in my tracks. "Oh."

"Is that a problem?"

"No, of course not. But are you wanting me out?" I only just moved in, but I understand if they want their space, taking this next step in their relationship.

"No, there's no need for you to go anywhere. I was just

letting you know." He studies my face for a minute. "You're cool with it, right?"

"Fine with me. Cori's... interesting." *Confusing*, more like. "But I think we'll get along." Sitting down in one of the armchairs, I prop my feet up on the coffee table.

He smiles and leans back against the couch. "Yeah, I wish she'd come out of her shell, but she's easy to be with."

My breath hitches. "What do you mean, *easy?*"

"I mean... low maintenance. She's not needy or suffocating. And she's good at letting things go." But I hear the unspoken qualities he finds attractive: easy to manipulate. I think I see why she needed to vent out on the patio.

The ability to let things go can be a good quality until someone takes advantage of it, or until you sacrifice your mental health.

A couple of nights later, I have another strange encounter with my future roommate. Since Sam wouldn't knock before entering his own apartment, I assume it's her at the door. She emerges in leggings and a t-shirt, carrying two stacked boxes that tower over her.

"Here, let me take those." I jump up from my seat on the couch.

"Oh, it's okay, I got it." As she says the words, she stumbles backward.

Deciding to take a different approach with her than I did with her tire and the cleaning after my party, I step back, placing my hands on my hips. "Fine, if you want to be stubborn."

Her eyes widen slightly. But if she needs help, she shouldn't be afraid to ask for it.

I'm just as surprised when she responds, "Fine."

She looks around the room for a spot to put the boxes and, not finding one, heads down the hall. I follow, ready to catch her or the boxes should they fall, but she stops in her tracks halfway. I almost crash into her.

"Can you just maybe take the top one? I can't feel my arms."

I take them both and pass her on my way to Sam's room. I drop them against a wall and almost trample Cori again when I turn. She walks on light feet and I didn't hear her enter behind me.

She mutters a small apology.

"Why do you do that?" When she raises her eyebrows, I add, "Apologize so much."

Her only answer is a quick lift of her shoulders. She looks across the hall to Sam's closed office door. "Is he in there?"

I shake my head and her shoulders sag.

"Did you have plans?"

"No. Well, sort of, he was supposed to meet me at my apartment earlier to pick up those boxes and a few more. But he's not answering his phone."

I ask pointedly, "He do this a lot?" He's worked late almost every evening I've been home, but working late isn't the issue. He broke his promise to be somewhere and isn't answering his phone.

Typically, when people lie, they avoid eye contact, fidget, turn red. Cori looks me straight in the eye, the usual blank expression on her face, and says, "No." I'd believe her without a doubt if she hadn't scratched at her wrists and bounced her gaze around during every other word she's said.

"He's got a lot going on at work." But I don't think it's me she's trying to convince.

"You're allowed to be upset."

"I know, but there's no need to be. It's not a big deal."

We fall into silence. She bites the inside of her cheek, crosses and uncrosses her arms, and I watch, wondering what she'll do or say next. She hooks her thumb over her shoulder. "Well, I should go. Thanks for helping with the boxes." I follow her back, turning towards the living room while she goes in the opposite direction.

"Umm... Nick?"

I stop in my tracks and face her.

"It's okay with you if I move in here, right?"

I slip my hands into the pockets of my sweatpants. "It's Sam's apartment."

"Yeah, but you live here too. And I don't want to move in if it will make you uncomfortable."

I appreciate her thoughtfulness. Even Sam didn't ask, he simply told me. However, no part of me thinks she'll bother me in any way. I'm concerned I'll be intruding, but I leave that unsaid in case she misunderstands, taking it to mean that I don't want her moving in.

I want to reassure her, make sure she doesn't doubt my words, so I shrug my shoulders and say, "I really couldn't care less."

Her eyes dart around, seemingly trying to decipher my words, but I couldn't have been more plain.

"Okay, well... bye then." She walks out the door and I return to my spot on the couch. I flip through movies until deciding on one about Vikings, but twenty minutes later, there's another knock on the door followed by the turn of the door knob.

Cori reappears in the living room. "Umm...." She breathes

heavily, but it seems to be more from irritation than physical exertion. "My stupid car won't start. Is it okay if I wait here for a little while? I can stay in Sam's room."

"Why would I care?" I meant it as, *You don't have to ask my permission for every little thing,* because she has no reason to feel like she'll disturb me by simply existing. Problem is, I don't think she takes it that way.

Her face scrunches slightly as she says defensively, "I was just checking."

I pause the movie and stand. "I can look at your car if you want, figure out what's wrong with it."

Shaking her head, she turns for the hallway, unable to escape me fast enough. "I already know what's wrong with it, just can't afford to fix it." Alrighty then.

When Sam's bedroom door shuts, I sit back down and resume the movie, but it isn't long before my stomach starts rumbling. There's not much in the fridge to make a meal out of, so I get my phone out to order food.

The polite thing would be to ask Cori if she wants something too, and maybe we could eat together and get to know each other. Find some common ground so we don't have to walk on eggshells or avoid each other once she moves in. I head for Sam's bedroom and knock. When she opens the door, she's wearing my sweatshirt again, and I momentarily forget why I'm standing before her.

"Did you need something?" she asks after a minute of me staring.

"I'm going to order food and watch a movie. Want to join me?"

She blinks rapidly, surprised at the invitation. "N... no, that's okay. Thank you though."

"You have to eat at some point."

"I'll just eat later when Sam gets off." Her phone dings

then. She holds it up, the glow illuminating her subtle features, but whatever it says on the screen has her shoulders slumping.

"Let me guess, he won't be home 'til late."

She bites her inner cheek. "He's having dinner with a client."

"So what'll it be? Preferably something close that can be delivered, but I don't mind driving to pick it up."

She nods, relenting. "I'm not picky."

"You're deciding. I'm perfectly fine with whatever you want. And I'm paying," I add, sternly pointing my finger.

Crossing her arms, she says, "Well, I don't even know what you like."

"I'm fine with whatever you want."

She throws her arms down. "Well, at least pick a type of food."

"Nope. I'm fine with whatever you want."

"Fine. Tacos, then," she says, testing me, and I grin, enjoying seeing her flustered.

"Okay, sounds good."

"From the food truck down the street." She watches me for some sort of reaction, but my only reaction is relief that she finally picked something.

"Okay, sounds good."

She narrows her eyes and I wonder if she's tricking me.

"Wait, what's the deal with the food truck? Are they known for food poisoning or something?"

"No, it's amazing. But Sam doesn't like it and never lets us order from there."

"*Lets?* Do you need his permission?"

"Well, no."

"I'm guessing you like to pick your battles." She nods slowly. "But I think good tacos are one of the few things in life worth fighting for."

She considers that thought, then levels me with another challenging look. "On that note, I'm ordering four tacos."

Again, she waits for me to say something I won't. Instead, I lift my shoulders. "Order ten if you want, you'll get no judgment from me."

We order the tacos, and despite Cori's protests, I pay for them. I thought it might tame some of the weirdness between us, maybe get us closer to a point where she's comfortable around me. But the friendly gesture gets lost in the translation, and she thanks me more times than I can count.

"No, you don't have to pay me back," I say for the millionth time. "Now, what do you want to watch?" I hold my hand out for her to lead the way to the living room, but she shakes her head.

"I'll just stay in here. I've got some stuff to work on."

"Like what?"

"Like... stuff."

Crossing my arms, I lean against the door frame. I'm not going anywhere until she answers. "Homework? Are you in school? Or, something for your job? Or, a hobby?"

Her eyes bore into mine.

"Why is it a secret? Is it embarrassing?"

"It's not a secret, it's just, nothing important."

"Then why can't you tell me about it?"

"Why do you care?" she counters.

Without realizing, my face inches closer to hers. "Because we're about to be roommates and you can't even sit in the same room as me to watch a movie."

She scoffs like the reasoning should be obvious. "I don't want to intrude on your space."

"If I want to be alone, I'll go to my bedroom. But the living room, kitchen, all of that is public domain. Why do I have to explain how roommate situations work, don't you currently have one?"

"She's my sister, it's different. And she's rarely home. And I know how they work, I just don't know how *you* work."

"So, come get to know me."

"Fine."

"Fine," I repeat, and she rolls her eyes as she passes me on her way to the couch. Once we're seated, I reach over the space between us to hand her the remote.

"You're picking what we watch."

She leans away like I'm holding out a dead rat. "No, you made me choose what food we ordered."

"Quit being stubborn and just pick."

Her eyes widen. "*You* quit being stubborn and just pick."

I can't help the amusement that spreads over my face. I lay the remote down on the couch, determined not to lose, then I cross my arms. She does the same.

"I guess we'll just sit here in silence, then."

"Fine by me, I love the silence," she says, smartly.

I take this moment to study her. Her socked feet are curled underneath her, appearing at ease, until I look at her shoulders, tense and raised to her ears. The tips of her fingers poke out from her arms, fingernails neat and natural. Strands of brown hair, fallen loose from her bun, frame her round face.

"What's your favorite animal?" I ask. If we're going to get to know each other, might as well start with the basics. As you age, people stop asking questions like this. I wish they wouldn't.

"Elephants."

I wave my hand for her to go on. She lets her arms fall in an irritated gesture, but the muscles around her lips twitch as the scowl on her face fights for its life. We're getting somewhere. "They're brilliant, fascinating creatures. Is that enough? Or do you need an essay?"

"I like ducks."

She snorts before her hands self-consciously fly up to cover her face. She clears her throat and schools her features, and I can't help but smile. "Why ducks?"

I point to her. "Same reason you just did that. They're funny. Their little waddles and funny-sounding quacks. And the way their feet sound slapping on the ground."

She nods in agreement but falls silent. I reach over and playfully shove her shoulder.

"That's not how this works. We take turns asking questions. It's your turn."

She rolls her eyes and after a minute or two of thinking, she finally asks, "If you had to stay in a haunted castle alone for 30 days with no TV or internet to win a million dollars, would you?"

"Oh, okay, we're getting deep already." I rub my hands together, thinking of my answer. "I'd like to think I could. If I'm allowed to go outside to, like, a garden or courtyard or something, then yeah. But if I have to stay inside the walls at all times, no."

I wait for her answer, but I already know she could probably spend a year there and not even notice the lack of company or internet. I smile knowingly.

"You'd spend your time reading and be perfectly happy, wouldn't you?"

"Yep."

I shake my head before taking my turn. "Name three things on your bucket list."

"Honestly, I'd kinda like to spend 30 days alone reading in a haunted castle."

I chuckle lightly.

"I'd also love to open a coffee shop, and I think it'd be really cool to go on this train ride that takes fifteen days to go from the west to the east coast. But those are unrealistic, obviously."

"It's not obvious—why are those unrealistic?"

"Well, when would I have a whole fifteen days to travel? And coffee shops are expensive and not exactly smart." She repeats the question back to me to avoid elaborating.

"Go to a Super Bowl game. Figure out what I want to do with my life. And get my pilot's license. My uncle has a couple of planes, and it'd be cool to have my license and go flying with him. I've gone a few times but just as a passenger. It's why I have this tattoo." I pull up the sleeve of my t-shirt and point to the plane above the mountains on my shoulder.

Her eyes slowly skim over the ink down my arm, taking in each line. She opens her mouth to say something, but a knock at the door interrupts and we both rise to answer it.

"I'll get it, you sit," I order teasingly. She nods but walks to the kitchen instead of obeying to get plates and drinks.

When I set the brown bag of tacos on the coffee table, Cori picks up the remote, keeping her eyes on me while she flips the TV on.

"I'm turning on The Office," she says, testing me like she did before we ordered the food.

"Fine by me. I've never seen it."

After a dumbfounded expression befalls her, she enters into a tirade about how you can't judge the show on the first few episodes. Her theory is that the characters act awkward and weird because they're still getting used to having cameras in their face from the fake documentary they're making, and I have no idea what she's even talking about.

"All that work I went through to get you to talk more, and now I wish you'd shut up."

She throws a piece of chicken at me from her taco. I pop it into my mouth and laugh at the snarl her upper lip curls into.

Cori ends up eating only two of the four tacos. I triple-check with her that she only leaves them uneaten because she truly is full. She claims that two tacos usually fill her up, but it's nice to have extra for "insurance purposes."

S am finally walks through the front door around ten and falls into an armchair. In his gray suit and purple tie, he looks every bit the privileged man who everyone moves out of the way for.

"Sorry, Babe. I had to work on a proposal. I'm glad you came anyway." *Proposal?* I thought it was dinner with a client, but maybe he had to do one before the other.

I open my mouth to ask, but Cori speaks softly, "It's not a big deal. My car wouldn't start when I went to leave. That's the only reason I'm still here."

"Why didn't you just ask Nick to jump you?"

"Because it's not my battery." Gone is the woman I was just watching TV with, the one giggling at nothing in particular because, according to her, the show "just gives off happy vibes."

"Oh, okay. Well, sleep here tonight. I was thinking, though. It'd be better to move everything on the same day, don't you think?" Sam suggests, untying his tie and unbuttoning his sleeves.

"No, but I'll move what I can by myself and save all the big stuff. Just don't forget, I have to turn in the keys on Saturday morning."

"Which Saturday? I can help, I have a truck," I offer.

But Sam says, "Just save it all. There's not much anyway. You're getting rid of most of it, aren't you?"

She nods, giving up on the conversation, but I can see the shadow of a retort.

"What is it?" I ask, urging her to use her voice.

She looks at me, eyes wide and innocent. "What?"

"You wanted to say something."

Sam sits forward, listening, but Cori's gaze bounces between mine and his before she shakes her head. "No, nothing. Except that I'm tired and need to go to sleep."

Sam disappears, mumbling something about a shower, and Cori starts picking up plates and trash from the coffee table.

"Hey."

She pauses and meets my gaze. "What?"

"What was it that you wanted to say?"

"Nothing." She resumes cleaning, but I snatch up all the trash before she can and block her exit.

She runs her hands through the hair at her temple, breathing out a sigh as hot as my shame. I open my mouth to apologize for stressing her out, but she starts talking first.

"I just think it'd be easier to move everything slowly. Not everything will fit in Sam's car, and now mine is out of commission. And it'd be less work on the day of, just in case something goes wrong, like Sam's car breaks down, or,"—she shakes her head—"I don't know."

"You should let your feelings be known."

"It's really not a big deal. Most people move everything in one day. It's nothing to get worked up over."

Does she not realize you can communicate feelings without causing an argument? Or is she accustomed to people throwing fits anytime they're disagreed with?

"Fine. But at least tell me what it was you wanted to say on the balcony that night. When I told you to stop being shy." I don't ask out of derision, but curiosity. Maybe I'm ignorant, or maybe it's hard to understand simply because I've never been in her shoes. Besides, an opportunity has arisen to teach her a lesson.

"Why are you asking about this now?"

I don't respond because the answer won't encourage her to open up. She swallows down too many things she wants to get off her chest, and that should change before the weight crushes her. "I don't remember."

My silence and the tilt of my head tell her I know she's lying.

"Fine." She stands up straight, stretches her neck to each side as if preparing for a boxing match, and inhales a shaky breath. "People tell me all the time not to be shy, like it's something I can just switch off. But no one seems to see shyness for what it is—a personality trait. Everyone views it as a fear to get over or a problem to be worked out. A combination that just needs the right codes for me to click and swing wide open. I'm just shy. I'll always be shy. And when people tell me to stop being shy, they're telling me to stop being myself. They're telling me I'm broken, that something is wrong with me. Sure, I may talk more after I get to know someone, but it takes me a little longer to open up to people. And if you criticize me for being shy, what else are you going to criticize me for? If you're studying me and judging me before I come out of my metaphorical shell, am I always going to be under your microscope?"

Her breath saws in and out as she watches me wearily like I might argue or say something demeaning.

"Do you feel better now?"

"What?"

"Do you feel better? Does getting out the things you want to say instead of swallowing them down help you feel better?"

"No." Not the answer I expected. "I could stream a message to every cell phone in the world and people still wouldn't get it." She takes the plates to the kitchen and turns on the faucet. "Not everyone has the brain capacity to understand other people are different from them."

What has this woman been through that she's adopted such a cynical view of people?

"Well, just so you know, you're safe to be whoever you want to be around me. I may ask dumb questions to understand you better, but just tell me to shut up if I overstep or offend you. Okay?"

She doesn't acknowledge my offer of friendship, but when I tell her I got the dishes, she nods without a fight. I consider that a win.

Chapter 12
A Bad Sign

Cori

S am's apartment is fairly comfortable, but it isn't home yet, and I can't help but feel aimless as I walk out of my apartment for the last time. Turning in my keys to the office and stacking my boxes on the sidewalk are more bitter-than-sweet moments, but they shouldn't be. I'm leaving behind temperamental electricity and locks that stick, and trading up for a building with an elevator and an en suite laundry room. Since I just carried about thirty boxes and two bookshelves down four flights of stairs, the thought of the elevator alone should be enough to lift my spirits.

But it isn't.

"This is a bad sign," I admit out loud. "My boyfriend forgetting about me on the day I'm supposed to move in with him is a very bad sign." Sam was supposed to be here at eight to help me haul my belongings, but as the minutes creep closer to ten, I lose hope of having a smooth transition.

"No, it's not. Stuff happens. Sam is a great guy, he wouldn't just forget about you."

It's not like this is the first time he's stood me up. He forgot we had dinner plans one time, and I sat at the restaurant alone, cringing at the pitiful looks from the other diners and servers. He forgot to pick me up from work once when my car was in the shop and I had to walk home. He forgot about lunch with my parents one Saturday, and I had to answer their questions about why I didn't bring my boyfriend. His excuse was the same every time: *"Something important came up with work."*

Most of me is angry that he isn't here because... well, what the hell? But there's a small gnawing feeling in the pit of my stomach that something horrible has happened. Like a car accident, a stroke, or what if something happened to one of his parents?

"Why don't you just let Brian and I help?" Sage asks.

"Because it's not your problem. And you don't have room in his truck anyway." I send off another text to Sam, giving it a few minutes, hoping he finally responds. But if he didn't respond to the first hundred, the chances of him responding to this one are slim. "You and Brian go enjoy your day together. I'll just sit here and hope he shows up soon."

My car still isn't running, it still wore the spare tire, and I still had no money to fix it. It's parked outside Sam's apartment building where I left it, although I put it in neutral and pushed it over to a spot assigned to his apartment to avoid a tow fee. It was enough exercise to kill me, but unfortunately, I'm still here.

Sage pulls out her phone and presses some things on the screen before holding it up to her ear.

"Who are you calling?" I ask. She puts her hand over my face and pushes me away.

"Hey. Are you busy? Cori needs help moving stuff to Sam's because we can't get a hold of him," she says into the phone.

"NO, I DON'T NEED ANY HELP!"

But I guess they don't hear me because Sage thanks them and hangs up.

"Tyler is on his way."

I groan. Don't get me wrong, I love Tyler. Callum, too. They're—somewhat—mature men and they've never made me feel weird or awkward about being shy. Tyler did ask me once why I didn't talk a lot, but I answered with, "Why do you talk so much," and he said, "Touché," and that was it. But it's *because* I like him that I don't want to ask him to wake up early on a Saturday to do manual labor for me.

"Why are you so against people helping you?"

"Because help always comes at a price. Like how you've been driving me to and from work for the last few weeks, despite us having the same shifts, and you're making me pay for *all* of your gas." Or that time I asked Sam to run to the store for me when I had the flu, and he asked for a blow job as payment. Or when I got distressed glances from Dad because I didn't go off to a university the second I turned eighteen, and Dad still had to pay for my food and shelter.

"Your boyfriend's friends are an extension of him. If you can't get a hold of your boyfriend, you call his friends."

I really don't think that's how things work, but I don't say anything until, "Why do you even have Tyler's number?"

"We texted a bit before I met Brian. We almost hooked up a few times, but I got to thinking—what if he and Hailey got together? Wouldn't they be so cute?"

"If you want Tyler to have his dick bitten off, sure."

It isn't long before his truck pulls up, followed by Nick's. And if that's not enough, Callum steps out of the passenger side of Tyler's truck.

"I am so sorry. I didn't want to ask y'all to come help, but *Sage-*" I forget what I'm saying when Tyler gives me a noogie as if I'm *one of the guys.*

"Stop it. We have no problem helping you, that's what friends are for."

Callum steps up, places his hands on my shoulders, and bends to my height. "You're worth our time, Cori."

It's Nick's turn and he says, "Yeah, please call any of us if your dumbass boyfriend doesn't show up."

"So, he's not at the apartment?" I ask, hopeful that I'm wrong.

"No, he left around six this morning. I don't know where he went. I also didn't know you were moving in today, or I would have been here anyway to help. We all would have. I remember telling you to let me know when you needed help?"

"You said *if* I needed help. I didn't need help because Sam was supposed to be here."

He glares at my subtle avoidance, but I ignore it as Sage starts ordering everyone around.

I'm so overwhelmed with the emotions of the day that their sweet words almost push my tears over the edge. But I don't have time to think too hard about Tyler's nice, yet, annoying brotherly gesture, or Callum somehow saying exactly what I needed to hear, nor Nick's shared annoyance at Sam. So I take a deep breath and bottle it up for later.

With everyone now involved, it doesn't take us long to get everything loaded into the parade of vehicles. As payment for helping me, I promise to buy the guys pizza from Joe's later.

When Sam finally calls, I almost knock myself out when I slap the phone to my ear.

"Sam, where are you?"

"Hey, I'm at the golf course with a client. Is everything okay? I have twenty-two missed calls from you and a few from Nick."

My heart sinks. "So, you *did* forget that you were supposed to help me move my stuff in today?" I ask in disbelief. I'm relieved he's safe, but I had hoped I was wrong about him simply standing me up. *Again.*

"No," he more so asks than says. "You're moving in tomorrow. On Sunday."

"No, I told you I had to turn in my keys on Saturday because no one is in the office on Sundays."

"You told me Sunday." There's an air of finality to his voice.

"I did not!" I whisper-shout.

"I remember you said Sunday because I thought 'That's perfect, I'll still be able to golf on Saturday.' Look, I have to go. I'll see you tonight and we'll celebrate your first night at the apartment."

I roll my eyes and hang up without saying goodbye.

As I look over at Tyler, Callum, and Nick, I wonder if it's worth getting worked up over. They showed up for me and we got my stuff loaded, so there's not much of a problem. But the hollow feeling in my gut doesn't care.

Nick

"**Y**ou ready to go?" I shout to Cori.

Despite our friendly conversation the other night, she looks at my truck with disdain before glancing around for a reason not to be alone in a vehicle with me. The passenger seat of my truck is the only seat available after loading both Tyler and my backseats down with Cori's boxes. Large, heavy boxes that we men could barely lift with two people.

"You either ride with me, or you stay here. Your choice."

I open the passenger door, just in case, and lean against the truck while she decides. Thankfully, she doesn't spend too much time stalling and hoists herself inside, and I make a mental note to install a stepladder. I close her door before running around to the other side finding Cori's seat belt already buckled, her hands clasped politely in her lap, and her body rigid as I start the engine.

"You can relax, I'm an excellent driver. No accidents, knock on wood, and only one speeding ticket."

"I'm relaxed," she says, as if I'm imagining her shoulders by her ears again.

"Tell your face." I straighten my leg to get my phone out of my pocket. "We should probably exchange numbers so that if something like this happens again, you can call me."

"I'm not planning on moving again anytime soon."

I level her with a look. "You know what I mean. If he ever leaves you stranded again."

"Fine."

I create a new contact, naming it *Roommate,* and hand my phone to her. Taking her phone, I see what she assigned as my name in her contacts: *Roommate.* I laugh as our heads snap up and the hint of amusement appears on her face.

I type my number in, then reach over the center console to open the music app on my phone. "And play whatever you want."

Hesitantly, she scrolls for a few minutes before finally pressing play on a hard rock playlist. As I pull into traffic behind Tyler, we listen to the first part of the song, a heavy guitar intro fading as the lyrics begin.

"Is this the kind of music you actually listen to?"

"Yes."

"I would have guessed you listened to... I don't know, punk or indie rock."

"I do." She stares out her window, apparently not in the mood to elaborate.

"Are you going to explain? Or leave me in suspense, like you do with everything else?"

She turns in her seat and sighs. "I listen to all kinds of music. Leona Lewis, Breaking Benjamin, Riley Roth, Staind, Patsy Cline. It really just depends on the song and what I'm in the mood for. Right now, I'm in the mood for guitar riffs and heavy lyrics." She raises her eyebrows as if to ask, *Is that enough of an explanation?*

"Yeah, I guess I'm the same way." We fall silent, listening to the guitar solo before the bridge.

"So what the hell is in these boxes? Are you taking the brick from your old building with you? I saw a few missing." I have to say I'm relieved she's leaving that place. I don't know how it hasn't been condemned yet.

"No, it's books." I should have known.

"How many books do you read in a month?"

"Probably about four or five."

I whistle to show my surprise.

"That's not a lot compared to most passionate readers. But it's all I have time for."

"Considering I don't read any, it's an abundance. Wait, how many books do you *buy* a month?"

"Okay, but you have to understand that buying books is a totally different hobby. Especially for someone like me that doesn't have much extra money. I have to be smart and shop sales when I have gift cards, or when authors run promotions. I also resell the books if I don't like them enough to keep them. And that money funds my book buying further. It's like a sport."

Chuckling, I point out, "That wasn't an answer."

She sighs again. "Over the past month, I bought ten books." My eyebrows shoot upwards and I open my mouth to exclaim a word of shock, but she raises her voice before I can do so. "*But* I only spent four dollars on them all. Now, I'm on a book-buying ban for the rest of the year because my bookshelves will crumble if I put any more weight on them."

"And you haven't considered the library?"

"Of course, I love the library. But I enjoy reading indie authors, and the library doesn't always carry what I want."

I shake my head.

"What? You don't have a hobby? Something that takes a lot of your time and money?"

Scoffing, I reply, "Of course, I do. Everyone has hobbies. I hang out with friends, I watch sports games, um... I eat. And sleep." Scratching my head, I rack my brain for an actual hobby, something I'm passionate about. I used to play fantasy football, but I stopped after my injury. Growing up, football *was* my hobby. The only thing I had time for. Work and simply surviving has taken up most of my time and energy the past couple of years, I guess I never picked up anything else to replace it.

Instead of answering further, I bypass her question. "So, will this move bring you closer or further away from your job?"

She shoots me a knowing look but plays along. "It's adding twenty minutes to my commute. Bringing it to about forty-five with no traffic." Longer than my drive to work, but typical for this area as most people drive closer to the city for work.

"Do you enjoy the work? Sam said you worked at your dad's diner?"

Shifting in her seat, she stares back out the window at the concrete buildings we pass. "That's a difficult question to answer."

I want to laugh at her ability to overcomplicate everything. "It's yes or no, I think that's pretty simple."

"I used to love it because it was my grandma's diner and it had a family feel where everyone was a friend and no one bitched because the cook took longer than five minutes for their chicken. Now, it's just a roadside diner and a black hole of a job that's slowly sucking the life from me."

I want to tease her, tell her *"My mistake for asking."* Instead, I offer some helpful, although unsolicited, advice. "So, change it."

She scrunches her face up. "I'm trying. I've applied for jobs and gone to interviews."

"Have you considered improving the job you currently have? Bring back the family feel to the diner? Or, maybe turning a hobby into a career? What kind of things do you like to do in your free time? Besides, read."

"What about you?" she counters defensively. "You said you wanted to figure out what you wanted to do with *your* life. Why don't you think about that before telling *me* what to do?" Crossing her arms at the tension smoldering in the air around us, she turns back to her window. Clearly, that's a sore subject.

I should feel dismissive, or hurt that she threw that back in my face, but I don't. I feel... like we're getting somewhere. "Okay, how about this? We can be each other's accountability partners. You do something with your life, I'll do something with mine. And we'll check up on each other's progress. You know, keep each other accountable."

"Fine."

A chuckle rumbles from my chest. "Is that going to be the title of your memoir?"

A strange, full-bodied noise from the passenger seat wipes the smirk from my face and my foot almost slams on the brake.

"Was... was that a *laugh* I just heard come out of you? I wasn't sure you knew how to make that sound."

I grin from ear to ear as she glares at me, her face back in its natural, detached state.

"I'd like to point out that, while you might find me irritating, your shoulders have relaxed, your head is leaned back on the headrest, and your arms are casually resting on the door and center console." As I say the words, she collects herself back into her seat, hands once again holding each other and resting in her lap. Still, her body isn't stiff, afraid to take up too much space.

She doesn't verbally acknowledge my observation. Instead, she sidesteps and changes the conversation. "Can you keep a secret?"

"Sure. But why are we whispering?"

She rolls her eyes and raises her voice to a normal volume. "That *stuff* I was working on the other day... it's a blog." I furrow my brows, unsure what that has to do with secrets. "I post recipes for coffee drinks, homemade creamers, and syrup. And I have a whole cozy, coffee aesthetic thing going on social media."

"What's the name?"

"I'm only telling you because of the whole... accountability thing. I'm exploring different avenues. If I never find a job, maybe I can do something with this. If this doesn't turn into anything more, maybe I can eventually get somewhere with a job. Or, maybe my dad will finally listen to my ideas for the diner," she adds, more so to herself than me. "My family doesn't know about it and I don't want them to."

"Well, thank you for telling me about it. I still want the name, though."

We're quiet for the rest of the drive, while she thinks about whatever the hell goes on inside her brain, and I think about what I'm going to do next. Besides the jealous and wishful thinking on the balcony that I want to do *something* besides bounce from job to job, I haven't done anything. Like Cori said, I can't give advice if I've made no progress myself.

Chapter 13
Be More

Cori

The boxes are hauled upstairs, and I begin unpacking right away. There isn't much, Sage is taking most of the dishes and kitchen appliances because Sam has everything we need, and Brian doesn't. There are the books, of course, a few decorations, an abnormal amount of coffee mugs—some of which were Grandma's—clothes and other linens, and enough office materials to supply a small business. We donated the furniture and anything else we had that Sage and Brian don't need. With all of my eggs in one basket, I'm left praying this arrangement works out.

"Y'all have done enough. Don't worry about it," I say as the guys begin peeling off tape and unloading the boxes.

But Callum looks at me with a stern glare as Tyler says, "Cori Lorraine, we talked about this earlier."

I shift my weight onto one foot, poking my hip out. "How do you know my middle name?"

He grins deviously. "Oh, Sage's told us lots of stuff about you."

Callum takes a box of coffee mugs to the kitchen, while Tyler opens a box of books. He slides it towards the hallway before opening another box of books. I watch him, amused, as he opens a third, then a fourth, and rolls his eyes. "Don't you think this is a tad excessive?"

"It's pronounced *impressive*. I know it's a difficult word, but say it with me slowly. *Im. Press. Ive.*"

He considers my joke for a moment. "Maybe stick to reading. Leave the joke telling to the professionals?"

I grin until I see Nick studying me with an intense, unreadable expression.

After the pizza arrives, the guys eat and I escape to Sam's room. Organizing the books is therapeutic, but it doesn't take me long to reach the last box.

Except, it doesn't contain books like it appears. It holds journals. I simultaneously admire the memories and glare at the reminder of what a failure I am. Because some journals have poems or novels inside—stories I've written poorly, then set aside to forget about. But some are empty because I stopped looking for the inspiration to keep writing.

I pull one out, a light pink cover with the words, "Live, Write, Repeat," stamped on the front. I know what's inside without opening it, but I do so anyway, to the halfway mark, finding the last poem I wrote.

I scream and flail about,
Drowning in tears as I shout
Your name, time after time.
My existence feels like a crime.
What are you even looking toward
To leave me here, alone and ignored?

Maybe I should just disappear,
Since you already pretend I'm not here.
From just being me, I'm swathed in shame.
For no matter how loud I scream your name,
Thrash about, writhe, and fret,
All I see is your silhouette.

I'd love to have the confidence in myself one day to again put something out into the world, something made up from what fills me inside. But these journals only serve as a reminder of finding the poetry book in a donation pile. A reminder of Mom and Dad's indifferent reaction to my published poem at nineteen years of age. A reminder that all I have to give is shadows and emptiness.

And nobody wants that.

I place the journal back inside the same box it's resided in since that Christmas when I retired my pen and stopped writing altogether. Then I slide the box beneath Sam's bed. When I die, someone will pull the box back out and shake their head at what a shame it is that I couldn't write more. Do more. Say more.

Be more.

It's nearing two p.m. when I hear the front door open. Hesitantly, I go out to the hallway, finding Sam, every hair in place and light blue shorts still perfectly ironed. He holds a small gift bag.

"Hey, babe," he says, taking off his shoes. He wraps me in a hug, kisses my forehead, then hands me the bag. "Did you get everything unpacked?"

"What is this?"

He smirks. "Look and find out."

I tilt my head when I see his car keys inside.

"You're welcome. Does that make up for me not being here today?"

"I don't understand."

"After you called me, I had your car towed to a shop. Don't worry, I'm footing the bill. They're working on it as we speak. Probably won't be done for another week, though, then I'll have to take it to the tire shop. So you can use mine in the meantime. I'll carpool with Dad."

I'm speechless. The keys, a gag to silence any complaints I might have had about him not showing up today. He'll fork over a bunch of money for me, and I can't do anything but accept it.

"I didn't want you to do that," I say. "I wanted to pay for it myself."

"When? Next year? The proper response is, *'Thank you, Sam, you're amazing.'*"

Suddenly, Nick's voice floods my head. *"Does getting out the things you want to say instead of swallowing them down help you feel better?"*

"Thank you. Truly, I appreciate it. But, you know, this isn't the first time you've not shown up and then blamed me for giving you the wrong day or time." I feel everyone's eyes on me, and weirdly, that's why I'm feeling brave enough to say it. They're the eyes of the people who were there for me today. The people who had to show up because Sam didn't. "And Nick's party, you swear you told me about it, but you didn't."

"You know, I ended the meeting early to come home to you."

"Meeting? I thought you were golfing?"

"Yeah, we were golfing while having a meeting. I don't go golfing with clients for fun, Cori."

"Okay? So, you left early. You still left me stranded this morning."

"Did I? Because it looks like you made it here just fine." He holds his hands up. "But I'm still the bad guy."

I don't want to brush it off just like every other time. I want an apology. But I don't get one. Sam rolls his eyes and storms off to his room. But I guess it's *our* room now.

So I follow.

When I walk in, he's sitting on the bed with his head in his hands.

"I had a shit day, okay? Can we not do this?" He brings his head up to look at me. "I swear you told me Sunday. And I spent all day with that asshole when I would have given anything to help you move into my apartment, and the dick didn't even take the deal."

I want to give him a hug and make him feel better. Maybe because I love him and hate seeing him so defeated. Maybe because I don't see a solution unless I cave.

My emotions betray me. I'm constantly caught between positives and negatives without being able to find a lane to stay in. Sam is a great boyfriend. But he's also a terrible boyfriend. He's sweet, but arrogant. He's caring, but sometimes only does and gives things so he won't have to hear me complain, like with the car.

But don't I give in for the same reason? I hate confrontation, and sometimes it's just easier to let him have his way than to hear him drone on and on. That's why I hardly eat in his presence—so I don't have to hear his lectures about nutrition. Why I lay with him before sneaking out to the living room to read—because he whines that he falls asleep faster with me there, but can't sleep with the lamp on. It's why I keep my mouth shut when I have something snarky I want to say— because the following argument is not worth my energy.

But I don't really care that he's tired and that he wasted his entire day on a hopeless case. Maybe he deserved that client dangling in front of his face like bait, only to be sorely disappointed when he chomped down on it. Maybe that's what you get when you tell me to wait to move everything in one day and then don't show up to help.

But do I have any right to be upset? I will be living here rent-free after all. I did convince him to let me pay some of the bills, the equivalent of almost half of the rent at the old apartment, but it's still not equal to what he pays. I let out a sigh and sit beside him, laying my head on his shoulder.

"I'm sorry. It's not a big deal, everything worked out. We have amazing friends, you know."

His arm comes around me, his head on mine. "Yeah, we do. I'm glad they were there to help."

Maybe we can make this work. I don't know why I have such difficulty silencing the doubts when this is Sam we're talking about. If our relationship could survive a seven-year separation, we can survive anything.

Right?

Chapter 14
Here Goes Nothing

Cori

T he Monday morning after Move-in Day, I wake up too late. My body doesn't care about the extra mileage during my new commute and is still in sleep mode when my alarms blare before the sun declares a new day. Stumbling around, eyes still closed and hair sticking up in all directions, I dress halfway, planning to finish on my walk to Sam's car. Running a brush through my hair, I bump into door frames and wall corners on my way to the kitchen. While I wait for the coffee to brew, I lean over the counter and rest my head on my crossed arms.

"You know, if you went to bed earlier, you might not be such a disaster in the mornings," drawls a deep, amused voice.

My head jerks up at the sound to find Nick leaning against the counter, one hand resting in his pocket, the other holding the handle of a coffee mug. He brings the rim to the smirk on his lips and drinks.

"How long have you been standing there?" I ask.

"Long enough to see that you're a disaster in the mornings."

I stand up straight and rub my eyes. "I am not."

He looks at my bra bulging underneath my shirt, then at my

pink underwear peeking out from the opening of my pants, before raising his eyebrows at me. Holding his stare, I quickly reach up my shirt to clasp my bra at my back, then button and zip my jeans before crossing my arms.

"Are you running late?"

"Technically, no. But I like to arrive fifteen minutes early, just in case."

He takes one last gulp from his mug before placing it in the sink. Passing by me on his way out, he pulls a chunk of my hair from where it sticks to my cheek, a smug grin slowly spreading over his face.

Once he's out the door, I groan, humiliation cramping my stomach, before running to the bathroom to scrub my face clean of dried drool. I promise myself I'll rise with my first alarms from now on, instead of pressing the snooze button repeatedly until I don't have a second to spare.

But by the time Friday arrives, that has yet to happen. As if to rub it in my face that I have no willpower, Nick has had my coffee already made and waiting on the counter in a travel mug for me every day this week. Along with the same smug grin on his face.

This morning is no exception.

"Thank you. Once again," I say after I've grabbed the cup from the counter.

Already dressed in the gray, grease-stained coveralls he wears to work, he leans against the counter, his preferred spot for drinking his coffee. "No problem. Once again."

"I won't need coffee tomorrow, though."

"Oh, you finally going to wake up on time?"

"No," I say defensively, then blow out a breath of frustration. "I mean, *yes*, but I don't have to be awake as early. I have tomorrow off."

"Two Saturdays off in a row? Lucky you."

"After today, I'll have already reached forty hours for the week." Plus, Saturdays tend to be busier and Mike likes to save those shifts for his favorites.

His forehead creases as he washes out his mug. "I don't understand their scheduling. They schedule you for doubles all week, then take your weekend shifts away because they don't want to pay you overtime?"

"Yeah, well. As my dad says, '*If you don't like it, find a real job.*'" I hold up the coffee in thanks and say goodbye before heading out the door, but he follows me.

"But it is a real job," he counters as we walk quietly down the tiled hallway.

"*I* know that, but he doesn't think so."

"Is your dad the one that does the scheduling?"

"No, it's the manager, Mike. But he doesn't spend much time on it. He just writes some random names down and adjusts it as needed throughout the week." Dad doesn't do anything with the diner, except complain about what a burden it is.

"It sounds like there's a lot of room for improvement there. Hint hint."

I think back to the conversation we had in his truck when we moved my things, about his encouragement to make my job less miserable of a place to be. But Dad's already shut down my ideas several times; if I present them again, the only thing I'll accomplish is pissing him off.

I tell Nick this as we descend the steps and walk toward his and Sam's vehicles; mine is still in the shop.

"Guess you'll just have to piss him off." I stop but he continues to his truck and waves over his shoulder.

Just what the hell am I supposed to do with that advice?

As I clocked into work, I naively assumed my shift would go as any other: I'd take orders, deliver food, wipe tables, cry in the bathroom a few times, scream in the walk-in at least once. I'd do the best an awkward, socially anxious introvert could do to serve customers without having a mental breakdown from all the human interaction.

In my years as a server, I've developed a talent for disassociation that helps tremendously, but there are still moments of pressure that I have yet to conquer. I have no issue serving larger tables, or having all of my tables occupied at once, but I do have issues with sales competitions. And Mike announced one starting today among the servers to improve sales and show Dad that the diner is worth keeping.

Inside the normal menu, there's an insert advertising limited time, special items, such as strawberry lemonade, mozzarella sticks, and a burger with some secret sauce. That pressure sets in when Mike stands over your shoulder at each table to ensure that you're convincing the guests to order these items and not taking no for an answer. The pressure is made worse when you're lectured in between tables because you're falling behind in the competition and told you just need to try harder. The pressure becomes unbearable when Mike asks if you should be demoted to washing dishes because *"you suck at sales."*

"You know what, Mike?" I throw down the rag I was using to wipe down a table, sick and tired of hearing his nagging for the past six hours. The cleaning wasn't doing any good anyway, the stains from the past fifty years still coat the laminate top. "I know I suck at sales. Wanna know why? Because the food sucks. No one wants gray mozzarella sticks or questionable fajitas from a *diner*."

He raises his eyebrows at me and I start to panic. *That's your boss you're yelling at.*

I lower my voice and soften my tone, "My sales numbers on these *special items* may not be where you want them, but why don't you ask the regulars how I am as a server? Why don't you look at my overall performance, how I'm always running other servers' food for them, how I pick up extra shifts, how I keep my section clean and don't spend all my time talking and flirting with the cooks?" I fight the urge to say, *'Like Sage.'*

As a shy person, I try to talk to my customers as little as possible. I ask what they want, I get it for them, and I leave them alone to eat. I'm here to serve, not to make friends. If the customers ask for recommendations from our menu, I have no problem giving them. But if they don't, they most likely already know what they want, and no amount of begging will convince them to order something extra. It's just a better experience all around if I leave them in peace.

Mike stares at me, a silent question on his face of whether I'm done with my outburst.

But I'm not.

This is my chance. My chance to get my ideas heard. If Dad won't listen, maybe Mike will. Dad always tells me I don't have ambition, but I do. I have loads of ambition and amazing ideas and they all fester inside with no relief because I lack confidence to put them out into the world. Or, when I muster up the courage to do so, they're shot down before they're fully spoken.

I take a deep breath and ignore the impending heart attack and the fire about to burst from my cheeks.

Here goes nothing.

"What is our biggest seller?" I ask.

"The pancake breakfast," he answers slowly.

"And what goes great with breakfast?"

He shrugs and says with attitude, "I don't know, what?"

"Coffee. Which is what I'm good at upselling." When a customer asks for coffee, I follow the request with clarifications. *"Coffee? I can definitely get that for you. Would you like hot or iced? Maybe some caramel and milk?"* And if they don't order coffee, but they order pie or breakfast, I ask if they'd like coffee to go with it. It's much smoother than, *"Would you like an appetizer? Maybe some cheese fries that look nothing like the picture on the menu and will leave you with the shits for days because it's barely edible?"*

Suspicion creeps over his features, so I continue. "If we stopped trying to add random items to the menu and simply expanded on the items that already sell well, we'll do a lot better. Offer flavored coffee instead of just plain black. Offer fresh ingredients on the items we already make and improve their taste. And put me behind the counter to make the coffee drinks and serve the customers there—it'll save time for the other servers and we could even work on doing more to-go business. We could offer ready-to-grab sandwiches and fruit cups and have seasonal flavors and-"

His hands come up to cut me off as he closes his eyes and shakes his head. "Slow down, you're all over the place. What are you talking about?"

"These are my ideas on how to make this place great again. I have tons more, plenty of ideas to improve sales and bring back the happy, friendly atmosphere that existed when Grandma ran this place." I leave out who's to blame for why the diner's in the state it's in, partly because I don't want Mike to hate me and shut down my ideas, and partly because it's as much Dad's fault as it is Mike's. Maybe more so.

Staring off at nothing, he taps his fingers against his chin in thought. And since I've already gone over Dad's head, I keep going. "You know, while we're trading ideas back and forth, you seem stressed. You work here six days a week and never take a vacation."

"Where are you going with this?"

"You need an assistant manager."

His eyebrows jump. "And you think you should get that position."

"Why not? I'm the owner's daughter. And I just told you a bunch of great ideas. I can work behind the counter for the first half of the day, then do some assistant-type duties for the second part of the day. I can work in your place on your days off and help you out with whatever you need."

Mike strokes his chin while he studies the counter in thought.

"I should run it by your dad, first."

Shit. "Better to have all the information first, you know? The sales numbers from coffee and such before telling him? Otherwise, he'll just reject the idea. Besides, you're the big boss man here, he trusts you to make the decisions, right?" I'm not great at ego-stroking, but that should work.

He nods, pointing his finger. "Alright. Get me a sample menu and I'll think about it." He walks back into his office, leaving me gawking at his back.

Did that really just happen?

Oh my God, it did.

I look around, but no one stands close enough that could have overheard my almost success. Or anyone to confirm that I did in fact wake up this morning and I'm not still lying in bed, blissfully dreaming. Except, I can't be dreaming because my dreams are almost always nightmares, and I resist the urge to fist pump the air while I stand alone and smile at nothing.

Okay, a sample menu. I'll make one that we can start with

using ingredients we already have, and another with drinks we need syrup and sauce for. I'll also make a spreadsheet with the cost of supplies and possible prices. My mind starts writing to-do lists and planning out my day off that I will be spending working after all.

It's small things like this that are so much harder for me—voicing ideas out loud to people of authority. Staying silent is the safer option because the threat of rejection is too scary to consider, like all the times Dad has interrupted me and brushed me off without letting me finish speaking. And that makes the simple act of speaking up that much more triumphant.

I immediately pull my phone out to text Sam and Hailey the good news, but I change my mind and put the phone away. I don't want to celebrate too early, because what if I jinx it? What if Mike ends up saying no? What if Dad shuts it down again before we can prove to him that it'll succeed? Or, what if it doesn't end up succeeding after all?

What if Dad is right and I have no idea what I'm talking about?

Chapter 15
Burnt, Dirty Water

Nick

" **A** nd that's pretty much it. There's a pool, a gym, and a courtyard downstairs. Are you satisfied now, Mom?" I joke.

Her lips quirk. "I'm sorry, you're a twenty-four-year-old male living with another male the same age. I just wanted to ensure you were living in a nice, clean environment, and not a cesspool with pizza boxes and chip bags everywhere." Mom had a day off of work, so I left the shop early to take her to lunch before bringing her to Sam's for a tour.

"No, you raised me better than that." I'll admit, I tend to overlook dust and dirty underwear on the floor without the threat of flying shoes from Mom if I didn't pick up after myself.

But since Cori moved in, she has kept the apartment clean from what I suspect is a desire to keep Sam happy. From my own desire to pull my weight around here instead of relying on her to do everything for me, I try to get to chores before she does. And it's become a game between us. Several times, she's opened the microwave to clean it or gone to vacuum the carpet, only to find it already completed. As payment, I'll come home to find my laundry already switched to the dryer or folded. So

I'll retaliate by cleaning the coffee machine or wiping the shelves in the refrigerator.

Instead of being thankful, she reprimands me and views it as a challenge to be faster. Sometimes, I wonder if I truly want to help out around the apartment, or if I simply want to irritate her.

"I know I did. I just wanted to make sure you knew it, too." She opens the refrigerator. "We should have gone by the store on the way back from lunch. You need groceries."

"No, we don't need anything."

"All you have in here are vegetables. Where's your cookie dough or cheese or sweet tea?"

I laugh. "Yeah, well, Sam has become a stickler about almost anything with calories. Unless he's the one eating it. Speaking of, do you want to wait around for him to get home?"

"I'd like that. It's been a couple of years since I've seen him, does he look any different?"

"No, he just wears suits now." We walk into the living room and take seats on the couch. "Oh, did you want a drink? Water or coffee? Cori has all kinds of flavors in there. There's a pecan one that's pretty good." I head to the kitchen, but we can still hear each other over the bar counter separating the two rooms.

Mom waves her hand. "Oh, I don't want to drink her coffee."

"She won't mind." I grab the bag of coffee grounds and start working the machine. When I moved in, it took me forever to learn how to use it. There are knobs and levers and a hundred different spouts for different things, but I finally got the hang of it. Now I try to have it made for Cori every morning when she finally emerges from her bedroom, if only to rub in my ability to wake up on time.

"So it hasn't been awkward, then? Having her here?" she

asks, admiring the knick-knacks and photographs on the shelf by the TV.

"It is a little. I still don't have her quite figured out. One moment, it's like pulling teeth trying to get her to have a conversation. The next, it's like you're friends after all. Then she gets all awkward again. She doesn't like help because she doesn't like owing people. She's constantly worried about bothering me, to the point where she asks if it's okay to enter a room I'm already in. And she's always stiff. But if you ask her why she's shy, she doesn't mind getting testy."

"But you're being nice to her, right? She sounds a little anxious, maybe insecure," she asks as if I'm in Kindergarten and Cori is the new kid in school.

"Am I being *nice* to her?"

Mom rolls her eyes. "I'm only asking because I know what it feels like to be insecure that you act... scared to..."—she moves her hands around, searching for the right words—"bother or burden people."

Because of my dad. My dad did that to her. "How did you get over it?"

She lifts a shoulder before speaking, her words slow and stiff. "You never really get over something like that. And, you know, everyone feels that way to some degree about something. But some people lie to themselves about it and some are honest. And some take those insecurities out on other people, while others take them out on themselves. I think with time, most of us learn to live with our insecurities, or at least not let them get in our way."

I think back to my past conversations with Cori. There were times that my words might have come across more gruff or harsher than I intended, but I'm not going to coddle her. She should learn to stand up for herself.

Once the coffee is done, I add cream and bring it to Mom.

She studies the mug for a moment before saying, "Classy, Nick." But her lips tip up in a grin as she takes a sip.

I smile. "It's Cori's." I could have served Mom's coffee in any one of the mugs in the cabinet, maybe the white one with bluebonnets or the souvenir from The Alamo. Instead, I'm feeling devious and serve it in one that says, *"Here we fucking go again. I mean... good morning!"*

"I think I might like her." She takes another sip. "This is really good."

Someone walks through the front door, and the sound of sweet, feminine humming almost has me rising from the couch in alarm. Cori doesn't hum, so who could that be?

But it is Cori who appears around the corner wearing her uniform—a black t-shirt with the diner's logo and jeans.

She stops in her tracks, eyes widening just slightly when she sees Mom and I sitting on the couch.

"Oh. Hi."

"Hey. Did you have a fight with the gravy again?" I say, pointing to a large stain on her thigh.

"Yes, it seems to happen every day."

I chuckle. "Mom, this is Cori. Cori, this is Mom." We both stand up and Mom playfully slaps my arm.

"My name is Elaine, you goof. It's nice to meet you, Cori." Cori steps forward and shakes Mom's extended arm.

"It's nice to meet you, too." Mom and I share a look at Cori's tense shoulders.

"I made Mom a cup of that pecan coffee."

"Yes, I hope that's okay," Mom says.

"Oh, of course. That's what it's there for." She grins timidly. "Do you like it? It's one of my favorites." Her fingers pick at each other.

"I love it. Nick, you'll have to show me the label before we leave, so I can buy some for home."

I nod and Cori hooks her thumb over her shoulder. "Well, I should go shower and change. It was nice to meet you."

"You too, hon," Mom replies. As Cori walks away, Mom asks how Callum is doing and if Tyler is behaving himself.

I'm answering her when the front door opens again. There's a thud, probably from Sam dropping his briefcase, and he lets out a long sigh as he walks around the wall.

"You're home early," I say in greeting.

"Yeah, Cori's car is finally done. Had to pick it up from the shop before they closed." A grin spreads over his face when he notices Mom.

"Elaine, what a nice surprise." He walks over to where she sits on the couch and takes her hand in his, kissing the back of it. "You look amazing. Much too young to have a twenty-four-year-old." He's right. She's only in her early forties, hair still her natural dark blonde, and skin still mostly smooth around her eyes and mouth.

But I stand for better leverage as I lightly punch his arm. "Dude, don't kiss my mom."

"Oh, stop it. He's being a gentleman," Mom says.

"Would you like one too?" Sam asks and starts towards me, lips pursed.

I escape towards the door, calling out to Mom, "Alright, you've seen him, let's go."

"What are y'all doing?" I ask once I come back inside from walking Mom to her car. Cori, hair wet and curling from her shower, sits next to Sam on the couch, their faces illuminated by the soft glow of her phone screen.

It's the phone that answers, "Who was that?" in a woman's voice.

My eyes widen. "Oh, shit. Sorry."

"That was my roommate, Nick. A guy I went to college with. I told you about him, right?" Sam asks while Cori mouths, "Run! It's my mother." She shoos me off with her hands, but it's too late.

"Oh, yes. Hi, Nick. I've heard a lot about you," the woman says.

"I've heard a lot about you as well, Ma'am." I shrug at Sam and Cori's shared looks of confusion because neither of them has ever mentioned this woman to me.

"Do you have plans tomorrow night? The kids are all coming for dinner, and we'd love to have you as well."

A family dinner? "Oh, are you sure? I don't want to intrude." I'm praying she changes her mind as I rub the back of my neck.

"The more, the merrier. Besides, I need some furniture moved around upstairs, and you and Sam would be perfect for the job."

"Oh okay. Can I bring anything?" A free meal in exchange for manual labor is a fair trade. Besides, it might be fun to learn more about Cori, maybe see a chubby baby picture or two.

"No, Cori will bring mac and cheese, you and Sam just bring yourselves. I have to run, but I'll see you all here at four."

"Well, I guess I'm making mac and cheese," Cori says as she hangs up. "Did you not understand what I was telling you?"

I breathe out a laugh and take a seat in an armchair. "It can't be that bad, can it?"

"Have you ever had your nails pried from your fingers while someone drilled screws into your shins?"

Sam rises from the couch. "Jesus. What the hell is wrong with you?"

"My parents," she answers with emphasis.

"So, anything I should know before dinner with your family?"

She considers her answer for a moment. "I have an older sister who's married with a baby. And you've met Sage. I also have two younger brothers who will probably inhale their food, then bolt to play video games or something. My dad will ask you a million questions about your job because it's not just me he's critical of, so try to stick to one-word answers. And my mom *really* likes compliments. Also, she often comments on my being fat."

A cough escapes at the discrepancy between her direct words and nonchalant tone. "Oh."

"I'm hungry, what's for dinner?" Sam asks, resuming his seat on the couch with a cold beer now in his hand.

Cori stands, but I ask, "Why don't you make him cook for a change?" Normally, she cooks on the nights she's off of work, but only because she beats me to the stove, and I cook on the nights she works. It's usually something easy and burnt, but honestly, not much different than anything Cori makes for us. We'd all benefit from a cooking course.

"Because I'm the king of this apartment and I let you home-less people live in my castle." I can't help but wonder if any seriousness lurks behind the joke.

Cori and I exchange a long look and I try to send her a message, telepathically. In case she doesn't understand, I widen my eyes and jerk my head in Sam's direction as if to say, "*Stand up for yourself.*" And if that doesn't work, I plan to race Cori to the kitchen and battle for cooking rights.

She's not weak by any means. I've seen firsthand how riled up she can get and heard her demand better for herself, but she doesn't do it often enough.

Cori clears her throat and starts scratching at her wrist.

"Umm... you know, it would be nice to know you could feed yourself if something ever happened to me."

"I fed myself just fine before you and Nick moved in."

She crosses her arms over a baggy t-shirt with a band name I don't recognize. "Eating take-out that your assistant ordered before you left work doesn't count. But you could practice while I'm here, in case you have questions or need help."

"I did that with my mom before I moved to college," I tell him.

"So your mom's to blame for your inability to not burn food? Noted." He takes a long sip from his can before setting it on the coffee table and stretches his back. "Don't tell her I said that."

"No, I'm calling her right now. She wouldn't have driven too far, she can turn around and come kick your ass."

I get my phone out, but not to call Mom. I need the camera handy because, to my utter surprise, he's removing his tie and walking to the kitchen. Cori moves around the other side to meet him by the pantry, and he opens the door.

"Okay, so what am I making?"

She moves a bag of rice and a can of something around on the shelf to peek behind it, so I intercept. "You have to decide. And do all the prep yourself."

"Fine. I'm just warning you, though—you're going to love what I make. It will be one of the best meals you've ever tasted and you're going to want me to cook every night. But that's not going to happen. We *all* need to pull our weight around here."

Cori and I both roll our eyes.

"Now, go to your rooms, I'll call you out when dinner is ready."

"What if you have questions?" Cori asks.

"I'll come ask. Now, go. I don't want to be filmed"—he

points to my phone, then to Cori—"or watched by Anxious Anderson."

Cori and I head for our separate rooms, sharing a look of apprehension before walking through our doors. I take out my phone again and tap on her contact.

> Me: What do you think we're going to have to eat?

Roommate: Take-out. That's why he sent us to our rooms-so we wouldn't see him order it.

I wonder if she hears my laughter through the walls.

> Me: What are you doing to pass the time?

Roommate: Blog stuff.

> Me: I still haven't gotten the name.

Roommate: I'm aware.

> Me: ...

Roommate: Fine.

Roommate: Coffee Break

I take out my laptop from my backpack and type *Coffee Break* into the search bar. I find a website that's nice and easy to navigate.

I'm impressed and I send her a text telling her so before signing up for her newsletter; I'm promised a "Printable recipe booklet" for doing so. After clicking through to her social media accounts and scrolling through the cozy, neutral-themed photos, I have an overwhelming desire to curl up in a blanket with a cup of coffee and read a book. She never shows her face in the photos or videos, but I recognize Sam's countertop and some of the mugs used in the most recent content. I hit the follow button on each account, figuring I could support her by sharing, liking, or commenting on stuff she posts.

I hate the taste of coffee; it's burnt, dirty water to my taste buds, and only manageable with a cup of sugar mixed in. But most of these recipes, except for the weird berry-flavored ones, sound pretty good, and I send a few to Sam's printer. I head there now to fetch the papers, stepping out of my door at the same time as Cori.

She stills at the sight of me as if caught in the act of something she didn't want witnessed. She's so odd. She gestures down the hall for me to pass by her, but I tell her I'm going to Sam's office across from their bedroom.

"Oh. Me too." We remain where we stand, each waiting for the other to go first. She's unsure of me once again, like any comfort she may have found around me is fleeting. It seems like we take steps backward any time we aren't around each other, and I have to repeat any reassurances I've already made to help her not feel anxious.

Finally, she opens his office door. She walks with quiet steps to the printer and takes hold of the papers, looking for the ones she printed. Holding up the recipes, she raises her brows.

"They look good. I want to try them," I answer simply. There's one for a Churro Latte, Oreo Frappuccino, and a peanut butter coffee creamer that sounds weird, yet intriguing.

Sam pokes his head inside and Cori jerks her hands down, still holding the stack of paper. The movement makes her look guilty. Of what, I'm not sure, and I give her a questioning look as Sam announces that dinner is ready.

"I'll be right there," she says. Sam goes back out and Cori hands me the recipes without a word before taking whatever she had printed to Sam's room.

A few minutes later, we all meet in the kitchen, where Cori

and I take in the scene. The kitchen is spotless, with no pans or cutting boards in the sink, and light granite countertops gleaming as they did before. Then we see the plates on the table, two of which have pasta with shrimp, and the third has a bed of dry greens topped with a naked chicken breast.

"Francesca's?" Cori asks. It's a restaurant a mile or so down the road.

"Yep," Sam answers, not bothering to lie. "You're welcome."

She clicks her tongue and pulls out the chair in front of the salad. "Well, I guess you've got the money to eat out for every meal, so there's no real need for you to know how to cook."

Chapter 16
Friends

Cori

"We also have reason to celebrate," Sam says, taking his seat and twirling his pasta onto his fork.

The metal clinking against the plate fills the silence as we wait for him to continue. "The Houston Review is doing an article about me. Not the company, just me. It comes out in a couple of weeks."

The smile that tugs on my lips is genuine as I reach over to grab his hand. "Sam, that's amazing. I'm so proud of you."

Nick slaps him on the shoulder in congratulations.

"I wasn't going to say anything yet, but I couldn't wait. And I'm the only one there that's had an article written about him. Except Dad, of course."

"We'll have to buy a frame for it and,"—I look around the living room for a spot to display it—"we could hang it there, beside the photo of the Houston skyline. Leave room on the other side for another future article."

Sam could never grin sheepishly, but he fakes a good impression of one now. "I already bought a few frames. I'll give a copy to my parents, maybe hang one in both of my offices. Do you think your parents would want one?"

"Um, maybe." I'd say no, considering they gave their own child's poem away, but this is Sam. They love Sam. I know they love me too, but having an article written about you is a big deal, and they'll be as proud as I am. Maybe more so.

"We should invite everyone out to celebrate, maybe next Friday." He waggles his eyebrows at Nick. "Maybe invite Kenna?"

Nick's body tenses at the idea. Mine does too, and I decide to be honest about it. "Kenna makes me uncomfortable."

"Why?" Sam asks, furrowing his brows.

I want to say *Because she looked at me like I was prey.* Instead, I answer, "I just got a weird vibe from her. I liked Erin though, she can come."

"You don't feel insecure around her? You know we slept together. A lot."

"Well, you're not interested in her anymore, right?"

He shakes his head. "No, although I wouldn't reject the idea of inviting her to our bed." He chuckles.

I'm often at a loss for words, but I doubt anyone would know how to respond to that.

"Learn to take a joke, Cor," he says, noticing my gaping mouth.

Completely unconcerned, he describes his interview with the journalist at lunch today, and how the article will highlight all his success in a short year at the company. And being so young makes it all the more impressive.

The urge to announce my own good news has my heart racing. I shift in my seat and push my food around, preparing to make the announcement. But, no. I shouldn't take this moment away from him. Besides, it'll look the same as this dry salad next to his creamy pasta—not worth mentioning.

"You okay?" Nick asks me once Sam is done talking.

"Me? Yeah, I'm fine." I take a bite, only the second bite of the meal. He isn't convinced, although Sam doesn't seem to notice.

I swallow and clear my throat. "Actually, I'm great. I sort of had some success at work today too, and it's way too early to get excited, but I am anyway. But we can talk about it another day, I'm just so proud of you." I smile and rub Sam's arm to further sell it.

"Just tell us. Big tip?" Sam asks like that's the only success I could've had.

"No, but... well, I asked Mike about making some changes, and he told me to get some more info for him. If he likes what I show him, we may implement some of the ideas and it would really improve things. For sales and me."

Nick's lips spread into a cocky grin. He knows he had a hand in encouraging me, but I avoid meeting his eyes, partly to keep from giving him the satisfaction, partly to keep myself from smiling back.

Sam narrows his eyes. "What are these ideas?"

I jump into it, describing too many details. It probably doesn't make sense by the time I'm finished explaining, but I'm excited and nervous.

Only for him to say, "But it's a diner, not a coffee shop. You don't have the right type of customers for flavored coffee. You get truckers and drunk people that want grease."

"Everyone from the town goes to the diner, as well as people who stop in off the highway. And I sell flavored coffee all the time already." I have so much more to add, like how the expansion from Houston is reaching us and in a few years, the town will be unrecognizable. The time to prepare for that growth was yesterday.

"Well, what does your dad say about it?"

I lift a shoulder, glancing down at my plate as if looking for the answers in the green mix. "I'll get the information to Mike first, then we'll talk to Dad."

"I just don't understand, why waste your time on this. If you want to make coffee for a living, go work at a coffee shop." He takes a drink of water and stands.

"Or, she could open up her own coffee shop," Nick adds. I know he means to be helpful, to thin out the tension.

But it only adds fuel to the fire as Sam snorts. "Yeah, okay."

"What? She could do it."

"With what money? She has no collateral. And the only job she's ever had is serving. She knows nothing about running a business."

"She's taken classes. And she knows more than you think."

He puts his plate in the sink and comes back to stand behind the chair he vacated. "How would you know? Even her dad would tell her she's not cut out for it. And classes only get you so far-"

"Okay, I'm right here," I interrupt. "And I'm not opening a coffee shop. I know better."

"Thank God," Sam mutters. "As for becoming assistant manager, you're not qualified for that either."

"I know enough to fill in when Mike isn't there. Besides, no one else has an interest in the diner. Who's it going to go to when Dad is too old? I was just trying to do *something*. Have some sort of purpose, some sort of accomplishment."

"Well, what about your blog? All your followers? That's an accomplishment by itself." My eyes snap to Nick's. "That proves you know coffee."

"What blog? What followers?"

I can see the moment Nick understands his mistake. "Oh, shit. I'm sorry, Cori." But it isn't his fault, it's mine. I'm the one keeping secrets from my boyfriend. I told him my family didn't know, but didn't specifically say that Sam was included in *family*. Because it's ridiculous.

"You have a secret blog? Why would you keep that from me?" Sam asks, like he's just been handed ammunition for future use.

"It's nothing. I just post recipes online. I knew you'd think it was dumb. Just a waste of time."

I finally meet his piercing stare.

"I mean..." He laughs without humor. Saying without saying that he agrees. "How much time do you spend on it? A lot? Could you be using that time to go to school, work out..." He waves his hand around because he can go on and on with all the different ways I could be bettering myself.

I stab the romaine and spinach leaves until my fork is full and put it in my mouth. I don't taste anything, not that there's much to taste. It's simply a tool to distract myself, to keep me from crying as my face heats and pulses with shame. It works. After a minute, I no longer hear Sam's continuation of my failures.

Although Nick has already finished eating, he remains in his seat, watching me with narrowed eyes. He interrupts and contradicts Sam occasionally, but I don't hear what words are spoken. Eventually, I meet his gaze and grin like it's no big deal that my entire existence is a waste of space in the world. But to voice such a thought out loud would be a pathetic display of self-pity.

Because if we're unhappy with our circumstances, we should just change them. Right?

If you're unhappy, just be happy.

If you're stressed, just relax.

If you're shy, just don't be shy.

It's that easy. Isn't that what everyone says?

"I'm just looking out for you, Cor. I only want you to succeed," Sam finishes.

After dinner, Sam lies down in bed to finish what's left of a baseball game while I slowly wash the plates we used. Nick grabs the dish towel, ready to dry when I finish scrubbing at nothing, his mouth opening and closing at a loss for words.

Finally, he finds them. "What the fuck?"

I meet his gaze to determine if he's wondering about my actions, or what Sam said. "What?"

"You just sat there and let him criticize you."

Oh, the irony. "So you're going to *criticize* me for it?"

I scrub the plate a little too hard and it slips from my grip, hitting the other plates in the sink. The clash reverberates through the air. Miraculously, it doesn't break and I pick it up to rinse it off, then hold it out for Nick to take.

"I don't mean to criticize you too, but you let him walk all over you."

What exactly was I supposed to do? *"I'm just looking out for you, Cor. I only want you to succeed."* How does one argue with that?

"Can we just not talk about it, please?" My cheeks could fry eggs. One would think I'd grown accustomed to the sensation by now, but my worst fear and clearest reality is shame.

He finally takes the plate from my hand. "Fine."

"Fine."

Silence falls between us as I clean the white sauce from the second ceramic plate, but he ruins the peace as I hand the plate to him.

"So, how was the salad?"

"Good."

"How? There wasn't anything on it. It was just chicken and leaves."

"Yeah, well, the dressing that usually comes with it is full of sugar."

"And?"

I lift a shoulder. "It's what I always order from Francesca's."

There's a clang as he stacks the dried plates together. "What *you* order? Or what he orders for you?"

I turn the water off and face him. I hate confrontation, but he's determined to get on my nerves today. And after the struggle to keep myself from exploding at dinner, my patience is running thin. "What's your problem?"

"Nothing. I just don't like that you're self-conscious about food. Your weight isn't anyone else's business, and there's nothing wrong with sugar now and then."

"Good thing it's none of *your* business, then, huh?"

He sets the towel on the counter and leans down. "Yeah, you're a big girl, right? You can handle yourself?"

Not breaking his stare, I say, "I'm handling *you* right now."

Despite the tension between us, his lips twitch at my word choice until he can't hold back his amusement any longer. His smile spreads wide, flashing his white teeth.

"Ugh." I turn back to the sink and flip the water back on to wash the remaining plate. "You know what I mean."

I'd love more than anything to be one of those women that doesn't take any crap from anyone, especially a man. Like Sage —she does what she wants when she wants and lets every criticizing comment and judgment roll off her shoulders. She doesn't spend hours overthinking decisions, having been born knowing what she wanted from the world. But I wasn't born decisive and confident. And I don't know how to be that way.

As I've said before, confidence feels like arrogance to those who don't come by it naturally. A combination of inferiority, fear of failure, of being in the wrong, of accidentally being disrespectful, and of feeling too much at once all keep me in my place.

Once the last plate is washed and dried, I wipe the counter down and turn to leave. But Nick grabs my arm.

"I'm sorry." His brown eyes, like an espresso with a hint of caramel, bore into mine. But I don't know what he's apologizing for. He must read my face because he adds, "For everything. Accidentally telling him about the blog, then being an ass afterward."

I take a small step backward and shake my head as I look away from the intensity in his eyes.

"You don't have anything to apologize for. I shouldn't have kept the blog from him." I won't mention the rest because, while he was frustrating me, he's right—I should be stronger. I should stand up for myself. But at the same time, Sam's right—I shouldn't waste my time on things that won't get me anywhere in life.

"Yes, I do. Because I caused you... pain? Discomfort? I don't know what you're feeling, but whatever it is, I did that. And I'm sorry."

I don't know what to do with my arms. I cross them, but that feels too defensive. I uncross them, only for them to dangle at my sides like I've never had arms before. I'm not used to people apologizing for the way they've made me feel, and I don't know what to do with that either. My feelings are usually brushed off or dismissed as dramatic, leaving me stone-faced and numb.

He extends one of his large, calloused, hands. "Friends?"

I nod. "Friends."

The next morning, I wake with a jolt at five thirty and scramble around for ten minutes until I remember, I don't have to work today. My muscles soften, a lazy grin appearing as I let the jeans I was about to put on fall to the floor, and slide back among the layers of bedding. Sam is already gone, probably at the gym, leaving me with the whole bed to myself. I struggle to fall asleep almost every night but slip into blissful sleep with ease now and don't rise again until almost nine.

The sun blares through the cream-colored curtains enough that I squint on my way to the bathroom. I brush my teeth, not bothering to fix my hair or change out of the oversized t-shirt before going to the kitchen. Nick sits at the table typing something on his laptop. But when he lifts his head, his lips quirk to the side and he closes the computer and crosses his arms.

"Good morning," I say as I get out a coffee mug.

"I'm glad you're getting more comfortable around me."

I press the brew button on the coffee machine. "What is that supposed to mean?"

"Well, it looks like a bird got caught in your hair and died fighting its way out. And you're not wearing pants."

Turning to face him, I lift the hem of the t-shirt. "I have shorts on. The shirt is just big."

He snorts. "And your hair?"

"You're one to talk." I stand before him, hands braced on the back of a chair, and raise my brows at the locks of dark hair sticking up on the side of his head. His hand flies up to feel, and his expression humbles.

"Oh."

I fetch my coffee, add a couple of tablespoons of my homemade cinnamon roll creamer, and pull out a chair to join him at the table.

"What are you doing?" I ask, blowing the steam from the surface of my drink.

"I was taking an aptitude test, but I got distracted by news headlines." He pulls his laptop towards him and opens it. "I'm sure there's some brilliant science behind these questions, but I can't see it."

"Key word there is *brilliant*. Which you are not." Friends joke around like this, right? I do with Hailey and even Tyler. But now that the words are out there, I panic. I peek at him over the rim of my mug to assuage his reaction. He grins, thank God.

"I see the claws are out this morning."

A thought occurs to me as a comfortable silence descends, how we look sitting across from each other. If I were to write a poem about us, I'd start and end it with the same two lines:

The moon is dust, the sun is flame,
But they rise and fall the same.

"It's funny—you and I are very different, but we're also very similar," she says.

I lift my face from the screen. "What do you mean?"

"Our personalities are different, what makes us, *us*. You're not paralyzed by shyness or insecurity, you were probably a *cool kid* growing up, and even our hobbies are different. But neither of us knows what to do with our lives."

"I'm more insecure than you think." I see what she means though—our pasts are different, yet we're at the same stop in the road.

"I know it's ridiculous, I know the injury wasn't *really* my fault. But I can't help but wonder if Mom feels like everything was a waste. Everything she did for me growing up. All the money spent on cleats and pads when we could barely afford our bills. I was so selfish and I didn't realize it until everything was over." Mom has been the absolute best mother, always sacrificing, never complaining. The kind of mom who's proud of me regardless of what I do. But every time she says the words, a stone sinks low in my belly. I haven't done anything to be proud of.

Cori remains silent, not taking her eyes off mine. I worry I've taken us too deep into my issues, that I've unsettled her.

Finally, she says the last thing I expected her to say, "I can see that." She must see the confusion on my face because she adds, "I mean if I were in your shoes, I'd probably think the same thing."

I assumed she'd tell me to stop being stupid, to stop tearing myself up over an injury I had no control over. I'm not sure how to feel about being told the opposite. That I *should* feel guilty.

"I blame myself for literally everything," she says, voice barely above a whisper.

"But you shouldn't."

"You can tell me that all day long." She lifts her shoulder. "Just like I could tell you all day long that your injury wasn't your fault. But it won't change how we feel deep down."

I glance off into the distance, my eyes losing focus as I think about her words.

"I'm not saying I agree with your feelings, exactly. For the record, I don't think you have any reason to feel guilty. But I know how self-blame works. I feel guilty for just existing most days." I meet her stare and she just shrugs. Like it's perfectly normal to be ashamed for existing.

"But, why?" Does she have some dark secret, some horrible sin that she committed that I don't know about?

Her eyes narrow at my tone, but she doesn't answer.

Did she take and take from her mom until she had nothing left and no energy from working several jobs just to pay for an extracurricular activity? Is she the reason her mom didn't go to college, or the reason her dad drank their money away until he finally lost it and just abandoned his family?

My blood is boiling with frustration at this woman. She could have everything she'd ever dreamed of if she'd only get up and take it. Instead, she lies down and lets people walk all over her.

She doesn't have any immovable boulders blocking her path to happiness, only herself.

"You and I are *nothing* alike. Sure, we may both be locked in a cage, but you have the key in your hand. You can reach out and unlock your door." I stand from the table and grab my laptop, adding before I start for my room, "Mine was welded shut and the keyhole filled in."

"That's just one door."

I halt in my tracks. "What do you mean?"

"The door to football may be welded shut, but you have the key in your hand also. And you have other doors leading you from your cage. We all do. You just don't know which one to go through. Neither do I."

My hand runs through my hair while I stand there like an idiot. All of this metaphor talk has my head spinning.

In truth, I don't want to admit that I'm holding myself back too. I want to continue blaming my injury. I want my jealousy of men like Sam to be justified because I can't accept that simple explanation—sometimes life just isn't fair.

Slowly, I set my laptop back down on the table, but I remain standing.

"You're right."

"I know," she responds quickly.

I meet her eyes and snort at her sudden cockiness, and her returned, close-lipped smile smooths out any lingering tension.

I think back to what Mom said yesterday, about everyone being insecure about something. It's why I finally admitted it moments ago.

Some take those insecurities out on other people, while others take them out on themselves.

I took it out on Cori just now.

"I'm sorry," I say while she picks at her coffee mug.

She bites her cheek and says softly, "It's okay. It's nothing I haven't said to myself before."

I shake my head. "It's not okay, Cori. And you shouldn't accept that from me or anyone." I'd love to understand, to know what in her past has made her feel so unworthy, but I don't want to push. I open my laptop once again and turn the screen to her. "Truth is, it's been a rough morning. I was filling out the questions and opened a new tab to search something. Then I saw this headline."

She reads the headline out loud. "Offensive tackle Grant Peters signs $63 million contract extension." The words spoken aloud pierce my heart. "Peters. He was the player that fell on you?"

I nod. It's irrational to blame him. It's not any more his fault than it is mine. But jealousy doesn't care about semantics. It only considers the fact that he's living my dream.

Chapter 17
The Merciful Queen

Cori

This macaroni and cheese might be what finally overworks my heart, sending me to an early grave. What if the salt doesn't get stirred in right and someone gets a clump of it in one bite? What if someone finds a hair or piece of fuzz in it? What if I drop it on the way there?

Because they prefer different types, I'm making a creamy macaroni and cheese for Mom and baked for Dad. I'm currently on my third attempt at the baked, and it's looking a little too brown on the top. The creamy macaroni and cheese is too creamy, so I added more cheese. But then it was too stiff, so I added more milk, and no matter how little I add, it takes it too far. I don't have enough ingredients to remake the dishes, so these will have to do. I just hope that everyone will leave the food alone and not point out everything I did wrong, like usual.

I quickly move around Sam's kitchen, cleaning up the droplets of milk and stray shreds of cheese on every counter. His kitchen is like a dream compared to my old one. I'm so used to the dark and the ancient appliances that I had to learn how to cook with an oven that heats to the temperature I set it to, and a microwave that doesn't randomly start itself. Unfortunately, 'easy' doesn't equal 'quality,' and my stomach twists at the thought of presenting my culinary disasters to my parents.

I've left myself with just enough time to get dressed, and I head to Sam's bedroom to plan my outfit as if I'm strategizing for battle. If I show up in my usual jeans next to Sam's slacks and buttoned shirt, Mom will ask why I have no respect for her showing up in an outfit I'd wear to a concert. If I wear the blue dress that flares past my hips and hits just below my knees, Mom will comment on the stretch marks on my calves again. But if I wear my black pants—Sam's favorite pair because of how they hug my ass— and the most expensive blouse I own, I just might make it out alive tonight.

I leave Sam's bedroom but dart back inside to stick a few pieces of sour candy in my pocket. Just in case.

When we arrive at Mom and Dad's after an hour of uncomfortable silence, Nick takes the food from my hands, insisting on carrying everything himself. Mom greets us in the kitchen, beaming up at Sam before hugging him tightly.

"Stunning as always, Sarah," he says. *Kiss ass.*

He introduces Nick, whom Mom also hugs and thanks for coming before pointing to a spot on the counter for the dishes. Then, she directs him and Sam upstairs to join my dad and brothers.

Once they're gone, she turns to me. "I hope it's okay that I asked him to come. Solomon wants the wooden desk upstairs moved to his room and it's too heavy for your brother and Dad. You know how bad his back is."

"Yeah, it's fine." I hug Stephanie, who sits on a stool picking at a veggie tray before kissing her ninth-month-old, Georgie, on his soft head.

Mom examines my outfit, and I squirm, unsure of where to put my arms. Squinting her eyes, she says, "You look like you're going to a job interview. And those pants are much too tight. I keep telling you to cut out bread and sugar."

I rub my fingers through the hair at my temples, accidentally pulling a few strands loose. "Yeah. I know."

"Why did you bring two different kinds of macaroni?" Stephanie asks, lifting the cover on each dish.

"Well, Mom and Dad don't like the same kind, so I brought one for each of them."

Mom looks at me with her brows furrowed. "That was sweet of you." I don't know why because I've always been the most thoughtful of my siblings, but her tone suggests surprise. Yet, it's that simple comment, that small declaration, that has me feeling more noticed than I've felt in a long time. But she ruins the moment by adding, "Hopefully it tastes better than the spaghetti you made for dinner that time a few years ago."

When Sage arrives, she passes right by me making a beeline for Georgie and giving his head a sniff. She takes him in the other room and doesn't reappear until Mom calls everyone to eat after the guys are done moving the furniture around upstairs.

When we form a line to fill our plates, I avoid most of the carbs, taking small spoonfuls of vegetables and the smallest piece of chicken. I'll sneak a roll later. I still don't know why our presence has been requested other than needing furniture moved, but Mom decorated the table with a burgundy tablecloth and a bouquet of tulips in the center. I'm praying they're not about to announce a divorce. Or that they're selling the house and buying an RV to travel the country. On second thought, that might not be so terrible.

We're barely in our seats before Sage asks Mom and Dad, "So, is someone dying or something?"

"We can't just invite everyone for a nice family dinner?" Mom asks. "None of you come to visit unless we demand you to."

Ignoring her, Dad says, "Stephanie is the one who requested a family dinner first, and then Spencer also has news of his own."

All eyes find Stephanie, who smiles and bounces in her seat, holding Adam's hand. "We're having another baby!"

Shouts of congratulations erupt from everyone all at once, along with exclamations about how Georgie will be the best big brother. And relief that everyone is healthy.

"Your turn, Spencer," Dad says.

"Oh, okay. Well," Spencer says, timidly, as he pulls an envelope from his lap. "I was a–"

"MY BABY WAS ACCEPTED TO NHU!" Mom shouts impatiently, stealing the spotlight from Spencer.

A chorus of various cheers is sung from the table with perfectly timed squeals from Georgie, who's still on Sage's lap.

"Does this mean you got the baseball scholarship?" I ask. NHU is a tough school to get into unless you have a sports scholarship, and I doubt very much Spencer got in on his grades alone. Not that he's unintelligent, he just doesn't care.

He nods. "Late acceptance. Someone dropped out."

I return his grin and say, "Congrats, little bro. I'm proud of you."

"You'll be closer to us, then. If you ever need a designated driver, call Cori. Since I'll probably be drunk somewhere, too." Sage laughs at her own joke and Mom shakes her head.

As the excitement dies down, Dad steers the conversation to his favorite topic. "So, Nick, what do you do for work?"

"I'm working at a machine shop for now."

"Supervisor?"

"Uhh, no." Nick glances over at me from across the table.

"Not yet, anyway?" Dad asks.

"Sure. Maybe," Nick says, taking my advice to keep his answers simple and boring so that Dad gets tired of having to draw answers out of you.

Dad goes around the table asking everyone how their jobs are going.

"I actually sort of have my own news," Sage announces. "I'm opening an online store and am already set to attend a festival as a vendor in a couple of months."

Dad narrows his eyes as he chews. "And what exactly are you selling?"

"Cute t-shirts, hand towels, mugs, pretty much anything I can make with my new sublimation printer. I figured I'd turn my drawing skills into something I can make money with."

"Okay, I have more news. I wasn't going to say anything until I had an author copy to show you, but I'm publishing a novel," Stephanie squeals. There's another round of cheers and squeals, but my mouth drops open in shock.

"You wrote a book?" I ask dumbfounded. Stephanie doesn't read, and I've never known her to enjoy writing.

"Yep. It's really not that hard. Pretty much anyone can do it." *Not that hard.* Nothing has been hard for Ms. Perfection. Her entire life has been a breeze.

"I guess the pressure is on me now to publish something," Sage starts. "Mom will put your novel by the book with Cori's poem in it, and I can't be the only daughter without something on Mom's shelf. I guess I could make a book of artwork or something. Oh! Can I design your book cover or do character art?"

Nick looks up at me. "Poem?"

"She wrote a poem. It was published in a book a few years ago," Sam answers for me.

"That's amazing. Can I read it?"

But I can't find my voice among all the commotion to give him an answer.

Sage jumps out of her seat, tugging an unsuspecting Georgie along. "I'll go grab it." But the book is at Sam's.

The only noise in the room, while we wait for Sage to return, is the clink of forks against knives and the nauseating sound of chewing.

Sage finally comes back into the room. "I can't find it, Mom. Where is it?"

"Oh. Umm..." She looks at my dad, who keeps his eyes on his plate while he eats. "Well, it should be on the bookshelf. It's not there?" But her voice is high-pitched, and she wrings her hands like I do when I'm nervous.

Sam jumps to her rescue. "Don't worry about it, I have a copy, you can read it when we get home." I push my plate away, the food sinking like bricks in my stomach.

Nick leans over the table to ask, "Am I still able to purchase one?"

His support is thoughtful, but it doesn't ease my nausea. "There's no need. It's not like I get the royalties."

Chatter resumes, most of it going to Stephanie to ask about her novel. It's a heartwarming tale about an older woman searching for her blood relatives after learning she was adopted. I'm so happy for her, and everyone for all the success they've had recently. But as I hear the plotline, what little I've eaten starts working its way up my esophagus. Is this jealousy? Am I really feeling jealous right now? God, I am pathetic.

"So, did any of you know about Cori's blog?" Sam asks. Every single eye falls on me, and mine shoot to Sam. Except he's slicing into his chicken as if nothing is amiss.

"What blog?" Stephanie asks.

When I don't answer, Sam explains, "She shares recipes

for making coffee drinks at home. Lattes, macchiatos, affogatos, homemade syrup and creamers. I didn't know about it either until last night." He shoots an irritated look at Nick. "But it's a nice website. It's a little too feminine, but it looks professional." *But.* As if something can't be feminine *and* professional.

I'm only just finding out that he looked it up. It's nice to hear he's impressed, but his icy tone has me wondering if he's doing this to hurt me.

"She also told me about her conversation with Mike," Sam tattles. Then emphasizes for maximum punch, "About becoming assistant manager and adding more coffee to the menu."

Dad lays his silverware down. "You discussed it with Mike? But I already told you no."

"We need an assistant manager, Dad. It makes sense for it to be me. I've been there the longest, I grew up going to this diner, and Grandma and I always discussed me taking over one day."

"Maybe so, but I own the diner now. And I said no."

"Fine. As for the coffee part, I was just trying to use what strengths I have to help you and me both. And my strengths lie in coffee."

"It's not a coffee house, Cori," Dad says with a piercing stare. I am so sick of hearing that.

While he drones on and on, my eyes move to a painting on the wall depicting the face of a woman with her eyes closed, something Sage painted in high school. It's unique because, despite the change in colors, the paint strokes all blend perfectly as if she only used one downward stroke and a face just appeared.

If I don't focus so hard on her face, I may succumb to the flames licking up my own, triggering the tears like a sprinkler system that floods when the alarms start screaming. I'm just so tired of not being enough for them.

I'm brought back to myself when Mom asks, "Why didn't you tell us about the blog?" Hurt resonates throughout her tone.

"Why would I tell y'all anything? I only ever get criticism in return." My hand inadvertently raises on its own to point at Dad. But I instantly will the words back inside, and cower waiting for the metaphorical backhand. It comes as a glare that could burn my skin from my face if only Mom had the power.

"So, what else aren't you telling us?" Mom asks, her expression hard and determined.

Because I'd learned from the best, I turn the tables. "Do you remember the book Sam asked to take home after Grandma's funeral?"

Her eyes lose focus while she thinks back to that day.

"It was the book with my poem in it. You threw it in a donation box. Sam held it up, and you told him to take it if he wanted it, because you had no idea where it came from."

She swallows hard, caught with nowhere to run. "Well, aren't I just the worst mother ever." She keeps her eyes on mine, daring me to agree, challenging me in the emotional warfare that is our relationship. She always wins and she knows she'll do so again.

Several voices ring out at once to bring her comfort, but I stay silent. What should I say? I'm not sorry, but I also don't want to be the cause of any pain. With five kids, my parents lived in chaos exactly like this dinner. There was always someone grounded, dishes everywhere, dirty clothes hanging from the picture frames. Mom and Dad were overwhelmed, but I was the peace. The one they could depend on to behave and follow the rules. I helped with cooking and housework, I stepped quietly so I wouldn't overstimulate Dad while the others stomped through the house like elephants. I always cleaned up after myself, and got ready to leave quickly, and never made them repeat themselves.

So I say it. "I'm sorry, Mom. I didn't mean to make you feel bad." It was wrong of me to ask non-readers to hold onto a poetry book, anyway. They'll keep Stephanie's though. But hers is a novel. It's different. That's what they'll tell me.

Mom is quick to forgive as long as you take the blame and apologize, so she flashes a victorious grin. "It's okay, sweetie. I forgive you." The merciful queen ruling over her dutiful and terrified subject.

I turn to Sage to keep myself from vomiting. I need something to hold to keep my hands from shaking. I reach my arms out to take Georgie, but she swings him to the other side.

"Quit hogging the baby. My stomach hurts anyway. Give him." Still, she ignores me.

Mom's eyes find my uneaten plate with hardly anything on it to begin with, and her face brightens. "Oh, you're finally taking my advice, I see."

Then, Dad says, "Who the hell made this?" I glance over to see him inspecting the baked macaroni and cheese on his fork with his nose scrunched up.

And the walls start closing in and I struggle to find breath. I really am just a waste of space. A black stain upon the white carpet, usually ignored, but occasionally looked at with consternation.

I look at the painting again, but it's too late—there's nothing there to save me.

I take a piece of sour candy from my pocket. I knew I'd need it. Knew I'd let all the comments get to me. Knew I'd have to battle an oncoming panic attack because if I escape to be by myself, someone will say something about my dramatics.

Discreetly, I stick it in my mouth. Everyone's too preoccupied with their own voices to notice.

The sour shock on my tongue and the tingling under my jaw pull every thought and feeling to where the candy sits on my taste buds. Like when you touch the glass of a plasma ball globe and all the lightning-like tendrils go to your finger.

Except someone does notice—Nick. His eyes, like a cup of coffee, filled to the brim with concern, watch me diligently. With enough of a grip on myself to do so, I tighten my lips into what I intend as a grin. To let him know I'm fine. But he sees right through me.

Chapter 18
Aimless Arrows

Nick

No wonder.

I can't help replaying the awkwardness from last night while I throw a football around with Cori's little brothers. Sam's God complex as he cast judgment upon Cori's choices. The way Cori's shoulders slumped at Sam's first hint of disapproval. The blank stare that moved over her face like a fog rolling in. Then a reenactment between her and her father. While I just sat there making it worse, unable to find the right words to hold on to her as she slipped into herself.

After dinner was over, Cori and Sage washed the dishes. I had volunteered to help, but when Spencer and Solomon asked me to play catch, Cori told me to go with them. After half an hour, she steps outside the back door behind Sam, who rushes out to the lawn to intercept a throw meant for Spencer.

"I'm taking a break," I say, now that Sam's there to take my place. I walk toward the covered patio, where Cori watches from a brown mesh chair, and gulp the rest of my iced tea. She looks up at me and straightens her lips in what I've come to recognize is her way of offering a friendly smile without actually smiling.

There are a million things I want to say to her now, but I can't find the words. An apology isn't enough. I want to get her away from here, but it isn't my place. Besides, they're her family. Even if she walked out now, there'd still be other family dinners, other holidays in which she'd have to endure the doubt they have in her abilities.

"So, that's your family," I finally say, as I watch a small gray bird fly out of one of the trees in her parents' backyard.

"Yep."

"I'm so sorry. About last night. And this morning."

"You already apologized. Everything's fine anyway."

I study her, the tension lingering in her posture, the light still dimmed in her eyes. "No, it's not. Especially not after dinner."

"Yeah, well. They're right."

I scoff. "How can you think that?"

"Because I'm twenty-three and I've done nothing with my life." She looks down at her fingers picking at each other.

I keep saying I'm not going to coddle her, but maybe she needs it. "You're *only* twenty-three, you have plenty of time." But she continues as if I said nothing at all.

"Like you said this morning, I've let my insecurities keep me locked in a cage. I don't take risks, I don't venture out, I stay safely within the bars. I say no to everything for fear of not succeeding or not being good enough. And I don't really know what I'm doing wrong, but I'm also not smart enough to know how to fix it."

I get the feeling she's venting more so than answering my question, so I stop trying to refute her claims and simply listen while she continues. Sam and Cori's brothers stand far enough away that they don't notice the slight rise in her voice or the rush in which the words come out.

"I don't feel as prepared for life as I should have been.

177

When we were kids, the adults talked big crap about how you can do anything as long as you put your mind to it. So I got good grades and followed all the rules, only to grow up and discover there are rules I didn't know existed. And at that point, it was too late. You know, you have to start seriously thinking about your future when you're like, ten? Any later and it's too late, you've missed your chance. Life doesn't care, it keeps moving and piling crap on top of you until you're so far beneath the surface, there's no way you'll reach the top in time.

"Remember the interview I went on about a month ago? Well, it actually went great, I *thought*. But I still got the rejection email. So I emailed them back asking for feedback, or a reason as to why they went in another direction. She responded over two weeks later and said if I was more outgoing, they'd be able to overlook my lack of experience and degree. But they wanted someone who would work better in a team, and she felt that I was just too reserved. So, I don't have experience,"—she ticks off her fingers— "I don't have confidence, I don't have a bachelor's degree, I don't have enough money to pay for school and to take more time off of work for classes. I feel like I'm tied to about fifty different ropes all being pulled in different directions with equal force, so that I can't move in any direction at all." She's out of breath as her face falls into her hands.

Something tells me these aren't thoughts that are shared with many people, and I'm not sure if I should feel honored that I'm hearing them, or like an ass for bringing them out.

I want to hug her, tell her she's wrong about all of it. Tell her that the right job will come along and not to give up hope. Not to think so negatively about herself. But I don't because she's not in the mood to hear solutions—she's in the mood to get some steam out before it cooks her from the inside out.

Besides, who am I to give such advice? Like she said, we're more similar than you'd think. Pressure to do something meaningful pins us in place. Pressure to find a job we care about, to make life feel like it's worth the lows because we're doing something that we love. Neither of us knows what direction to start walking in, but that doesn't mean she's worth any less because of it. And I realize now the reason she doesn't fight for herself. She doesn't think she's worth the effort.

She puts her hands down and takes a deep breath. "Can we just not talk about it anymore?"

Unsure if she means the blog, the proposal, or her low opinions of herself, I nod anyway and silence falls upon us.

When we can no longer handle the suffocating heat, I follow Sam and Cori inside the living room. Everyone waits for a pot of coffee to brew before eating the peach cobbler that warms in the oven.

A black cloud still hovers above Cori, but she wears a fake smile for the sake of her family.

"Hey, Nick," Sage calls to me from where she stands by the white-painted brick fireplace. "Wanna see Sam and Cori in matching Easter outfits?" Her devious expression has me intrigued.

I look over to see Sam glaring at Sage and mouthing, "*Don't you dare,*" and Cori looking at the ceiling as if in prayer.

"There's nothing I would love to see more," I answer as I rise from the loveseat. The photo Sage hands me shows two kids, probably eight or nine. Cori wore a yellow dress with pink flowers, and Sam wore a suit jacket and shorts made from the same fabric.

"Our moms thought it would be cute to make them dress alike," Sage explains.

Cori sits forward on the couch and holds her hands up. "Okay, but what she's not telling you is that all of us kids had the same outfits. Except Solomon, because he didn't exist yet. But of course, she only shows you the photo of Sam and me."

"Please tell me there are more photos of them," I ask Sage. She flashes a sly smile and pulls a scrapbook off the shelf.

Even after we've all eaten the peach cobbler Stephanie brought for dessert—except Cori who only had coffee—Sarah and I sit side by side on the loveseat, flipping through pages of the scrapbook. Cori and Sam glare at us from the couch with their arms crossed and I can't resist snapping a few photos of them with my phone. And their youthful, ornery faces in the scrapbook provide just as much entertainment. Clearly, they spent most of their free time together. Even during some holidays and family events, Sam could be seen among the four, and eventually five, Anderson kids. He fit right in, almost better than Cori.

"How did you and Sam become friends?" I ask.

"He wore a Hornets jersey to school once in first grade. I told him to get in the trash can." She doesn't elaborate and I fail to see how that led to a years-long friendship.

After a minute, Sam chuckles and explains further. "We argued baseball for a while. I can still picture her standing there, one hand on her hip, the other pointing a finger in my face. Then I asked if she'd want to watch the upcoming Hornets/Stallions game at my house and she promised me I'd switch teams by the end of the game. The rest is history."

I can see that. Cori's passion for the things she enjoys could easily grab hold of anyone's heart.

On one page are two photos taken just seconds apart. In the first one, Cori was wearing a birthday crown and sitting next to Sam in front of a cake with chocolate icing and candles. In the next, Cori's happy expression had morphed into one of shock, her eyes crossed to look at the chocolate icing on her nose. On the next page is Sam's birthday, the photos almost the same, except the chocolate icing covers Sam's nose.

I look closer at another photo of the two of them, I'm guessing preteen-age, dressed as each other for Halloween. Cori wore a short, blond wig, along with a full football uniform, while Sam wore a brown wig, a graphic t-shirt, jeans, and white vans.

Neither one of them has changed much, with a few exceptions. Sam's personality still takes up more space than it should, but his arrogance seems to have grown along with his height. The biggest difference is in Cori's eyes, innocence glittering from the sky-blue in the pictures, but the lightness is gone now, transforming her irises into a gray storm.

After we arrive back at Sam's, I open the fridge to put away the leftovers Sarah insisted Sam and I take home, then think better of it. Cori hardly ate anything at her parents' and coffee doesn't count as a meal.

I ask her if she's hungry and she glances at Sam before answering as if to ask for permission to eat.

"Yeah, I am, actually." I'm relieved she doesn't say no.

"You're not full yet?" Sam asks.

"She ate like one green bean. You didn't notice?" A loving boyfriend doesn't miss his girlfriend distressed enough to push away her plate. Or overlook her seeking confirmation from her mom and boyfriend before deciding she better not risk taking a serving of cobbler.

Sam keeps his gaze on me as he says to Cori, "Go ahead and eat, babe. I'll wait up."

Except, he doesn't. I shower and change my clothes, and when I come back out, Sam is passed out on the couch while Cori washes the dishes she used.

I lean against the counter and cross my arms, watching her dry the plate and fork and put them away. She changed clothes at some point while I was showering and, once again, wears my sweatshirt. I don't know why I haven't told her it's mine yet. Maybe because it's just a sweatshirt. Maybe because I know she'd be unnecessarily embarrassed and never wear it again. And what a shame that would be.

She leans against the counter, mirroring my stance, and it's a few minutes before I have the nerve to say, "I want to read that poem." I raise an eyebrow, daring her to say no.

She scrunches her nose. "Counterproposal. What about a more recently written poem? One I'm not quite as ashamed of?"

"You still write?"

"I've recently found the inspiration again, but it comes and goes. I actually wrote it this morning."

I want to ask where this newfound inspiration comes from, but I don't want to scare her away. "Okay, then. Deal."

She leaves, then hands me a brown, leather-bound journal once she returns. But before I can grab it, she hides the journal behind her.

"But," she warns, pointing her finger at me. "Don't be mean if you don't like it. Poetry is very subjective, and everyone has their own preferences of style and rhythm."

"Just give it to me," I say, playfully. "I can barely write a full sentence, let alone poetry. It doesn't take much to impress me."

She considers my words for a moment before handing me the journal, her finger slipped in between the pages marking the spot I should look.

Aimless Arrow

I'm an arrow pulled back and ready to fly,
Ready to soar through a cloudless blue sky.
I wasn't made to sit idly by,
While everyone else around me rose high.
I was made to do great things.

But a ruthless timidity darkens my way,
Veiled promise lets talent decay.
I'm too tired and wired at the end of each day,
Pent-up ambition is here to stay.
Rooted and growing and gnawing and choking.

The answers to life have been written in codes.
The pressure to prevail builds until it explodes.
My armor takes hits faster than my weapon reloads.
The weight crushes my soul until it implodes,
Since my doubt appears to be stronger than hope.

Dreams tried on and discarded like clothes,
With every change of outfit, my insecurity grows.
I put on a smile but it's just a pose,
As my mind succumbs to that familiar place that it loathes.
Because nothing fits, making me unworthy.

I'm an arrow pulled back and ready to fly,
Ready to soar through a cloudless blue sky,
To hit my mark, to flourish, to defy.
But as the hand lets go, it all goes awry.
There is no target on which I could land.

I go to sleep feeling as if she had ripped me open and copied the words that were painted on my soul. I've never felt as seen as I do now, laying in my bed, wrapped in contentment from the simplicity of relating to another person. Because sometimes all we need is to know that we aren't alone.

When I wake the next morning, I walk out to the kitchen, starving for a hearty breakfast. I find Cori already awake and sitting at the dining room table, coffee cup sitting beside her while she scribbles something down in a notebook.

"Good morning. You're awake early."

She smiles and returns the greeting. "Yeah, but I might have to take a nap in a little while." She yawns into the crook of her arm. "I couldn't sleep, so I got to work."

"Got to work on what?" I ask, fetching two skillets from the cabinet and bacon and eggs from the refrigerator.

"It's for the diner. A list of drinks and their ingredients. Along with costs."

"So you're going ahead with it? Even though your dad forbids it?"

She nods.

I can't help the smile that appears or the warm joy that spreads through my body. "Good. I'm glad. Once you get the facts to Mike, maybe he'll talk your dad into accepting the idea."

"Yeah, well, I'm making it seem more of a big deal than it actually is."

While the bacon cooks, I walk over to her chair. "No, you're not. You're taking initiative. Giving ideas. *Good* ideas. Your dad has to see that and realize your potential. It starts with one idea, and soon you'll have all kinds of them to help the diner improve. You're paving the path toward leadership and maybe he'll realize that and put you in charge if Mike ever leaves, or instead of him. Or, maybe he'll give you the diner."

She snorts, but her eyes still lack that luster I saw in those photos. "Now you're the one dreaming big."

"No, I just believe in you."

The air sizzles and pops, and I almost mistake the intensity in her gaze as the cause.

Walking over to check on the bacon, I ask, "Is there anything I can do to help? I don't really know anything about coffee, but I can fetch you cups of it while you work, make copies, highlight some stuff." I grin. "I can be like your assistant."

I hope she understands how much I support her and how badly I want her to succeed.

She chews on the inside of her cheek, seemingly considering something. "I had another idea. One that I know for sure Sam wouldn't approve of, so I wasn't going to say anything until I did some more research on it." I nod for her to go on. "But that company that I interviewed for sold bags of coffee beans, some whole, some ground. And they had people you could work with to develop your own blends. I was thinking, since I already post about coffee recipes, that I could start selling coffee too, and promote my own brand through my recipes. I need to figure out how much money I'd need to start, but if I'm running it from home, it shouldn't be an outrageous amount. Sam wants me to save my money now that I'm not paying as much towards rent and I could use it towards that."

"I think that's a great idea. And I can tell you already that you'd have a customer from me. And probably my mom too."

She smiles softly, but averts her gaze, suddenly shy. After getting to know her and her family members, I imagine she's so desperate for support that it makes her uncomfortable when she finally receives it.

"Can I ask, though, what is your obsession with coffee? Why, of all things, are you so passionate about it?" Before she can get defensive, I raise my hands. "And I'm only asking because I'm curious. Not because there's anything wrong with being passionate about coffee."

She rises from her seat to stand beside me at the stove. "I don't know, I guess because Grandma's house always smelled like coffee. She always took a moment from housework, the diner, working in the yard, or whatever she was doing around three p.m., and had a coffee break. And if I was with her, she'd use that break to tell funny stories about her childhood or about people she knew from town because, back then, everyone knew each other. It was a community, not just a town full of strangers. And while my siblings were drinking chocolate milk in the mornings, Grandma and I were drinking coffee together. Decaf for me, of course. She'd clink her glass against mine and call me her drinking buddy." She grins. "I guess, I felt important in those moments drinking coffee with Grandma. Like I mattered."

"You do matter, Cori."

"Sure. But I truly felt it then."

The air is thick with her silent admission—that she doesn't truly agree that she matters *now*. It's an exhausted subject anyway, so I change it. "I wish I could have met her." If only because she's an inspiration to Cori and someone who showed her the love she deserved. "And I won't tell Sam. I promise."

"It's not that I want to lie to him. And I feel bad asking you not to say anything. It's just, I need to do some planning before he finds out. And it may not even happen. It's just an idea." I don't think it's me she's trying to convince.

"Well, you're not asking me not to tell him. I'm telling you I won't. And I agree that it's better if you wait to tell him."

"Thank you. So, that's my update. What's yours?" I furrow my brows, so she explains. "Are we still accountability buddies?"

"Oh, that. Right. Well..." I run my hands through my hair.

"I haven't made any progress, to be honest." The deal we had made completely escaped my mind.

"That's okay. You're at the hardest part. The field is too open, there are too many directions you could go in, and you won't know it's the wrong way until it's kinda too late." She rubs`my upper arm consolingly, but pulls her hand away too soon, leaving my arm cold from her absent touch. "You have a good job now, one that doesn't seem to crush your soul, so there's really no rush for you. Like you told me the night of that interview, and like my grandma used to say, the right thing will come along at the right time."

Chapter 19
Just Looking Out for You

Cori

I n typical Cori fashion, I stick my head in the sand and choose to pretend the events of the last few days never happened. It's the only way I know how to cope.

Before clocking out, I give the spreadsheets and lists to Mike, who barely glances at them before grunting and disappearing into the office. I try not to let his lack of enthusiasm get me down, as I rush to the frozen strawberry margarita waiting for me.

"Hey, I went ahead and ordered a drink for you. And queso," Hailey says as I slide into the booth across from her. She takes a bite of a tortilla chip dripping with cheese.

I didn't have time to go home to change before coming to the restaurant, and still wear my t-shirt with the diner's logo and jeans, but it isn't much different than what I normally wear anyway. Despite us being the same clothing size, Hailey's healthy relationship with her mother is evident in the lace tank top she wears, openly displaying her arms.

"Thanks. It's been a week." I take a sip through the straw— a small one, so I won't get a brain freeze. The frozen tartness shocks my taste buds, like a defibrillator to my mood.

"Why? What's going on?"

Normally, I filter out most of Sam's berating comments, but I need to vent. So, I let it all out. Every word he said, every horrible feeling, every time I wanted to cry, but didn't.

"God, he's such an ass," she says when I'm done. She waves to our server to request a second round, the first having disappeared somewhere during my spiel. "Can I please just let loose on him? Give him a piece of my mind?"

I snort. "Are you saying you've been holding back on him so far?"

"Are you kidding? I've been an angel."

Lifting an eyebrow, I say, "Sure you have."

But the moment sobers. "Seriously, though. Are you finally going to leave him now?"

"I'm not going to end my relationship over one disagreement. That's a little dramatic, don't you think?"

"No," she deadpans. "He's a pompous ass. Actually, he's a narcissist. He criticizes your every move, he brushes off your feelings, he belittles you when you *do* stand up for yourself. I could go on and on."

That's a tad extreme. "He doesn't treat me any differently than everyone else in my life."

She tilts her head, lines appearing on her forehead as some lightbulb appears to come on. "Is that why you're with him? Because you think that's what love is? Because you think you deserve to be treated that way?"

I feel my finger itching to scratch at my wrists. She's supposed to be my safe place, the one person I don't have to hide from or lie to. But the walls close in on me.

"You're anxious around him, always walking on eggshells, jumping when he says to. Just like with your parents," she says more to herself. "You feel guilty for not being perfect, you feel like a burden anytime you ask for help-"

"Can we change the subject? We came here to let off steam, not make it worse. And you're kinda making me feel like shit right now."

Her shoulders deflate. "I'm sorry, I just want you to be happy."

"I am happy. But even happy people need to vent, that's all this is."

She watches me, unconvinced but, thankfully, drops it.

A couple of hours later, we're buzzed enough that calling for rides home is necessary. I call Sage, but of course, there's no answer. Not wanting to bother anyone else, I pull up a ride-share app on my phone, but Hailey begins calling someone at the same time.

"Hey, Cori and I are a tad blitzed." She speaks in a higher voice to sound cute. "Could you maybe come pick us up?"

She tells them where we are and listens for a moment, ignoring me as I mouth, "Who is it?"

Suddenly, her face straightens and she raises her voice into the phone. "No, please don't send him." But I guess it's too late because she brings the phone away from her ear, groaning.

"Who was that?"

"Well, I called Callum, but I guess he had the phone on speaker and Sam is with him. And Sam said he'd come get us right as Callum hung up." She clicks Callum's name again on her phone. When he answers, she says, "Please don't let Sam come." But she growls in frustration when Callum informs her Sam already left.

"You're really not interested in Callum romantically? He's really cute," I say.

"No, I like having a platonic relationship with a guy. It's nice. Plus," she lowers her voice to a whisper. "I've been sworn to secrecy, but he has a crush on someone." We both giggle like little girls gossiping about who likes who. I guess the only difference is, we're on a bench outside the restaurant instead of a playground.

"Who is it?"

"Nope." She zips her lips and locks them with an imaginary key. "Can't say."

"Erin?" I get a stone-faced glance. "Not Kenna?" Again, she gives nothing away. Most likely, it's someone I don't know anyway.

Sam arrives twenty minutes later, and Hailey scowls at him as we get in his car.

"Take these." He hands each of us a plastic bag. "I don't want any vomit in my car."

"There's vomit in here already. In the driver's seat. And if you don't want any more, cover your ugly face, so I don't hurl from the sight." I grow uneasy with every word Hailey says, but thankfully, Sam is being a good sport and only shakes his head with an amused smile.

"Good to see you too, Hail."

"I've told you a million times, don't call me *Hail*. And what is your problem anyway?"

"Hailey, please stop." I would have turned in my seat to meet her gaze, but I'm prone to motion sickness. And with nothing but alcohol, sugar, chips, and cheese in my belly, I didn't want to risk it.

"No, it's time he got a wake-up call." She leans forward, putting her hands on the back of his seat and glaring at him through the rearview mirror. "Do you realize how lucky you are to have a woman like Cori? You don't deserve someone even half the woman she is, yet you go around telling her that her ideas are stupid? And tattling on her to her parents? What the fuck is wrong with you?"

"Hailey," I groan, gripping my stomach as if that would help keep the contents inside.

"Is that how you feel, Cori?" Sam asks. I'm losing control of the situation, but I don't know how to reel it back in. I open my bag and hold it underneath my chin.

"Of course, that's how she feels. What do you think we spent the last couple of hours talking about? But she's too nice and considerate of your feelings to say anything because that's how kind she is. And you're too blinded by your inflated ego to realize what you're doing to her."

His voice is deadly when he asks, "And what am I doing to her, exactly?"

"Killing her soul," she says, her tone lifting at the end. "Killing what little self-worth she has left. Killing her happiness."

Sam only nods, slow and terrifying, and I can't hold it in any longer. I lose control of my strength into the plastic bag.

When we get home after dropping Hailey off, Sam closes the door behind him and leans against it. I can't wait for him to say anything, though, as the taste in my mouth twists my gut. I walk to the bathroom to brush my teeth, then crawl into bed, wishing I could stay forever beneath the comforter. The mattress shifts from Sam's weight as he sits on the edge, his hands clasped between his knees.

"Can we talk?" I don't think he'd buy it if I gripped my stomach feigning pain again, so I accept my fate and sit up.

"I'm sorry, she was just drunk."

"Alcohol has a way of drawing out the truth. And she wasn't that drunk."

"I'm sorry. I'll talk to her tomorrow." My eyes burn and my head throbs.

"And what are you going to say, exactly? As Hailey said, you're soft. You don't like hurting feelings. So what good is it going to do if you talk to her?"

I narrow my eyes, partly because I'm confused, partly because they sting from exhaustion. "Then, what exactly would you like me to do?"

"I don't know, Cori. I've tried to be nice to her, I've tried to ignore my disdain for her because she's your friend. But she can't come between us like that again. Whatever problems you have with me, whatever problems we have together, need to stay between us. You can't go around complaining about me to other people. I let you move in here because it was the next step in our relationship, but it's not going to work if someone comes between us."

The words lash out like a whip across my skin, stealing my breath. *I let you move in here.*

He stands, unclasping his watch from his wrist. Hands on either side of the dresser, his head hangs between his tense shoulders.

"Are you even happy with me?" His voice is drained, so I'm quick to answer. Quick to end his suffering and ease his mind.

"Of course, I am. You know I am." Rising from the bed, I wrap my arms around his waist and lay my head on his back. But he brushes me off and turns, a scowl staining his handsome face.

"Would you be honest if you weren't? You made me look like a *fool* in front of Nick because you can't even confide in your *boyfriend* the details of your little hobby." I inch backwards, but keep my features stoic; I won't let Sam see how terrified I am. "Maybe you need some time to think about it. Maybe your moving in here was a mistake. Maybe you weren't ready."

Where would I go if he ended things? What would I do? He's the only thing I've done right in my life, according to my parents. I can't let this relationship fail.

I just want this conversation to be over. I want to go to sleep and wake up tomorrow morning with all of this dealt with and put away for good. Thankfully, all the years of bringing Mom back from the edge of an emotional breakdown have prepared me for this moment.

"Sam, I need you to hear me. I'm sorry. I love you. I am happy with you. I've given up my apartment for you. I've given away most of my things to move in here. If that doesn't prove that I'm here for the long run, I don't know how else to tell you. I just felt bad and needed to vent to someone who would understand and not tell me that I was being irrational. Okay?"

He stares at me for a long moment. "I don't think you should hang out with Hailey anymore. She's poisoning your brain and turning you against me."

"She's my best friend."

"I'm just looking out for you, Cori. You're easy to manipulate. I wouldn't want her doing that to you." With that, he heads to the bathroom, and I fall into bed shaking.

Chapter 20
Uncle Jonah

Nick

" A re you wanting to continue with your previous major?" The counselor keeps her eyes on her computer screen, her fingers darting loudly over the keyboard. It's a question I expected, and the answer is on the tip of my tongue, but I zone out.

Several pens stick out from a cup on her desk, one with a flower taped to the end. I have to hold my hand back from reaching out and feeling the petals.

When I don't answer, she glances at me over the rim of her glasses before pulling the form I had filled out when I arrived to her face. "It says here that you were a sports science major."

"Yeah, sorry. No, I don't want to continue with that, but I'm not sure what I'd major in. I don't have to decide just yet, right?"

She looks back at her computer, types something, clicks a few times, types some more. "Most of your credits transfer, you'd only have to retake three classes. I'd suggest having it narrowed down at least. Most of what you have left are major classes."

The whir of the air conditioner kicks off, sucking all the air from the room. Three extra classes that I'll have to waste money on. Then there are the major classes, for a career I can't envision for myself.

"Are you wanting to do something sports-related? Like sports medicine or analytics? Or, would you rather go in a completely different direction?"

I've only recently reached the point where I can watch sports on TV without ending up a blubbering mess; I can't plan for another sports-related career.

I keep my eyes on that flower, a daisy maybe, I don't know flower types. But it's pink and way too big for the end of a pen. I want to know what it looks like when she's writing with it. Does it bounce around like-

"Mr. Porter?"

My head snaps up and I realize I've zoned out again. "I'm sorry?"

She repeats the question patiently. "Do you currently have a job?"

"Yeah, I actually just started as a machinist not too long ago."

"That's a good job, good growth opportunities. But you want to get away from that?"

I lift a shoulder. "I just can't see myself doing this for the rest of my life." I know I sound like an idiot, but it's the only way I know how to explain to a stranger the fear I have of never finding myself. The fear of accepting defeat and succumbing to a discontented and regretful life. I'd already done that when I ran home after my injury, and I moved back here intending to continue on the same way. But something I thought was dead inside of me had awoken and was ready. I just didn't know what for. Just like Cori's poem.

She nods, but the furrow of her eyebrows gives away her concern for me.

Ms. Owen, the admissions counselor, sighs and tosses her glasses onto the desk. "Can I give you some advice, Mr. Porter? Less than fifty percent of college graduates end up in the field they studied in school. I majored in music theory and composition before completely changing my path after I was unable to find a job. I probably shouldn't be saying this, as an admissions counselor, but college isn't for everyone. There are so many careers and trades that don't require a degree. Look at your hobbies. Can you turn any of them into a career that you would enjoy? If not, make a list of jobs you'd think you'd like, and look up job listings for those positions to see if there's a more versatile degree, like business or psychology, that might be accepted for those positions."

Simply to end this unproductive misery, I tell Ms. Owen that I'll think about everything she told me, and I go home not feeling any better than before I walked into her office.

T he next morning, I wake, not looking forward to a Saturday full of thinking. I need out of the apartment so I call Mom and ask if I can visit.

"Of course, I have no plans. How'd the meeting go with the college?"

"Sucked."

"Oh? Why?"

"Just did."

"Okay..." She draws out the word. "Well, since you don't want to talk about that, what do you want for dinner?"

"Whatever's easiest. We can just order pizza or something."

Then I hear that voice again followed by a distant shushing as if Mom covered the speaker. It was definitely a male voice, definitely real, but it wasn't close enough for me to hear what it said.

"Is that your boyfriend?" I ask, feigning uninterest.

Mom laughs nervously. "What? I don't have a boyfriend. It's just the TV."

My eyes narrow as I keep listening, but the line is silent. I wish she'd just tell me if she was seeing someone. I'd be happy. That's all I want is for her to be happy.

"So, dinner. I'll invite Jonah, unless you just want it to be us. I may need y'all to look at the sink in the bathroom."

"Sounds good."

We say our goodbyes and I receive a text from Uncle Jonah shortly after I hang up.

> Jonah: Your mom called to invite me to dinner. Do you have time before to come by and help me with something? I got a new plane.

Uncle Jonah's hobby is planes. He flies them, builds them, sells them, fixes them, whatever. Turns out, he bought a kit for a Hummel Aviation H5 and wants help putting it together. For as long as I can remember, I've stood alongside him working on his planes in the hangar on his property just outside of town. At first, I'd simply hand him tools. Eventually, I was old enough and had learned enough to do everything by myself while he drank a beer in a lawn chair five feet away.

That's where he sits now while I work on fitting hose clamps onto the outer wing tank. The local country station plays on a battery-operated radio, and the heat inside the metal building is suffocating. After an hour, my shirt is drenched in sweat and I have to take it off to find what little relief I can.

"Can't you get this thing air-conditioned? I know you can afford it," I say. "At least a fan or something. I'm over here dying while giving you free labor, and you're lounging around like you're on vacation."

"Oh, hush. You'll live." As if to mock me, he props his feet up on the chair next to him. "Your mom said you went to talk to someone at the community college. How'd that go?"

"Fine," I answer, still not in the mood to talk about it.

"Well? What'd they say?"

I run a hand down my face and recount the meeting to him while he stares thoughtfully out the open door and across the field, taking mouthfuls from his beer can every so often.

He remains quiet after I'm done, and I fit the second clamp on the other side of the tank.

"Do you even wanna go back to school?"

"I mean,"—I shrug—"I'm not doing anything else with my life. Might as well."

"You don't sound excited. You should be excited about what you choose to do."

"Yeah, I'm sure you're really excited to do. . . whatever it is you do on the rig." I wipe my forehead with the back of my arm. "I'm just worried about wasting all that money and time on something else that might not work out."

My injury was more than just the dead end to my career, it was a failure. It doesn't matter that it wasn't my fault. If only I had moved out of the way faster, before the 250 lb lineman fell on my leg, forcing my foot to the right and my knee to the left. If only I hadn't been in that spot. If only I had trained harder after the injury. If only I had run faster while Coach studied my progress.

If only, if only, if only.

"Nick, everythin' we do in life is a waste of time. We all die anyway and we can't take any of the accomplishments or relationships or money with us when we go. Might as well do what you want and damn the consequences. With reason, of course." He winks.

When I was a kid, I wished Uncle Jonah was my real dad, especially on nights when Dad would come home shit-faced drunk. He never laid a hand on me or Mom, but he'd yell so loud the walls would shake like the hands of God himself had a hold of our double-wide.

As I let his words soak in, I realize those childhood wishes of sharing his blood don't matter. He's my dad, regardless of how much I look like the man whose last name I share.

"You know what you should do?" he asks, the lines around his eyes more defined as he squints up at me through the light filtering in from the open door.

"What?"

He gestures with his head towards the parts in my hands, but I don't get his meaning. "Aviation mechanics. There's a school in Houston. I think it takes a couple years, but once you're done, you'll be licensed to work on planes and can get paid for it. And you already know a bunch."

When I thought of mechanics, my mind usually shot to automobiles. Why had I never considered planes before?

He points to the tattoo starting at my shoulder. "You even have a monoplane tattooed on you already. I think it's fate." He chuckles, taking another drink of his beer. "Besides, I'm leavin' my planes to you when I die anyway. It'd be nice to know they're goin' to someone who'll know how to keep 'em runnin'. Oh, that reminds me. You're goin' to need your pilot's license too. But that's easy to get." He scratches at his nose as if he's telling me what he had for breakfast this morning and not that he's leaving me his most precious possessions when he dies.

I tap my palm with the fuel filler neck in my hand a few times while I consider the option. "What's the school called?"

"I don't know, somethin' Aviation somethin' Institute. I'll google it for you." He pulls his phone out, and after finding the webpage, hands it out for me to fill out a request for information.

I shake my head. "I don't know if I want to yet."

"Just fill it out," he insists. "All they'll do is probably call you and set up a tour or meetin' or somethin'. You can go and find out more information, and then decide." He stands up from the chair. "While you're doin' that, I gotta pee."

"Hey, real quick. Do you know if Mom is dating someone?"

He cocks his head, then looks around the hangar. "Not that I know of, why?"

I explain the voice I heard in the background during the two phone calls.

"I think you're readin' into things that ain't there, but if she is datin' someone, she'll tell you when she's ready."

There I go again, selfishly making everything about me. All this time, I figured Mom didn't think *I* was ready for her to be dating, but maybe Uncle Jonah is right. Maybe *she's* the one not ready to share the news.

I nod. "Yeah, okay."

I think some more about the conversation we just had while I fill out the form.

When I had my sleeve drawn up, I asked for the plane to be added to the design above the mountains. Uncle Jonah and I never flew above mountains during the flights he'd take me on, but the plane alone made the tattoo special. While I'd never consider piloting as a career because of the stress involved, I love working on planes. All this time, I thought it was because I enjoyed spending time with Uncle Jonah, but now I realize I actually enjoy the work. I enjoy working on cars as well, but there's something special about aircraft, something unique.

But two years? A lot could happen in two years. Hell, a lot could happen in two minutes.

Chapter 21
You Used to Be Fun. What Happened?

Cori

The next day, I wake up alone, unsure of what to do. What Sam said... there couldn't have been truth to it. My gut tells me his stress and exhaustion fueled his argument because I can't comprehend how an innocent vent session turned into potentially dropping my best friend.

After work, I spend the rest of the day in bed working on my website, waiting until evening to call Hailey. I needed that time to think, but when evening comes, nothing is any clearer.

It doesn't matter anyway, because my phone rings before I can figure it out.

"Hey, I'm so sorry for last night," she says when I pick up. "Was he a total ass when you got home?"

"He was upset and needed reassurance, understandably. But I don't blame you, either. I shouldn't have complained about him the way I did."

"Did he tell you that? Cori, that's manipulation."

There's that word again.

"You have every right to bitch about him as much as you want, he can't tell you not to. A decent boyfriend would hear those complaints and change how he treats you. Although, decent boyfriends wouldn't treat you that way in the first place, and men like him don't change."

"Hailey," I groan, rubbing my temple. "Can we please not do this? Please?" My voice shakes with desperation and the need for her to understand.

"Fine. But you need to think about what I said. About why you allow him, and your parents for that matter, to treat you like they do."

"Because they're right!" I say too loudly, the admission bursting out. "I'm a failure. A waste of space." My eyes spill over now, and I furiously swipe at my face, the wetness against my burning cheeks overstimulating me.

The line is quiet for a moment until, patiently, Hailey says, "Cori. You are not a waste of space. Are you kidding me? You only think that because of how they treat you. I guarantee if you got away from Sam and told your parents off, you'd start to feel so much better about yourself. You know how moldy fruit causes other fruit around it to mold as well? Hey, why don't you see a psychiatrist? Isn't Tyler's mom one?" While I know she's trying to comfort me, trying to make me feel better, she's telling me that my feelings are irrational, just like everyone else. And I know they are, to an extent. Instead of throwing myself a pity party, I should just get up and change my life, right? The problem with that is, I'm slowly losing the will, the hope, the care. "You're depressed, Cori. You need help."

"I'm not depressed, Hailey. I feel exactly as happy as I've been my entire life." As for therapy, not a chance. Opening up, and allowing myself to be vulnerable to a stranger, who doesn't actually care, but only sees me as a case number, a problem to be solved? No, thank you. It's not like I could afford it anyway.

"My point. You're with Sam because that's what you think love is. Because that's what you've been shown by your parents. You've been in survival mode your whole life, with little energy or motivation to do anything else. Probably the only reason you have the energy to read or work is because people like me and your Grandma have to undo some of what they do to you."

I open my mouth to protest, to tell her she's wrong, but haven't I said that before? That Grandma was my anchor?

"And where would I go? I live with him now. I've changed my address, I have no money for a down payment and first and last months' rent, or new furniture. I'm staying here, Hailey. You need to accept that." I recognize the absurdity of staying with someone simply because I'd already changed my address, but there are more reasons to stay than there are to leave. I do love him and we have so much history together. Surely that counts for something.

She exhales a heavy breath. "You know what? Fine. Go live your unhappy life with him, then."

"Hailey-"

"No, just stop. I can't sit back and watch you hate yourself while you continue to let him treat you like shit. I've got my own problems to deal with. I'm done."

The line goes silent.

I pull the phone away from my ear, my mouth opening in shock when I see the home screen.

She hung up on me.

"I'm done." What did she mean by that? Did she simply mean the conversation and we'll reconvene once we've calmed down? Or our friendship?

It's easy to like someone who knows exactly who they are and what they want out of life. Easy to love those who have already reached the finish line on their self-discovery or healing or whatever type of journey they're on. There aren't any low points because they have all the answers already.

There's a poem here, but I have no energy to write it down. Or finish it, for that matter. The words, a cruel whisper strong enough to bring me to my knees, but just another thing left unfinished.

No one likes the insecure,
The gray clothes, the unsure.
No one has the patience
For my self-unacceptance.

I've always known this, but the rejection still hurts.

Nick

I arrive back home late after dinner with Mom and Uncle Jonah. The apartment is completely dark except for the moonlight that shines through the large windows, illuminating Cori, who had fallen asleep in one of the leather armchairs. She looks troubled, even in sleep, her forehead pinched and fingers twitching. The blanket on her lap slowly slides to the floor, same with the book from her limp hand draped over the arm of the chair.

I take the book and close it, placing the bookmark where her thumb had separated the pages before laying it gently on the coffee table. I know Cori's love for her books—she does not take kindly to rough handling. Then, I pick up the edges of the blanket and place it properly over her shoulders so that she's completely covered, save for her face. But she wakes, probably from the sudden warmth encasing her arms. She blinks a few times as if she can't place my face, or is simply confused seeing me upon waking.

"Hey, sorry. I didn't mean to wake you. I was just covering you up so you wouldn't be cold."

She looks down at the blanket, eyes still bleary and watery from sleep. Sitting up, she rubs them and yawns.

"Thank you. I didn't mean to fall asleep out here. I was reading and I guess I dozed off."

I sit down on the couch. "Reading puts me to sleep too."

She narrows her eyes. "Ha. Ha. Where were you all day?"

"Uncle Jonah's, then Mom's for dinner. I uhh, may have an update. You know, for the whole accountability buddy thing. Nothing concrete, just an idea I'm exploring."

She smiles and sits up straight, ready to listen.

"You know how I've helped my uncle work on his planes all my life. Well, today he suggested I look into aviation mechanics, and I honestly don't know why I'd never considered it before."

She nods.

"So, he looked up the website for a school in Houston where I could get my Airframe and Powerplant license to work on aircraft. I filled out the form for information, so I'll see if they call, but... I'm kind of excited." A grin spreads over my face as Cori reaches out to squeeze my hands, her softness a welcome contrast to my rough calluses.

"That's exciting."

"I may not even want to go through with it, I still have to see what all it requires." I shrug. "But I don't know. I just feel..." I don't have the words. Lighter? No... energized maybe?

"You have a goal in mind. Something to use your energy towards. A target for your arrow, if you will." I marvel at the sound of her small laugh.

"Yes, exactly." I laugh myself, and can't help admiring the

crinkle of her nose when she smiles a full smile, or the clearness of her eyes as they twinkle with delight. How does Sam not spend every waking minute trying to bring this out of her?

I clear my throat, shifting in my seat. "Uh, so how was your day?"

Her face sobers instantly, remembering something that isn't near as happy as this moment. "Oh. It sucked, actually."

"*Sucked*, as in we need dessert while we talk about it? I think there's still some ice cream in the freezer."

I hook my thumb over my shoulder, but sorrow seizes her expression, her eyes becoming glossy as they fill with tears.

"Oh, shit. What happened?"

I want to take her in my arms, hold her as she cries and talks me through the argument between Sam and Hailey, then her and Sam, then her and Hailey.

But it isn't my place. I can't be the shoulder she weeps into or the comfort that envelops her. I really shouldn't be the person she confides in either, but she needs someone.

Her boyfriend only ever shows her doubt and disrespect. And now her best friend is leaving her alone in a shitty relationship she doesn't deserve. I've overlooked too many of the comments Sam has made towards her. Comments like, *"You should probably change into something more attractive."* Or, *"Lighten up. You used to be fun. What happened?"* I know I haven't heard the worst of his remarks, but I've just stood back and remained quiet and, while I'm ashamed of that, I'm also torn. She's her own woman, a grown woman who could and should fight for herself. If she's never taught her worth, she'll never know what she deserves.

"Cori, I know we're finally on neutral ground, but you know where I stand."

She lifts her face from her hands, and her eyes, glistening with unshed tears from the pain that consumes her, bounce between mine. Once again, I fight to stay in my seat, refraining from scooping her into my arms.

"So, you agree with Hailey, then?"

"Well... yeah." Nervous that our friendly camaraderie may have just shattered with those words, I wait for the backlash.

"So, you agree with my parents and Sam?"

"What? No, how did you come to that conclusion?"

She rises, throwing the blanket into the chair and angrily swiping at the tears sliding down her red cheeks. "Because everyone has an opinion about my life and my choices, and I can't even hear my own voice inside my head anymore. I'm so busy trying to please everyone else, and I don't have a damn clue as to what I want." With that, she storms off to Sam's room, leaving me torn in too many directions to count.

On one hand, she stood up to me. She let me know she was angry and why. But why can't she do that with Sam? Why is it me that she pushes away when I only want her to be happy?

And how do I help her if helping only pushes her away?

Chapter 22
Everything is Peachy

Cori

A rms wrap tightly around my abdomen as Sam's cologne attacks my nose. I turn the water off from the kitchen sink where I stand washing the dishes.

"Next weekend marks one whole year that I've put up with you," he says into my hair tied up in a bun.

I turn around so I can get a better read of his emotions and find out if that statement is a joke or if he's serious. It's hard to tell with him. We've hardly spoken over the last week, except for when speaking was absolutely necessary. It's better to give him space when he's upset and wait for him to come to me.

His mouth is curved into a grin, and I figure it's safe for me to joke back.

I groan. "It's only been a year?"

He laughs and squeezes my body to his. "Let's do something special. We can go to the beach house for the weekend. Maybe go dancing while we're down there." His parents own a beach house on South Padre Island. I used to spend weeks with them there as a child, my hair a few shades lighter from the sun by the time I got back home.

"Counteroffer, we could just go to the beach. No dancing."

Don't most women have to drag their men dancing? How did I end up with one that enjoys it?

"Karaoke?"

"Ew."

"Will you wear a bikini? Instead of that weird long-sleeved shirt you have that shows nothing?"

The fact that it shows nothing is the whole point. I burn to a crisp with the strongest sunscreen applied hourly. The long sleeves are necessary, as are the shorts. I have one of those body types that no one wants to see spilling out of a bathing suit—thick thighs, too much butt, and one breast bigger than the other.

The house backs up to a private beach for residents—the only reason I agree. "Fine."

"Can you get off for the whole weekend?"

"Shouldn't be a problem if I work doubles all week."

"Good. That means I can get some extra work done, too." He kisses me on the head and walks away to his office.

I begin the climb up eighteen wooden steps to the yellow, four-bedroom house, my hair whipping in and out of my face with the wind, and I feel fourteen again. The July before Sam and I started high school, the Bennetts brought me along as usual on their annual summer vacation, where they spent a month at this very beach house. As Sam and I barreled up the steps nine years ago, we thought of nothing except the carefree days ahead that we'd spend swimming, fishing, lounging, and burning beneath an unforgiving sun.

I expect to find the same over the next day and a half, plus dinner, and possibly another earth-shattering kiss. On our last trip here, while his parents were upstairs packing the rest of their things, he pulled me into the shadows and kissed me—my first, and what would become the standard for all other kisses that came after it.

What I don't expect to find when we reach the top of the stairs is Nick's ex-girlfriend, Kenna, and Sam's ex-lover, Erin. They're dressed in bathing suits, sitting in the chairs beside the glass patio table, drinking something pink on ice.

I look to Sam for an explanation, but his face is void of one as he asks how was their drive and where is the guys' truck.

What guys? What truck? What the hell is going on?

"They're making a beer run," Kenna answers.

I follow Sam into the house, and the second the bedroom door is shut behind us, I turn on him.

"What the hell is going on? Why are they here? Why are the guys here?"

He cocks his head and furrows his eyebrows like I'm the one not making sense, and swings his suitcase onto the thin sand-colored blanket covering the bed. "They're here to celebrate. We planned this the night we had Francesca's, remember?"

"I thought we were celebrating our anniversary, not your newspaper article. Besides, I told you that Kenna makes me uncomfortable." Honestly, I thought the idea of making a big deal out of one year of dating was ridiculous. I figured dinner and actually spending time together would be sufficient, but when he offered the beach house, I wasn't dumb enough to decline.

He lets out a snort, pulling clothes out of the suitcase and carrying them to the dresser. "*Getting a bad vibe* from someone can't make you *uncomfortable.* And we are celebrating our anniversary. And the article. We can celebrate multiple things at once."

"So, when you were asking me about coming here, you were intending to invite them but let me believe it was just going to be us?"

"Uhh, no? Like I said, we planned this the night I told you about the article. But I also reiterated they'd be here when I asked if you wanted to come."

"*No*, you didn't."

"Calm down. Why does it matter?"

"Because you're lying to me." And completely disregarding my honesty about my discomfort around Kenna. Even if I've only been around her once.

He pins me in place with his glare. "I am not. You're the one that doesn't pay attention." Mom always tells me I live inside my own head too much. I often zone out, losing myself in a daydream; it's entirely feasible that he *did* tell me and I simply didn't hear it.

I follow him out to the living room, hot on his heels anyway. He takes a bottle of sunscreen from the counter and squirts it into his hand before handing it to me and gesturing to his back.

When I don't immediately rub it into his skin, he turns to face me again. "Are you really going to ruin this weekend over this? Do you realize how much more fun we're going to have with a full house than spending it by ourselves? This is my vacation too, Cori. I have two days completely off of work, and I'd rather not spend them watching you read the entire time, or taking naps. I'd like to enjoy myself too."

I don't get to respond, though, because the door opens and Kenna walks in, freezing when she must feel the tension sizzling in the air.

"Uhh, is everything okay?"

Sam looks at me and cocks his head, waiting on my answer.

"Everything is peachy." I slap the sunscreen onto his back, roughly spreading it around.

"Easy there," he says, but I don't ease up because I want to be done as fast as possible. The second his back is covered, I set the sunscreen back on the counter and head down the hallway.

I hear Kenna ask, "What's wrong with her?"

Back in the safety of the bedroom, I shut the door and reach for my phone to call Hailey. Then I remember what she said about *being done*, whatever that meant.

I sit down on the bed, shoulders deflating, just as Sam opens the door. He stands in the doorway, clearly wanting to be outside, but feeling obligated to check on me.

"Can you just be happy for once? All of our friends are here to celebrate us." When I don't respond, he throws a hand up and points to the phone in my hand. "Invite your sister if you want. Maybe she can catch a ride with Nick. He only works a half day today, so he's driving down after he gets off."

I stand to unpack my bag. There's no point in taking out everything just to put it back in when we leave Sunday morning, but I need to keep my hands busy before I find them wrapped around Sam's throat. Metaphorically, obviously. I'm not a monster.

Assuming I'm letting it go, he kisses me on the forehead before walking away, and I close the door behind him a little too loudly.

I call Sage and sit back on the bed while the phone rings. I don't know why I'm doing this because she and Sam will gang up on me, pressure me to drink or smoke, and I'll comply because it's the easy thing to do. Because people like you when you're easy.

"Hey, sis. What's wrong? You never call me."

"That's because you usually don't answer. Can you get your shifts covered for this weekend and come down to Sam's parents' beach house? You can ask Nick for a ride down here, Sam said he's not coming until later."

"I thought it was just going to be you and Sam. For your anniversary?"

I rise from the bed and begin pacing the room. "Apparently, I was mistaken. Everyone is here."

"Then, hell yes! Brian already has the weekend off, and I'll ask Dad to tell Mike I need off if I can't get someone to work for me." She's the only one Dad will do that for, but she's never had a problem getting her shifts covered anyway, because all the servers love her.

Once I hang up, I don't know what to do with myself. I can't spend the whole weekend in the bedroom; Sam would never forgive me for that. But how am I supposed to walk out there and act like nothing is wrong? Am I being crazy? I come out of my own head, just enough to picture the beach house from the sky. Three people enjoying the breeze coming off the water and soaking in the sun on the balcony while I sit alone sulking in the bedroom.

Disoriented and wretched, she sits all alone,
Leaning into the darkness to which she is prone.

I stall as long as possible, applying sunscreen slowly and tentatively, switching outfits several times, reapplying light pink toenail polish, and taking deep breaths. Thankfully, I packed my long-sleeved swim shirt and shorts just in case I needed them. And because I don't want to wear a bikini in front of two women who wear one much better than I, that's what I wear when I finally emerge outside.

As I had hoped, I spent long enough inside that Callum and Tyler are back from the store. I walk to an empty seat and Callum greets me with a friendly grin while Tyler attempts another noogie until I elbow him in the ribs. I decide Sam is right—we will have more fun with them here than by ourselves.

Besides, he can be entertained by them, leaving me free from his every whim.

"Cori?"

I realize I'm staring off at the ocean, not paying attention to the conversation, and look up to see which of the two women had spoken my name. My face heats beneath everyone's watchful stares.

"I'm sorry, what?"

Kenna is the one who answers. "We were talking about the plans for tonight, once Nick gets here. We were thinking of doing karaoke tonight and dancing tomorrow."

I look over at Sam, the smug grin on his face. With everyone here, I'll be overpowered in my declination of karaoke and dancing.

The official date marking one year together isn't until next Tuesday, and I find myself wondering if we'll make it after all.

I brace myself when he opens his mouth to talk. "Come on, don't be a buzzkill. You don't have to sing or anything, just come along and watch. It'll be fun." He reaches over for my hand, but I move it away just in time. He recovers, placing his hand on my shoulder like that was his plan all along.

"Oh, don't worry. I'll get her to sing," Kenna says, once again a hyena staring down a gazelle. Scratch that, I'm not a *gazelle* in any way; more like a warthog.

"Yeah, I mean, whatever y'all want to do. It is your weekend after all," I say, pointing to Sam.

He laughs, playfully shaking my shoulder. "It's *our* weekend, silly."

"Oh, is it? I didn't know." I cross my arms over my chest, wishing I could just melt into this chair. The air is hot enough, I probably could. "But karaoke sounds great. Dancing too," I say sharply, because I know better than to say otherwise. I wouldn't dare suggest not going simply because I don't want to; that would be incredibly selfish. The problem is, I won't be allowed to sit on the sidelines. I'd have no problem going if I could, but I will be expected to participate, regardless of how anxious I feel.

The crashing of the waves is the only sound, while unsure eyes dart to each other across the table.

"We can do karaoke or dancing anytime we're back home. Let's enjoy the beach, build a bonfire, and grill some food." I send a thankful grin to Callum at his suggestion.

While everyone discusses the plans, I escape downstairs. I sit in the sand far out enough that the tide reaches my toes and breathe in the salty breeze. Stress seems to blow away with the wind coming off the water, and I'm perfectly content to spend the remainder of the weekend in this very spot thinking about nothing. I sit there too long, though, because my butt goes numb. I stand to stretch my legs and let them take me down the shoreline about a mile and back, then another in the opposite direction. While I walk, I keep my eyes down for shells out of habit.

I pick up a spiral shell and peek inside to make sure a hermit crab hadn't claimed it as its home. The inside is a deep purple color, but the outside is a pale pink, making it one of the most beautiful shells I've ever seen.

But I drop it back onto the sand and leave it behind.

Every year I came with Sam and his parents, I'd take home buckets of shells, intending to turn them into jewelry or fill jars as a keepsake. But after Sam moved away, the sight of the shells only brought pain and loneliness to the festering hole deep inside. I don't want to risk that happening again. Just in case.

As I start walking back to where I had laid out my towel, a presence appears at my right. Out of my periphery, I see dark hair, a shirtless torso, and black swim trunks—Nick. I've stayed out here longer than I realized if he's already arrived.

"Hey," he says.

I hesitate before meeting his eyes, but there's nowhere to hide from the conversation we need to have. Regardless of how I felt, he didn't deserve my snapping at him last Saturday, and I've avoided him since. I try not to stare, but his arms are crossed over his wide chest, bringing definition to his thick forearms and biceps. His shoulders droop as if he's dreading this as much as I am.

"How are you?"

He looks down at his feet and nods. "Good."

At the same time, we both say, "Look, I'm sorry-" We share a smile.

"You have nothing to be sorry for," he says. The depth and softness of his eyes have me taking a step toward him, desperate for the comfort and safety they provide.

"Can we just forget it?" I ask.

He studies my face for a silent moment, looking for something and, at first, I don't think he's going to agree. I nervously gnaw on my lip until he finally nods.

"I have one question though. After I picked up Brian and Sage, she mentioned something about you being upset when you arrived and saw Kenna and Erin."

"That's not a question."

He cocks his head, seeing through my attempts to stall.

"It's not a big deal. I just didn't know Sam had invited everyone along this weekend."

He runs a hand through his hair. "Shit, Cori. Look, we can probably find a couple of hotel rooms, let me go round everyone up." He turns to do just that, but I grab his arm and pull him back.

"No, I'm glad y'all are here. I just don't know Kenna or Erin very well, and you know how I am with strangers."

"You're seriously glad? Or you just don't want to cause an argument?"

"Nick, please. I *am* glad. It was just a shock because I was expecting Sam and me to be alone. But Sam was right, we'll have more fun with y'all here. If we're alone, we'll probably just spend the whole weekend arguing."

He cocks his head again, giving me a stern look, and I know he's thinking back to what he said to me last weekend. I start scratching at my wrist and he pulls my hands away from each other.

"I'll try to lure everyone else away for something so you and Sam can at least have some alone time at some point."

"Thank you, but it's not necessary. I'm not even looking at this as an anniversary celebration anymore. He and I can celebrate at dinner or something on Tuesday."

He narrows his eyes. "Wait, is that why we're here? He told me and the guys that he wanted to celebrate a huge contract he just got. And, of course, the article."

I sigh and look out at the ocean, the waves rolling in one after the other. The deeper you get, the bigger they are, the more you struggle to stay above the surface.

"Who cares why we're here? Point is, we are. And we're going to have fun, right?"

"Sure." But he doesn't sound the least bit convinced. He looks back toward the direction of the house. "Everyone was getting ready to come down, wanna head back to your spot?"

I nod, and we start walking in silence until Nick nudges my arm. I look up and he smiles, raising his eyebrows and jerking his head in front of him. Somehow, I know he's challenging me to a race, so I take off.

Unfortunately, he was an athlete in college and he wins. He stands by my towel, arms crossed, foot tapping in the sand, and that stupid, smug grin on his face as I finally approach. I collapse on my towel and grip my side. It wasn't quite a mile that we ran, but I'm pretty sure I'm dying anyway.

He laughs, helping me to my feet, and glances up at the sky. "You know, I've now seen you smile with your teeth a whole three or four times. Why don't you do it more often? You have a beautiful smile."

"*Don't smile with your teeth, Cori. Not until we fix them,*" Mom said.

"*Why don't you get braces?*" Sam said in eighth grade. But Stephanie needed a car, so we couldn't afford them.

"*You'd be so pretty if you smiled more,*" my ninth-grade science teacher said. So I smiled. "*Oh, never mind.*"

"I don't know. Just don't." When I turned eighteen, I paid for my braces. By then, however, the instinct to shield the world from my smile, and myself from criticism, was ingrained in my DNA.

Chapter 23
Like a Monkey on a Stage

Cori

There's no one in sight when I finally rise the next morning and stumble to the kitchen for coffee. At least, not until Erin appears and says much too brightly, "Good morning!"

I jump, almost spilling the scalding liquid as I bring it to my lips.

"I slept so well, did you? I love the sound of rain when I'm sleeping. I usually sleep with a sound machine, but I forgot it at home. I hope it rains again tonight. Is there more coffee?" I'm fond of the sound too; it gives me something to listen to when I can't sleep.

I fetch another cup from the cabinet and fill it for her.

"Thanks so much. I woke up to find a text from Kenna. Apparently, she and your sister left early to go shopping, and the guys went fishing, so it's just you and me until they get back. What do you want to do? I was thinking we could sunbathe, read, and search for sea glass. Then maybe come back and take a nap? I really love naps."

I laugh. "Me too. All of that sounds great."

She pulls a platter of fruit from the refrigerator and we pick at it until our coffee is gone. Then we get dressed—I wear my bikini this time—and we head for the sand. We spend the day exactly as she said, although we end up talking more than reading while we lay out on our towels in the sunshine. It would be easy to feel self-conscious around her—she's beautiful and thin, confident and smart, but I'm not focused on my flaws at all. She has a way of warming you from the inside out and, by the time we return to the house for our naps, I feel as if we've been friends for years.

Only as I'm opening the door and hear my phone ringing from the back bedroom, do I realize I left it behind. I rush to answer it, concerned it's Sam and scared of all the calls I've missed.

But it isn't Sam, it's my dad. He never calls, usually having Mom relay any message he has for me. And it's almost always work-related.

"Hello?" I say, nervously.

"Cori."

"Is everything okay?"

"I know you're with Sam this weekend, but I wanted to talk to you about this whole coffee menu idea." I close my eyes and sit on the edge of the bed, expecting another lecture and wholly unprepared for his next words. "I called Mike to make sure he shut the idea down, but we had a lengthy discussion about it all. He emailed over the spreadsheets you gave him, and I have to say I was impressed. I didn't expect all the information you provided, the estimated project cost, even the customer segmentation and sales reports from the past few months. It would seem those little classes you took *did* pay off."

I don't say anything, not entirely sure Erin didn't smother me with her beach towel, sending me to the afterlife.

"I uhh..." He starts and stops a few times. I've never heard Dad trip over what he has to say. "I wanted you to know that I'm proud of you for taking the initiative, and I look forward to hearing more of your ideas in the future."

My heart skips a beat and I can't get my mouth to close. I had hoped he'd be impressed, but it was human nature. A childish need to have your parent's approval, not a realistic consideration.

"Dad, thank you. That... I'm so... glad, um. That means... a lot. To me." My eyes burn as tears form.

"I know it's fast, but I want to roll out the new insert on Monday. Mike said he was prepared." Over the past week, Mike made a small order for extra items while I made the final touches on the menu insert and sent the design for printing. We were planning to start Monday anyway, the sooner, the better.

"Yes, we're prepared. Even with the new drinks added to the system, we're not making many changes after all." It's a simple rearrangement of the dining room map while I take the customers behind the counter instead of dividing them up among the servers.

"Okay, good. I've got to run now, but I'll talk to you later. Love you, Cor."

"I love you too, Dad."

When everyone returns from their outings, we walk back to the beach to play a game of volleyball. But when Sage, who played throughout high school and one semester during college, gets too competitive and yells at her team, Callum picks her up and dumps her into the ocean. He walks back toward us, dusting his hands off.

"So. Dinner?" He barely gets the words out before Sage trudges up behind him and paints his back in wet sand.

Tyler and Brian take off for the house to put meat on the grill, and I lean back on my towel while Sam and the women start another game of volleyball. Callum goes back to the water by himself and Nick appears to my right.

Sunglasses shade his eyes, so I can't read his expression as he stares off into the water.

"How much crap do you think I'd get if I picked up my book right now?"

His lips twitch and he shakes his head.

I command my hands to remain clasped together, instead of running my fingers along the dark lines covering his left arm.

"If I had the time and money to travel, I'd rather visit heavy woods with mountains within view," I say, admiring the trees and river inked into his skin.

"Same. The mystery and beauty is what sort of drew me to this design."

My eyes roam up to the plane on his shoulder. "Have you flown over mountains with Jonah?"

"No, a few rocky hills, but no mountains. Maybe when I get my license. Would you ever come up with me?"

I've never flown before, not even commercially. Would personal aircraft be more or less scary than commercial? "Maybe."

"The first time I flew with Jonah, I was seven. He was so excited to finally share his love of flying with me, and I was hyped because no one else I knew got to fly in a personal plane. We went up in the one his dad gave him, a Cessna 172 Skyhawk. It was expensive and still is his favorite plane.

Anyway, we mainly flew over places I knew, just to see the aerial view of familiar homes and buildings. We saw mine and Mom's house, where Jonah grew up, my school. About thirty minutes into it, I threw up. But I knew how special the plane was to him, and I didn't want to vomit all over the nice interior. So, I held it in my mouth, even as it slowly leaked out into my hands."

He laughs at my face, scrunched up in disgust. "He turned around immediately, and as soon as the doors were open, I let it all out onto the concrete. He didn't say much on the drive home, but he stopped to get me 7Up. I felt so bad. And I thought he was mad until I overheard him telling my mom how *he* felt bad, how he was scared he'd traumatized me and ruined planes for me forever."

"Aww. How long did you wait before flying with him again?"

"We went back the next day. I told him I wasn't going to let a little vomit scare me away from flying again. He made sure to bring several bags, just in case, and more 7Up. And I needed it."

Our laughter has Kenna approaching and asking what's funny.

"Cori said your voice sounds like squawking seagulls," Nick says without an ounce of regret.

I jolt, smacking his arm and assuring her that I said no such thing. The last thing I need is for her to feel insulted.

Nick only grins while Kenna glares at him before sizing me up. Finally, she claps her hands. "Why don't we go dancing, like I suggested yesterday?"

Cheers of agreement come loudly from Erin and Sage, but a silent groan from me.

"And you,"—she points to me—"are dancing with us. I don't

care how drunk we have to get you beforehand, you're dancing. I don't want to hear none of that *I'm shy* bullshit." Laughter breaks out.

Sam moves to crouch beside me. "Yeah, Cor. There's nothing to be scared of, it's just dancing."

My cheeks blaze and I force my feet to stay in place as all eyes fall on me, including Nick's. I can't see beyond the sunglasses, but his lips are thinned into a tight line, and a noticeable vein pulses in his neck.

Sam nudges my arm. "Come on, Cor, relax. Take a joke."

There's no way to play this and still come out on top. I have to betray myself to save my dignity. So I play along.

"I'm not sure what y'all are talking about, I love dancing."

Laughter breaks out again, thinning the tension, but I still feel Nick's gaze burning my skin everywhere it touches.

I used to pray to God every day to take away the anxiety I feel around people so that I could dance like no one was watching, or sing at the top of my lungs without a care in the world. I would pray that my mind would quiet so that I could jump in the water without thinking of all the sharks or eels or unnamed monsters that lurked in the depths waiting to bite. I used to pray that He'd turn me into someone who Sam didn't seem to be ashamed of and someone who could hold their own in a conversation, demanding that their boundaries be respected.

Eventually, I stopped praying. I couldn't see the use.

—

After dinner, nine of us fight over one bathroom to get ready, and we arrive at a western dance hall and saloon an hour later. To my dismay. You'd think I'd prefer being able to disappear into a crowd, to blend in with the masses, and that I'd feel uncomfortable in more intimate gatherings where I run a greater risk of becoming the center of attention. But my idea of letting loose does not involve getting wasted in a hot, crowded room where I feel like every eye is watching me. Judging me.

Because I didn't plan to go dancing, I only have a long-sleeved maroon dress I packed to wear if Sam and I went to dinner. It's Sam's favorite but it stands out among all the blue jeans and tank tops worn by the other three women who somehow knew to pack for a dance hall.

"First, tequila," Tyler announces after we pay the entrance fee. He takes off to the bar, and the rest of us gather around a wooden table just off the dance floor. It's hard to see or breathe much through the haze of cigarette smoke, and the lighting is almost nonexistent from the little lamps at each table.

"So, are you actually going to dance with me? Or do I need to find someone else?" Sam asks. I hate the pressure of every-one's eyes on me. Hate the fear of being filmed and turned into an internet meme. Hate that I get so lost in my self-awareness that my body starts to physically disconnect. Hate that I can't move my body fluidly and carefree like *normal* people. But I also hate being labeled as uptight, boring, or *buzzkill*, just because our ideas of fun didn't match.

I'm lost in my head, watching dancers of all ages twirl their partners around, that I don't notice when Tyler reappears, carrying a tray loaded with shots.

"Cori? Want one?"

Kenna takes a glass in her hand. "Just give her one, she needs it."

"No, thank you."

"Just take it," Sage insists.

"Come on. Don't be a buzzkill," Sam pushes.

"She doesn't want to, leave her alone." Sam glares at Nick, so I jump in to defuse the situation.

"Fine, I'll take one, but then I'm done." I grab a glass in my hand and throw it back, resisting the urge to scrunch up my face as the liquid burns its way down my esophagus.

"Come on, just one more." Sam holds out another shot glass. "Drunk Cori is so much more fun."

Avoiding Nick's piercing gaze, waiting for me to decline, I extend my hand out for a second. Like a monkey on a stage, might as well dance.

I don't mind two-stepping since the steps are the same every time and I don't have to flail about to some hip-hop song, so I agree. But just because I prefer it doesn't mean I'm not stiff as a piece of wood as Sam eyes me with suspicion, waiting for me to run back to the table in panic. I can't get him to understand that if he'd relax, I'd relax. But he watches my every move, either looking for something I'm doing wrong or because of a self-fulfilling prophecy.

As he watches me, I'm hyper-aware of every person around us. Three guys lean against the railing that separates the dance floor from the tables, beers and cigarettes in hand, watching. A guy and a woman in jean shorts and cowboy boots lean into each other at a nearby table, watching. A couple in leather vests with motorcycle patches take a swig of their whiskey, watching. The rational side of my brain knows they're watching everyone out here spin around, but the irrational side is much louder with its claims that all eyes are zeroed in on me.

The pulsing in my brain makes it hard to hear the bass thumping from the speakers just feet away, and my vision fogs, but not from smoke this time.

Sam's voice pierces through but doesn't help to calm me. "Will you unclench? It's hard to dance with you so rigid."

"I'm trying, but you're watching me like you expect me to make a fool of myself."

"I'm expecting you to look lovingly into my eyes while we dance romantically to a love song. Like all the other couples." So I do. It's completely forced, and Sam ends up rolling his eyes, but at least he smiles, and it helps to see his dimples appear. "It's not the same if it's sarcastic."

Somehow, we manage through three songs before I'm bursting with the need to find the bathroom and a brief moment of reprieve. I stay a little longer than necessary in the stall to recuperate as much as possible before heading back out, but any longer and Sam might think I was going number two. When I come back out, he's talking to some people at the bar, so I head to the table. Nick, Tyler, and Callum are dancing with Erin and Kenna, while Brian twirls Sage around. I sit down at the table alone, wondering how much shit I'd get if I pull my phone out to read an e-book.

I decide the risk is worth the few moments of escape. I get about halfway through a chapter before Nick plops into the booth across from me, a sheen of sweat covering his forehead.

"Why are you reading right now? Where's your boyfriend?"

I glance back at the bar, but he isn't there anymore. He isn't anywhere on the dance floor, either. "I'm not sure."

Nick scoffs. "Wow. What a dick."

"Why is he a dick?"

"Because you're sitting here all alone."

"We've known each other for a couple of months now, Nick. Long enough that you should know I'd much prefer it if Sam left me alone to read." I mean it as a joke, but Nick's eyes bore into mine, unreadable and intense.

"Then why are you even with him?" he asks, and I feel his deep voice all the way to my toes.

My brain frantically searches through all the possible responses to that question. *I love him* would just elicit another question of why, and I doubt, *because I just do,* would be sufficient. It doesn't matter anyway because Erin slides in next to me. And I don't owe Nick any more explanations on my relationship with Sam anyway.

I still feel his gaze burn my skin like lasers as Erin asks me, "Will you come with me when they do the next line dance? I love line dances."

I agree, if only because Erin asked so nicely. But also because she doesn't make me feel panicky; I feel safe around her like I do with Hailey. Or, *did*.

When Erin grabs my hand to drag me back out, Nick follows, and soon everyone in our group, except Sam and Kenna, are lined up and dancing. A fast song follows and Tyler pulls me into him, saying, "We'll keep you entertained until your boyfriend comes back in. He had a work call."

He distracts me enough with his goofiness that I don't feel as anxious, though I'm not sure if one could even call it dancing. We stumble around in a circle as we fight to keep our knees buckling from laughter. Next, I dance with Callum, who is just as stiff as I am, but owns it better.

When a slower song comes on, I step off the dance floor heading for the table, but an arm reaches out to grab me. My eyes follow along dark ink and muscle until they peer into Nick's.

"My turn," he says, his tone lilting upwards in question. I nod, and we stand in position with my left hand stiffly placed on his shoulder and my right hand lost in his. There's nothing romantic about it; even Sage dances with Callum to our right while her boyfriend sits at the bar. But my heart nearly beats out of my chest as I glance around for Sam.

Nick's jaw is tilted down, resting against my temple. I don't think he's heard any of my breathless apologies anytime I trip over his feet until he says, "You don't have to apologize so much, you know."

"I know, I'm sorry."

He pulls back, leveling me with a pointed look.

"Uhh, sorry. Ugh! I don't know what's wrong with me!" I hide my face in his chest and his laughter shakes both of our bodies. I'm not sure when it happened, but my hand has wrapped itself around his neck and I become too aware of the heat emanating from his tan skin. I move it back to his shoulder, but can't help but notice how broad and strong and hard they are. Curling my fingers into my palm, I rest my wrist on his shoulder instead, to prevent myself from feeling too much of him.

But that only brings my focus to other parts of my body. Like my hand in his. Or his other hand burning a hole through my dress where it rests at the small of my back.

The song, "The One Thing I Can't Say," is one of my favorites, but is not helping the situation I find myself in.

"A cold hand grips my heart in a pain I've never known,
When you leave with him and I'm left all alone."

My palms are sweaty, and I'm sure to drop from a heart attack any minute from the electricity in the air. It's just the song making me feel this way, I know that, and I repeat the thought to myself over and over. I know that I don't *really* want to lean into his neck or tilt my face up so that my mouth would be just an inch away from his. I'm not *really* lusting after my boyfriend's friend, or feeling heat between my legs. It's just the song. And I feel relief when he leans down to my ear and suggests we sit down before the song has finished.

Until I consider the possibility that he somehow knew what

I was thinking and is only trying to get away from me. If I don't die from anxiety, it will be from mortification. Because there is no way he felt the effects of the song as much as I did.

> *"In a parallel universe, there would be no line,*
> *There would be no him, and you would be mine."*

Because it *really was* just the song. That's it.

Chapter 24
Not Mine to Reach For

Nick

C ori and I return to the table because... well, I'm not
entirely sure what the hell that was. Cori's touch burned
me to the point of pain, and I found myself leaning in closer to
her. Intoxicated by her flowery scent, I forgot for a minute
where, and who, we were.

Intoxicated. That's it, it must be the alcohol. Except I forgot
—I haven't had anything besides water to drink because I'm one
of the designated drivers.

It must have been the song. The lyrics were far more
romantic than they should have been while dancing with your
roommate's girlfriend.

*"My first and last thought every day,
Is the one thing I can't say,
I love you"*

I don't know what I was thinking. The three of us guys
were simply trading dance partners, and it was time for Cori
and I to partner up. She seemed to be enjoying herself, now
that Sam had disappeared, and I wanted her to realize the

impact of the people one surrounds themselves with. It was innocent.

Until it wasn't.

We sit at the table now, neither of us saying a word, not even looking in each other's direction. I've never wanted a drink more than I do now.

And where the hell is Sam? Did he see us dancing together? Is he mad? Will I have a home to return to after this is over?

I'm usually calm and collected, but my thoughts spiral, the buttons on my shirt tightening around my neck. I tug at the collar and roll my sleeves up. It's boiling in here. Is this what Cori feels like when she's anxious? Did she feel the same tension earlier? Is she still feeling it, sitting across from me at the table?

I finally steal a glance at her as she faces the people dancing. The definition of calm, until you look closer. Her knuckles are white from her fisted hands, and her gray, unfocused eyes fixate on a specific point. Her chest rises and falls quickly and... *Stop staring at her chest!*

Brian comes back to the table and I jump up to hug him. He stiffens, probably because I've barely said five words to the guy, and suddenly, I'm latched onto him like he's my life raft.

After I peel myself off, his eyes narrow. "Are you drunk?"

"No, sorry. Just happy to have you hanging out with us, man." I slap him on the arm and sit back down, while Cori watches the exchange with an unreadable expression.

I stay at the table as Erin drags Cori back to the dance floor. Kenna has disappeared, but everyone else is still on the dance floor by the time Sam finally reappears.

"Where the hell have you been?"

He slaps a small stack of bills against his hand. "Had a work call, then got pulled into a game of pool. Hustled some guys."

"Seriously?"

"Yep. I won twenty bucks." He fans out the one-dollar bills. He was gone for a whole hour. For *twenty dollars.*

"So, you made a big deal about having to babysit Cori at the table while you missed out on dancing, for what? While she's been out there most of the night."

He doesn't answer, though, because Cori and Erin come bouncing over, laughing until Cori's face falls when it lands on him. How does she not realize how shitty he makes her feel?

He repeats what he told me before handing her his winnings, then kisses her on the forehead. "You can have it. For school."

"Uhh, thanks, I guess."

"Are you having fun?" he asks her.

"Yeah, I am, actually."

Yeah, 'cause you weren't around. I excuse myself to the bathroom and splash cold water on my face. Shaking my head like a dog, I hope the pieces of my brain will fall back into the right places. Kenna stands against the wall outside the bathroom when I exit.

"What do you want?" I ask.

She twirls her necklace around her finger as she studies my face. Her low-cut tank top might have done some damage at one point, but it sparks nothing in me now.

Finally, she says in a superior tone, "You're in love with her."

"What? Who?" I scoff. "I'm not in love with anyone."

"Yes, you are. I saw you two dancing. It's a good thing Sam didn't, because the tension was so hot, my underwear almost melted."

"You should probably see a doctor about that."

She smirks. "And you know as well as I do that she and

Sam are not compatible. So do us all a favor and tell her how you feel."

"I'm not in love with her. Even if I was, he's been my friend since college. I could never make a move on his girlfriend." Encourage her to leave him for her own happiness? Sure, I can do that. But if she leaves him, it needs to be for herself and no one else.

"Why not? It didn't stop him." She pushes off the wall and walks away. Leaving me reeling from her words while the walls of the hallway close in.

It didn't stop him from *what?* Was he who she cheated on me with? I take the spot against the wall that Kenna just vacated, ignoring people as they walk past me for the bathroom. I think back to the morning I went over to her house. Sam hadn't been home that morning before Tyler and Callum left for practice, and he'd been avoiding me for months. Could it have been because he was sleeping with my girlfriend?

Cori walks down the hallway, stopping when she sees me.

"Hey, are you okay?" Her eyes are full of worry at my face leeched of blood as I struggle for breath.

I panic, unsure of what to tell her, and worried Kenna or Sam might find us alone in the hallway. I push off the wall to leave.

"I'm fine," I say as I pass her.

I find Erin at the bar and sit down on the stool next to her. "Please tell me you have a single friend you'd think would be good for me."

Her face lights up and she puts her hands together. "Let me think, there's a fellow cheer coach I know from another school district or a cousin you might like." She pulls up photos of both women and, while they're both beautiful, there's no excitement when I see their faces. "Okay, what about this one? She's another math teacher at my school." She turns her face for me to see the brunette with glasses, but again, nothing. "You're a tough one. But, I think I have the perfect one now." She shows me the screen one more time.

"Umm... that's a picture of you."

"Yep."

"You want to date me?" I ask, nervously. Don't get me wrong, I like Erin, but she's always just been a friend.

"Why not? We're both looking. I haven't dated anyone since I broke up with my boyfriend a few months ago, but I'm ready to get back out there. And we already know each other well."

Looking back at our table, I see Cori back from the bathroom and sitting beside Sam. She smiles softly as he kisses her forehead, and she leans back against his chest while they watch Tyler and Callum dancing with a group of women.

"You know what? You're right, why not?"

I spent the rest of last night and this morning in a fog. After Sam locks up the beach house, Sage and Brian hop into Sam's car because I'm not ready to leave. Not ready to go back to Sam's only for him to disappear and leave me alone with Cori. I walk down to the beach, stick my toes in the sand, and pick apart a piece of dried seaweed that had washed ashore.

What happened last night, Cori, and what Kenna said, then the whole Erin thing... there isn't enough space in my head for it all.

In my periphery, Callum appears a few feet away, but he doesn't approach. Instead, he crosses his arms and watches me, probably giving me time to think before he comes over to impart his wisdom.

"I thought you left," I call out.

"No, I was waiting for you to get in your truck." Finally, he sits down. "What's wrong?"

"Nothing."

"Okay." He doesn't push because he knows I'll open up anyway. And I do, filling him in on everything that happened last night, except the weirdness with Cori.

We sit in contemplative silence until the piece of seaweed is no more.

"Are you going to confront Sam?"

"I don't know." What would be the point? Although, now that I'm thinking about it, that bastard had the nerve to suggest Kenna and I get back together at my party, and again at dinner when he announced the stupid article. Which he wouldn't be featured in if his father was someone normal.

"Has Sam always been so..."

"Conceited with an overestimated sense of superiority and self-importance?" he finishes for me. "Yeah, but it seems to be growing with age."

"He acted as if he didn't know she cheated on me. Acted surprised at the news." He'd said, *"Oh, shit. I thought you broke up because you left town without telling anyone."* What a dick.

"As for Erin, you sure you want to go there?"

"I don't know, but it's one date, maybe. We haven't planned anything yet. Might as well see if something more comes of it. I could use the company. And distraction."

"From Sam? Or something else?"

"I just, I didn't expect it to still hurt so much. Football, I mean. Coming back here, I thought enough time had passed."

"You said something yesterday about aviation mechanics. Are you not as excited about that as you let on?"

I grab another piece of dried seaweed and start tearing. "I am, but that seems to be the problem—what if something else happens? Another injury? And I spend all of that money for nothing."

"Well, if something else happens, you'll deal with it then. And you'll be more prepared to handle it because you've been through it before. Look, life is always going to throw you around. That's one of the few things that's certain."

"It's just that I failed at the one thing I knew how to do. I let my mom down, Uncle Jonah. They won't admit it, but I did. I'm the reason my parents couldn't go after their dreams, and I took so much from Mom's youth to go after mine."

"You didn't let anyone down. You didn't fail at anything. This happened *to* you. It hurts because you had no control over it." Not true, but I don't argue.

"Fine, but what if I should go back to college and get a degree, or just stick it out with my current job?" On the way down here, I drove under the "Be Someone" sign in Houston, the famous graffiti above I-45. I want to be someone. I don't need fame, I don't need money, but I want to be someone worth all the sacrifices Mom made for me.

He sighs. "Look, I can spew inspirational bullshit all day. But the point is, football is over, and you need to stop whining like a little bitch about whether or not to go to that school. Just do it." He stands and brushes his pants off. "Problem solved. Now, you're going to buy me lunch on the way home as a thanks for all the motivation."

I gawk up at him. "You know, you're supposed to be the caring one. The gentle giant. But you're kind of a dick."

"Yeah, cry me a river. I can only be the wise, soft mother of the group for so long, but even mothers lose their patience. Didn't your own threaten you with a shoe if you didn't get off her couch after you lost your scholarship?" He lifts his rubber shoe-covered foot. "Well, this is my shoe. Would you like to get to know it better?"

I extend my hand so that he'll help me up, but he ignores it and starts walking. "You're cranky when you're hungry." But I see through his tough act. He's always been intuitive, knowing exactly what we need when we need it. The time for comfort had come and gone. What I need now is a swift kick in the ass.

I stand and rush to catch up to him. "Hey, am I sunburned? My skin feels tight."

His hand comes down on the back of my neck with a smack, and I cringe at the sting. "Does that answer your question?"

"A verbal answer would have been preferred."

After burgers with Callum, I stop by my mom's house. *Stop by* is a stretch; I had to drive an hour out of the way, but I want to avoid going home as long as possible.

I pull into the gravel driveway and park next to my uncle's truck, assuming he's here to help Mom replace the bathroom faucet I never got around to fixing for her. They've been friends since they were kids, so it's just as likely that he's simply visiting and having coffee.

As I suspected, when I enter the house, they're not in the living room or kitchen area. I head back to Mom's bathroom to let them know I'm here and see if he needs any help, tilting my head in confusion at the closed bedroom door. I reach out to turn the knob.

Then I hear a moan.

Jerking back as if I've been burned, I'm paralyzed for a

second until I hear another moan that sends me into motion. I rush back to the living room and sit on the couch, covering my ears with my hands. The walls of the double-wide are paper thin, but I can't hear the noises any longer, except for what replays in my head.

Was that what I think it was? I can't imagine any other reason my mother would be moaning in her bedroom with Uncle Jonah, but my brain won't accept it. Was it *his* voice I heard on the phone saying my mom's name? Surely, they would have told me if they were together.

I stay on the couch, revisiting every strange occurrence. Like when I woke up one morning and Uncle Jonah was here at six a.m. He looked as surprised to see me as I was to see him in mine and Mom's kitchen wearing nothing but boxers and pouring coffee into a mug. He said, *"Uhh, hey, Nick. I... I'm just here to shower. I uhh... my water is turned off."* He was jittery and nervous, but I didn't see any other reason he'd be there, so I accepted it.

Or the time when I found one of Mom's shirts at Uncle Jonah's house. He claimed she must have dropped it when she came to do laundry because her washer was acting up.

I'm not sure how much time passes, and my heart races when I hear Mom's door open. Their voices carry down the hall, growing louder and louder until they fall silent at the sight of me on the couch with my head in my hands.

"Nick," Mom says. "Honey, when did you get here?"

"I'm not sure," I answer without looking up.

"Uhh... I was lookin' at... uhh... I was helpin' your Mom..." Uncle Jonah starts.

"He was changing the faucet in my bathroom," Mom finishes, calm as can be.

"I know what he was doing." I finally raise my head to look up. They look guilty, cheeks flushed and shoulders caving in. I lock eyes with Uncle Jonah. "Why don't you have a seat and tell me exactly what the hell is going on."

He glances at Mom, brows pinched, before looking back at me and taking a seat.

He takes a deep breath and rubs his palms on his jeans. "Well, I love your mom. Always have."

"And how long has this been going on?"

"Well, you were about twelve, I think."

Twelve years? I'll admit, it stings a little. All that time we could have been a family.

But we *are* a family. Maybe I didn't know they were together, but we've spent every holiday together, every birthday and major milestone. Even at random family dinners with Mom and me, Uncle Jonah was always right there.

"And why didn't you just tell me?"

"We were goin' to tell you when you got to your teens, but I don't know, for some reason we just didn't. Then, we were goin' to tell you before you left for college, but we didn't want you upset and pissed at us right before you left. Then, the injury happened. We've kinda just been waitin' for you to find yourself."

"And you never considered that it would make me happy?"

He tilts his head. "Does it?"

"Are you kidding? I'm fucking ecstatic!" Allowing the smile I've been fighting to spread over my face, I stand and open my arms.

It takes him a second to understand I'm not going to hit him, and he returns my smile and embrace.

Mom furrows her brows. "So, you're okay with this? Even though we didn't tell you after all this time?"

"Yeah, I am." I let go of Uncle Jonah and sit back down. "Truth is, I used to pray that you'd sit me down one day and tell me that Uncle Jonah was my real dad. And now he sort of gets to be my real dad." I probably shouldn't have said that, because Mom's eyes fill with tears.

He looks lovingly at my mom, wrapping his arm around her shoulders and kissing her temple.

I point my finger at him and give him the most threatening look I can muster. "Assuming you don't break her heart, that is."

He chuckles. "I waited for her for too long to do a dumb thing like that."

I take them both out to dinner to celebrate, letting them know it's perfectly okay to be as disgustingly sweet with each other as they want. It is weird, seeing them kiss and hold hands and gaze into each other's eyes, but a good weird. Everything has finally fallen into the right place after a long time of being wrong. Then, I make the drive back to Sam's feeling much lighter than I did during my earlier drive.

Like I thought, it was Uncle Jonah's voice on the phone. That time when I found him in the kitchen, he had stayed the night but didn't expect me up so early. And when I found Mom's shirt at his house, she had spent the weekend with him. I'm just so happy that Mom is happy, that Uncle Jonah is happy, that the muscles in my face are sore from smiling.

My dad knocked up my mom when they were in high school, and was overall miserable with how his life turned out. As a result, he'd go through low periods where he'd fall asleep drunk in a ditch with no clothes on. The next week, he'd clean himself up, bring my mom apology flowers, find a job, and be a dad. But that would only last a few months until something would set him off again. He'd go back to spending every penny he could find on alcohol or lottery tickets, and occasionally disappear for weeks on end. And yet, Mom stuck by him. I still don't really know why, especially when Uncle Jonah was right there and willing the entire time.

I always wondered why Mom wouldn't date anyone after Dad left, and why Uncle Jonah never got married. Now I know.

Maybe I should be more upset about the secret being kept for twelve years, but if my instinct is to be happy at the news, I won't force myself to feel something I don't.

Until the guilt sets in.

I'm the reason Mom got stuck and still lived inside that double-wide with the stained, peeling wallpaper. I'm the reason they didn't live together, the reason they waited so long to be together. The reason Mom even married Dad in the first place. My injury and emotional turmoil were the reasons they hid it for even longer.

As the shame seeps into my skin, I find myself wishing I had a vice to reach for and desperate to get home to Cori.

But she's not mine to reach for.

Chapter 25
Things I can't talk about with Sam

Cori

> Me: Where are you? Please tell me you've left already, the reservation is in twenty minutes.

> Sam: Won't make it. Got stuck in a meeting

I sit on the edge of Sam's bed, already dressed in a long-sleeved black dress that reaches my knees, but with a slit up to mid-thigh. It's tight, showing every curve I have, and is another of Sam's favorites. He bought it for me to wear to his office Christmas party last year. I usually avoid looking too long into mirrors, but after an hour of practicing positive affirmations while peering into the glass, I finally talked myself into wearing it.

I slip my feet out of the four-inch heels and put them back in the closet along with the dress, wipe the makeup from my face, then pull my leggings back on.

The bed, with its mint-green comforter and cotton sheets, calls to me to burrow underneath and sleep my disappointment away, but my stomach also calls for me to eat my feelings. Slipping Sam's navy sweatshirt over my hair, back in its usual messy bun, I head for the kitchen. But I stop at the sound of the TV in the living room.

Nick has been acting weird since Saturday night. Yesterday, I had looked forward to telling him all about the first day with the new coffee menu, but he didn't come out of his room all evening. My suspicions that he noticed my strange emotions while we danced grow with every tense moment that we don't talk. With the possibility that he's avoiding me, I'm afraid, once again, to go out into public domain and unintentionally disturb him.

I stand in the hallway, wondering if I can sneak into the kitchen, grab food, and hightail it back to Sam's room without being noticed. Unless I should toughen up and not worry about unnerving him. Or, if I should forget food, ignore my rumbling stomach, and go to bed. However, God decides for me, and His decision is none of the options I considered. As Nick appears in the hallway, he stops in his tracks when he sees me standing there. His eyes fall to Sam's sweatshirt and his shoulders visibly sag with clear disappointment at running into me.

"Uhh, sorry. I was just coming to get food really quick."

He studies me before a smirk creeps over his lips. "What did I tell you about apologizing so much?"

Bypassing the weirdness is a great plan, but I'm not sure how it will work long-term. "To not to?"

Laughter bubbles out of his chest. "Yes. To not to."

But the moment ends. He runs his hand through his hair, making it stick up at odd angles. "It's your anniversary today, isn't it? One whole year with Sam?"

I shrug. "Yeah, but it's just one year of dating. It's really not a big deal."

His lips thin into a straight line. "Still weird that you're spending it alone, though. Where is he?"

I look down at my socks. "Work."

Out of the top of my eye, I see him nod as he slips his hands into the pockets of his gray sweatpants.

"Wanna order tacos and talk about the latest news and gossip?" I love that he knows exactly how to cheer me up. I mean, *like.* I *like* how he knows me so well. It makes him a great friend. Yeah.

I meet his eyes and a grin takes hold of my lips as I ask what he knows.

"Well, before I get to the juicy stuff, the aviation mechanics school called me yesterday, and we set up an appointment to tour the facility next week and go over tuition and all the boring crap. I asked Uncle Jonah to go with me and he's excited."

"That's great."

"Yeah, I just... I don't know. Callum thinks I should just go for it, but I'm still scared."

"Well, it's just a tour for now. You can decide after you see it and have more information."

"Yeah, I guess you're right. Anyway, now, for the good part. Remember my Uncle Jonah? Apparently, he and my mom have been together for years and just didn't tell me."

I don't know how to respond to that. He's smiling, but only just hearing that they've been together for years doesn't sound so happy. "Oh?"

"It's good news," he clarifies, noticing my unsure expression. "I kept trying to convince Mom to get back out there and date. For years. And I've always thought of Uncle Jonah as my dad. Now, if he and Mom end up married, he will be." He scrunches up his face. "I guess I should stop calling him *uncle,* huh?"

I laugh. "Probably."

Standing in the hallway, both of us leaning against the wall,

I listen to him explain how he found out. He talks about his mother some more, and Jonah, but his face falls as he confides in me the self-hatred he feels for being the cause of their sneaking around.

And the desire to go to him, to pull him into my embrace, is almost stronger than I am.

"Nick, you know it isn't your fault. You have no reason to feel any guilt about it. They're both grown-ups and they both made their choices."

"But it was because of me. All of it." He struggles to retain that unwavering wall of confidence he normally has, but I'm glad he's opening up and bearing his soul. Especially to me.

"Maybe so, but that doesn't mean you had any control over any of it or that you should feel any shame. I'm the master at feeling guilt for things I shouldn't, so believe me."

He looks at the floor as I had done earlier, and I step forward to tilt his head up, forcing his eyes to meet mine. But the connection of our skin, my fingers to his jaw, sends a shock through me and I jerk my hand back.

It takes a minute to remember what I had intended to say. "Look, I understand why you feel the way you do, but as an unbiased third party, your mind is lying to you. They hid it because they love you. And because they love each other. Maybe it wasn't the right decision, but none of us really know the right decision in most situations until it's too late."

His eyes dart around my face, and his chest rises and falls with quick, shallow breaths. But he looks down and takes a step backward, coughing. "I guess you're right."

"Of course, I am. I'm right about everything."

He laughs. "Well, that whole statement was wrong, so try again."

I haven't filled him in on the phone call with Dad yet, so I jump into it, partly to distract him. As I recount the conversation, he listens intently, the tightness ebbing from his features as he puts aside his concern to pick apart another day.

"We rolled out the new menu yesterday. It's only the second day, but people seem to like the drinks. I'm hoping it does well enough that we can justify buying an espresso machine." Honestly, if that's all that I get out of this deal, I'll be happy.

"Look at us, huh? Things are falling into place," he says with an easy grin. "What did Sam say about it?"

I haven't told Sam about anything, and I won't until it's all settled. I plan to tell him after we have a sales report that proves I was right and after I start assistant manager training—if that happens.

Nick must read my face because he says, "You haven't told him yet? I understand if you haven't, but don't you think you should feel comfortable telling your boyfriend, especially after an entire year, about your success? Even if it isn't completely decided yet?" I don't answer that either, and he asks, "Have you spoken to Hailey?"

I pull out my phone and click the internet icon. "So, about those tacos you promised me..."

He sighs, but we're back to normal after more than a week of weirdness between us, and I don't want it to return. I don't want our relationship to become strained like it did with Hailey. I like being able to talk to him, about the heavy things, the things I can't talk about with Sam.

My heart races as the mouse hovers over the "submit order" button. I'm only ordering samples, but if I don't like the taste, I'll be wasting eighty dollars. I just know there is something here. Maybe not money exactly, but something I could care about. Something to look forward to, a reason to wake up in the morning. If my parents can support Sage in selling homemade crafts online, why couldn't they support me in selling coffee?

I won't have to stick to online, either: I could sell coffee to the diner. I could even ask the gas station by Mom's to carry some bags; they also serve as the grocery store. There are options and growth opportunities, and I couldn't be more excited.

I close my eyes and click, then peek through to double-check I hit the right button. Once I see the order number, I exhale in relief before printing the receipt. Now, it's time to work on my application for my business license, and think about possible coffee flavors. I've ordered samples of their basic flavors—breakfast blend, dark roast, and a few others. And if I like those, I can work with their experts to create my own, like a raspberry vanilla, or cinnamon mocha.

After I finish my blog to-do list, I move on to social media sites for the diner. Mike tasked me with creating an online presence to help with advertising the new drinks and any other changes. It will be a lot of work keeping up with my own side business and the new socials for the diner, but for the first time, I trust myself to be able to handle it. The doubtful voices that demand to be heard over all else are losing their strength. Still shouting, but harder to understand through the box I've packed them in.

Along with the new coffee options, Mike created an online survey for customers to fill out to receive a coupon for their next meal. No one likes surveys, but I can't help the smug grin I flash Mike anytime a response comes through, because they all say the same thing: the coffee is good but the food sucks. A few responses have said the coffee could be better, with higher quality roasts and more flavors, but that only further proves my point—people want coffee. And investing more in this idea is the right way to go.

However, the only person I have to share this news with is Nick. By the time Sam arrives home each night, he goes straight to bed walking past the plate of food I set aside for him just in case, and is too tired to talk about his day.

I shut my laptop now to go prepare that dinner he'll ignore when I smell garlic already wafting from the kitchen. Following the scent, I find Nick stirring something in a stainless steel pot.

"Hey, sorry. I was going to cook, but I got sidetracked working on some stuff for the diner."

He looks up. "It's not a problem, you know that. I'd just be sitting on the couch anyway."

Rolling my neck and stretching my back, I tell him about ordering the samples.

"Think you can convince Mike to order coffee from you if you go through with it?"

"I'm going to try. I need to do the math, see if it would be cost-effective first."

"Still, you'll have a customer in me and Mom and most likely Tyler and Callum. I'll work on selling for you to Erin-"

I smile as he lists the names of almost everyone he knows. Even old teammates and people from his job.

The excitement dies when he asks, "Will Sam be home for dinner today?"

"Who knows? I'm just worrying about myself these days. If I see him tonight, great. If not, perhaps tomorrow."

His gaze lingers for a moment too long before he turns the stove off and dumps pasta into a strainer in the sink.

"Just say it."

"No. I'll keep my thoughts to myself."

I drop it and get glasses out for water while he spoons pasta onto plates along with ladles of sauce. We eat on the couch watching a baseball game, as we have almost every night. Eating at the table feels too intimate without Sam, just the two of us with only each other's eyes to look at.

Chapter 26
She's Not Cori

Nick

After we finish eating, Cori grabs her book, and I continue watching the baseball game. Neither the bullpens, nor defense, for either team do what they need to, and too many runners land on base.

I steal a glance at Cori when the station cuts to a commercial, her hair tied into a messy ponytail and her socked feet curled beneath her. Her lips twitch at something on the page.

"What are you reading?"

She shows me the cover depicting a ship and bubbles beneath the water, as if someone is drowning. I ask what it's about and she gives a seven-minute speech about the main plotline. A simple, *"Pirates,"* would have sufficed, but I'm glad she took me on the scenic route. I drink up every word, every smile, every animated gesture as she talks with her hands.

"Does that answer your question?" she asks after she's done explaining.

"That answered questions I didn't even ask."

She grins and returns to her reading. But as interesting as the game is, it becomes increasingly harder to look away from her. Based on the slight shifts in her expression, I can almost read the words from the page on her face.

The crease in her forehead, the quickening of her breath and eyes racing across the page, the tiniest lift of her brows in concern. I can't pry my eyes away, and I find myself desperate to read the same words as her. To know what it is that makes her bite her bottom lip and shift in her seat. To know what makes her breaths shallow, the rapid rise and fall of her chest that I pray is bare underneath my sweatshirt.

I still haven't told her it's mine, although now I want to so she'll think of me every time she puts it on.

As if a bucket of ice water falls on me, I jerk my head back to the TV. What the hell is wrong with me, and where did these thoughts come from? This is another man's girlfriend. *Sam's* girlfriend. Sam, one of my best friends from college. Although, I'm not sure that means much anymore.

It's been a while since I've had sex, that's all it is. Erin and I have texted quite a bit and set a date for tomorrow night. I don't know where it will lead, but hopefully towards a bed. If I can stomach it.

I grip my gut now, the food settling like a stone at the thought of tomorrow night. Nervousness about starting something with Erin after being friends throughout college? Or dread because it's the wrong direction to go in?

I also haven't told Cori about what Kenna implied. I don't know if it's even something she needs to know, or if I'd be telling her because I want her to act on the news. I'm at a standstill, searching for the right thing, but with no clue where the right thing lies or what it even looks like. Typical.

As for Sam, I haven't seen him much over the past week and a half. I don't know how he'd react if I confronted him, but more importantly, I don't know what I'd say. It was years ago, yet the news is fresh, and by confronting him about it, I'll be crashing through the dam holding back my emotions.

I won't mention my current suspicions about his late nights.

When Sam does get home, tired and hair mussed like he'd run a hand through it too many times, he roughly asks Cori if she is going to spend the remainder of the evening with him or his roommate. She rolls her eyes and stands, following him to their bedroom and leaving her book behind.

I pick it up and flip to where her bookmark lies, going backward and skimming pages until I find it.

His hands, calloused and strong from wielding his sword, rolled the stockings down my legs. He had a gentleness about him, a softness unlike any of the other men here. His hair was shorter than the long, wild manes worn by his people. I ran my fingers through it, the dark, feather-soft locks a welcome contrast to the rough stubble scratching my legs as his lips trailed upwards. He bypassed the area that craved his touch, leaving kisses along my belly until they reached my breasts. He took one peak into his mouth, the other between his thumb and finger, and my back involuntarily arched, my center searching for the friction I so desperately needed. He reached up and slammed his mouth onto mine, his tongue greedily taking what it wanted.

Finally, he grabbed my thighs, pulling them up around his waist, and I could feel his eagerness through his trousers. Reaching down to free himself, he ran his knuckles along my seam before meeting my eyes and licking my wetness off his hand.

I clawed at his hips, not opposed to begging him, until he complied and lined himself up to enter. Slowly, he slid in, filling me completely, thrust-

"Whatcha readin'?"

My head snaps up finding Cori leaning a shoulder against the wall, arms crossed and a sly smile tugging at her lips.

"Uhh..." Guiltily, I toss the book back onto the coffee table.

She laughs and walks to the kitchen to get a cup of water and I do the same, needing something to do with my hands.

"I just, you know. Figured I'd see what all the fuss was about. You seemed to be enjoying it so much earlier."

She takes a sip of water then meets my eyes. "I was." Grinning again, she turns to leave and says, "Good night, Nick."

I stare at the space she just vacated for an amount of time I'm unaware of, pinned in place by her words and the ornery gleam in her eye. When I gain control over my body again, I take my water to my room and brush my teeth. I lay down in bed, staring at the ceiling before caving and reaching for my phone to purchase the ebook version. I want to finish that scene, and maybe read the rest of it in case there are more scenes like it.

"So? What'd you think?" Jonah asks. We walk outside where the sun slaps us with its awful heat.

I look up at the sign above the door, *Aviation Institute of Mechanics*. We'd just completed the tour, and now came the hard part: deciding. The next semester didn't start until January, though, so I had time.

Admittedly, nothing felt so right as when I walked through the facility. Except football. We saw the classrooms and discussed tuition payments. Then we walk through the hangar where the students work on real airplanes.

"I think I might do it," I answer.

"I'm glad," he says, slapping me on the back. "Look, I want to pay your tuition."

"No, there's no need. Especially if I can pay monthly. You helped me and Mom enough when I was a kid."

"But you don't stop bein' a parent just 'cause the kid grows up. You said you'd always wished I was your real dad. Well, I always thought of you as my real kid." He shakes my shoulder before opening his arms. It's more of a bro hug, as little touching as possible, but with all the emotion and healing of a parent enveloping you in their arms. "And your mom requests your presence for dinner next weekend, or whenever you have time."

"Is everything okay?"

"Yeah, she just wants to discuss what to do with the house."

The house? I study his face and his unreadable expression slowly slips into one of joy. "Is she moving in with you?"

"Yeah." We hug again, slapping each other on the back harder than necessary. "It's about time. She's over there most of the time anyway."

"Well, just tell her to burn the house. I don't want it."

He sighs. "I know you've always hated it, but you hated it 'cause you assumed your mom hated it and she didn't. She loves that house. That's why she's held onto it all this time. You know, she bought it herself. Well, with help from her parents. It may not have been fancy, but it was hers. I don't think she'll mind if you want to sell it, but she wants you to have the money from the sale at least. Or, you could keep the lot and build a house on it."

When I think of that mobile home, I think of it as a prison. One where Mom was abandoned and stuck living a life she hadn't planned on. One where I was stuck after being thrown out of school. But Mom has never acted as if she hated her life. She smiles more than anyone I know, more than people like

Sam who have everything and have reached every goal they've ever set. Maybe she didn't live the life she planned, maybe she didn't get everything I thought she deserved, but maybe happiness can be found anyway.

"Think on it," Jonah says, getting his keys from his jeans pocket and unlocking his truck. "And I'll get you the check for tuition."

"I don't need it," I call after him.

"Too damn bad. At least let me pay for half. It was my idea after all." He climbed in his truck and drove away as I got in mine, eager to share the events of the day with Cori. But my head falls back on the headrest when I remember I have that date with Erin tonight.

Erin sits before me in a low-cut black dress with spaghetti straps, her cat-like eyes, glittering forth from her glowing skin. Her lips, red and plump are every man's dream as are the long, thick eyelashes she bats my way. Several heads turn toward us as we follow the hostess to our table, eyes filled with envy of me. And it does feel good to be walking with her, to be the reason for the sneers from some of the other guests.

We spend most of the meal discussing normal first date topics: family, work, hobbies, etc. We know most of these things already, but we're getting to know each other as more than friends. We reminisce on moments from college, share a few laughs, and try each other's meals; she has the salmon, I have the tenderloin.

When the server asks if we want dessert, I almost order some to-go to share with Cori. But ordering dessert for one woman while on a date with another is probably inappropriate.

Because, while Erin is one of the most beautiful women I've ever laid eyes on, she's not Cori. And while this date has gone about as well as a date can, I've waited anxiously for the end, so I can get home and spend a measly five minutes in Cori's presence, simply to ask her how her day was.

I don't know when it happened, or even how I allowed myself to fall for my roommate's girlfriend. But I did, and I can't deny it any longer. I fell so hard that not even the goddess in front of me has any effect on me, physically or otherwise.

She has nothing on Cori's stormy eyes that give away her every emotion, now that I've learned her tells. Nothing on her smile when I'm treated with a rare genuine expression of joy. Nothing on the way she demands my every thought and concern, like what she's doing at any given moment, or how the day is treating her, or when I'll see her next.

Except I do know when it happened—slowly over the last few months. And I do know how—she opened herself up to me. She bared her soul, her wonderful soul that not many people get to see. Like a rare artifact discovered by a starving archeologist so close to giving up, I found her, my reason to keep digging, to keep hoping, to keep fighting. Only those most worthy get to know the treasure that is her being. Like how animated she gets watching game shows, shouting the answer as if she's a contestant herself. How fast and high-pitched the words come out when she's sharing her strong opinions on certain topics. How she almost always sits criss-cross even when sitting at the dining room table. How she hates bare feet and always wears the thickest socks she can find.

When we reach Erin's car at the end of the date, I give her a side hug instead of meeting the kiss she offers, and the air turns cold.

"Are you not into me?" she asks bluntly.

Closing my eyes, I prepare myself for the truth. I can't be a coward now. "I'm really sorry. It's not you, you're amazing and beautiful. I just don't think I was ready for this."

She bites her bottom lip. "Is there someone else? Or is it the fact that we know each other?"

I don't know how to answer that. Rubbing the back of my neck, I sigh. "I sort of realized I have feelings for someone, but I can't be with them."

"Someone you dated back home?"

I don't confirm, or deny.

Nodding, she consolingly touches my elbow. "I understand. I sort of still have feelings for my ex, but I was hoping I'd start to feel differently if I forced myself to move on."

"It's not Sam, is it?" I ask, praying they haven't started something behind Cori's back.

"God, no. The guy I broke up with a few months ago."

"Is there any hope for a relationship with him?"

She thinks about it for a moment, before answering. "There might be, but I'm prideful. I'm not sure how to ask him without embarrassing myself."

"Life is short. You'll forget embarrassment, but you won't forget regret."

"What about you? You said you can't be with this person, but is there any hope for the future? A year from now? Two years from now?"

"I'm not sure. She's with someone now. I can't see it lasting, but I have no idea how she feels about me." I leave out that It would probably ruin a few friendships, but they might already be ruined anyway.

"How about I make you a deal? I'll try with my ex, and you don't lose hope for being with this person."

It's a deal not unlike the one I made with Cori when we

both said we'd try harder at doing something for ourselves and our careers. But the things we promised to do were sort of inevitable. This one has much more risk. "I'm not sure I can make that deal."

"Well, then I'll leave you with this: Life is short. You'll forget embarrassment, but you won't forget regret." A chuckle escapes me as she smiles and slides in the door I hold open for her. As I push to close it, she reaches out her arm to stop it.

Narrowing her eyes, they dart around my face, searching. "It's not Cori, is it?"

My non-answer is answer enough as I look to the ground.

"Whoa." She sits back in her seat and looks out her windshield, eyes unfocused. "Okay. So... your best friend's girlfriend."

"I mean, *best* friend is a stretch. But, yeah."

"Okay, so I'll leave you with this then: tread very carefully and don't do anything stupid. She'll need to come to the decision to leave on her own. But I agree with you, I don't see it lasting. Sam is... well, he's an ass." She closes her door, but opens the window and adds, "And I'm always here if you need to talk."

When I get back to Sam's, the apartment is quiet and dark, except for the light above the stove. As I pass by Sam and Cori's bedroom, I don't hear any noise, thankfully, but the thought occurs to me that I can't stay here. Once I lay in bed, I pull up an apartment search online. But how am I supposed to leave Cori here alone? Because she will be if I'm not here to keep her company.

Chapter 27
Let's Get Two Things Straight

Cori

O n the day that the samples are supposed to be delivered, I rush home, reminding myself to breathe. But when I open the mailbox, there's nothing inside. Smacking my fore-head because the package would be too big for the mailbox, I rush to the front office. But they don't have it either. I double-check the tracking information, and it confirms the package had been delivered earlier in the day. I look around the door before heading inside to tear the apartment apart, yet still can't find it anywhere.

As a last resort, I text both Nick and Sam, asking if they'd seen a package. Nick responds right away that he hasn't been home yet. And Sam, although he never responds, wouldn't have been home yet either. So I slump onto the couch, disappointed.

It must have been a mistake, and I talk myself out of worrying about it for the time being. It might show up tomor-row, maybe even the day after that. If it doesn't, I'll contact the company and see if they're able to send another without me having to fork over another eighty dollars. In the grand scheme of things, it's not a big deal. But I hate looking forward to some-thing all day, only to have it not happen.

I get to work on social media sites for the diner and updating plugins for the blog. It's a few hours before Sam walks in the door, carrying a medium-sized box.

"What did you order?" he asks, tossing it onto the bed before loosening his tie.

"Oh, thank God," I exclaim, grabbing it to double-check the label. I look up at Sam, who stands with his hands on his hips waiting for his answer. "Umm, it's just some coffee."

"From a roaster?" He points to the sender on the label. "You're skipping the supplier now?"

I guess it's time to be honest. "I ordered some samples to see if I want to continue with this roaster, or find a different one."

He blinks at me. "For what, exactly?"

"A side business I'm starting."

Scratching his head, he seems to be contemplating different options for his response. "So, I don't make you pay rent and I pay for your car problems so that you can save your money, and you waste it on this?"

I almost laugh. "Are you serious?" I don't know why I bother asking. Of course, he's serious. It's the reason I didn't tell him until now of my plan. Why I didn't tell him about the blog.

The bed shakes as it bears his weight, and he grabs my hands in his. "Look, you've been depressed about not finding a job for a long time. You've doubted yourself and that's made your self-worth crumble. I see it, Cori. I see you. But this is not worth your time. You'll spend loads of money getting it off the ground, only for it to crash."

I yank my hands back and level him with a glare. "Forgive me if I don't listen to you, but I've done my homework. I know what I'm doing. And I've already set the groundwork for it to succeed. So kindly, fuck off."

There's just as much anger as there is amusement in his laugh. "Fine. Waste your money. But don't come crying to me when it doesn't work out. Don't start moping around, hating yourself because you've failed once again." He rises from the bed, yanking on his tie and throwing it on the dresser.

"Can you put your laptop away now?"

I narrow my eyes and ask, "Why?"

"In case you haven't noticed, it's been a while since we had sex."

"Yeah, let me just bend over. Because I'm *really* in the mood now."

He scoffs. "You're never in the fucking mood."

"When have I ever turned you down?"

Rubbing his eyes, he sits back on the bed. "I'm sorry. It's just been a rough day." He looks up at me, his typically neat, hair disheveled. "I don't mean to take it out on you."

I don't know why I do it, but every time he looks at me with those pleading eyes, I cave. Maybe it's pity that his job is so stressful, maybe it's love because I want to take his stress away. Maybe because it *has* been a while since we've had sex, and I know it would help his stress levels tremendously and improve the tension between us if he found release.

But if I know myself—and, honestly, I don't very well—it's because it's easier. Just do it and get it over with so he'll shut up and go to sleep.

I push him back onto the bed, straddling him, kissing him, running my hands through his hair. He pulls my shirt off, then my pants. He unbuttons his own and pulls them down just enough to slip on a condom that I don't recall him grabbing, then I slide my walls down around his penis. But thoughts intrude. Did I leave the oven on? Can Nick hear us? Does Sam think I look fat from his angle? And I struggle to reach climax.

Sam's tan, chiseled torso beneath me should be the only thing I can think of. I don't know if it's anxiety, the inability to quiet my brain, or what, but I need to relax and live in the moment. So I begin narrating every action with the voice inside my head, so there's no room to think of anything else.

I'm running my hands down Sam's chest through the opening of his shirt. I'm leaning down and kissing him. I'm sitting back up so I don't squish him. Sam flips me over.

"You take too long to finish in this position."

I'm face down on the pillow. I move my face so I can breathe. He nears my entrance from behind.

I let out a moan. Fake, but he buys it. A few more. He grunts. He stills.

He rises from the bed. The trash bag rustles as he throws the condom inside. A tear escapes, but I brush it away before he notices. He walks back into the room.

"Did you even enjoy that?"

"Yes, of course." I know lying to him is wrong, but which is worse—being the cause of his stress or lying about enjoying sex with him? Maybe they're equally wrong.

He goes back into the bathroom and starts the shower.

"You didn't get soap today?" he calls out.

I turn, finding his head poking out of the door. "No, I didn't know we were out."

He sighs and closes his eyes as if praying for patience. "All I ask of you is to take care of the housework and shopping while I bust my ass all fucking day. And you can't remember a tiny thing like soap?"

"I. Didn't. Know. We. Were. Out."

"What the fuck am I supposed to use, huh? Hand soap? Shampoo?"

I throw my clothes back on as quickly as I can, frustration getting the better of me.

"Can you see if Nick has an extra bar in his bathroom?"

I don't answer as I stomp off to the guest bathroom. A soft sliver of light glows underneath his bedroom door, but I won't bother him. Rummaging through the cabinet, I find a whole package and take a bar back to Sam. Neither of us says a word while I place it in his hand and escape to the kitchen. There's a candy bar in my purse for emergencies such as these. I skipped dinner and need to eat something, to curb the rumbling in my stomach and the ache in my chest.

Leaning against the counter, one arm crossed against my chest, I nibble on the chocolate. At some point, my eyes fill with tears again. I will them away, but not before a shadow appears in the walkway, propping a shoulder against the wall at the entrance to the kitchen.

"I'm not in the mood for you tonight," I announce without looking at him.

"Woah. Care to explain what *I* did wrong?"

"You're so hot and cold. Just like Sam."

I finish the candy bar and throw the wrapper in the trash can, but when I approach Nick, he doesn't budge from where he blocks the walkway.

"Excuse me."

"You're not going anywhere until we discuss what you just said." He crosses his arms now over his broad chest. After I roll my eyes I stare at the tattoo on his thick forearm.

"First, I apologize. I've been trying, but clearly failing, at hiding my feelings better than that. Second, what happened for you to not be *in the mood* for me?" I gnaw on my lip instead of answering, and he adds, voice soft and comforting, "Talk to me."

I shake my head. "There's nothing to talk about, I'm just in a bad mood." I'd love to share with him the details of the argument between Sam and me, but I think there's a line somewhere of what I should and shouldn't share with my boyfriend's roommate. I've probably crossed it by now.

"Did I tell you I finished that book you were reading?"

Puzzled by the sudden change of topic, my eyes narrow and lift to his. "I bought an e-book copy."

I snort. "You really liked that scene you read the other night, huh?"

I almost ask if he'd like to join our book club, but the reminder of my strained relationship with Hailey hits me like a punch to the gut. I clear my throat and ask instead, "Would you like to have a discussion about it?"

His lips quirk as he leans in, voice gravelly. "Just tell me when and where."

There's something in his tone and his expression, something more than just a joke. My smile starts to thin as he stands up straight and hooks his thumb over his shoulder. "I, uh, noticed a shopping bag from the bookstore in the living room yesterday, that wasn't there before. I thought you were on a book-buying ban."

I tap my chin and lower my brows. "Hmm. . . I'm not sure what you're talking about?"

"Magical book fairies don't exist, you know."

"Okay, but I used a gift card, so I didn't really buy anything."

He raises an eyebrow. "But you don't have any more room on your shelves."

"With a little imagination and creative stacking, I can make them fit."

He laughs and shakes his head.

I throw my hands up in the air. "Well, what was I supposed to do? They were having a sale!"

"Oh, so you're a victim?"

"Yes! I'm not strong enough to resist the lure of a book sale." A smile breaks through when I can no longer fake seriousness. "Want to see what I got?"

"Of course, I do."

We go to the living room and I pull out book after book, explaining why I bought each one.

Afterward, Nick asks, "You bought *eight* books?"

"Did you not hear me about the sale?"

His deep chuckle reverberates throughout my body. But a veil of sobriety smothers the moment, killing my smile.

"What just happened?" he asks, taking a step towards me, face pinched in concern.

"How did... how am I... I mean, I was..." I take a deep breath and try again. "Why is it so easy with you?"

His shoulders fall as if he knows the answer, but doesn't want to say it.

My eyes narrow. "And what did you mean earlier when you said you thought you were hiding your feelings better than that?"

He runs his hand through his hair as he opens his mouth to answer. But he closes it and shakes his head. "I've told you before what I think about Sam, but I've been trying not to mention it anymore."

A gentle touch of suspicion graces my skin, just enough that I wonder if he had a different answer the first time he tried to speak.

"I don't understand why you're with him. Can you finally answer that, please?"

My voice is barely a whisper. "Because I love him."

"But, see, I have turned it over and taken it apart, looked at it from every angle, and I can't come up with a single explanation other than you don't understand what love is."

"I do," I say, my voice full of hurt from the sting of his words. "See? You're just like him. We're joking around one minute, and arguing the next." But even I can see the differences.

He takes another step towards me, chest heaving and brows

pinched as if he's in pain, and I back up until I hit the wall behind me. He brings his arms up on either side of my head, bracing himself against the wall and caging me in.

It takes every ounce of strength not to grip his shirt in my fist and pull him closer. Because even though his hard chest is almost flush against mine, it's not close enough.

He leans in, the smooth teakwood scent from his skin enveloping us both. His lips, just a breath away from mine, have every ounce of my attention. How easy it would be to grab his neck and pull his mouth down to mine. To wrap my legs around his waist and have his strong arms holding onto my thighs.

His voice, a gentle caress down my spine, awakens every nerve when he says, "Let's get two things straight. One, I am *nothing* like Sam. And two, you can be sure you'll never be in tears after I fuck you."

Not *if*—a promise.

Before I can melt into the floor from the tension, he pushes off the wall and walks away, leaving me shaking with need.

I'd feel guilty if I thought for one second that Sam actually stayed late at the office to *work*.

After searching for guidance among the stars, I leave the peace of the patio to return to Sam's room. He's still awake, keeping his eyes on his phone as I close the door and climb underneath the covers.

His skin burns mine when he reaches over to hold my hand, but not in a good way. "About earlier. It's just been a rough day-"

I yank my hand away. "You have a *rough day* every day. At

some point, you've got to learn how to handle it better than taking it out on me."

Through Hailey and Nick, through all of his *rough days*, through all the times I've felt lonely despite Sam sleeping a foot away, the world seemed to be telling me this isn't right. Why do I hold on so tightly, ignoring every warning?

"In case you forgot, I have a job that puts more stress on me than you've ever dealt with in your life."

"I know that, but you chose it. Isn't that what you always tell me? You and Dad. I *chose* to work at the diner. I *chose* not to go back to school for my bachelor's."

"Were those not choices you made?"

"Obviously. But that's the other thing you always tell me. If you're that unhappy, if you're that stressed, change it." Maybe he'll cut the cord, so I don't have to. I don't agree that I deserve better, but maybe it's time to let go so that Sam can be happy. Maybe it's not the job, but *me* causing him so much stress.

He sits up straight, a fighting stance, and I think, *here it comes*. "I make more money at twenty-four than you'll be making at fifty. I'm on track to leading my team in less than a year. I'll own the company when Dad hands it over. Why would I change any of that?"

"Because there's more to life. Despite what you and Dad think, money and success are not everything. What is it going to get you in the end? If that's how you want to spend your life, go for it. But you don't get to take it out on others when it becomes too much for you to handle."

But if he does end us, where would I go? Not just physically, but mentally. What do I do with all the memories of us? The scrapbook with Sam in almost every photo, my first kiss, my childhood best friend. Ending us means spoiling all of that. Don't I owe it to myself, both current and younger versions, to hold on?

"Have I really treated you that badly?" His shoulders cave in, eyes shining with tears, and my defiance fizzles out.

And the guilt sets in.

I find myself sliding over to lay my head on his chest, wishing I could take his pain away with just my touch.

I'm supposed to be his peace, the one he can count on not to make his stress worse, yet I was planning my getaway, ready to file away our moments together.

"No, you haven't. You've been wonderful." Sam holds me tightly, his chin resting on the top of my head.

"I think we just need some quality time together. What do you think? Your birthday is coming up. How about you take my card and buy the closest seats you can find at a Stallions game?"

I jerk back to study his expression. "Who else will be coming with us?"

"No one. Just us. And tens of thousands of other fans, but I'll only be talking to you."

"And you'll get off in time? No meetings or dinner with clients?"

"I promise."

My head falls back onto his chest. Maybe we can be salvaged after all. But even here in his embrace, there's a Nick-sized division between us in the form of his masculine soap drifting up from Sam's skin.

Chapter 28
Tired of Waiting

Nick

"I'll need first and last month's rent and a non-refundable deposit," the property manager says. I sit in his office, looking at the two different floor plans currently available for an insane amount of money. I was planning to use that money towards my future, towards tuition, but I guess I'll have to reconsider enrolling in the school for my A & P license. I could still pay the tuition monthly, but with this chunk of money missing from my savings, the risk is now greater.

"We won't have this one available for another month, but if you're okay with the one bedroom, it will be free in two weeks."

"One bedroom is good. Am I able to go look at it?"

"Yes, but it still needs some patches on the wall and some cleaning."

"That's fine, I just want to get a feel for the space."

He walks me up concrete steps to the third floor and to the very last door. As soon as I walk inside, the smell of fresh paint hits me. Paint that's probably covering up mold or something so they don't have to deal with the problem.

It's a small apartment, but perfectly sized for one person who won't be home enough to justify the cost. I don't have any furniture except the bed and dresser in my room at Sam's, but I'm not opposed to eating over the sink and watching TV in bed.

When we get back to the office, the thought occurs that I should give Sam some sort of notice before signing any paperwork. I did promise that I wouldn't leave again without informing anyone when I came back to town; maybe I'm taking the coward's way out. But if he slept with Kenna, he didn't tell me before doing so. Or, *after.* So I give the guy my ID and sign my name several times throughout the lease agreement.

I've started carrying antacids in my pocket to have on hand quickly, and when I walk inside Sam's apartment, I shake a few from the bottle to soothe the burning in my stomach. Cori walks into the living room as I'm popping them in my mouth. She normally changes out of her jeans the second she arrives home, but she wears a pair now along with a Stallions jersey, and her brown hair is free of its usual ponytail. She's riddled with anxiety as she starts pacing, checking her phone every five seconds.

"Is everything okay?" I say, sitting on the couch and flipping on the pregame show.

She lets out a manic laugh and answers a little too loudly, "Everything is perfect!"

"Then why are you marching through the living room?"

"Well. You're going to be shocked at what I have to tell you, so you might want to sit down."

I look down at the couch I'm already sitting on and wonder if she's officially lost it.

"Sam was supposed to be home an hour ago so that we

could go to that game." She points to the TV. "As usual, he's not here, and I can't get a hold of him."

I sigh, digging my fingers in my eyes. This shit is getting old, how does she not see it?

"Go to the game without him."

She swings around, shooting a mortified look in my direction. "By *myself?*"

I almost say, *"Why not?"* but this is Cori.

"I've never been to a game before. Tickets are expensive. But Sam bought some so he could take me, and I've been so excited I can barely think about anything else. And now that it's finally here, where is he?"

I shake my head, warring with myself. But the devil on my shoulder wins. "Do you have access to both tickets?"

"They were sent to my email."

Standing, I rub my hands together. "Then let's go to the game together."

She stands still, contemplating the idea. "Do you think that's a good idea?"

"No," I answer honestly. But I'm more concerned with her seeing the game than I am about my own comfort or doing the right thing.

Her shoulders relax and she exhales more evenly. "Are you sure you don't mind coming with me?"

I tilt my head and level her with a look. She should know by now I'd cut my arm off to feed her. "Like it's a downgrade from watching the game from home. Let me just go change really quick." The jeans I'm wearing are fine, but I want to put on a jersey.

"Thank you, Nick. But you have to hurry because I'm tired of waiting. I'm sure I've already missed out on the free bobble-head they were handing out to the first ten thousand people."

A proud smile spreads over my lips. "Yes, ma'am."

After paying an astronomical amount just to park my truck and walking at least a mile to the gates, I ask if she wants to wait, just in case Sam shows up last minute. It's already the last minute, but this is Sam we're talking about.

"No. If he shows up, he can buy another ticket and sit by himself." She pulls her phone out of her pocket and turns it off.

I almost do the same to mine, but I want access to the camera in case I need it.

Since this is her first game, my eyes are glued to her face to catch every expression of awe. For a baseball fan, walking into the park for the first time is a whole experience by itself. Besides the memorabilia and team history on every wall, the energy from the fans is unmatched, and I get to witness the very moment the current hits her. The lingering anger from Sam's absence melts away until nothing is left except awe at the swarm of bodies, all decked out in team merchandise, and all here for one, united reason.

We stop by a concession stand before heading to our seats, and I try not to cringe at the prices. But it's her first live game, and I'll spend any amount Cori wants. I'd do the same if it were her hundredth game.

"Do you want a hot dog?" I ask.

"No, I'll just get some water."

"You can't watch a live baseball game without eating a hot dog," I point out. "It's a national law."

"I thought that was cracker jacks?" She smirks.

"Those too." I give the man at the counter our order of two sodas, four hot dogs, and two boxes of cracker jacks. But when I pull my card out to pay, Cori elbows my ribs out of the way to slip hers into the machine. She forgets that I have almost a foot on her and at least seventy pounds. Simultaneously, I yank her card out of the machine and wrap my arm around her waist, lifting her in the air. I tap my card instead of inserting it, and the payment goes through before she wiggles out of my grip.

She adjusts her shirt down in adorable frustration as she tries to fight the grin from forming on her face. Pointing her finger at me, she says sternly, "I'm going to get you back for that."

"I'd like to see you try."

We get to our seats just in time for a child from a local youth league team to shout, "Play ball," then it's baseball time. The first few innings are uneventful; a few hits land runners on base, but don't turn into runs. However, things pick up in the fourth, when a runner waits on second and another on third.

Chatter continues, but the smack from the ball meeting wood reverberates throughout the park and everyone falls silent to see where it lands before deciding whether to cheer or shout obscenities. Time slows as the ball flies through the air, teasing those of us biting our nails below. Finally, it arches downwards right into the hands of a teenage girl, and cheers obliterate the silence.

Looking around the ballpark at the excitement, Cori doesn't physically react as much as everyone else, but the pure joy is evident by the smile on her face. I get my phone out and snap a picture of her to show to Sam later. Just in case the desire to rub it in his face doesn't dissipate. I get another picture of her smiling down at the field before I'm caught red-handed, and the sound of her laughter muffles everything else.

Like the song of a siren to a willing pirate from the dark depths of the ocean, I drown in the sound. And the sight of her bright, full smile that reaches every inch of her face.

Before she notices me staring, I jerk my gaze back to the field and clear my throat.

"So, what now?" I ask, simultaneously afraid and hopeful of her answer.

I don't have to elaborate because there's only one thing I could mean. "I don't know."

We watch another batter strike out before she says, "I know what I should do, I just don't know if I have the strength to do it."

"Because you don't know where you're going to live? Because you don't know how to live without him in your life? Or because you don't think you'll be strong enough not to cave when he turns the blame on you until you're the one apologizing to him?"

Everything I wanted to say to her the other night when I found her crying in the kitchen floats back to the surface. *Everything is so much easier with me because I'm right. You don't love him. Maybe you did at one point, but dreading his presence isn't love. And he doesn't love you. Making you feel like everything is your fault and that you're nothing without him isn't love. Desperately trying to spend every available second with someone or making unavailable seconds available for someone, that's love. Supporting someone in their dreams, lifting them up, and being excited for them when they succeed, that's love.*

But I swallow the words down again.

We shouldn't be talking about this here. Sam did her a favor by not ruining her first baseball game with his physical presence, I shouldn't be bringing him here in conversation.

"Let's talk about something else. I haven't told you how the tour went."

Her face remains blank while I walk her through the information I was given and describe the facility. When I'm done, she pulls out a folded piece of paper from her back pocket. "So, are you going to enroll?"

"I still don't know. I have until January to decide. That's when the next term starts. But I'm starting to think I should keep the job I have. Try to advance and save my money. I don't know, I keep going back and forth."

Hesitantly, she hands the paper to me and gnaws on her lip. I try to take it, but it won't budge from her iron grip.

"Don't read it until we get home. But it's a... poem." Finally, she lets it go. I hold it, fighting the urge to read it now. "I'm not great at verbally expressing feelings or giving advice, but I've been thinking about what you said in the hallway, about feeling guilty for spending money and time on football when it didn't work out. And I was inspired to write a poem about it. I hope you understand it." Her eyes fly to mine and widen before she adds quickly, "Not that I think you're too stupid to understand it, but I hope that I chose the right words so that the message is clear. And not confusing."

I laugh. "I'm sure you did." I slide it in my pocket. "Thank you."

"I haven't had a chance to tell you how the coffee samples turned out." I wait for her to continue. "They're amazing. All the flavors were amazing. I still have some grounds left, if you'd like to try them."

"I'd love to. So you're going ahead with it?"

"Yep. I have to save up some money first, it's a few thousand to get started. But I'm excited."

I thank God the twinkle appears back in her eyes as she talks about her business plan, and pride swells in my chest that she's not allowing Sam to keep her from her goals. Even if this plan is a smaller version of her coffee house dream, it's something.

She continues, sharing updates about the diner, and how sales improve by the day.

"But it's going to take time to see real change," she says. I can't help thinking about how I've already seen *real change* in her since that night we met. There's still a long way to go, but I can now see the day when she won't brush off and dismiss any compliment. I can envision her setting clear boundaries and telling her mom and dad off for crossing them. I can imagine her knowing with certainty what she wants and taking it.

The next inning adds a run to the visiting teams' score and the fifth inning starts. Then, our pitcher is hit on his arm by a ball. We wait with bated breath to see if they'll pull him to have his arm checked out when Cori starts frantically shaking her head and waving her hands. I follow the gaze of her wide eyes and see our faces on the fucking kiss cam of all things. Of course, she's saying no.

Of course, we aren't going to kiss, not even on the cheek or anything. She's not mine to kiss. But I can't help but look back at her to see what she'll do. I know she does so jokingly, yet disappointment consumes me as Cori scrunches up her face and covers mine with her hand. Thankfully, the camera moves on to another unsuspecting couple of fans and leaves us alone.

She looks at me and laughs. "That was funny."

Yeah. *Funny.*

When the game ends 4-1 Stallions, we fight our way through the stifling tide of heavily perfumed bodies until we burst forth from the doors into the cool night air. We walk side by side, enjoying the silence, but still riding the high of victory through the fans around us.

When we arrive at my truck, I open the door for her, like I did when we left Sam's apartment earlier. I'm wondering if Sam opens her doors for her when she captures my gaze before stepping into the truck. I can't breathe while I wait for her to say whatever is on her mind.

"I'm going to do it. Tonight."

I don't need elaboration, I know exactly what she's referring to. She's going to end things with Sam.

I have to remind myself that her words don't mean we'll be together. We can't be. Not yet, if ever. But she'll be free. Her happiness, her confidence, her ambition won't be stifled by some dick who thinks he's spun from gold.

Despite the reminder, there's nothing but the sound of my heart thumping. I don't allow myself to smile because I know this won't be an easy journey for her, but my chest swells with joy at the thought of her out of his grasp.

I nod my understanding and close her door before running around to mine. As I buckle my seatbelt, Cori turns her phone back on. New notifications continue dinging their arrival as I pull out into traffic.

"What?" Cori mutters as the phone keeps going off.

"Is he mad?" I can picture him coming home late, kicking off his shoes and throwing his briefcase to land wherever, expecting Cori to be waiting to jump into action for whatever he needs.

But she gasps, breathily murmuring, "Oh, God."

"What is it?"

Tears already fill her eyes. "Sam was in a car accident."

Chapter 29
Anytime, Sweetie

I t's been a dream of mine to watch the Stallions play in person ever since I was a child. Sam went to games all the time when his Dad had season tickets, and my dad took my brothers at least once a year. My parents couldn't afford tickets very often, and since my brothers were boys and actually played baseball, they got to go while I stayed home.

But for most of the games, Dad watched from home with all of us kids and a mountain of junk food on the coffee table. It was the one time Dad wasn't irritated with us for one reason or another—unless we stood in front of the TV blocking his view. Watching those games with Dad are some of my favorite memories, and to that list, I planned to add this night. With Nick.

Until I turn my phone back on.

Nick drives me to the hospital and we rush inside. Mr. Bennett, still in his suit from work, argues with a nurse at the desk. Mrs. Bennett sits perfectly still, one hand mindlessly grasping her necklace. There's an open magazine in her lap but she doesn't appear to be reading anything, most likely too lost in her worry to notice the page.

I say her name as I approach and her head snaps up. It takes a second before her watery eyes focus on my face.

"Oh, Cori, I'm so glad you're here." She stands and latches onto me. "We're both going crazy. They won't tell us anything, and we've been here for an hour already." We hold each other for a moment, desperate to reach a reality in which this is all just a huge overreaction.

Mr. and Mrs. Bennett have been a second set of parents to me since I met Sam. I went on vacations with them, I spent holidays at their house, I'm standing next to them in several of their family photos, just like Sam in mine.

"I'm so sorry. My phone was turned off, or I would have been here sooner. Do you know anything at all?"

"Nothing. Sam called us, he told us he was in a car accident and was coming to this hospital. He said he couldn't get a hold of you. He didn't sound great, but the phone cut off before he could give any details. We don't know how bad his injuries are, or where he was when the accident happened." Her blue eyes, the same ice-blue as Sam's, spill over with tears and I rub her arm consolingly.

"You did talk to him though, so we know he's alive, right?" Nick asks from behind me.

"Yes," she answers. No one mentions the fear of Sam having injuries that may not have taken him immediately. "But the nurses don't seem to know anything, as if he's not in the system."

Mr. Bennett, swearing under his breath at not getting

anywhere with the lady at the desk, pats my shoulder in greeting while he tells his wife to try Sam's phone again.

He doesn't answer.

"He bought tickets for the game tonight, but I was so mad when he didn't get home in time. So Nick took the extra ticket, and I'm so sorry. I never should have turned my phone off."

"Don't feel guilty. He's been pulling a lot of late nights lately, and I know how frustrating that can be," Mr. Bennett says, rubbing his wife's back, like they've had arguments over this very subject.

I fall into a chair as my own guilt buckles my knees, blowing the breath from my lungs. If his dad says he's pulled a lot of late nights, then maybe he actually *is* working.

Suddenly, Mrs. Bennett turns to me. "Oh, Cori, Happy Birthday. I'm so sorry I didn't call earlier."

Nick's eyes, wide with shock, fly to mine. "It's your birthday?" After I nod, he asks why I didn't say anything.

Shrugging my shoulders, I turn back to Mrs. Bennett. "Thank you, and don't worry about it." We have much bigger things to worry about at the moment than my dumb birthday.

The tension weighs down on all of us as Mr. Bennett paces, checking in with the nurses every five minutes. Nick leans against the wall, and Mrs. Bennett takes the seat next to me. All of us stare at nothing.

The plain white walls are adorned with TVs and generic photographs of potted plants. It takes less than a minute to look at every single thing within sight and, before I realize, I've grabbed a magazine as well, simply to have something to hold.

The very same second that Sam's car slammed into another, I was considering a future without him in my life. I was *planning* that future. I had it all worked out—I'd rip off the bandage, then run home to my parents' house. Presumably, they'd let me inside, and I'd stay there until I figured out the rest. And if they didn't, I'd sleep in my car. Maybe get a gym membership for the showers until I could find an apartment.

I lose track of time guiltily wondering if I accidentally manifested this accident. But my thoughts are interrupted when Nick asks, "Can I get anyone anything? Coffee? Water?"

Mr. and Mrs. Bennett decline, but Grandma used to say coffee helped with any ailment. If exhaustion or headaches pained you, the reasoning is obvious. But if you were cold, sad, or lonely, the warmth and weight of the cup provided comfort. It's not the warmth, but the illusion of feeling close to her in this bleak moment and the desperation of needing something to do with my hands that has me rising from my seat in search of coffee.

But just as Nick and I turn down a hallway, we hear the double doors open and Mrs. Bennett cries out, "Samuel!"

I run back into the waiting room and Mrs. Bennett rushes to Sam, checking him over. Cuts mar his face, his neck, his hands, and some blood stains his light blue shirt. But there are no stitches or bandages that I can see. He has no cast, not even paperwork in his hand.

He turns his head, his eyes meeting mine before hardening and filling with betrayal as they move to Nick's presence beside me.

"I'm fine, Mom. Just banged up a bit." He hugs her gently, wincing a bit, before hugging his dad.

"What happened?" Mr. Bennett asks.

"I was trying to get home in time to go to the game with Cori, and someone ran a red light."

Then he walks out the door without another glance in my direction. I rush after him into the lit parking lot, calling his name, but he shouts, "Cori, I need some space away from you right now."

I stop, unsure what he means by *space*. "You... you want me to stay somewhere else tonight?"

He continues walking, winding between parked cars.

"Sam, please. I was so scared-"

He whips around and scoffs. "I'm surprised at that. Considering you didn't care enough to answer your phone." He takes another step backward and wrenches open the back seat of his dad's Mercedes.

"I'll go home with Mom and Dad. You go with Nick. That's what you'd prefer, isn't it?"

Anyone can miss a phone call because they're asleep, don't have a signal, their phone is dead, or they just don't hear it ring, but I specifically turned mine off. That's the difference between my infraction and all the times I couldn't reach Sam. And I can't do anything to make it up to him except give him space until he's ready to forgive me.

After Nick drives us home, I lay down on the couch, too tired and sad to change my clothes or find a blanket. I shiver from the blast of the AC vent blowing directly on me as I fall into a restless sleep. Eventually, the air stops, and I finally sleep deep enough to dream, but the dream is a nightmare, the same one I've had since I was a kid. I'm in the driver's side of a car trying to slow it down as it plows into fences, mailboxes, other cars, even houses and people. The brakes don't work, the steering wheel is too sensitive, and I'm hysterical.

Based on the harsh sun glaring through the window when I finally wake, it's about ten a.m. There's no sign of Sam, but a blanket covers me and Nick sits in an armchair scrolling on his laptop.

Noticing my open eyes, he says, "Good morning. I know I don't have to ask if you want coffee." He chuckles and rises from the chair.

"I can get it." I follow him into the kitchen.

"I haven't gotten you a gift or anything yet, so let me get your coffee at least."

"You don't have to get me anything. Plus, you came with me to the game, and even paid for the food."

He smirks at me. "I already ordered it. I've had a gift idea for a while, I just figured I'd have some notice before your birthday came around."

Shaking my head, I grin and thank him for his consideration. It's hard to feel down around Nick, or like you don't matter because he's always so thoughtful. Even when you don't deserve it.

He hands me my favorite clear, curvy mug.

"Do you want to talk about last night?" he asks.

"Nope." I blow on the steam.

"Okay, but aren't you suspicious? I know we didn't get all the information, but if the accident happened on his way home, before the game started, wouldn't he have been out by the time the game ended, especially if all he had were cuts? And why couldn't the nurses find his name in the system?"

"I don't know, but once Sam gets home, I'm sure he'll explain." Except I don't really want him to. I just want this to blow over. No matter how you look at it, I'm the bad guy here.

"Or, he'll lie. Or, twist the questions around instead of providing answers, so you feel you're to blame. Like he did last night."

I know that better than anyone, but I don't want to deal with it. My head falls forward. "Nick."

"Cori." He steps in front of me and tilts my head up, his thumb grazing my jaw. "Please don't give up. Please don't accept his lame ass excuse. Demand answers until you get them."

I pull away from his touch, away from the eyes I could easily spend forever staring into, and go to Sam's room. I have to get ready for work, ready to smile at a bunch of strangers as if I'm not empty inside.

When I get back to the apartment after my eight-hour shift, Sam still isn't home. I call Hailey to pass the time while I wait for him, but she doesn't answer. I try not to let it hurt—it's late and she might be asleep. I try Sage next, but she doesn't answer either. As a last resort, I call my mother.

"Well, this is a nice surprise," she says upon answering.

"How are you? How's dad?"

"What's wrong? You sound close to tears."

"I am." I start pacing my usual track around the apartment anytime I have to make a phone call.

"Sweetheart, tell me what happened."

I tell her everything. Not some of the more intimate moments, or the plan to break it off with Sam, but everything else.

"He won't return my texts, and he hasn't come home yet." I sniffle.

She starts softly, "Well, sweetie, instead of being there for him when he needed you, you were at a baseball game with his roommate. I mean,"—she snickers—"did you expect him to understand that?"

"Not exactly. Based on all the other nights that he got caught up with work, I assumed last night was no different."

"But it's his career. It's not like he's off drinking or gambling or something."

"I know, but-"

"Listen, I know it can be lonely. But you can't expect him to just drop his work for you." Her tone is gentle, yet nauseating. "This is one reason why we keep telling you to go back to school or find something to keep your mind occupied while Sam is off making all that money that pays for your home. And your car, last I heard. You need a separate identity from just being Sam's girlfriend."

I stop pacing. I don't know what to do with all the rage inside from the conflicting advice and brushed-off feelings I just confided in her. I should have known better than to call Mom. Just a few days ago, I started to feel better than I had in a long time. Like I wasn't flailing about in mud, struggling to breathe.

"Do you feel better, sweetie?" Mom asks as my head slides back under.

But the only thing I can say is, "Yes. Thanks, Mom."

"Anytime, Sweetie."

After the phone call, I scrub the stove, clean out the refrigerator and pantry, and wipe down the windows —mindless tasks. I don't remember if I eat or not before I go to bed alone.

The next day, I work a double before busying myself with more chores. Right as I'm about to sink into bed, giving up hope that Sam will come home tonight, he finally walks through the bedroom door. He wears black athletic pants and a plain white t-shirt, the dark bruises standing out on his left arm.

"How did you get home? I texted you to let me know if I could come get you."

"Dad took me to get my car."

His answer has me blinking. "Your car? You can still drive it?"

"I wasn't in my car during the accident. I was in a coworker's. We were driving back from a meeting with a client at a restaurant, and he was going to drop me off."

I think about what Nick said, about demanding the answers and not letting him push off the blame, but I don't want to know the answers. I just want to hold him. So I rush to him, gently laying my head against his chest, and allow myself to cry. My body shakes from violent sobs as I let it all out—the guilt from being with Nick when Sam needed me and the bite of exhaustion from restless sleep.

"I'm so sorry."

"Hey, it's okay," he whispers into my hair. "I was just frustrated, you know. I do so much for you and it feels like I've had to beg for your attention. But I think we could both be better at communicating our plans to each other."

His arms wrap around my waist, squeezing a little too hard, but I don't protest. Nor do I protest when he starts planting sloppy, desperate kisses on my mouth and neck, or when he lays down on the bed. I do pull back to check that he's been cleared for sexual activity, but when he nods and pulls my body down on top of his, I give him what he needs.

He needs distraction, release, love. Every move of my hips is an apology, every kiss on his neck, his jaw, his lips, a promise to be better.

But when my eyes lock with Nick's, my own orgasm starts building, and I chase it with abandon.

Chapter 30
A Good Reason

Nick

I'm glad Sam's okay, but of all the nights for him to have a car accident, he sure picked a good one. Cori finally saw what I'd seen, what Hailey had seen, over the last few months and was ready to start demanding better for herself. Ready to stop wasting her time. But all that progress was thrown out the window because Sam knows how prone Cori is to absorbing all the blame.

After Cori runs off to Sam's room, my body buzzes with restlessness. I can't just sit around and wait to see what happens; I want to help her pack her things up in the cardboard boxes she hasn't thrown out yet because a car accident shouldn't change her mind. But sitting around waiting to see what will happen is all I *can* do.

To distract myself, I decide to make the drive to Mom's to finally have that talk about the house. I stand before my dresser, picking out clothes when I see the folded paper Cori gave me last night sitting next to my wallet. All the t-shirts in my drawer are pretty much the same, so I blindly grab one and pull it over my head before snatching up the poem.

I sit on the edge of my bed and take in each word three times.

Stories Written From Stories Told
New chapters can't begin
Until old chapters end,
We are made from the ashes of our past.
To allow us to dream on
After the dream is long gone,
The lessons learned build us to last;
To withstand the hell,
Then say farewell
After the winds calm from their rage.
So insert your key,
Push off and flee,
And don't look back at your cage.

At the bottom, there's a note: *Encouraging words have a nauseating effect if you're not ready to hear them. But I think you're ready now.*

She's right about one thing—I've heard from others, and myself, how football was just a chapter and that new and exciting things awaited me in the future. But when your dream is yanked away right as you're about to grasp it, you don't want inspiration or encouragement to keep going. You want answers. You want justice. You want life to return to you what it took because we all forget how unfair life can be.

Ashes of our past. Well, my dream certainly went up in flames.

Lessons learned. What exactly is the lesson that I learned by having my dream blocked off? To keep going? Again, not what I want to hear.

The only other lesson I learned was how to play football. I

learned the rules, to keep my elbows tucked in, to maintain a straight spine.

But that's not entirely true. I also learned dedication, team-work, punctuality, leadership, discipline, perseverance. All valuable lessons for any job. Or, life in general, I guess.

The more I think about it during the drive to Mom's, the more I realize the *lessons* she might have been referring to. Because football taught me a lot, but Mom taught me more—my dreams are worth fighting for.

Mom never once told me not to do something because it might not work out. And maybe that's just it. Maybe Mom didn't waste her money on football equipment or fees, maybe she was investing in her love and support for me. Maybe the lesson is that anything in life can be worth doing, can be worth loving, if only for a single second of joy.

Cori was right when she said that she and I are similar, about neither of us knowing what to do with our lives. But she was also wrong. She had two parents in her home, but there was double the love and support in mine from my mom alone.

So maybe football wasn't a waste of time; maybe it taught me my worth.

But why did it have to end? Why couldn't football have been my destiny, or fate, or whatever bullshit word you want to use? *To allow us to dream on after the dream is long gone.*

Most likely, I'll never get a clear answer as to why it had to end, but maybe therein lies the explanation I'm looking for—sometimes, shit just doesn't work out. And if whatever new thing I decide to tackle doesn't work out either, I'll survive because I know how to persevere.

Maybe Mom's love and support taught me something else. Maybe it taught me how to show the love and support for Cori that she doesn't get from anyone else.

And maybe that love and support will lead Cori somewhere else someday, even if it's not towards me. Maybe, once she rises from the *ashes* of her relationship with Sam, her confidence in herself will be an impenetrable force.

That's all I want for her.

Mom and Uncle Jonah, or whatever I should call him now, sit on a bench on the front porch. As I walk up the sidewalk, an image intrudes of gray-eyed children running up the stairs to visit their grandparents for the weekend. But I shake it out of my head before I can see the face of the woman who holds my hand.

Uncle Jonah has his arm around my mom's waist and lifts his chin off of her shoulder when I jokingly tell him to get off my Mom. They both stand for hugs and I smile at how happy Mom is. Her skin glows with a brightness that hadn't been there when they had to hide their relationship from me. But a weight still lingers on her shoulders.

"So, the house," I ask, sitting on a chair across from them.

"Yes, we need to discuss the house. We also have some news, but first, let's discuss your t-shirt."

I look down and notice for the first time which one I grabbed from my drawer. "Oh. Oops."

Uncle Jonah laughs at the words across my chest. *"Choking hazard. Package may contain large parts."*

My lips quirk upwards. "Sorry, Mom. It's actually Sam's shirt. Must have accidentally got mixed up with my laundry."

She rolls her eyes, most likely not believing a word I said. But I don't need to announce to the world how big my dick is because I don't need to compensate for being one.

"What news do you have?"

Mom waves her hand dismissively. "Oh, we can discuss it later, let's just enjoy the day."

"Is it something bad? Is someone sick or something?" My eyes flicker between both of them, but their faces give nothing away.

"No, we just have some news, that's all. But we can talk about it later."

"Can you at least tell me if it's good or bad? Or neutral? Or what it involves?"

Mom shakes her head and smiles at my persistence, but looks at Uncle Jonah before meeting my eyes.

"Okay, fine." She pauses, taking a deep breath. "I'm pregnant."

I choke on nothing. "Pregnant?" I ask. "Who's the fath-" I look at Uncle Jonah, who grins. "Oh, right."

There's pride fighting the guilt on his face, and I would laugh, but my brain struggles to comprehend the words Mom just said.

"You're not... you know... past the age where you can have a baby?" I ask gently, so as not to offend her.

"No, I'm only forty-one. Which isn't an ideal age to have a baby, but we've already done blood tests and genetic tests and everything, so far, looks great."

"How far along are you?"

"I'm 22 weeks." She must see the confusion on my face because she elaborates. "A pregnancy is forty weeks." My eyes reflexively look at her belly, but her shirt hangs loose on her body.

"At first, she thought she was entering menopause a little early, but..." Jonah pulls a strip of paper out of his pocket and holds it out for me.

I have no idea what the hell I'm looking at in the first few photos, but in the fourth, I finally see the silhouette of a baby.

A perfect, little baby.

"Why didn't you tell me when you told me about... you know, you two?"

"Because we figured it'd be too much at once. And we were waiting for some test results to come back," Mom answers, reaching for my hand. "We know this is crazy. It's a lot, it's shocking. But it's not going to change anything. You'll always be my baby. It's just... well, now we'll have a little girl to love."

I'm not worried about anything changing. I'm worried about how they'll both be almost sixty by the time this baby goes off to college. Mom had me when she was sixteen, but that was twenty-four years ago. She should be having grandkids soon, not children of her own. And I'll be almost fifty when this baby is my age.

"Wait. Did you say, girl?" I look from Mom to Uncle Jonah. "It's a girl?"

They both nod, Mom's eyes glistening with tears.

Well, shit. Another image appears uninvited, of a tiny little hand holding mine, her curly pigtails bouncing as she walks beside me. She looks up at me with eyes as green as the grass to match Mom's, and suddenly I want a little sister more than anything. Our family has always been small; Mom doesn't have any siblings and Dad's side of the family lives halfway across the country. We may be adding one little person to our family, but I know that little girl will be our whole world.

As for Mom, she'll be getting the family she always deserved. The one she was always meant to have if I hadn't gotten in the way and forced her to marry Dad. Maybe my whole existence is a mistake.

Is this what Cori feels like? A glitch the world was forced to find space for? Is this why nothing works out? Not Dad, not football, not school, not moving back and living at Sam's. Maybe I throw people off their own paths because I was never meant to exist, and the world has to throw me off of mine to correct the holes in destiny.

Here, in front of them, after they've shared such wonderful news, is not the time for an existential crisis. They deserve to be happy. I won't ruin it for them again.

Eventually, Mom rises to find a snack, leaving me alone with Jonah, and my knee bounces as I think of the right words to ask my question.

"Somethin' wrong?" he asks.

"Um..." Running my hands through my hair, I clear my throat and stretch my back. "How did you do it?"

He cocks his head.

"All those years, when Mom was with Dad. How did you deal with it? Watching her stay married to someone who didn't deserve her?"

"Well, it... it wasn't easy. It hurt. I tried to convince her to leave him, but she kept thinking she needed to keep her family together, for your sake."

God, that hurts.

"Where is this coming from?"

"Nowhere, just curious." His eyes narrow, and I give it up. I tell him how I've fallen for someone else's girlfriend. How I always seem to want what I can't have. How I feel helpless and desperate for Cori to wake up and see what I see.

His face remains unreadable throughout my spiel, but he won't judge me. He's been in this boat before.

"You know I'm a firm believer that everythin' happens for a reason. And,"—his face morphs into a sympathetic expression—"that's kinda the only advice I have for you. You just have to wait and see what happens. And know that if she's meant to leave him, she will. If you're meant to be together, you will be. Sorry, I know that doesn't help much. This is just one of those things where there ain't any clear answers."

This isn't news, but I couldn't help hoping he had some magical trick up his sleeve. I nod before dropping it, and ask, "So, all those lectures about using protection, and you just forgot to follow the advice yourself?"

Jonah chuckles. "You forget, I've been with your Mom for years now without knockin' her up. At least one out of a million condoms was bound to bust."

My hands fly up to cover my ears. "Okay, gross. Stop talking."

It was late when we finished dinner and I decided to stay the night. I helped Jonah with his plane some more the next day, avoiding the subject of Cori, and drove home Sunday evening.

The apartment is quiet when I arrive home. Neither Cori nor Sam are in the kitchen or living room, so I grab a bottle of water and head for bed. I use the light filtering from their open door to guide my way down the hall. But as I pass their room, I catch a glimpse of Cori on top of Sam, and I stop in my tracks, quickly pulling myself back out of sight.

They should know by now to close the door when they have sex. But it's not accidentally seeing something I shouldn't that has my heart clawing its way out of my chest.

It's the fact that they're having sex at all.

Because if they're having sex, that means Cori has thrown away all plans to leave him.

I don't think she saw me, her body faced the direction of the door, but her head was down looking at Sam. I lean against the wall and slowly peek around the corner to make sure I can pass without her noticing. But her eyes snap to mine.

And she doesn't stop.

She keeps moving on top of him. She rides *him* but her eyes are on *me*. Her mouth is slightly open, her hands on Sam's chest to brace herself. Her full breasts, covered by a black bra, bounce in tandem with her movements. And my feet are glued to the floor. I can't move, can't pull my eyes away. But I get the impression she doesn't want me to.

My face heats, my heart beating wildly out of control. I try to swallow, but can't get my body to do a single thing I demand of it. I have to grab onto the wall for support as my dick threatens to bust out of my jeans.

I wait for Sam to notice her attention on something besides him, but he doesn't. My eyes break away from Cori's only to follow Sam's hand as it trails up her body, over her breasts, inside her bra.

I don't know what the hell is happening. My brain barely registers the sight in front of me before my hand starts moving toward the bulge straining against my jeans. My breath comes out heavy and fast as Cori quickens her pace. She closes her eyes for a second before they fly back open and land on me. Her ardent gaze caresses my body, and I know every touch she plants on Sam's chest is meant for me.

I pull my hand away from my pants, disgusted with myself, but I stay put. Pretty confident that I'm helping her orgasm build, I don't want to ruin it for her. I can't imagine what a fly on the wall would think of the sight of my head peeking around the corner, watching like a creep, admiring her curves. But what I wouldn't give to be the one underneath her.

Finally, her eyes roll back in her head for a moment before meeting my gaze again, and we share the moment while her perfect body trembles.

Her release is mine too as I break free from her hypnosis. I walk straight to my room to pack my things. I can't stay here another minute, not after what I just did. I'll go back to Mom's if I have to, and wake up extra early on Monday to get to work.

But I call Callum instead.

"Can I crash on your couch?" I ask once he answers.

"Yeah, is everything okay?"

"No. I'll be there in a little while." I hang up before he can ask any more questions. I'll be able to confide in him without judgment, maybe even get some advice, if there's any to be given, but it'll have to wait until I'm out of here.

I quickly stuff everything I'll need for the next week into a bag, then sneak off to the bathroom to grab my shampoo and crap before heading toward my escape.

I snatch my keys off the table and reach for the doorknob when I hear Cori's voice behind me. "What are you doing?"

Turning, I find her wearing my sweatshirt of all things, arms crossed over her chest.

"I'm going to stay at Callum's."

"Why? Because of what just happened? I'm sorr-"

"Cori, don't you dare apologize. You did nothing wrong." I let out a shaky sigh. "There are several reasons why I can't stay here. One, I'm moving into an apartment next week anyway-"

"What?" The air stills. "When did you find an apartment?"

My eyes fall to the floor. "Friday"

"Were you going to tell me?"

"Yeah. At some point. But everything happened." Her arms tighten around herself as she shuffles her feet. "I assume you're going to stay with him."

She takes long enough to answer that I almost turn around and walk out the door. "Do I have a good reason to leave? Sam has done so much for me, he's good to me in his own way. You don't have to see it or understand it."

"You don't need a good reason to leave him. If you don't

want to be with him, don't be." Is that really what she's holding out for? A *good reason?*

Again, she considers her answer. And when she opens her mouth to speak, I ask, "What do you want, Cori? Not what Sam wants, not what your parents want, what do *you* want?"

"I have what I want."

Her words sting as the doubt creeps in. Did I imagine everything? Did I push her to her decision Friday night? Maybe she really does love him, maybe I don't know her as well as I thought. I'm certain I didn't imagine Sam's mistreatment of her, but maybe she truly wants to stay with him despite it all. It's not right, I know that. But if she doesn't want to leave him, there's nothing I can do.

"Then, can I have my sweatshirt back?"

"Your what?" She looks down when I point. "This is Sam's." Her breathing quickens when I shake my head. "I've worn this in front of you a million times. Why didn't you say anything?"

My eyes pierce hers. "I liked seeing you in it."

She doesn't blink. She doesn't breathe. She doesn't move. Until she rips the sweatshirt off her body, black, lacy bra gone with nothing replacing it, and throws it at me. "Goodbye, Nick."

"Cori-" But she's running down the hall to Sam's room.

To Sam.

Chapter 31
This Isn't a Coffee Shop

Cori

Guilt swirls in my belly. In my attempts at being the woman Sam wants when he initiates sex, the one who doesn't worry about turning the lights off or laying a towel over the sheets, I ignored the open door. I was the woman who went along with the spontaneity. But when Nick peeked in, I couldn't pull my eyes from him. No matter how much I commanded my eyes to look away, to stop, to cover myself, I couldn't.

All the times Nick was home when Sam wasn't, all the words of encouragement Nick offered, kept my eyes glued to his. Thoughts of how it'd feel if he were the one underneath me snuck in uninvited, and it resulted in the best orgasm I've had in a long time. Of course, it could be attributed to having one at all. Or, it could be that I wasn't staring at a blank wall or praying for it to be over. Instead, an intense, dark pair of eyes shared that passionate moment with me, and we weren't even touching. But now I feel about as low as a person can.

After all, who was responsible for that orgasm, Sam, Nick, or me?

And what did he mean he *liked* seeing me in his sweatshirt? What did he mean when he backed me against the wall? *"You can be sure you'll never be in tears after I fuck you."* There's no way he's fallen for me. Maybe he's lonely, or sadder than I realized. He'd have to be, to want me.

I laid in bed last night so conflicted about how to feel that I didn't feel anything at all. After a sleepless night, I drove to work, prepared to pretend like last night didn't happen. Determined not to let his words affect me, determined to ignore the pull of gravity and stay upright. I don't need Nick or his belief in me, or his comforting shoulders.

Now, as I open the door to the diner, carrying a file with recipes and the social media account information Mike asked me to bring, I try summoning the excitement I've had since we rolled out my ideas. I haven't cried on my drive to work in a few weeks, finally feeling like I had a purpose, that I hadn't given up on life, as Dad likes to say. But today, I just wanted to hide under the covers.

Mike and some other servers are gathered around an unfamiliar woman in uniform when I walk back to his office. I didn't know we were hiring anyone new. Her blonde hair is held back in a neat ponytail, a cheerful smile lighting up her pretty face.

When Mike spots me, he gestures for me to join them. "Cori. This is Tessa, and of course, you know Kiersten already." He points to a server I've worked with for years. "We're moving Kiersten behind the counter instead. Did you know she used to work at a coffee shop? Your dad and I thought she'd be better at the counter, you know, for when we add more drinks to the menu and roll out the premade breakfast sandwiches."

"Wait. What?"

"Well, we're hoping to have more to-go business. And with more coffee orders, we'll need someone experienced."

"Okay, and what about me?" My heartbeat picks up. Is it finally the moment? Do I get to start training for assistant manager? Full-time instead of half a day?

"You'll return to the floor. As normal. And Tessa here is the new assistant manager." He smiles like it's good news. As if a fire doesn't rage inside me, ready to burst forth and consume everyone in my path.

I jerk back as if physically pushed from the realization—this was their plan all along. To use my ideas and free labor before ripping any hopes of advancement from my naive, inexperienced hands.

"What's wrong?" he asks. "Isn't this what you wanted?"

"What did you need these for?" I ask breathlessly, holding up the binder.

"Well, we need the recipes for Kiersten to use, and Tessa's going to run the social media accounts."

The hot blood in my face boils over, spewing the words before I can tame them, "If Kiersten is so much more experienced than I am, she can use her own recipes. And if I'm not going to be compensated, you're not getting the passwords to the accounts."

His mouth hangs open. "What do you mean, *compensated?*"

"I did all of this work off the clock. With the assumption that it would be *me* taking the assistant manager position. We talked about it being *me*, remember?"

"Yes, but in the end, your father wanted someone with experience. He thanks you for your ideas, but... come on, Cori. You're a waitress. That's all you've ever been. You have no other experience to offer us."

"You used to be a server. For two years. Then, you were promoted. That's how it works. I've been here for five. And I know more about this diner than you or Dad *combined*." My voice is shockingly calm, despite my entire body shaking with anger and nerves.

Everything I've done was for nothing. I mean, it helped my dad out, but... that's just it though. It helped Dad.

Everything I've done is microscopic compared to the accomplishments of other people in my life. In truth, I've done nothing except entertain dreams I have no business dreaming. I'm not a barista. And this isn't a coffee shop.

So I take my file with my recipes and log-in info, and I walk out the door. Dad will tell me later that I gave up once again. That I stopped fighting. But why do something if I no longer see the point?

Once I get back to Sam's apartment—because it's always been *Sam's* apartment, never mine—I go to *Sam's* room. I take my notebook, the one with notes on different coffee suppliers with their prices and flavors, and the pros and cons of using them as my roaster. Then I go to *Sam's* kitchen and grab the remaining coffee samples from the cabinet. And I throw it all into *Sam's* trash can.

I crawl underneath *Sam's* covers, where I can cry and not be shamed. But no tears come. I have no one to blame but myself, and I'm tired of being upset about it, but I don't know how to fix it. That's the problem, isn't it? I don't know. I don't know myself or what I want or what I feel or what I think. I don't know what to do or where to go or when to do it. I don't know what's right or wrong. And I don't know the reason to keep trying to figure it all out.

Nick

Shamelessly, I slept with my sweatshirt over my pillow last night.

I asked for it back before I could stop myself with every intention to shock her. But I was the one who couldn't pry my eyes from her chest, or close my mouth until she was already gone. I almost left it behind on the table in the hallway. Then I caught a whiff of my soap mingling with Cori's coffee and floral scent, and I couldn't part with it. So I brought it with me to Callum's one-bedroom apartment, slept on his short couch with the peeling leather, and dreamt of Cori.

I told him everything when I arrived, every detail, every feeling between Cori and me, every long look shared, and every demeaning comment I'd heard Sam say. To cheer me up, he invited Tyler to watch a baseball game with us after work today. Yet, all I can think of is the game I saw with Cori two nights ago. Was that only two nights ago?

My phone rings, interrupting the game. The name on the screen is Sam's, and I debate letting it go to voicemail. But I man up and answer it as I walk out the front door for privacy; God only knows how ugly this conversation will be.

"Hey, I can't get a hold of Cori, can you go see if she's in my room? She's probably sleeping again. She's always fucking sleeping."

She's not *always* sleeping. And if she is, it's because her low self-worth keeps her awake at night.

"I'm not there. I moved out," I answer, calmly.

"What do you mean you *moved out?*"

"I mean, I moved out."

"When? Why didn't you tell me?"

"Why didn't you tell me you slept with Kenna?"

The line is silent as he thinks about how to worm his way out of this.

"She was lonely. You were distant, only focused on football and you ignored her. Sorry if I wanted her to be cared for."

I almost laugh. What kind of answer is that? "Can you just do me a favor? Can you just treat Cori right? You're an ass to her and she doesn't deserve it. She's too good for you and you know it. Step up, be a man, and treat her with respect. And encourage her to continue with her coffee business. Don't crush it like you do everything else."

I should hang up now, but stupidly, I don't.

"Are you in love with her?" he asks, tone dripping with accusation.

I decide it's time for honesty. "Yes."

"And you have the nerve to be pissed at me because I was the one Kenna cheated on you with."

"The same reason you just gave me for sleeping with Kenna, is the same reason I have for falling for Cori." I understand it's not justified. I understand I'm still in the wrong. But he has no right to talk.

He laughs, a cruel, mocking, sound that sets my nerves on fire. "And yet, she stayed with me." More laughter. "Kenna chose me over you, and now Cori. Man, you can't catch a break."

"Because you manipulate them, Sam. Believe me, I will be

praying that she leaves you. Not for me, but for herself." I end the call and let my head fall in my hands.

After a moment, I go back inside and resume my spot on the couch. From my left, Tyler rubs my back. I look at him.

"Sorry, is that weird? It felt like a back-rub moment."

"I think it's a stiff drink kind of moment."

Callum jumps into action. "I can do that."

After he hands me a glass of scotch, I tell them what Sam said over the phone.

Just as disgusted as I am, Callum picks his phone up to call Cori to check on her, but she doesn't answer. He sends a text instead, letting me see the screen.

> Callum: Hey, just checking on you. How are you doing?

While we wait for a response, hoping we get one at all, he asks, "Should we tell Cori? About Kenna?"

"I have no idea." I've debated myself, since the beach house, about whether or not I should tell her. "I don't know if it's my place or if she'd rather not know. If it's even something she needs to know."

"I would want to know. Especially since he keeps bringing her around." We drink in silence, refilling our glasses when we've drained them.

Tyler sits up. "Wait. You don't think they're *still...*"

I shake my head, another thing I've warred with myself over. "He's gone all the time. It's highly possible."

"I don't want to just turn my back on, what? Five, six years of friendship? I understand why you would, but what do *we* do?" He gestures between himself and Callum. "I don't want to be friends with someone like that."

I don't have any more answers than he does.

"Shit. Sorry, I'm making this about me."

"I could use the distraction. Let's talk about your hair next."

His hands fly up to his head. "What's wrong with my hair?"

But my phone dings with a text, and we all scramble to see it.

Roommate: I need you.

Chapter 32
What Hurts the Most

Cori

It's evening by the time I decide to face reality. I get out of bed to use the bathroom and get some water. My phone is on silent, and I check to see if anyone cares at all that I walked out of my job this morning.

There are eleven missed calls: two from Sage, two from Mike, one from Dad, three from Mom, two from Sam, and one from Callum. I have four voicemails, but I ignore those, instead reading the text messages.

> Sage: Where did you go?
>
> Sage: Mike is pissed.
>
> Sage: Dad is pissed too.
>
> Sage: At least talk to me, I didn't do anything wrong.
>
> Dad: Cori, call me back immediately.
>
> Mom: You've upset your dad. Call him back, please.
>
> Mom: Cori Lorraine, you're acting like a child.

> Sam: What the hell are you doing? I've called you ten times.

> Callum: Hey, just checking on you. How are you doing?

I ignore them all and busy myself with chores, because what else am I good for? I am here to quietly serve others. That's what Mom meant when she told me to find an identity other than *Sam's girlfriend.* Do what he needs done, but don't expect anything in return. And fall to my knees with gratefulness when he blesses me with his attention.

My hands are wet and soapy from the water when my phone rings. It's Sam this time. I use my nose to press the green button, accepting the call. It takes a few tries, but I finally get it and shout, "Hold on," while I work on hitting the speaker button. "Okay, I'm good. Are you on your way home?"

"No, I have to work late again."

"I understand." I'd avoid me too if I could.

"What the hell have you been doing? I've called you a hundred times. Didn't we just have this issue?"

"I'm sorry, I didn't hear my phone." A half lie.

"I was calling because I ordered your favorite from Francesca's, to make up for me having to work late again. It should be delivered soon."

"Oh, thank you." Ugh.

"I'll always take care of you, Cor. I love you."

I hear a thud as if he chunked his phone, but he forgot to hang up. I sigh, trying to hit the button with my nose again, but the screen is dark and I can't get it to light back up. I turn the water off, dry my hands, and reach for my phone. But my hand stills when I hear an impalpable female voice.

Sam's response is clear. "Yeah, I've got a couple of hours at least."

I don't know how long I'm locked in place, listening. There's more talking between her and Sam, but they're further away from the phone making their words unintelligible. The laughter, however, the playful giggling, is crystal clear. Then moaning. Unmistakable moaning. And banging, the steady rhythm of two things rocking against each other. Like a jar against a counter. Maybe a fist against a table.

Or, a headboard against a wall.

Slowly, I raise my hand to end the call. Then I slide to the floor against the counters, the realization settling like ash. Not the realization that he's seeing someone else—I already knew. Deep down, I knew. But the realization that I don't care.

I don't care that he's cheating on me. I don't care that it's not me he wants. I don't care if my childhood memories are now ruined. I don't care about making a scene, or doing the right thing, or acting reasonably.

What hurts the most is that I've done this to myself. If only I were more confident in myself, if only I knew my own mind, if only I knew what I wanted out of life. If only I stood up and went after it. Then I wouldn't still be here to be cheated on.

It would be so easy for me to leave. Not just Sam's, but this life. I could build a new one, maybe in a cabin in the woods, or a private island. Maybe I'll send a postcard now and then, just to keep them from looking too hard for me. Not that anyone would; I'm not needed.

After Mom and Dad had Stephanie, they prayed for a boy. Instead, they got twin girls. Not just one unwanted girl, but two. Of course, they loved us. In their own strange way, they loved us all the same. But they don't need me. I'm the middle child, unsuccessful with no personality, and when I die, some will ask, *"Which one was she?"*

"The shy one," the others will reply.

The boring one, the expendable one, the one with no valuc.

I most likely don't have a job anymore. But even if I did, there are a million other servers just like me who can fill the position just fine. Better, even.

And Sam. He has someone else to see to his needs now. Maybe he's had them all of this time.

What I don't understand is, why not end it with me first? Why juggle me and another woman simultaneously? Is that the reason he's so stressed—trying to keep his lies straight and his lovers separate?

A knock sounds at the door, but I ignore it.

Instead, I look around at the sink still full of dishes and counters that need wiping. I think of the laundry that needs to be switched. A comfortable bed that calls to me. Books upon books that want to be read. A TV with any show you can think of to watch. But I don't want to do any of that. I don't want to sit on the floor, I don't want to talk to anyone, I don't want to be alone, I don't want to do anything. I don't even want to do nothing.

My phone dings. I reach up to grab it and see Sage's name on the screen.

> Sage: How's Sam doing after the accident he was in? He was in someone else's car, right? Maybe Kenna's? Apparently, she was in an accident too. Let me know if I need to kick his ass. Or hers.

Along with the text, there's a screenshot of Kenna's latest photo shared on social media. The date shows Friday. Her face is cut up, and she lies in what looks like a hospital bed, based on the tan side rails beside her head. The caption says, *"Red means stop. Now I have to buy a new car."*

No. What truly hurts the most, is that I've denied myself the one thing I want, while Sam has denied himself nothing.

I've gone after things I wanted before. But only when I felt I deserved them, and only when I thought the timing was as perfect as it could get. Like dessert, only after I ate a balanced meal. Or a new book, only after working extra shifts. Well, I'm still *technically* involved with Sam, so the timing couldn't be worse. However, as I've already declared, I don't care.

For once in my life, where I overthink every decision until I end up not deciding at all, I don't care.

There's a knock at the door, followed by the sound of it opening.

"Cori?" Nick calls out.

He finds me, still in the kitchen, still on the floor. He must have found the bag of food outside because he places it on the counter. Kneeling in front of me, he caresses my cheek, and I lean into the warmth for a moment.

"What do you want, Cori?" he had asked me just last night.

I'm ready to admit my answer. *You.* So I take it. No over-thinking. Just action.

I lunge at the love in his eyes, my mouth crashing against his. In an instant, he's lifting me off the ground and I'm wrapping my legs around his waist. All I know is his tongue stroking mine in a hurried frenzy before he sets me down on the counter. Hands everywhere. Tangled in my hair, mine in his, so feather-soft. Down my back. Possessively, yet softly, around my neck.

I don't know if this is wrong; it only feels right as he plants soft kisses at my ear and down my throat, sending volts of electricity to every nerve ending.

But he stops. He pulls back. Our breath comes out fast and heavy, dancing together in the few inches between us.

He opens his mouth. To stop this. To say we shouldn't, that it's inappropriate.

Before he can, I blurt out, "He's cheating on me. And I'll be damned if I'm going to stop myself from being with you just because of a technicality. I've denied myself so much of what I want because I didn't feel deserving or whatever. So, just kiss me." The longer he stares at me without moving, the more doubt creeps in. "Unless you don't want to and I misread things, or imagined-"

His finger covers my lips. "You imagined nothing. I've wanted you for a while now, and you know it. But I think I should tell you something first." His Adam's apple bobs as he swallows, and he pulls away.

Too much has occurred today, and I don't want to sit here and listen to whatever news is making him hesitant. He won't meet my eyes, and that can only mean the news will shatter me.

"I think he may be sleeping with Kenna. The guys and I... we think it's Kenna."

I search his face. "What do you mean? You knew?"

His eyes dart between mine and his breathing quickens. "No. I mean, not for certain. But the guys and I were talking-"

"About *my* relationship?"

"No, about our *friend*."

I hop off the counter, looking around for what, I don't know. I suspected, so it only makes sense that they did too. But it still stings.

"Cori, I would have told you if I had known for certain, but I didn't want to alarm you over a possibility."

I know he would have, and taking one glance at his face extinguishes the shame and hurt.

"Look, it's not a big deal. I know you would have told me. It just sucks, that's all." He pulls me into him, and I bury my face in his chest.

I already know it's her, but I want all the information I can get. "What makes you think it's Kenna?" I ask, enjoying his warmth and strong arms wrapped around me. I feel like I'm in a strange dream. One that starts and ends as a nightmare, but with so many highs and lows in between that I won't be able to make sense of it in the morning.

His voice shakes. "Umm... well, *that* you might get mad at."

I pull back. "Why?"

"She told me at the dance hall that Sam was the one she cheated on me with." He jumps into the explanation. "I didn't know if I should tell you because it happened before you and Sam got together. I almost told you a few times, but... in the end, I didn't."

Calmly, I say, "It's okay. I understand."

"You do?"

"Yeah. I don't know what I would have done in that situation, either."

He can sense something is wrong though, his gaze is searching, and his body is tense.

"I also understand now why you came. Why you kissed me. Why you've slowly been worming your way into my heart." He's only just given life to the very fears I'd stifled. How could I ever think, especially after what just happened with Sam, that someone like Nick would be attracted to me?

"What do you mean? I have feelings for you. Cori," he reaches out, but I back away, "This, us, has *nothing* to do with that."

Toneless and emotionless, because my brain is doing what it does best and detaching to protect itself, I say, "No, you did so for revenge. Sam slept with your girlfriend, so you were trying to sleep with his."

"Cori, that's not fair. Revenge has nothing to do with it." He grabs my shoulders, but I shake off his grasp and stumble backward.

"Cori. Please. I swear to you."

But I can't think of another explanation. I allowed myself to think maybe he cared, maybe he saw past my flaws, but why would anyone overlook everything that's wrong with me?

I can't watch his lips tremble. Either I'll cry, or I'll move towards him. And neither option is preferred because decisions shouldn't be made while my head spins.

I just found out my boyfriend is cheating on me and I'm devastated. Only, I'm devastated because another man's feelings for me aren't what I thought.

I'm so stupid.

"Please, just give me some time." I walk to Sam's room with Nick right behind me.

"Okay. Yeah, okay, you're right. You're feeling a lot of things right now, and you need some time to process it all. But do not think for one second that I don't care."

I close the door in his face and move around packing a few things as quickly as I can. Clothes for a few days, toiletries, books. But when I'm done, I can't get my feet to move.

Where am I going to go? I can't go to my parents' house because Dad's there. I can't go to Hailey's because I ruined that friendship. I try calling Sage but she doesn't answer.

A white corner pokes out from a book lying inside my bag. It's a book that belonged to Grandma, a collection of popular—albeit, creepy—fairy tales, bound in leather. Necessary to pull me out of my own nightmare.

I pull it out and open it to a photo of Grandma and me, around eight years old, stashed between the pages. We sat on the porch swing, both oblivious to the camera because we had our noses in books. I smile as tears well up. Tears for the little girl in the photo and tears for Grandma, because of what I'd done to her granddaughter.

Returning the book inside the bag, I decide. I'm going to the place that always smelled like peanut butter pie and coffee, where popcorn and ice cream were acceptable dinners on Sunday night, where it was impossible to be anything but happy and carefree. The place where trouble can't reach me.

I'm going to Grandma's house.

Chapter 33
Only Memories Remain

Cori

The highway splits the fields of corn as if it's a bridge leading to the secluded island ahead where the sharks can't reach you.

I haven't been back here since before Grandma passed away. How painful will it be to find all of her belongings sifted through, her furniture given away? To walk into the kitchen and not find her twirling the bottom of her coffee cup on the table, her chin sitting in her other hand as she stares dreamily out the window?

I've been on the road for an hour when I finally turn onto the country gravel road. Fireflies illuminate my way as I drive past acres of farmland, a couple of cow pastures, and some old, weathered barns. It takes five minutes to reach their driveway, and when I make the turn, I see what I've always seen when the cornstalks part: the bright blue house, starkly breathtaking against a cloudy gray sky. And Grandma and Grandpa swaying in the porch swing.

I throw the car in park and jump out as Grandpa descends the steps and invitingly opens his arms. Running up the sidewalk, I'm eager to be wrapped in one of Grandpa's bear hugs, but as soon as I approach him, he disappears.

He fades.

Into nothing.

I blink at the space he occupied for a moment before my eyes fly to the porch swing. But Grandma's no longer there either, and I feel so, so stupid. I don't remember the last time I ate and I'm probably dehydrated. If that wasn't enough, I'm an emotional wreck. I got so lost in my desire to be hugged, to lean on someone else for a little while, that I forgot—only memories remain to greet me.

Because loneliness and pain follow now, even to Grandma's house.

I run back to the car to get the bag I left behind in my temporary moment of insanity, and walk back up to the yard. The rain holds off, but the wind roars, whipping my hair in my face and blowing me back to a time when I was five.

The wind was fierce and I struggled to stay upright as I walked up to the house at Grandma's call, but I was blown backward onto my butt. That happens when you're smaller than the force pushing against you. Smaller and weaker. Grandma just laughed and rushed out to help me up and walk me inside. But she's not here to do that anymore.

I'm at the steps when I hear a rustling from the garden. It sat, tall and green, just off the side porch and a dog jumped out. It was Otie, Grandma and Grandpa's bull terrier, pouncing on the old watermelon rinds Grandpa had just thrown out. I laugh, then I'm startled by Sage, twelve years old, telling Spencer to look through the metal pipe that holds the slats of the porch swing. He did, and a frog jumped out onto his face, then he screamed and ran around until it finally leaped off.

I step onto the porch and unlock the front door with the spare key found under a rock in the flower bed. A blast of coffee-scented air hits me as I step inside, and walk past Spencer and I, playing with marbles in the front room. Past my siblings and I eating popcorn in the living room, crowded around a movie playing on their tiny TV. Past Sage and I, surfing down the staircase on storage tote lids.

In the kitchen, Grandma sat at the table, her chin in one hand, mug in the other, and a game of dominoes laid out before her, ready for game night. Grandpa held up the coffee pot, his eyebrows raised in question. I nod and grab the plastic cookie jar usually filled with Grandma's homemade rice crispy treats and a clean coffee cup, but when I set the items down on the table, they fall to the floor.

Staring at the cup and cookie jar, my brain is incapable of understanding. The table isn't there. Because Grandma and Grandpa aren't there.

Once again, I'm reminded that I'm all alone.

I lean down to pick up the mug and empty cookie jar, shaking my head and thankful the rug cushioned the fall, but when I stand up, nothing is as it was before. I see everything clearly now, not how I wish it were still. The wallpaper peeling off the walls, a crack forming in the wood of one of the window frames, the wood floor in the corner chipping away. The house falls apart, all the clutter of my grandparent's everyday lives disappearing along with any hope of my rescue. I wanted an escape, not a harsh reality that things can never again be what they once were because the magic of grandparents is gone.

As I scan the room, my eyes fall on the screen door to the side porch. I go to it and fling it open, unsure if my mind is playing tricks on me. The garden. It turns brown, then gray before my very eyes. The corn stalks fall and dry up. The door to the cellar caves in, and weeds shoot up around it.

I step off the porch, following the destruction to the back of the house. The paint from the chicken house dissolves into the air, leaving weathered wood behind; the same happens to the once-white barn. The tires deflate on Grandpa's enclosed trailer parked off to the side, weeds growing up from underneath.

I run to the two trees that stand side by side, leaning against one, trying to catch my breath. But I fall. Just like the table, they aren't there. They've been cut down at some point, probably so they didn't interfere with the power lines above. I stand up and take off, running away from their disappearance, away from reality, because I've surely lost it now.

Then I hear the hum of a tractor. Back from a long day out in the fields, Grandpa pulled his tractor into the front barn. I run to catch up to him, to jump into his arms where everything is safe and sure. But when I get to the door, it's empty. Completely empty, not even the old feed sacks litter the ground anymore. Not even the old front door is leaned up against the wall. Not even the doghouse sits in the corner.

I turn around and see the taillights of the maroon car, this vision an invention of my brain. During this memory, I was inside that car looking out at my grandparents and seeing them together for the last time before Grandpa passed away.

I look at them now, as I saw them then. They waved as they watched us pull away. They sat down on the swing. They pulled each other close and watched the fireflies guide us home.

The edges of their memory dissolve into the air.

And I fall, without the cushion of childhood bliss to catch me.

Nick

My knee bounces, my knuckles ache from being cracked repeatedly, and my shoulders are tense and full of knots. After she shut the door to Sam's room in my face, I reluctantly got dressed and left, hating myself. I knew she needed space, and not just because she'd asked for it, but because the light disappeared from her eyes, just like at dinner with her parents. I texted her after I got back to Callum's and asked if she'd let me know if she left and when she safely arrived wherever she'd go. I've sent a few more texts and called her, but it's been two hours and I have yet to receive anything. I'm going insane.

Callum slaps my shoulder. "Man, relax. I'm sure she's fine."

I shake my head. "She was pissed. But the scary kind where you don't really feel the emotions until a bit later and it all comes crashing into you." I didn't tell them we kissed. And would have done a lot more had I not pulled away. But I told them what she knew about Sam, and what I had admitted.

I stand and pace the living room like Cori does when there's too much nervous energy in her body to handle. Like when she's on the phone with her parents or waiting for Sam because they're running late for something.

Tyler is completely unbothered, eating chips straight from the bag, cheese dust covering his fingers and his mouth. Little flakes float to the couch, where I'll be sleeping tonight.

"Why are you such a fucking child?" I snap.

He looks at Callum, then back at me. "What the hell did I do?"

Sighing, I sit back down on the couch. I shouldn't be taking it out on him. They've done nothing but be here for me. "Nothing. Sorry."

I reach for my phone again, but texting her once more isn't going to accomplish anything. Besides, she may be driving and unable to use her phone.

"I've never felt like this before," I admit.

"Like what? Anxious?" Callum asks.

Like she's driving off with my heart. Like I can't focus because my entire being is wherever she is, and I can't even imagine my own surroundings because she could be anywhere right now. But I don't admit that out loud.

Instead, I say, "Yeah."

My phone rings and I whip it up to my ear so fast it hurts. "Hello?"

"Is she with you?" It's Sam again, the last person I want to speak to at this moment. His voice is terrifying, full of venom and rage.

Rubbing my eyes and breathing deeply, I respond, "No, she's not."

"Tell me the truth, Porter. Give her the phone," he commands.

"She's not here."

Sam shouts through the phone loud enough that Tyler and Callum can hear. "I know she is, don't make me come over there!" He doesn't realize I never told him where I was staying.

"She discovered you were cheating on her and she left you, but she didn't come here. I don't know where she is."

Callum snatches the phone from my hand. "Sam, she's not here. We're sitting here worrying about her, waiting for her to let us know she's safe somewhere. But you can bet that when we find out, we won't be telling you." He ends the call and hands the phone back.

I'm done waiting. I grab my keys and slip my boots on.

Tyler stands from the couch and puts the chip bag away in a cabinet.

"Where are we going?" he asks, washing his hands and wiping his mouth.

"I don't know, but I have to start looking somewhere."

Callum puts his hands up. "Just stop. You're only going to waste gas. Have you tried calling Sage? Or Hailey?"

"I would if I had their numbers." I snap my fingers as a thought occurs. "Her grandmother's. That's probably where she went." I grab the doorknob and start to turn it but stop. "I don't know where the farm is."

"I have Sage's number, I'll call her," Tyler says. He puts it on speaker and my heart races as it rings.

"Hello?"

"Do you know where Cori is? Have you spoken to her?" I ask without greeting.

"Hi, hello, how are you doing? I'm good, not that you asked."

I roll my eyes, waiting for her to go on.

"She tried to call me earlier, but I missed-"

"Seriously? What if she needed help?"

Callum pushes on my chest. "Calm down."

"If you'd let me finish..." Sage adds. "I missed her call, but Mom just called and the security alarms went off at the farm. She had a neighbor drive by and they recognized Cori's car. I'm almost there now."

"See?" Callum points to my phone. "She's good. Now chill."

"I'm sorry, Sage. I'm just worried about her." I run my hands through my hair, gripping a little.

"Yeah, me too. She was pretty pissed when she walked out of work this morning, then the whole Kenna thing. She didn't respond to my text, but I imagine it was upsetting."

Tyler's eyebrows furrow. "What text? And why did she walk out of work? Because of Sam?"

"No, because of Dad. And Mike," she says, like it's obvious.

When she realizes we don't know what she's talking about, she explains that Cori was overlooked at work for the assistant manager position. And that Mike and her dad have the nerve to be upset with her because she took off with some important information and the other recipes. *Her* recipes. Not theirs.

"And I texted her a screenshot of Kenna's last post on social media. The one where she's lying in a hospital bed?"

I flex my fists, anger coiling down my spine. Not just at my dumbass ex, but it meant so much to Cori to have her dad accept her ideas, and to feel like she was part of the diner, not just some employee. It took a lot for her to put herself out there and make her ideas known. She wanted to feel essential, to have a purpose. She already had that, but too many people in her life made her feel otherwise.

She's out there dealing with the rejection all alone, and I hate myself for doing what I did. Although, I'm still unsure where I went wrong. Should I have told her earlier about Kenna? Or not at all?

Tyler hangs up the phone after I give Sage strict instructions to keep me informed. But I don't ask where the farm is because Cori's asked for her space and I have to respect that. Regardless of how much I want to go to her and hold her. And tell her I love her.

Chapter 34
Sweetheart, Have You Been Drinking?

Cori

The sky opened up and poured on me while I sat in the yard, but I barely noticed. The moon appears now, full and bright. At some point, Sage arrived and made me drink water. She hasn't said a word, though, at least not one I've heard.

Eventually, the tears run out and the fear creeps in. I hear rustling in the corn stalks a couple feet away and there could be anything waiting to jump out and attack. It won't be Otie this time, I know that now. So I finally stand, brush myself off, and walk toward the porch. Sage follows.

"You can go home now. I'll be fine."

"Oh, really? You've barely responded to my presence, you're drenched both from rain and tears, but you're fine?"

"Yes. I'm fine. The water helped. And I need to eat."

"There's no food here, but I can go pick up something from the gas station. I think it's still open."

She turns me by my shoulder to look closely into my eyes. "Are you going to be okay for a few minutes?"

"I'll be fine. Go." I push on her arms and walk up the steps to the porch swing.

Nothing is stopping me from staying out here all night, just me and the entrancement of the sky. The stars are many and vibrant in the clear country with no other light to dull their sparkle, now that the clouds are gone. Maybe that's what I need, I think to myself as if I need any more convincing—to get away from all those voices that speak over my own and cloud my judgment. To learn how to recognize what my own voice even sounds like.

The stars twinkle as if someone is winking. Like Grandpa used to wink at us when he'd play a prank on Grandma or Dad.

Maybe it's him now, telling me I'm thinking in the right direction. Maybe he's telling me I can still find peace here, even without them. Maybe I can find it in the strong, cool breeze that caresses my skin. Or in the hum of the cicadas or soft sway of the trees. Maybe in the view of the expansive stretch of land so far out I almost believe I can see the curves of the Earth. It's this humbling view that reminds me how small I am and how minuscule and unimportant my problems truly are.

Those minuscule and unimportant problems become raging wildfires because I continuously breathe life into the flames. Simultaneously, I brush off the things I shouldn't and carry loads that only weigh me down. It's those comments from Sam or my parents, about my weight or my job, that aren't worth my time thinking about. Instead, I could use the energy I spend trying to be better—according to their definition—and use it to fight for the things that truly matter. Like setting boundaries or trusting my instincts.

Hailey had said, *"I can't sit back and watch you hate your-self while you continue to let him treat you like shit. I'm done."*

And Nick. *"Then, can I have my sweatshirt back?"*

I know it's a strong word and a slight exaggeration, but they were right to *abandon* me. Because even I had abandoned myself. I saw myself as a lost cause, not worth fighting for. But there's a responsibility in living whether you ask to be born or not. Not just to breathe, but to *live*.

I come back to myself here under these stars and make a promise to seek therapy, to fight for myself, and to never abandon myself again. I've found comfort in the sadness and the anxiety. Safely confined in the cage. For so long, I've been blind, unable to understand the point of anything. I swim and swim, exhausting myself trying to stay afloat, and for what? But I have that answer now—me.

A couple of days pass. Sage stayed the first night but went home the next morning with the promise of keeping Mom and Dad away for a while. Other than a trip to the store, I've spent most of my time on the porch swing admiring the view of nothing but green fields. Occasionally, a tractor will slowly drive by, a cow will moo in the distance, a bird will sing. Sometimes it's a short staccato, other times a graceful melody. Otherwise, there's nothing but the wind and soft rustle of the leaves as the trees sway.

There was an incident with a snake while I hung laundry on the line, but I managed it with a good scream as I ran back to the porch.

The land is healing; I've always thought so. The moment I set foot on the ground, it's as if the soil recognizes me, like a ley line. The blood, sweat, and tears, dissolved into the Earth throughout the years while Grandpa worked the fields, recharges my soul. And there's a whisper on the wind, as it blows the loose tendrils of my hair back and drifts across my skin, that says, *"You belong."* There's nothing but peace to be found here. Now that I've eaten and gotten some distance, that is.

The house is mostly empty, no beds, towels, or dishes remain. Tools and paintbrushes, random pieces of wood, and a few broken items litter the space, but if I find myself bored and itching to do something, I clean. I've slept in a pile of blankets I bought at the store and used mostly disposable dishes, but an idea pops into my head. What would Mom and Dad say if I offered to fix the place up in exchange for free, or at least, discounted rent?

Now that I think about it, they'll probably decline. Dad, the man who didn't trust me to do a job I'd already proved I could do, would only ask, *"What do you know about remodeling?"* And that's if we were on *good* terms.

As I watch the clothes on the line swing on a breeze rolling through, Mom and Dad's car pulls up the driveway. I try slinking back into the shadows on the porch, sidling up against the wall toward the door, hoping I can hide before they spot me. My car is out front, but maybe they'll think I'm out exploring the back pastures.

However, Mom hops out of the car before I can get inside. "Cori Lorraine, we saw you already!"

Damn.

"I was just going to make coffee," I lie. Except, I forgot. I haven't had a drop of coffee since I arrived because there's no coffee maker. I've destroyed my stomach lining with the amount of ibuprofen consumed just to keep the caffeine headache manageable.

I lean against the column supporting the roof so that it may support me as well. Mom and Dad approach, expressions of impatience upon their faces, and cross their arms in unison.

I swallow the lump in my throat.

"Sage said to give you a few days. Well? It's been a few days."

I shrug a shoulder. "What exactly is your question?"

Mom jumps in. "She said you and Sam got in a fight."

"Sort of. I haven't spoken to him, but I found out he's cheating on me." It takes Mom a moment to understand the shocking news clashing with my calm demeanor. When the light bulb goes off, her shoulders slump inwards and her arms fall to her side.

"Oh, no." She walks up the steps to me with open arms and I fall into her embrace, letting the tears fall, not because of what I said, but because it was nice to have her react the way I had hoped. She strokes my hair and kisses my head, and I want to stay there in her arms forever. Until she pulls back and asks, "Why?"

I swipe at my wet face and ask, "Why does it matter?" It shouldn't matter why; he strayed. And I may always be at war with myself, I may always equally blame both him and me, but my *mother* shouldn't.

"Well, were you attentive? Were you supportive? There must have been a reason, he wouldn't be searching for something else if he was getting everything he needed at home."

I scoff. "You're right. I wasn't good to him. I told him his ideas were dumb and everything that he worked for was a waste of time. I told him that his job was worthless and that he wouldn't get anywhere in the world because he wasn't smart enough. I constantly made him insecure about his body. I worked late all the time so that he was left alone with dinner that he made growing cold on the stove, then bitched when the apartment was a mess. I also lied to him, because I'd forget to tell him something, but make him believe he was the crazy one that just forgot what I'd told him. Oh, and I invited people along with us when we went to the beach house without telling him."

They blink at me, then look at each other.

Dad says, "Some of that doesn't make any sense. Why would you make comments about his job or his body? Why would he be making dinner or cleaning?"

"Because those are all things he did to *me!*"

He shakes his head and starts pacing. "I don't believe it. If that's how he treated you, if it was that bad, you would have left a long time ago."

"Yeah, well, I didn't think it *was* that bad. I still don't, really, because that's how I've been treated my entire life. By you guys."

Mom laughs. "Sweetheart, have you been drinking?"

"Don't you see it, Mom? You talked me into dating him, then you talked me into moving in with him, all because I make awful decisions on my own and wouldn't be able to do any better than him. You made me feel as if I was nothing without him. And he made me feel the same." I jab my finger towards Dad. "Don't *you* see it, Dad? The way you laughed at my ideas for the diner? Then changed your mind, but hired someone else to make those changes with *my* ideas? Mike tried to take all the recipes I had and the login information, and I did all of that work for what?"

"That's completely different, and you know it."

"Is it, though? You don't support me. You don't have confidence in me. So why should I have any in myself? Why should I expect more for myself when you only expect less from me?"

He takes a step forward, voice raised to a scary volume. "I expected a lot from you, Cori. You were the one with good grades, the level head. You were the one who was supposed to go places. But you did the bare minimum in college, wasted my money on an associate's degree, and didn't even try for a bachelor's-"

"*Your* money? You didn't pay for my school. You told me you were on your own the minute you turned eighteen, and you expected the same from me."

His face straightens as he realizes I'm right, but he doesn't say anything else. That's not the point anyway.

"Regardless, we may have talked you into those decisions, but you still made the final choice yourself. You don't get to blame us, and you can't just run away to Grandma's house and ignore your problems. How many times did we call you? And you didn't answer once," Mom says.

Because not a word I've said makes any difference to them. One reason I don't talk much, besides the fact that I'm shy, is because there's never been any point. My house was always filled with noise, everyone's voices talking over each other. It was just a waste of energy to get mine heard. But even when I managed to sneak a word in during the rare moments of silence, no one cared what I had to say. Their own feelings or opinions mattered above all else.

I storm inside and quickly gather my things, shoving them messily into my bag. When I'm done, I stomp across the porch and down the stairs, leaving the clothes on the line behind.

"Then I'll go somewhere else." At this point, I have no idea if I'm over or underreacting. But I'm tired of being reasonable all the time. It's my turn to be crazy.

"Cori-"

I slam my car door, cutting her off, but there's one more thing I need to know. Stepping back into the blinding sun, I ask, "Is there a reason my name doesn't start with S like everyone else in the family? Or did the disconnect start before I was even born?"

"The *disconnect?* Stop being dramatic," Mom answers. "You've heard the story before."

"I haven't."

She rubs her forehead and continues. "We already had an S name for a girl or boy, but when we found out it was *two* girls, we couldn't find another girl name we liked. So your grandmother told us to stop being ridiculous, that the name didn't have to start with S. She recommended Corianne, the name she had picked out for your dad if he was a girl. But we didn't like the -anne part, so we dropped it."

Having expected a completely different answer, I swallow. "Oh." I like my name, but it's always bugged me that it doesn't match everyone else's. I figured Mom and Dad closed their eyes and pointed to a random name in the book instead of giving serious thought as they did with my siblings.

However, my favorite person in the world inspired, not only my middle name, but my first too.

Dad steps forward. "Cori, we love you. You do know that, don't you?"

Before the tears spill over, I choke out, "Yes. But I don't think we understand each other very well." I slide back into my car. Maybe I am dramatic, maybe my imagination is too active, but maybe rejecting my feelings too often has made me this way.

I leave them standing in the yard and set out for the next place. Which happens to be a gas station because I don't actually have a destination in mind. I fill up my tank and get some water for the drive, then get out my phone.

"Hey, how are you doing? We've all been worried."

"I'm fine. Umm..." I fail at keeping the emotion out of my voice. "Can I come over?"

"Of course you can. My home is your home whenever you need it to be."

Chapter 35
No Ice Cream for You

Cori

I 've never been to Tyler's house before; he and Callum always came to Sam's anytime they hung out. I must admit, I'm surprised at the light brown siding and blooming flower beds with dark mulch. Tyler is far from a grown-up, yet this is a grown-up's house. I pull in behind his truck, parked beneath a metal carport, and walk up the sidewalk to knock on his white door.

He answers it with a wide grin, and I walk into his open arms and close my eyes.

"Thank you for letting me come. I promise it will only be for tonight."

He pulls back, placing his hands on my shoulders. "I know I've said this before, but I don't care if it's three a.m. and you ask me to drive across the country just to give you a hug. I will do it."

And for the first time, I believe him. He's always been Sam's friend, not mine. But maybe I'm worthy of his friendship too.

"And you can sleep in the bed, I'll sleep on the couch. Please stay as long as you need." He turns to walk away, but I can't take his bed. Not only is that rude, but who knows who else has been in there?

"I get the couch, or no deal."

He looks back at me and rolls his eyes. "Fine. Maybe if you stay long enough, I'll clean out the spare bedroom and put a bed in there. I just want to say though, I was right." He smirks. "I always said that one of these days, you'd leave him for me."

For the first time in—I have no idea how many—days, I laugh. I was right too. Tyler is the person I need right now.

After Tyler makes dinner for us, homemade pizza because we can eat stuff like that at Tyler's without judging comments, someone starts banging on the door.

"Open up, Tyler Borseth!"

I look over at him. "Is that *Hailey?*"

"Sounds like it, but I'm not sure what I've done this time." *This time?* And how does she know where he lives when I only found out today? He sets his plate down on the coffee table and goes to open the door. I set my plate down as well and sit up straight.

Hailey marches right up to him, pointing her finger in his face. "You should have called me the minute she showed up at your door." Then her eyes meet mine, softening as she walks over to me. She takes Tyler's spot on his loveseat and gathers my hands in hers.

Tyler leans over and says next to Hailey's ear, "That's fine, I'll just sit on the floor."

But she waves him off. "Why didn't you call me?" she asks.

"I wasn't sure you'd answer."

Her eyes well up and her lip trembles. "God, I've been the absolute worst, haven't I?"

"No." I shake my head, adamant that she not blame herself. "You were right. This whole thing has been so pathetic. I was accepting less for myself because I didn't think I deserved better. I understand you not wanting to be there to watch."

She shakes her head, the tears falling fast. "No, that's no excuse. I never should have shut you out. I just haven't really been myself lately and it's just been a lot and I didn't handle it well-" She sobs and I scoot closer to her as Tyler moves to the armrest, laying a comforting hand on her shoulder.

"Tell her, Hailey," he whispers.

His face gives nothing away, so I look at hers. "Tell me what?"

Her green eyes shimmer with tears. "It's nothing. I want to talk about you and how you're doing now that you're away from him."

I remember then about something she wanted to tell me at Nick's birthday party, but we were interrupted because Sam hurt his hand. Then, she started to tell me again at my apartment, but Sam showed up with coffee and flowers to ask me to move in. And I feel awful. I didn't make the time to listen to whatever she was trying to say.

"No, tell me. Is this what you were trying to discuss at Nick's party?"

She looks down and nods. "My parents. They've been fighting a lot, Dad's been sleeping on my couch most nights and driving me crazy. They're in therapy, but I don't know if it's going to help."

"Oh, Hailey." I pull her to me. Hailey's parents were the parents I'd dreamed about. Always present, always cheering her on, always putting her first before their own emotions. But they're still people with problems and complex feelings.

"But I don't want to make this about me. I've been a bad enough friend."

"The last few months have been about me. *I've* been the bad friend. Talk to me."

Tyler stands and walks to his room, giving us privacy as she talks. But Hailey admits that he already knows everything because she turned to him when she and I weren't speaking. He went through his parents' divorce as a kid and can relate to some of it, although it's different as an adult. Not worse, not better, just different.

"I still hate his guts, though."

I smile and nod, although I'm not sure it's true.

"Wait, how did you know I was here?"

"Oh, so Tyler texted Sage, so that she wouldn't worry, and Sage told me. She also said your parents are pretty pissed at you, which I don't understand." I don't understand it either. I know I was rude and disrespectful, but isn't it justified? At what point am I allowed to stand up for myself without it biting me in my ass?

"So, what's the plan now?" she asks.

"I don't know. I'm just happy you're here."

She agrees and grabs Tyler's plate, digging in while we brainstorm my next move.

Sam is relentless in his pestering. He calls every hour and texts every half hour, begging me to let him explain. I'm not ready to speak to him because I'm so humiliated by the whole ordeal and don't know what to say.

The one person I want to hear from doesn't call. I know he texts Tyler often for updates about me, but he knows that I need time. Which only makes me want him here with me more because he seems to know me better than I know myself. He's caring, while Sam only cares about Sam.

Case in point, Sam shows up at Tyler's after a couple of days with bloodshot eyes and hair sticking up in every direction. Tyler's in the shower, so I'm unlucky enough to be the one who answers the door.

"Hey," he says, his voice weak and gravelly.

I cross my arms and lean against the door frame. "How did you know I was here?"

"Your mom."

Sighing, I pinch the bridge of my nose.

"Can I come in?" When I shake my head, he adds, "Please, just let me explain."

"There's nothing to explain."

"Don't you want to know the details? It wasn't just a meaningless affair. I mean... it-it didn't mean anything, but it was with someone sort of- look, it was Kenna. I was there for her when Nick ignored her, and she was there when you were..." He gestures towards my head. "Well, whatever the hell was going on with you. It was just a friend who comforted me. And it went too far."

"It was her car that was in the accident, right?" I already know, but I'm curious if he'll be completely honest.

"I was hurting, Cori. I just needed someone. You weren't there for me the way I needed you to be. With the accident, and with work-"

"How was I not there for you? I haven't been anywhere else. One time I didn't answer the damn phone. And I already knew it was Kenna."

"How?" he asks, surely to improve his stealth the next time he strays.

"Wait." Something hit me then. "Were you with her when

we were all in the waiting room? Is that why the nurses didn't know where you were, because you weren't actually admitted?"

The way his shoulders deflate and his hesitation in answering tell me all I need to know.

"So, were you actually on your way home, then? Or did you forget?"

I barely hear his admission. "I forgot."

I don't allow myself to feel the weight of that statement. There's more to uncover here. "Why did you invite her to the beach house? And Erin? Are you involved with her too?"

"No, Erin is just a friend. And I invited my *friends* to the beach house, Kenna is included in that."

"Then why did I not hear of her existence until Nick's party? Did you just reconnect then? Or were you using Nick's birthday as an excuse to bring her around?"

He swallows as his eyes fall to the ground. "We reconnected at the party."

"So, it's been going on since then?"

He nods. "But there was someone else before her." And something Grandma said, years ago when Sam and I were kids, comes back to me. *"That boy is too big for his britches. Nothing ever satisfies him."*

My gut was right on the day of Grandma's funeral. When Sam came back into my life and my family told me I was crazy for not immediately telling him yes. I hesitated because my insecurities told me to, proof I need to learn how to trust myself.

"Like I said, you were detached, depressed, I needed someone. And, from the sounds of it, you were quite busy yourself. With *Nick*." He emphasizes Nick's name, almost mockingly.

"I wasn't *busy* with him. He distracted me from *your* absence. And when you were around, you doubted me, you drew a wedge between me and my best friend, and you acted like my father."

This is usually the time that I give up my fight. The time that I assume all guilt. But I deserve better than this.

"You know, it's impressive. Impressive that you even noticed that I was detached. Impressive how you always come out on top. Impressive how you've managed to fool so many people. You're an ass. No, I wasn't perfect. But neither are you. And your need to manipulate everyone into thinking you are is why I want nothing to do with you. Have a nice life, Samuel." I manage to get the door shut just as the tears begin to fall.

Tyler stands just out of sight of the door, and comes to wrap me in his arms as Sam shouts from outside, "You have two days to get your shit out of my apartment, or I'm burning every book you own."

"Don't worry about him, I'll gather the guys and get your stuff for you."

"Thank you." I'm not sure if he understood through my sobbing, but his arms tighten.

I pull away to curl up on the couch and stare mindlessly at the TV playing a sitcom.

"We were all worried about you because we didn't know where you were, and Nick said you were pissed at him when he left after he told you about what Kenna said." The cushions shift with his weight. "Talk to me about it."

I don't know what to say. I don't want to cry anymore, I want to smile and laugh, the whole reason I came to Tyler's. But I remind myself that I'm not supposed to be afraid of the pain anymore.

"Nick has become my safe place, but I don't know why he's been so nice and supportive. Is it because he does have feelings for me, like he said? Or because he wanted to get back at Sam?"

"If you saw him when he got back to Callum's, you'd know

the answer without a doubt. He was a wreck. He was snapping at everyone, couldn't sit still, and not because you were upset with him, but because he didn't know if you were safe. And he didn't like that you were alone after having found out everything you did. And after Sage told us what happened at the diner, he was murderous."

It's nice to hear but still doesn't confirm anything. After some time passes, without the Sam and Kenna factors, we'll see what happens.

After a few moments, I say, "Sam was right. I wasn't good to him."

Tyler walks to the kitchen and takes out two pints of ice cream from the freezer.

I hold my hand out for one when he returns, but he shakes his head. "Both of these are mine. No ice cream for you until you correct what you just said. You won't listen to reason, so we're trying a new method."

"Okay, sure, I went through the motions of being a good girlfriend, at least until the end. I put up with a lot. But emotionally, I was barely there. And when I was, I didn't really want to be. Most of the time, I only did things to shut him up."

"Even so..." he gives me a pointed look, urging me to continue.

"Even so, he wasn't there for me when I needed him to be. And he said and did things to me that he shouldn't have."

He nods and hands me the ice cream. "Good enough for now."

"See? Right there. I didn't really want to say that, but I did so I'd get the ice cream."

He snatches it back. "Then no ice cream for you."

"Fine. I don't deserve it anyway."

"I don't think you were wrong, by the way. Turning to Nick for the comfort and support Sam wasn't giving you."

"What do you mean?"

"You and I both know Sam doesn't give a shit that you grew close to Nick. It probably made him happy because he had something to throw back at you. I'm not saying he never cared about you, but Sam's definition of *love* seems to be different than most people's. And if you didn't have Nick, who knows where you might be right now?"

I can't excuse my behavior. It was wrong. There's no way around it. But my relationship with Sam wasn't healthy, and maybe I can choose not to feel guilt over an emotional affair because I've done the right thing by ending it with Sam. Maybe, instead of dwelling on things like I typically do, I can choose to just ... drop it. Maybe I can choose to forgive myself and move on.

When I fake right for Tyler's ice cream container, he moves it out of reach, leaving the one between his knees open for the taking. I take a bite before saying with a mouthful, "You know, if I wanted deep conversation and meaningful advice, I would have gone to Callum's."

"No, you wouldn't have. Nick was there. He's not anymore, though. He moved into his apartment yesterday. I have the address if you want it."

"The timing is wrong."

"Didn't we just go over this? Who cares? Sam doesn't. Set your own rules for life, instead of doing things or not doing things because someone might consider it wrong."

Tyler consumes the entire pint, throwing me back in time to the night I met Nick. Then I put mine back in the freezer and go after what I want.

Chapter 36
Why the Hell Not

Cori

After I typed in the address Tyler gave me, GPS directed me to an apartment complex with red brick buildings. I followed the signs to a door on the third floor of a building in the back, where I stand now, hand raised to knock. But I can't do it.

Too many what-ifs whirl around, keeping me locked in place. Too many doubts and insecurities. I shouldn't be here, I'm not ready. But my phone dings with an incoming text from *Roommate,* a reminder that I need to change his name.

> **Roommate: Do you want me to open the door?**

He must be watching through the peephole. Nick wouldn't judge me if I ran away right now, and it's that very fact that has me replying, *Yes please.*

I knew I missed him, but I didn't realize how much until the breath is sucked from my lungs at the sight of him. He wears a black t-shirt and gray sweatpants, his damp hair sticks up in many directions, and the familiar scent from his soap takes over my senses.

"How are you?" I ask to distract myself.

"I should be asking you that." He holds my gaze. "Especially after this evening. Tyler texted me, said it wasn't pretty."

"It wasn't, but it's over now."

He shifts, allowing me to enter. It's empty except for a backpack leaning against the wall, and grocery bags on the counter.

"The only seating is my bed," he explains, slipping his hands in his pockets.

I slip my shoes off by the door.

"I don't mind the floor." I sit crisscross in what I assume would be the living room, and he sits across from me. "I'm sorry for the other night."

"Why would *you* be sorry? I'm the one who should apologize. I should have told you, I should have-"

I hold up a hand to stop the words rushing forth. "I know, but I also understand why you didn't. I'm mainly sorry for accusing you of wanting revenge. I was hurt in more ways than I can list and my emotions were all over the place. Whether I wanted to admit it or not, I felt sad at what Sam did and for how rashly I reacted."

"My only intention was to be with you in whatever way I could."

"And deep down, I know that. But I still need to learn how to silence those voices that tell me I'm not enough. I have a lot of work to do on myself."

"Well, I'm here to help in whatever way I can."

"Thank you." I pull at a loose thread on my sock.

"Oh. Guess who's pregnant?"

My head snaps up and a muscle in my neck pinches. I massage the area as a lump forms in my throat. Surely, it's not Kenna.

"My mom," he answers, and the dam breaks on my relief. I

don't think I'd care if they had kids together, or got married and lived out a fairy tale, at some point in the future. But a kid conceived while Sam and I were together would make me very uncomfortable.

"Wow. I didn't see that one coming."

He laughs. "Me neither."

"How do you feel about that? That's kind of weird. I mean, Solomon was born when I was thirteen, and even that was weird."

"It's definitely that. But, I don't know." He shrugs and looks at the carpet. "I'm really happy for them. And I know I'm going to love the baby. I kind of feel like an outsider, though. Like, I'm going to be forcing myself into their little family."

"Isn't that probably how Jonah felt all those years? And y'all wanted him part of your family."

He rubs his forehead. "My God, you're right. I'm being irrational."

"Life changes mess with your head."

He nods and, even though the silence is thick with tension and uncertainty, it's somehow comfortable. Because it's Nick.

"Hey, I got your birthday present. It isn't wrapped, though." His smile is so breathtaking that what he said doesn't hit me until he stands. I stand as well and wait for him at the counter. When he returns, he places a thin, cardboard box into my hands. I pull out a picture frame with the words, "First Dollar," and space to write in a date.

"For your coffee shop."

Gifted by the man who's never shown me anything but support. Who's only believed in me every second I've known him, despite the idea of opening a coffee shop being idiotic. Even if I were rich with millions of dollars to spare, even if I knew every in and out of running a business, opening a coffee shop would be foolish because of the huge names that already dominate the coffee community. But Nick's belief in me is tangible, wrapping my body in the warmest of hugs.

Sam has the clearest blue eyes I've ever seen in all of my life. But they're shallow and unburdened like he's never truly seen me, while Nick's are deep and full of love as if he's always seen all of me.

I lose myself in that depth now, unable to look anywhere else. Nick said he would be there to help in whatever way he could, but he's already helped so much. I stumbled around in the dark before I met him. He turned the light on for me.

"Do you not like it?"

"I love it," I whisper. Breath quickening, my lips part, and his gaze catches the movement. He moves to stand directly in front of me, arms braced on the counter on either side of my hips. I lean in, unintentionally, but so does he.

We shouldn't be doing this, it's too fast. But also, why the hell not?

With a gentle touch, I run my hands up his abdomen. They stop at his chest, feeling his heart beat wildly. I start to second-guess myself, but his lips finally slam into mine. He lifts me onto the counter and my legs wrap around his waist. I fist his shirt tightly, overwhelmed by him.

When my eyelids flutter open and find his dark eyes boring into mine, witnessing every moment of ecstasy flickering across my face, I can't breathe. Because it's *Nick's* tongue clashing against mine. It's *Nick's* large hands caressing my jaw. *Nick* carrying me to his bedroom, not once mentioning how heavy I am.

He lays me on the bed and straightens, ripping his shirt over his head and, for the first time, I don't shy away from admiring his toned body. The sight shoots sparks straight through my core. He lowers himself on top of me, and our hands slide down each other's backs, searching for confirmation that this is real.

His scorching touch comes around to my belly and dives underneath my shirt. Leaving a trail of goosebumps along my skin, he nears my chest. His hand slips underneath my bra and palms my breast, and I arch into the pleasure, my vision blurring and my cheeks heating. But not from embarrassment this time. No, this time it's all lust.

Like starving animals, we paw at each other, touching and kissing whatever inch of skin we find, and when he undresses me, there's not an ounce of shame. For the first time, as he kisses his way up my thighs to my center, as his tongue strokes up my seam, I'm not worried about taking too long to reach orgasm.

For the first time, as he flips us so that I'm straddling him, I'm not worried about dimming the lights to shield my body from view.

For the first time, as he flips us again and throws my legs over his shoulders, I'm not worried about hiding my fat rolls.

And for the first time, as I reach my second release at the same time he finds his, I'm not worried about being enough.

Afterward, I lay in his arms, content to stay there forever, skin to skin, his breath skimming over my neck. I have no immediate plans to leave, but I'll have to eventually. We've quenched our thirst for now, but Hailey was right: I need therapy.

I don't know how I'm supposed to talk to a stranger; I'd rather avoid therapy altogether. It's just one more thing I'm supposed to do, that's been suggested to me by someone else.

But I think it's one of those pains I have to go through to feel better in the end.

Because this jumble of emotions inside my head needs a professional to sort through it. For the most part, I know what I need to do to improve myself. But the *how* is what trips me up. And, most importantly, I need someone to listen. And I can't put that responsibility on Nick who has his own stuff to figure out.

We go long enough without speaking that Nick falls asleep. I don't want to leave him here alone like I did with Sam, so I turn the brightness on my phone as low as it can and get to work.

While Hailey was at Tyler's, we brainstormed a plan for me, and the first step in that plan is to find a source of income. I could return to the diner and grovel for my job back, or I could go after my dream. Because the time to trust myself, to stop being a wilted flower, has come.

After the coffee samples proved good, the decision was easy to go with that roaster. I don't need the notes that are probably still sitting in Sam's trash can, considering no one is there to take out the trash for him. All that's left to do is narrow down the flavors I want since my investment amount is lower than I'd hoped to start with and email the sales representative that I've been messaging back and forth.

Once again, the timing is all wrong. I don't have a job. I don't have much in the bank, and I'll have even less after I submit the order. I don't even have a home, and most of my belongings are still at Sam's.

But it's what I want and I've waited long enough.

Next, I send a text to Sage.

Me: I have a proposal: Let's go into business together. Ground coffee and coffee-related designs on your towels/shirts/signs.

Me: I understand if you're not interested, but I figured I'd ask.

While I wait for her to respond, the ideas start rolling in and I make a list. Sage and I can work the tables at the events she attends together and I'll help make the actual products. I could take a small coffee pot and give out samples, maybe a free coffee cup with the purchase of three or more bags. And offer a small discount to those who follow me on social media. There are so many neat things I could do for my customers, but I'm getting ahead of myself. I don't even have the product yet, let alone a single customer.

The second step involves finding a place to live. I write an email to Dad because I'm too chicken to have this conversation in person. I offer him rent in whatever amount he wants— within reason. If I do any work on the house, painting, or replacing flooring, anything I spend will come out of rent.

After the email is sent and my hands begin shaking, I start the search for a therapist. I bookmark a couple that offer therapy online, as well as a website for family counseling.

When I find myself fighting to stay awake, I put my phone down and cuddle up close to Nick's warmth, savoring this time with him. He can't be my knight in shining armor; I have to be that for myself. I have to learn to love myself before I can ask him to love me, and I can only pray that happens before he finds someone else. I'm hopeful, though, with his support and friendship the foundation of my healing, of finding a way to keep going.

Because, not only is my birthday gift symbolic of Nick's

belief in me, but it's practical for the final, and longest, step in my plan: opening a coffee shop right next to Dad's diner.

Chapter 37
No Fancy Shit

Cori

Seven Months Later

I look out at the cars lined up on the drive-through side, and the line of people on the walk-up side, then regret the time it took me to do so. Sage and I work as fast as we can to push out the orders, but people still come. As a server, I've been in the weeds, running around like I was on fire, plenty of times. But not once did I savor the rush like I do now, feeling more of a thrill than stress. I know it won't be like this every day, so I soak it up while it lasts.

"You know it won't be long before Mike finally calls Dad to let him know. If he hasn't already," Sage says behind me. Her hair, tied high on her head, is blue to match our shirts.

I smile and press the button to start the blender. "I can't wait 'til he does."

Surprisingly, Dad agreed to my deal and let me move into Grandma's house for the time being. I don't know if it truly was a weight off his shoulders, but he claimed it to be, and I've laid new flooring, removed wallpaper, painted rooms, and even knocked a wall down. I have no idea what I'm doing when it comes to remodeling. But I have Nick.

And Sage, occasionally. Her and Brian's relationship is rocky, on one month, off the next. When things are off, she stays with me at the farm.

My relationship with my mom and dad has improved tremendously. They agreed to attend a few family therapy sessions with me, and we've learned a lot about each other's boundaries and how to go forward. But there's still a war to be won with Dad, although with less ruthless tactics than I had originally planned.

Instead of a building, I decided a trailer would be the smarter choice. If sales aren't doing great in one area, I can move it somewhere else. I can also take it to festivals, if they allow food trucks, and drive customers to Sage's table.

The upfront costs were much lower than a building as well, and because I bought the enclosed trailer that belonged to my grandparents from Dad at a discount, I had even more money to put towards equipment. I asked the owner of the empty lot next to the diner if I could rent it for the week to prove my point to Dad, and today is my grand opening. For this location, anyway.

After this week, I'll rent a spot month-to-month closer to Grandma's house, which, as it turns out, isn't far from Nick's mom.

After Sage agreed to be my partner, we grew the brand by attending craft shows and markets and drove traffic to the website where we receive more orders by the day. It was slow at first but picked up after a few months, and every penny I saved went into the coffee trailer.

It's twenty feet long with a fresh coat of white paint, and the name, "Coffee Break" in black letters. There's a dark wooden ledge on the outside of the walk-up window, and a chalkboard menu on both sides.

As for Sam, he quit his job. He gambled away all of his money and now lives unemployed at Kenna's house. I think they're happy, though. He keeps the house clean and makes dinner while wondering if Kenna is actually at work or not. He texts Tyler and Callum every once in a while, but they haven't warmed back up to him yet.

I've forgiven him, though. Because I still believe that I could have been better. Thing is, we just weren't right for each other. I can't blame him for all the issues in our relationship because it's hard to be with someone who's insecure. I'm not accepting any of the treatment as what I deserved, just that I'm not blameless. And that's okay because I've accepted that I don't need to be perfect to be worthy.

Eventually, the rush slows and I serve the last customer in line. Dad stands about twenty feet away with his arms crossed. I smile and wave as nicely as I can and call out, "Welcome to Coffee Break. What can I get for you? My favorite is anything caramel and it pairs nicely with a chocolate chip scone."

He walks to the window, scanning the menu to the side with a judging eye.

"I see Mike called to tattle on me," I say, wiping down the surface covered in milk.

"You've made your point. Are you through stealing my customers?"

"You stole my ideas."

"I didn't steal them, you gave them willingly."

"Under the impression that I'd be compensated. With the position, at the very least."

He exhales loudly. "This was months ago, we've gone over this a million times. When are you going to let it go?"

"You hurt me, Dad."

My parents didn't seem to know what to do with a timid child, always telling me to "Stop being so shy," or "Speak up," or apologizing to people when I was reserved. I took it personally, feeling shame and regret that I wasn't who they wanted me to be. I may have tried to make up for what I lacked in personality by always following the rules, never making more sound than was necessary, taking up as little space as I could, and never being the cause of stress for my parents.

I learned not to defy them in any way, to give them what they wanted, and to look for their approval in everything I did. This only taught me to ignore my instincts and not trust my own feelings, because disregarding their suggestions only led to Dad's wrath and Mom's silent treatment.

Stephanie was right when she said, *"Your confidence is your responsibility."* As difficult as that lesson is to learn, and as much as I wish we didn't have to harden ourselves to shield against the cruel words that are sure to be hurled our way, I have to fight for myself. I used to say that Grandma was my anchor. When she was gone, I relied on Hailey, then Nick. But I'm my own anchor now. I've figured out how to be that for myself and learned so much over the past year. We all have.

Dad finally meets my gaze. "I'm sorry, Cori. I didn't think you'd be able to handle the pressure once business picked up after the trial was over. You were moody and standoffish. And I realize now why, but I thought it would be best to put someone with real experience behind the counter. Maybe it was the wrong thing to do, but I'd like to say it's what led you here. Because I always knew you'd do something amazing."

While his words set in, he looks back at the menu and peeks behind me inside.

"I had wondered what you wanted this trailer for. I saw a video of someone transforming a bus into a tiny house, I thought that might be what you were doing. How did you keep this from us?"

I lift a shoulder. "It's not hard when all we talk about are my failures." That was harsh because things have significantly improved with Dad, but I still needed to say it.

Another customer walks up and Dad steps aside to let me help them.

After they leave, smiling and holding a drink carrier with four coffee beverages and a bag with chocolate chip cookies, Dad steps up again and orders a cup of "normal coffee, no fancy shit." I decide to change the name on the menu as soon as the day is over.

"How do you have so many customers on your first day?"

Sage says behind me, "We advertised the crap out of the opening day." Through the blog, coupons, and flyers at a market held just down the road.

He nods and takes a sip, then raises his brows at the cup, impressed with the flavor. "So, do you think you'll actually make money with this?"

"Not a lot, but hopefully a livable wage. We make plenty of money from the website too, you know."

He studies me. "Is this what you've always wanted to do?"

"I've tried on many dreams, Dad. As you used to say, I was not made for customer service. It's painful, even now, to be in front of people and to talk to them all day long. But at least I get to talk about coffee. There aren't many jobs out there where you don't have to talk to people. And I trust myself to make it work because... well, I don't really have a choice now that I've invested so much. Plus, I have the greatest motivation pushing me onward."

He tilts his head, waiting for the answer.

"To prove you wrong."

That's how I know I'm doing better—because when Dad

tells me I can't do something, instead of believing him like the old me did, I want to give him the finger.

I even wrote a poem about my newfound confidence and published it along with a few others in a small collection.

But I Can

I cannot sing with substantial range,
But I can forgive and turn the page.
I cannot dance with sophisticated motion,
But I can feel deeply every emotion.
I cannot play an instrument with any virtuosity,
But I can show kindness and generosity.
I cannot use any dexterity to paint,
But I can withhold a futile complaint.
I cannot recall formulas from memory,
But I can show patience and empathy.
Sometimes, God keeps our skills undecorated,
But even the littlest sparrow is celebrated.

Dad laughs, then nods his approval. But it doesn't matter, because I don't really need it.

My attention moves on anyway, to the dark-haired man stepping out of his truck. I haven't seen him for a couple of weeks, not since he came to help me install a ceiling fan. I could have done it myself, but I'm terrified of electrocuting myself, and that may or may not be the excuse I used just so I could see him. He's also the one who helped with the renovation of the trailer. We put in the flooring, finished the walls, and installed cabinets together; it's not my idea of fun, but it was the most fun I've ever had.

We're just friends, nothing more. Although, there have been a few moments where things almost progressed further. I can hope for one day, but insecurities don't ever really go away

—you just get better at dealing with them. He doesn't share the details of his romantic relationships with me, but is it too much to hope there are no details to share?

We text each other often, usually funny memes, and gave each other Christmas gifts. For his birthday, I gave him a coffee mug with an airplane graphic that Sage drew and told him we'd get his mug collection caught up with mine soon. He looked pleadingly at the sky.

The frame he bought for my birthday last year hangs by the door of the trailer, ready for the dollar I had folded up in my pocket. I look at the frame now and wonder how I ever chose to stick with Sam. Nick showed me that I didn't have to be perfect to be deserving of love, even if I didn't love myself. Everyone needs someone like Nick in their life.

The conditions for my death remain—I don't want a funeral when I die. Maybe instead of a funeral, my family and friends can dance on my grave, or wherever they dump my ashes if I'm cremated. They'll have fun and no one can force me to participate.

I may be the quiet one, the less-expressive one, the one that gave up. But I'm also the one who came back to myself. In the end, I listened to that pull, that yearning in my chest, for something I wanted.

I never saw myself saying this, but I fought for myself. And in the end, I won.

Nick

"Hey," I say, timidly, approaching the window. "How's it been?"

"Amazing." Sage comes up beside Cori and drapes her arm around Cori's shoulders. "We've barely had a break all day. It's slowing down now, getting too close to dinner time."

"Don't you have class tonight?" Cori asks.

"Yeah, but I wanted to come see you on your first day."

Her cheeks flush in response.

"I was wondering if I could place an order?" I pull my wallet from my back pocket.

"Of course, but you're not paying."

"Then I'm not ordering."

"Then I'll just make a drink for you anyway. My choice."

"Fine."

She laughs and rolls her eyes before moving away from the window to drizzle something in a cup, and I use the distraction to hand Sage a ten-dollar bill. She puts the change in the tip jar without asking, but that's where it was going anyway. I shake my head and smile.

I don't notice that the man standing there is their dad, Stephen, until he says, "Nick, right?"

I tense, still pissed about how he treated Cori, but she's mentioned how their relationship has improved. And the fact that he's here, a Coffee Break cup in hand, says a lot. "Yeah. Good to see you."

"How's work? Still working at the machine shop?" I nod, and he asks another question. "You said you have class tonight? For what?"

I fill him in on the aviation technical school I've been attending for the past two months before Cori hands me my coffee.

"Oh, hey. Come in here real quick and help me," she says. I

say goodbye to her dad, who walks over to his diner, and meet Cori at the door of the trailer.

She takes the frame I gave her off the wall.

"Oh, hold on." I take out my phone and click on the screen. Mine and Cori's faces smile up at me from my background; it's a picture we took at the baseball game, the evening before everything went to shit. I press the record button, snapping photos as it captures a video of Cori laying a dollar bill flat against the glass.

After snapping the back on, she turns it around. "Oh, shit. It's upside down."

I laugh. "Leave it. Hold it up." She does and I snap a few more photos before Sage poses beside her. Then, Cori requests I take one of her and me.

"That's my new screensaver," I say afterward.

"Send it to me. It'll be mine too."

I grin and take her hand in mine as Sage excuses herself to greet the car that drove up.

I can't help but stroke her soft skin with my thumb as I ask, "I should get going, but are you going to be open on Saturday?"

"Yeah, I'll be here still. I move to the new spot on Monday."

"Can I come to help you?"

"I'd like that."

I bring the back of her hand to my lips while her other hand goes to the wall to brace herself. Smiling, I try not to let it go to my head that I still make her feel that way.

"I'm so proud of you. I hope you are too." I head for my truck, but I steal a couple of glances over my shoulder to see her watching every step I take.

When Saturday arrives, I wake up at my usual time and wonder how Cori is handling these early mornings. I picture her, hair sticking up in all directions, half naked as she stumbles through the house in the dark, and wish I could be there to see it in person. She opens the trailer at six but has about an hour's worth of prep beforehand. It's almost comical how Cori's personality is the exact opposite of what's required of someone running a coffee trailer —outgoing and early riser.

I can't thank her enough for allowing me to be there to witness the changes she's made in herself. She's still the shy, introverted woman I fell for, who reads more than she socializes and gets nervous talking to strangers. But she smiles freely and takes time to admire the beauty in the small things. She's present in the moment and holds her head up high—at least most of the time. And she went for her dream. It may not be a brick coffee shop, but it's more practical and seems to make her just as happy.

I can only hope the time has come when she's ready for *me* to make her happy.

I've invited her, along with Tyler and Callum to make it less awkward, out to Jonah's a few times, for dinner and to meet my baby sister, Natalie. Cori and Mom get along well and even talk occasionally over the phone. I jump at any opportunity to help her with work around her grandmother's house, but no matter how much time I spend with her, it's still not enough.

When I pull up behind the trailer, Cori's car is already here. I take a deep breath before stepping out of my truck and walking on shaky legs towards the trailer.

She turns her head and my heart skips a beat at the way her face lights up. Suddenly, the trailer is too hot, but it's a warmth I have no desire to run from.

"Morning. As soon as the coffee is ready, we're having

some. I don't know what I was thinking, opening a coffee trailer. I hate mornings. Low sales aren't going to kill my business, it's having to be here so damn early."

I laugh. "You should have gone into alcohol so you could sleep in."

"It's legal now to sell alcohol to-go. I should look into that. Although, I don't know the difference between scotch and whiskey, so probably not the route for me."

She gives me orders for preparations and we get everything set up. She waits until the end to brew the coffee so it's as fresh as it can be and hands me a cup once it's done.

"I was thinking, you can take orders and payment while I make the drinks. Does that work? I don't think we'll be as busy as we've been during the week, so you should be able to handle both windows."

I hope she's right. "Sounds good." I take a sip of the coffee—rich, nutty taste shining through the mocha flavoring—and wonder how I can become a full-time employee so that I can do this with her every morning.

"At my normal location, I won't open as early on Saturdays, but because we're next to a highway, I wanted to be open for those that have to work weekends."

She was right to open early because we're slammed for the first couple of hours. The traffic finally thins around ten with a few small breaks throughout the day, and we spend them cleaning and prepping, snacking and laughing. Too many times I have to pull my hands away from reaching for her waist or her hair. In such close proximity, we bump into each other and accidentally touch, and each time she smiles shyly up at me before averting her eyes and tucking her hair behind her ear.

When she finally closes the windows and switches the sign to closed, we wipe down the counters and put everything away in the cooler at the end of the trailer. She slips on a pink jacket over her cyan-blue buttoned shirt—the same blue as my sweat-shirt—and locks the door to the trailer. Wanting to prolong this moment as much as possible, we walk leisurely to her car, our hands brushing every so often.

Neither of us knows what to say when we come to a halt by her door. I'm not ready to leave her yet, but I don't know what she's thinking. She pulls her ponytail holder out of her hair, letting it fall over her shoulders, and I close my eyes breathing in the sweet scent of her shampoo.

Somehow, I summon up the courage. "Do you-"

"Would you-" she asks at the same time.

We laugh and she tucks a strand of hair behind her ear.

"Go ahead, ladies first."

"No, you go."

I know she will keep refusing until I ask first, giving her time to change what she was going to say if needed. "Do you want to pick up dinner and watch a movie or something? Your house or mine, whichever."

Her lips quirk upwards. "That's exactly what I was going to ask."

I swallow and my breath turns heavy at her smile. Inadvertently, I step forward and stroke her cheek.

Realizing what I'm doing, I step backward, mumbling an apology. But she grabs onto my hand and places it back on her cheek, leaning into my touch.

A gentle breeze glides in, ruffling her hair. I smooth it back down as her gaze bores into mine.

"You're all I think about." And I mean it. The image of her on top of me fills my mind when I'm in the shower. The memory of her laugh is what gets me through hard days. And knowing that she's away from Sam, setting boundaries with her parents, and is learning to love herself is what helps me sleep soundly at night.

Mom has never given me a reason to feel like a mistake, even though that's technically what I was. Sometimes, though, those dark thoughts don't care about reason, latching on and multiplying like a virus just because they can. I see her and Jonah with baby Natalie and sometimes wonder where I fit in.

Then I see Cori and I know exactly where I belong, even if we're just friends. Maybe Mom's life with me wasn't as lonely as I assumed. She and Jonah weren't officially together, but they still loved each other. And maybe her time spent loving me and protecting me from her secret wasn't a waste of her time. Who knows, if they hadn't waited, potentially things wouldn't have happened the way they did. Those chapters helped prepare us for the chapters ahead after all like Cori said in her poem—which now hangs in a frame by my bed.

My forehead rests against hers, our heavy breaths mingling between us. "But if you're not ready, I can wait longer. I can wait for as long as it takes. I just wanted you to know that you're it for me. I don't want anyone else."

She doesn't respond, and I can see the doubt on her face, the quick movement of her eyes as she overthinks. Her gaze falls to my lips, but still, she doesn't say anything.

"You don't have to make any decisions or give me an answer right-" Her finger crosses my lips.

Then, finally, her breathless admission grabs hold of my heart and squeezes in the most wonderful way. "I'm ready. I've never been more ready for anything."

She caresses the back of my neck and pulls my mouth onto hers, parting her lips to grant me entrance. My nerves ignite as she runs her hands down my chest and around my waist. I push her against her car door, the evening around us ceasing to exist, but she pulls back just enough to whisper, "Take me home."

Epilogue

Cori

Four Months Later

Despite the storm last night, the skies are clear today with temps in the mid-nineties. A little hot for an outdoor wedding, but the reception will be held inside Jonah's hangar that he finally got air-conditioned. Sage, Elaine, and I have been in Elaine and Jonah's bathroom getting ready for about four hours now and the ceremony start time creeps up on us.

Sage holds Natalie and sniffs her head. "If I could have the baby without the man, I would," she says. Elaine laughs.

She and I have grown close, bonding over our strong, but different, love for Nick, and our love for reading. She and Jonah are so different from my parents and I love being around them. I don't have to think of ways to respectively say, "Fuck off," when they criticize me or remind them of things the therapist said.

I'm already dressed in my navy blue bridesmaid dress, and we leave the bathroom to allow Elaine to slip into her simple maroon wedding dress instead of the traditional white. Nick knocks on the bedroom door before pushing it open. He looks me up and down, smiling and biting his lip before pulling me into him and nipping at my neck.

"Uhh, gross."

His head whips to Sage and Natalie, whose tiny fist is curled around Sage's dark red hair.

"Oh, hey. Didn't see you there." He chuckles nervously. "Is Mom almost ready? Jonah is nervous as hell."

Nick will walk her down the aisle to give her away, then he'll go to stand next to Jonah. He wears jeans and a navy vest over a white buttoned shirt. And I want to rip it off of him. I can't help but scan his body with my eyes while I answer. "Yeah, she's getting dressed now. Have you given him the papers?"

"Not yet. I'm waiting until I give my speech. Really punch him in the gut. Hey." He snaps his fingers. "Eyes up here before I carry you to the guest room." His smile is mischievous and adorable.

"There is a *baby* in here," Sage says, shielding Natalie from us.

The bathroom door starts to open and I scurry to grab my phone to snap a photo of Nick's face when he sees his mom. I get it out just in time to capture his eyes reddening and his expression morphing into one of endearment.

"Well, shit," he says, swiping at his eyes before any tears can fall.

Elaine slaps his arm playfully. "Nicholas. Language. There's a *baby* in here." Then, she smiles and opens her arms.

"You look beautiful."

"Thank you, son."

"So, is this marriage even going to be legal? I thought you were still married to Nick's dad."

"*Sage!*" I exclaim.

Elaine laughs. "It's okay, Cori. I was able to have a lawyer hunt him down and have him sign papers without me having to see him."

Callum pokes his head in the door. "Everyone's ready. We good to go?"

I hold my hands out for Natalie, but Sage swings her out of reach. "No. She's mine."

I prop a hand on my hip. "She's in the wedding. I'm supposed to carry her."

"Fine." After one more head sniff, she hands her over and leaves with Callum. I follow and line up behind Jonah, whose mom holds his arm by the back doors, and wait for the procession to start. When it's mine and Natalie's turn, I black out. My brain focuses too much on not tripping on the clumps of grass beneath the aisle runner, not dropping the six-month-old in my arms, and all the eyes that watch us, and I end up walking too fast to reach the front. But I breathe a sigh of relief when Nick and Elaine appear and all eyes go to her. My own watch Jonah as his stoic expression breaks, and he lets tears of love fall at the sight of his bride.

I tear up myself and then find Nick's gaze, and the rest of the world falls away.

—

After we all eat BBQ, it's time for speeches. Elaine tells me I didn't have to give one because Nick has enough to say for both her and Jonah, and I'm so grateful. But I am in charge of watching Natalie who decides to poop right as Nick starts his speech. I'm inside the house changing her diaper as fast as I can before Sage graciously takes over so I can get back out and listen.

Nick stands beside Jonah, whose arm is wrapped around Elaine. Laughter at something Nick said vibrates the room before Nick's expression sobers.

"I've said repeatedly how much Jonah is a father to me. I've even started calling him Dad, but now I want to make it official." Jonah looks at Elaine for an explanation, but she shrugs because she doesn't know either. "Many people don't know that you can adopt an adult, but you can. And the reasons to do so are usually in case of death, the biological father won't be contacted or given custody of any kids the adult may have. I don't know if I'll ever have kids, but just like Mom and Jonah want the world to know, through action *and* paper, that they're husband and wife, I want the world to know, through action *and* paper, that he's my dad. So,"—he pulls out the paper from a folder in front of him—"would you be my father?"

Jonah's lips straighten into a thin line as he tries to hold back more tears before he stands and grabs a hold of Nick for a tight hug. A few rough slaps on the back later, Jonah signs the papers and everyone cheers.

A little while later, Natalie's back in my arms again after Sage disappears with Brian. Nick finds me and kisses us both on the head. I stare up at him in adoration and complete and sudden realization that he's *actually* mine.

"Hey, why don't we practice making one of these tonight?" He waggles his eyebrows.

"*Practice?* With or without protection?"

"With. Are you nuts? I don't want a baby. Yet." He smiles and squeezes my waist. "Your sister would never leave our house if we had one before her."

He wraps his arms around me from behind. "Oh, you have BBQ sauce on your neck. Hold on, I'll get it." Just as I'm wondering how I got BBQ sauce on my neck, he sucks over the spot. "Oh, and over here." He moves to just beneath my ear and I almost melt in his arms.

"You're making me wet in front of all of these people." I mean with his saliva, but it's hard to think with his lips on me and it comes out wrong. He chuckles into my neck.

"Language, Cori. There's a *baby* right here."

As Mom approaches, shaking her head at us but grinning at our happiness, Nick takes Natalie from my arms and walks back to his mom and dad.

"So, how long before I get to be mother-of-the-bride again?"

"Ugh. I don't know, Mom. We only just started dating officially a few months ago. Can you let us be?"

"Fine, but he's the one. You know it, I know it." She holds her hands up defensively. "And I'm not trying to *pressure* you into anything, but you're so much happier with him. And lord knows, Sage can't make up her mind. I doubt she'll ever get married."

"Getting married isn't everything. It's not for everyone." However, because we understand each other better—thanks to the continued family counseling—I know what she means. It's her way of saying she wants us to be happy and to know we aren't lonely. "Who knows, Sage and Brian have been working through their issues. Maybe they'll last this time."

"No, they won't. Sage can't commit to a hair color, let alone a man."

Sage approaches from behind us and holds up her left hand, a small diamond inlaid in silver adorning her ring finger. "Is now a bad time to tell you we're engaged?"

About The Author

Amanda Courtney has loved books since before she could read. In high school, she published two poems, along with a small collection of poetry in 2023, and has dreamed of publishing a novel since childhood. She resides in Texas with her husband and twin boys, and is a baseball fan at heart and a football fan by marriage.

Connect with Amanda so you don't miss the novels for Sage, Callum, Tyler, and Hailey!

www.ingramcontent.com/pod-product-compliance
Lightning Source LLC
Chambersburg PA
CBHW030227120726
47903CB00005B/1389